Storm and Stone

Also by Joss Stirling

Finding Sky

Stealing Phoenix

Seeking Crystal

Storm and Stone

Joss Stirling

OXFORD
UNIVERSITY PRESS

OXFORD
UNIVERSITY PRESS

Great Clarendon Street, Oxford OX2 6DP

Oxford University Press is a department of the University of Oxford.
It furthers the University's objective of excellence in research, scholarship,
and education by publishing worldwide in

Oxford   New York

Auckland   Cape Town   Dar es Salaam   Hong Kong   Karachi
Kuala Lumpur   Madrid   Melbourne   Mexico City   Nairobi
New Delhi   Shanghai   Taipei   Toronto

With offices in

Argentina   Austria   Brazil   Chile   Czech Republic   France   Greece
Guatemala   Hungary   Italy   Japan   Poland   Portugal   Singapore
South Korea   Switzerland   Thailand   Turkey   Ukraine   Vietnam

Oxford is a registered trade mark of Oxford University Press
in the UK and in certain other countries

British Library Cataloguing in Publication Data

Data available

ISBN: 978-0-19-273568-3

1 3 5 7 9 10 8 6 4 2

Printed in Great Britain

Paper used in the production of this book is a natural,
recyclable product made from wood grown in sustainable forests.
The manufacturing process conforms to the environmental
regulations of the country of origin.

For Jane Stevenson

Chapter·1

A black eye. Great.

Raven Stone studied it in the mirror, lightly probing the developing bruise. Ouch. The strip light flickered over the wash basin, making her reflection blink like the end of an old newsreel. The tap squeaked a protest as she dampened a cold compress.

'You look about seven years old,' she told her mirror-double. Ten years on from the schoolyard of scraped knees and minor bumps, Raven considered the injury more a humiliation than a pain. She tugged a curl of her spiralling black hair over her face but it sprang back, refusing to hide the cloud gathering around her left eye. She wondered whether she could hide in her room until it faded . . . ?

Not possible. All the students were expected to attend the welcome-back supper and her absence would be noticed. Anyway—she threw the flannel in the sink—why give her enemies the satisfaction of knowing they had driven her out so easily? Cowardice was not part of her character résumé. She had far too much pride to allow it.

Raven stripped off her tennis kit and pulled on a towelling robe. She tossed the dirty clothes in the laundry basket by the door with a snap of the lid. It was tough keeping her promise to herself that she would be strong; easier when she had someone at her back. But the second bed in the room was empty—no heap of untidy belongings or suitcase as she had expected. What was keeping Gina? She was the only one Raven wanted to talk to about what had just happened. Raven flopped on her bed. How had it come to this in a few hours? Until the black eye, life had been skating along fine, a smooth place after years of rough. Westron, as run by the head teacher, Mrs Bain, had been weird sometimes, putting too much emphasis on wealth and parents, celebrity pupils and privacy, but teaming up with Gina, Raven had been able to laugh off most of those absurdities. She would have said no one in the school wished her ill. In spite of owing her place to her grandfather's presence on the staff, the other students had not appeared to mind her numbering among their privileged ranks. Now she knew better.

The realization had come out of nowhere, like the tornado spiralling Dorothy's house off to Oz. When Raven opened the door to the changing rooms, everything went skipping down the yellow brick road to Bizarre City.

Hedda's question had seemed so, well, *normal*. 'Hey, where's my Chloé tote?'

The other girls in the locker room getting ready for the tennis competition had made a brief search among their belongings. Raven had not even bothered: her little sports bag, a much mocked airline freebie, was too small to hide the bulky taupe leather shoulder bag. Hedda had been flaunting it all morning like a fisherman displaying a prize catch. The flexing, polished surface had gleamed like a sea trout in her manicured fingers: *so many pockets and you won't believe how much it cost!* Hedda had thought it a bargain but it had come with a price tag more than Raven's grandfather earned in a month as the school's caretaker. Something so pointlessly expensive had to be a rip-off.

'Hey, I'm talking to you, Stone.'

Raven felt a sharp tug on her elbow. Standing on one foot to lace her tennis shoe, she toppled to one side. Why had Hedda suddenly taken to using her surname?

'Whoa, Hedda, careful!' Raven balanced herself against the wire mesh dividing the changing areas and tied off the bow. 'You almost knocked me over.'

Stick thin and with an abundance of wine-red hair, Hedda reminded Raven of a red setter, sharp nose pointing to the next shopping bargain, a determined little notch in her chin that gave her face character. Hedda put her hands on her hips. 'Where have you hidden it?'

'What?' Raven was too surprised to realize what it was that Hedda was accusing her of doing. 'Me?'

'Yes, you. I'm not stupid. I saw you looking at it. It had my phone—my make-up—my money—everything is in that bag.'

Raven tried to keep a hold on her temper and ignore the hurt of being accused with no proof. She had had enough of that in the last school she had attended before coming to the UK. She tried for reasonable. 'I haven't done anything with it. Where did you last see it?'

'At the lunch table—don't pretend you don't know.'

The changing room fell silent as the other girls listened in on the exchange. A flush of shame crept over Raven's cheeks even though she knew she was innocent. Memories of standing before the principal in her old school rushed back. She felt queasy with the sense of déjà vu.

'I'm sorry: are you saying I stole it?'

Hedda tipped her head back and looked down her long nose at Raven. 'I'm not saying—I know you took it.'

Raven dragged her thoughts away from her past and focused on the accuser. What on earth had happened to Hedda? She had missed most of last term and had come back with what seemed like a personality transplant—from clingy, whingeing minor irritant to strident, major-league bitch. Raven told herself not to back down; she'd faced false accusations before and this time she wasn't a traumatized little girl.

What was the worst Hedda could do? Wave a mascara wand at her?

'So you think I took it? Based on what? On that fact that I just *looked* at it? Looking doesn't mean stealing.' Raven appealed to the other girls, hoping to find someone who would join her in shrugging off the accusation as absurd, but their expressions were watchful or carefully neutral. *Gee, thanks, guys.*

Then Hedda's friend, Toni, joined in the finger pointing. 'There's no point claiming you're innocent. Things were going missing all last term.'

'I had nothing to do with that. Some of my stuff was stolen too.'

Toni ignored her. 'We all noticed small things disappearing but didn't like to . . . I mean we *guessed* it was you but we felt sorry for you, so . . . ' Toni waved her hand as if to say *that was last term, this is now.*

'Sorry for me?' Raven gave a choked laugh. One thing she never wanted was anyone's pity. Even at her lowest moment after losing her parents, she hadn't asked for that.

Hedda got right up in her face. 'But taking my brand new Chloé? Now you've gone way too far. Give it back, Stone.'

Ridiculous. Raven turned her back on Hedda. 'And what am I supposed to be doing with these things I'm stealing?'

'Your grandfather has a new car—if you can call a Skoda a car.'

Toni snorted. Raven felt a surge of anger: taking a crack at her was one thing but Hedda had better keep her granddad out of it or there really would be trouble!

'So I, what? Steal from the rich to give to the poor? Now why didn't I think of that?' Raven's irony was lost on the literal-minded Hedda.

'Stop denying it. I want my bag and I want it now.'

Hoping that if she ignored the infantile rant Hedda would

back down, Raven shook her head and dipped her fingers inside her jeans pocket for a band to tie up her hair.

'Don't you ignore me!' With a grunt of fury, Hedda shoved Raven hard into the mesh, right onto a peg that caught the corner of her eye. Even though the hook was padded by clothes, Raven saw stars. Clapping a hand to her face, she swung round, temper threatening to gallop away riderless.

'Look, Hedda, I don't have your stupid tote!' She gathered herself in the defensive stance she had been taught. Raven had to be careful, knowing she could do a lot of harm with the self-defence training her father had insisted she take. It had come in useful for fending off the predators who roamed the corridors in her American public school, but she guessed it would be frowned on at refined Westron and would earn her a reputation as a thug.

'Yes. You. Do!' Hedda shoved Raven in the chest with each word so her back collided with the mesh. Someone giggled nervously while two students hurried out to fetch the PE teacher.

That was outside of enough. It was time Hedda learnt there was one girl in the school she couldn't bully.

'I've had enough of your idiotic—' (push) '—accusations!' Raven thrust Hedda back a second time, measuring out exactly the same force as Hedda had used on her.

Then Hedda went for a handful of hair. Big mistake.

'Just leave me alone!' Raven seized the girl's wrist, executing a sharp twist-and-bend defensive movement. But this was no fair fight: Toni snatched a hank of Raven's hair at the back and pulled sharply, nails raking the side of her neck. Raven shoved Hedda away and broke Toni's hold by a sharp chop to her elbow, making her arm go dead. She grabbed her tennis racket and swept it in front of her like a kendo sword, fending off both her attackers.

5

'Touch me again and you'll be sorry.'

Toni backed away, shaking her hand. 'Leave her, Hedda: she means it.'

But Hedda had not given up on her misplaced revenge. Deterred from a direct attack, Hedda went for Raven's belongings. 'Think you can steal from me, do you?' She upended Raven's bag, scattering all her things over her head. Raven's phone fell onto the floor and shattered, bits flying across the tiles. 'There! Suck on that, skank.'

'What? No!' Throwing the racket aside, Raven dropped her knees to collect the pieces before someone trod on them. It had to be salvageable—had to.

Hedda ended the gesture by throwing the empty bag at her, cord whipping her across the cheek. 'That'll teach you to steal. And I still want my tote back.'

The door slammed open. 'What is going on in here?' Miss Peel, head of PE, had arrived and was standing, arms crossed, in the entrance.

The girls in the changing room suddenly all became very busy, like a flash mob melting back into the crowd.

'Miss, Raven dropped her phone,' said Toni spitefully.

'That's not fair! You all saw Hedda do it!' protested Raven. No one spoke up in her defence, a slap that she'd have to absorb later when they wouldn't see the hurt. 'She dumped my stuff on the ground because she thinks I stole her bag.'

'I'm not interested in bags or phones.' Miss Peel folded her arms. 'I was told there was a fight going on in here.'

Hedda passed Toni a tennis racket. 'Not really. Just Raven making a fuss.' She rolled her eyes indicating that this was a frequent occurrence.

Miss Peel glared down at Raven who was cradling the remains of her now defunct mobile. 'You've been told hundreds of times that the school can take no responsibility for private

A bird—her namesake—cawed as it hopped and flapped untidily along the rooftop crenulations of the old castle that housed the school. The sound scraped against her hearing, a distraction from the maelstrom of hurt and anger that whirled inside her. *No biggie*. She would cope as she always did. This was peanuts compared to losing her mom to cancer and her dad to Afghanistan.

I'm sorry for your loss, that was what people said, like she had misplaced her parents. They said it, of course, because all words were inadequate and these were the ones society had settled on, but there were times she wished someone had said 'I'm sorry that your mom and dad died.' Told it like it was. Horrible. Gut-wrenching. Not a loss but a huge hole dug out of her middle. Mom had gone first. After her dad died, Raven's old life had been flushed away and an unspeakably grim transition period followed while the authorities fumbled her future. Granddad had been out of the picture—in hospital in England after a heart attack—so for a while the social worker dealing with her case had placed her with military friends of her parents, not realizing the couple was going through a stormy marriage breakdown. Emotionally there had been no room for a grief-stricken thirteen-year-old, leaving her prey to their bully of a fifteen-year-old son. Jimmy Bolton looked innocent, boy-next-door-charming, but his face hid a malicious nature. That was where she had learnt to run fast, and if she couldn't run, how to fight back so she could get away. Her old self-defence lessons had become daily survival tactics. She couldn't even escape him during the day as Jimmy had been in the senior department of her high school. The exact opposite of Westron, it had been underfunded, teachers overstretched and the students low on ambition. It was a place in which you endured rather than studied. When her granddad recovered enough to apply to be her guardian, Raven had thought that coming to Westron was a move to paradise—lawns, gardens, cool ancient building: it looked perfect. But then, even Eden had its snake, didn't it?

Enough brooding. Dumping the robe, Raven changed into a summer dress she had picked up for a fiver from the Oxfam charity shop in the local town over Easter. She smoothed it down, enjoying the sensation of the soft cotton flirting just above her knees. She doubted any of her classmates ever bargain hunted like she did. Bright orange, the colour suited her deep bronze skin tone. She accessorized it with a string of green and orange beads, also picked up from the same store but from the Fairtrade Craft section. She tugged off the label telling her about the women's cooperative in Bangladesh that made it, her mind briefly flitting round the world to a hot shed by the bank of a river that spent weeks in flood. It seemed really stupid to agonize over a smashed phone in contrast to that level of hardship. *Get a grip, Raven.*

The dinner warning bell sounded outside. Just as Raven was on the point of leaving her room, she almost stepped on an envelope that had been shoved in the gap under the door. Expecting some leaflet about term time activities, she ripped it open. Her photo fell out, features defaced by marker pen, a dagger sticking in her neck, spurting out blood. So not funny. Angrily, she scrunched it up and chucked it in the bin in the bathroom, not wanting it in her room.

The picture left a horrid taste in her mouth and a shaky feeling in her stomach. Somewhere deep down she was always the terrified girl who had lost her foundations along with her parents, and she worked hard so that side of her didn't come to the surface. Her old school had taught her not to show weakness—that was like blood in the water to the circling sharks. Only her granddad saw the true her and that was heavily edited so as not to worry him. Why had someone decided

9

to single her out for such spite? Even though she didn't expect a welcome downstairs, she wanted to be with other people to chase the image on the letter away.

Pushing through the heavy fire door in the corridor, she headed down the narrow stairs. The room she shared with Gina was up in what had once been servants' quarters. The school had four storeys in the main building, divided into boys' and girls' wings: the rambling fourth floor in the attics housed the boarders, the second and third floors were given over to classrooms; and the fancy, high-ceilinged ground floor that had started life as a medieval manor and grown to castle status under the Tudors. All in all, the school was home to three hundred live-in pupils. Westron Castle was just the English branch of the exclusive Union of International Schools. If you counted the other twenty-five schools round the world, and the alumni association, the students of the Union numbered in the tens of thousands, forming a powerful and well networked elite. Her granddad had been chuffed she'd been accepted; he thought that graduating from this school would set her up for life. And look how well *that* was going.

The gong sounded in the entrance hall. She was late. Picking up speed, Raven charged through door after door, leaving them swinging. Jumping the last few steps she reached the foyer a second before the entrance to the dining room was closed. The rule was if you got there after that point without a good excuse you had to forego supper. Fortunately tonight it was her grandfather on door duty. He raised a bushy eyebrow at her but held it as she slipped in.

'Thanks,' she whispered.

He patted her shoulder and disappeared off to his office by the kitchens, his little hunched frame soon swallowed up behind yet another fire barrier. The old architecture of the place had been brutally beaten to take on fire safety precautions, swing doors and fire escapes. She wished he had elected to stay to keep her company, but as usual he avoided the rigmarole of eating with the students; the resident teachers were not so fortunate. Their attendance was obligatory.

Raven slipped into the hall and closed the door behind her, feeling exposed without Gina by her side. As anticipated, she was the last to arrive and most seats were taken. This was no baronial style dining room with heavy oak tables, as you might expect from the decor, but a restaurant setting of circular tables that could be folded away when the space was needed for other activities. The students were supposed to learn the art of dinner party conversation in their groupings of ten, teachers sprinkled strategically through the room to encourage manners and intelligent talk. At least that was what the syllabus promised parents; in reality, the tables were closely guarded spheres of influence, markers of who was in and who was out. Teachers preferred to sit together at their own table and gossip, leaving the students to fight out their social battles without referees.

Raven's eyes swept the room. Though she was standing in the shadows, her late entrance had attracted attention from the girls. A number of them glanced her way then started whispering together. She could imagine what they were saying: *there's the thief. We always knew it was her.*

Which one had left the picture, she wondered? It was horrible to think someone had spent their afternoon working out how to upset her. Her money was on Hedda and her gang but, really, now she knew what the girls thought of her—the school's trailer trash—she had begun to see enemies everywhere. No one had stood up for her: she would always remember that.

The boys, thankfully, seemed oblivious to the undercurrents in the room. When she caught the eye of Adewale, a friendly

11

Nigerian boy in her year, he just grinned back and returned to his conversation. Shame there was no room at his table.

Not wanting another battle, she avoided taking a seat with any of the girls. Her normal place by the serving counter was occupied so she slid into a spare chair at the same table on the far right. It was a good place to watch the room and had the advantage that she didn't recognize the two boys already there, so they at least should be ignorant of the undercurrents.

'Hi. You new to Westron?' she asked brightly, pretending she wasn't worried by the atmosphere in the dining hall. She was attuned to danger, thanks to past experience in a rough school, and somehow the situation had subtlety changed. She was no longer so sure she was safe. It might not be drug-dealing seniors she had to worry about in the corridors here but something was . . . well . . . *off* about Westron post vacation. Worth thinking about later, but for now she turned to give the newcomers her attention.

The tousled-haired one on her right ignored her, apparently engrossed in a Sudoku puzzle. *Extreme level*. Great. She had put herself next to an Ultra-Geek—admittedly a handsome one. Hoping for rescue, she peered beyond him to the other stranger on Sudoku boy's far side.

'Hi, I'm Raven.'

This time her greeting did not fall on deaf ears.

'Hey, Raven. I'm Joe Masters.'

Not only did Joe have a lovely deep voice, East Coast accented like hers, but he had a smile that felt like the sun coming out to brighten her overcast day. His hair was shaved close to the scalp and his skin tone was only a couple of shades darker than hers. Total effect? Gorgeous.

'So, you . . . er . . . just joined us, Joe?'

'Yeah. We started today.'

12

We? Did that mean he came as a package deal with Sudoku? 'Oh. Awesome. I hope you settle in OK. I mean, it's a strange time to come, so late in the academic year.'

Joe tapped the fingers of his left hand lightly on the table, a pianist practising the bass line. 'Couldn't be helped, Raven. We got expelled from our old school.'

Raven wondered if he was joking; he seemed so cheerful about the fact. 'What?'

'The professor here blew up the labs. I was just an innocent bystander, your honour.' Joe's eyes were laughing at her expression.

'Oh, er, yeah right. Of course, you were. Totally.'

His expression told her he appreciated the irony. 'I always blame him. He never takes the trouble to defend himself. Do you, Kieran?' He nudged his friend.

'Hmm.' The boy filled in the grid with lightning speed. Raven suspected that he had to be making up the answers but when she surreptitiously checked the first box she couldn't fault it.

Waiting staff appeared with the first course, which entailed a dangerous ladling of hot soup over the shoulders of the students. As most of the servers were poorly trained locals drafted in for the meal, the older students knew to lean well back. The Sudoku boy did not take evasive action but impressed Raven by flicking up a napkin to intercept the drops with no seeming pause in his concentration.

'Is he always like this?' Raven asked.

Joe smiled indulgently. 'Hard to believe but yes.' He broke a roll into pieces.' You think he hasn't noticed you but you're wrong.'

'Yeah right.'

'No, it's true. Hey, Key, stop that and say "hi" to the nice girl sitting on your right.'

'Pathetically easy. I don't know why I bother.' The boy dropped the paper onto the floor between their chairs.

'You bother because if your poor brain doesn't have something to work on it starts to cannibalize its own cells out of sheer boredom.'

'Hmm. Not very scientific but you might have a point.' Sudoku sat up straight, revealing he was exceptionally tall. He had an enviable crop of loose chestnut curls and a face of angles and planes like some sculptor's exaggerated version of 'bone structure: British aristocracy'. Raven was reminded of a thoroughbred horse, all restless energy and skittishness. These two made the rest of the boys in her year look plain. She predicted that they were either going to be wildly popular with the guys who wanted to hang out with them, hoping to be at the front of the line for the girlfriend surplus, or—and this struck her as more likely—envied for being so fit.

'So turn your gargantuan mind on your dinner companion, Key.'

As Kieran looked worth the extra effort, Raven decided to help by restarting introductions. 'Hi, I'm Raven.' She held out a hand.

He glanced at it, then took up his soup spoon instead. 'I know who you are.'

Raven let her hand fall to her lap. Fine, be like that, Mr Arrogant. Clearly, he had put her in the surplus category already. That stung. A lot. 'So, I get it: I say my name and now you know everything there is to know about me! Gee: no need to say hello back or ask me about myself. Gosh, darn it, you must be so clever!'

Joe chuckled at her sarcasm. 'That's Kieran Storm for you. And believe me, he does know you—height, weight, life history. He probably even has a shrewd idea of your . . . um . . . shoe size.' He winked.

14

That seemed unlikely. The boy had not met her gaze yet, let alone given her feet or other parts any attention.

'I think I'm getting a fair picture of your friend, Joe. Six three, maybe six four. White British. Too intelligent for us mere mortals. Posh education at one of those English schools called public when they are private—Eton, Harrow or equivalent—until he was expelled.' She said the last with relish. She would have liked to have seen that.

Joe was highly amused. He stirred his tomato and red pepper soup in a circle, mixing in the crème fraîche. 'Go on.'

Raven made a guess. 'He needs you to dress him.'

'Right on target,' crowed Joe. 'That's me: his valet. How did you know?'

'You're wearing a Ralph Lauren suit . . . '

'A designer second,' Joe slipped in.

'And your friend has one too . . . '

'I know a very useful guy.'

'But his shirt is probably bummed from his dad's or younger brother's wardrobe as it doesn't fit—too short in the sleeves. I figured he threw it on this morning before coming here and since then he's been hard at work on his Sudoku until you forced him into the only decent suit he has. He couldn't be bothered to put on the matching shirt like you did and you decided the battle wasn't worth fighting. Am I close?'

'Hey, Key, you've got a rival. How many points does she get?'

Kieran raised his eyes to Raven's face for the first time. He had eyes of an uncanny pale jade green, almost alien in their intensity. Her heart did a little flip of shock as she recognized the visceral attraction she had felt from the beginning had just got ten times worse. Moth, her; flame, him: result, singed wings.

'Not bad.' His voice wasn't cold, more deep and distant,

as if it were a struggle for him to remember to relate to little Earth people like her.

'And that, Raven, is high praise from my man here. Congratulations.' Joe shook her hand across Kieran's meal then let go.

'Thanks.' Raven took a sip of her soup, attempting to regain her balance. 'So what did I get wrong?'

Kieran crumbled a piece of bread with his long fingers and scattered them on the surface of his soup. He shot another glance at her then concentrated on his bowl. 'It's my shirt. I've grown.'

Joe nodded. 'Yup, he never goes shopping for clothes. He will wear something until it falls apart or we hide it from him.'

'Who's "we"?' asked Raven.

Joe looked troubled for a moment. 'The boys at our old school. Yeah, them guys.'

'But you got him the suit?'

'It was given to me. We both share a generous . . . ' Kieran searched for a word. '. . . Godfather.'

'I wouldn't mind one of those,' said Raven, thinking of her phone. 'So I did only "OK" then. Let's see what you know about me.' She was intrigued what he would pick up as she was convinced she had not registered on his girl detector.

Kieran finished his soup before replying.

'Go on: the suspense is killing me.'

'As you wish.' Kieran pushed the bowl away and leant back in his chair to study her—to really study her. Raven had the feeling that no one had ever looked so closely at her before. It was like he was some human form of MRI scan, revealing all the layers.

'Fire away.' She crossed her arms, a little worried as to what she had invited.

'Raven Stone. Seventeen. Granddaughter of the school

caretaker, Robert Bates. You have been at the school for three years, which explains why you use both British and American English idioms. Parents deceased. One parent an American army officer—father most likely. Yes, yes, of course the father as the mother was British. Idiot.' He hit his forehead. 'Father was African American and proud of his heritage from the civil rights movement, but that is so obvious I apologize for mentioning it.'

'How did you . . . ?'

Joe shook his head, warning her to let Kieran continue.

'You are five three and would like to be taller. Size 8—or about American size 6, though the conversion equivalent is not exact. You don't have much money, shop at Oxfam, buy Fairtrade, read real books rather than eBooks. Shall I go on?'

He was good: she had to give him that, but Raven was irritated by his calm dissection of her habits and person. 'How do you know all this? Have you been in my room or something?'

'No. Everything I need to know is right here.'

'I suppose you know my shoe size too, Detective Storm?'

His eyebrow winged up at that sarcasm. 'Size 5. I can make an educated guess at other measurements if you wish.'

Joe swallowed a laugh.

'No thanks,' Raven said quickly.

'And you have had a fight with that red-haired girl over there about . . . ' Kieran brushed the bridge of his nose with a long forefinger, '. . . about her ridiculously large handbag.'

Raven was far from amused. 'I think you'd better stop before you spill all my guilty secrets.'

'Oh, you're not the kind to have guilty secrets. You are an open book—usually honest, preferring to be direct and physical rather than subtle and devious, but under that surface show of strength, there is a hint of shyness and fragility, such as now when you prefer not to meet my eyes.'

17

Naturally that meant that Raven had to force her gaze to challenge his. She immediately regretted it as his eyes seemed to draw her in like some kind of Star Trek tractor beam taking her little ship in tow of his *Enterprise*.

Joe put a hand over Kieran's mouth. 'You'd better stop, my man, before she plants a fist in your face.'

Raven looked down at the crumbs on the table top. 'How do you know about the fight—and all the rest?'

Kieran did not appear to understand that he had embarrassed her. He was enjoying the glow of his cleverness. 'That was simple: your clothes speak for themselves—label cut out at back of dress, cotton tag end still hanging so recent secondhand purchase. Bead work from Bangladesh. Fair guess that they were bought together as you matched them as an outfit, so that suggests Oxfam rather than a home-based charity. There is a branch in town. As for the fight, the girls over there have been looking in your direction continually since you came in—most comments have been directed to the redhead and she has been clutching that bag to her side all night as if expecting you to rip it away from her.'

He was right: the tote was back. All that fuss over something that wasn't even stolen! 'The jerk—she hadn't lost it at all!'

'She did misplace it,' Kieran continued. 'It had been removed by your grandfather when he found it under the table during clear up from lunch. He put it in the school secretary's office and asked her to tell the girl who owned it to collect it. I heard the secretary call the redhead over on my way in today.'

So that was why they still blamed her. They probably now thought her grandfather was in on her career as a thief, covering for her when she got caught.

Resentment fought with curiosity and curiosity won. 'How did you know we had a fight?'

18

Kieran paused as his bowl was taken away and the second course of lamb and new potatoes was placed in front of him.

'You have a slight scratch on the side of your neck that suggests a girl fight,' he gestured with his trim nails, 'and a rather fine bruise over your left eye. Actually, now I think about it, were there two of them? Yes, there were. You and two girls—probably after lunch judging by the age of the bruise.'

She watched with fascination as he dissected his meat with surgical precision. 'Anything else?'

'Your phone. It got broken or stolen.' He chewed on the lamb, piece by careful piece.

Raven put down her fork. 'How on earth do you know that?'

'Because that girl over there has been waggling her iPhone at you. The gesture suggests she has something that you do not.'

'Wow, well done,' Raven said flatly. 'So you are, what? Sherlock Holmes's love child?'

'Impossible. He is a fictional character based on the real life Joseph Bell, a medical lecturer from Edinburgh who pioneered . . . '

'Enough information, Kieran. She was making a joke,' Joe said softly.

'Thanks, you can get back in your box now.' Raven gave up on her meal. If her behaviour was going to be put under a microscope, she'd prefer it to be by a friend and in private. 'It was nice meeting you, Joe.'

Joe caught her sleeve. 'Before you go, Raven, was he right about the civil rights movement?'

Kieran snorted and added another teaspoon of mint sauce to his meal.

'Yeah, actually he was.'

'Bracelet,' muttered Kieran.

Raven turned her silver wrist band so Joe could see the inscription. *I have a dream*.

'Clearly an American piece from the 1960s referencing Martin Luther King's speech; date suggests a family heirloom.'

It was the last present her father had given her before he deployed out of country and into the path of a roadside bomb. Raven put her hand over it protectively.

'It's a nice piece,' Joe said.

Kieran swallowed his mouthful, appetite sharpened by the display of his intellect. 'Actually, it's only silver plate which means it's not worth much.'

'*Actually*, it's worth everything—to me.' Raven gave him her back and walked out.

Chapter· 2

'Oh, well done.' Joe gave Kieran an ironic round of applause. 'Way to go.'

Kieran was still processing the punch he had felt when he'd first noticed Raven, a boxer spinning from the knock-out not yet flat on the canvas. He made himself catalogue details to regain his mental balance.

The waiter began clearing the plates. He had long nails on his right hand, short on the left—guitar player in his spare time, then.

'Are you listening to me, Key?'

'Huh?' Kieran followed Raven with his eyes, noting she was rather neatly put together. He wondered what it would be like to touch her hair—in the interests of scientific enquiry of course. He sipped some water and sat back as the dessert was put in front of him. He excavated the apple pie; the pastry had been made out of vegetable fat and margarine—not butter.

Joe gave him a shove. 'I despair of you sometimes.'

'Why? What have I done now?'

Table manufactured in Sweden. Cutlery in Sheffield. Plate not silver, like the bracelet.

'Key, did you or did you not just totally piss off the first female we've spoken to since arriving here?'

Kieran blinked at his friend, struggling to comprehend. Give him advanced algebraic equations any day, human maths never added up satisfactorily. 'She asked me to tell her what I knew about her so I did.'

Joe punched him in the ribs. 'Don't you ever edit what you say? Check it for the offence it might cause?'

Kieran rubbed the sore spot on his side. 'Explain.'

'You basically told the girl she was a fight-prone charity case dressed in rejects whose prized possession was nothing more than junk.'

'But that's the truth. I don't see why people can't face up to it. And I did not say it like that.'

Joe pushed his empty plate aside and accepted dessert from a waitress with a clever compliment that had the girl smiling. He turned his attention back to his friend. 'Look, Key, there's truth and there's truth. Some things are OK to say right out—"gee, I like your dress", or "oh my, you're a pretty thang". Other stuff, you keep to yourself—"hey girl, you're dirt poor", "man, you are one ugly bug". Got it?'

The hall door closed behind Raven.

'She wasn't ugly.'

Joe rested his chin on his hand and sighed. 'I'm giving theoretical examples. And no, she wasn't. I'd call her very cute.'

'Not just cute. Really . . . nice looking.' That didn't do her justice. He had never had such an instant tug of attraction to anyone before.

'Shame she hates your guts already,' Joe smirked. 'I'm the one she likes.'

Kieran's irritation flared. His friend had an advanced degree in flirting. 'Joe, you will back off Raven Stone.'

'Whoa, coming over all territorial, are we?' Joe studied him with amusement. 'Gonna start beating your chest next?'

'Don't be an idiot.' Kieran snapped his napkin in Joe's face, making his friend flinch as the end flickered a millimetre from the end of his nose. He could do the same move to greater effect with a bullwhip as well Joe knew. You would've thought he'd get over the wincing after having been Kieran's partner in circus skills class last summer.

'So what's going on? You, reclusive Kieran Storm, the mystery among us Yoda boys, have finally deigned to notice a girl and are staking a claim?' Joe took a heaped spoon of his ice cream and smacked his lips appreciatively.

'I'm not.' He was. 'I just don't want you messing up our mission here with you doing your usual thing.'

'Which is?

'Getting their hopes up with your charm. Leaving a trail of broken hearts. You know you do it, Joe, as we never stay around for long.'

'I can't help it if I'm a chick magnet.'

'Wait a minute, ladies and gentlemen—wait while I move out of the shadow of this man's ego.'

'My ego has nothing on yours.'

Kieran smiled complacently. 'But mine is justified.'

'Keep telling yourself that. You, my friend, are heading for a fall: one day you are going to meet someone who's going to take you down a peg—or twenty.'

'Not going to happen. We don't have relationships while on a mission.'

'We'll see. You'll find you can't ace everything life throws at you.' Joe gave his friend an evil grin. Kieran could tell Joe was up to something. The recruits at the Young Detective Agency—or Yodas as they called themselves—trained together so had a fairly good idea of each other's strengths and weaknesses. It was necessary so that, when they went out as a team, they went prepared. Kieran knew to be suspicious when Joe looked pleased with himself.

'What are you up to, Joe?'

'Nothing. Just our mission.' Joe was acting innocent—too innocent. 'As the A stream representative, you apply that immense brain of yours to what links a series of corrupt decisions of global significance and this very benign-seeming school. Batting for Team C,' Joe mimed an imaginary baseball stroke, 'I'm the one who is supposed to get up close and personal with our sources of information.'

Kieran preferred not to think about Joe being close and personal to Raven Stone. He wasn't worried about what Joe did with the other students, but something about her had slipped past Kieran's guard. Probably the hint that she wasn't as tough as she tried to appear; he found the combination of hard shell, soft centre fascinating. 'And that's all you're doing?'

'Do you doubt me? I was the one tasked to find out why the parents of some of these students have suddenly fallen so spectacularly off the straight and narrow path.'

C stream, the Cats, as the agents with skills like Joe's were nicknamed, were selected for their ability to blend; one result was that they were never short of girlfriends or boyfriends, thanks to their charming ways. Kieran's own A stream, tagged the Owls, were teased for their high IQs and low sweet-talking scores. The charm and the brains: that was how they were seen at the YDA.

Kieran stabbed his apple pie. Personally he preferred five minutes of straight talk with a girl he fancied than Joe's hour of clever manoeuvring and flattery—anyone with any sense would.

But was Raven sensible?

Put it aside: this was about the mission, not about an irrational instinct that had flared up inside him. He distrusted emotions. The last thing he wanted at Westron was a girlfriend, as serious relationships were forbidden while on a job. What was needed now was for him to focus on his mission.

'OK, how we going to go about this? Do we need to adjust any of our strategies now we are on site?'

'I don't think so. We'll proceed as Isaac told us. I'll check out those who have parents mixed up in this scheme, see if they spill anything about what connects them, other than them all having kids at the same school; you get into the database and find any hint of Westron being knowingly involved.'

'That red-haired girl who has it in for Raven—Hedda Lindberg?'

'Already memorized the roll?'

'Naturally. First thing I did on arrival.'

Joe gave him an exasperated look. ''Course it was. What about her?'

'She might be a good place to start. Her father went from legitimate gem merchant to smuggler of blood diamonds overnight.'

'Interesting. OK, I'll check if she knows anything.'

'Good luck with that. She looks pretty toxic to me.'

'I'll be careful.' Joe stood up. 'Will you be OK on your own?'

Kieran folded his napkin in a precise square. 'You have to ask?'

'Oh yeah, Mr I-am-an-island is fine with his own company. I forgot. See you in our room then.'

'I'll have my preliminary results on the email traffic by then.'

'Great. Don't forget we're gonna have to attend lessons tomorrow and check in with Isaac at midday.'

Kieran was already running some tests on Westron's wireless network on his tablet computer. 'Like that will be hard for me.'

'I know you have Science qualifications up to your ears, so that's why I enrolled you for the Drama, Art, English, and Dance AS level courses.'

'You did what? I'm not prancing about in a leotard!'

'Shouldn't have handed over the form-filling to me, should

you?' Joe intercepted Kieran's thump with his forearm. 'Come on, Key, it'll be fun.'

'For whom?' Kieran imagined squashing his dessert bowl on to Joe's face—so tempting. Then again, how hard could all that arty stuff be? Nothing surely to the extreme difficulty of pure mathematics, and he'd mastered that without breaking a sweat. He rose to his feet. 'You will die for this, Joe, and no one will find the body. I have several completely undetectable means of disposing of a corpse.'

Joe looked worried for a second, knowing Kieran probably did. 'You could see it as a challenge. You complained about not being tested earlier.'

'You imagine that this is going to test me?' Kieran raised a brow. 'Think again, my friend, think again.'

From her vantage point on the visitors' sofa by the office, Raven watched the students file out of the dining hall while she pretended to read a newspaper. She had meant to return to her room but curiosity about the new guys kept her hanging around in the foyer.

'Oh my gosh: they are fa-bu-lous!' exclaimed Mairi, a girl in her dance class, blessed with an abundance of freckles and frothy auburn hair. 'Did you see them?'

'You mean Mr Hottie McTottie and Mr Scorching Tightbuns? You could hardly miss them. What can I say but wow!' laughed her friend, Liza. *I'm with you there, sister.* 'They've just joined Westron. Hedda said they were expelled from their old school.'

Mairi grinned. 'Even better. I just love bad boys.'

'Me too. I wouldn't mind helping them settle in, if you know what I mean.' Liza waggled her eyebrows, still giggling.

'Raven had a go.'

'She's quicker off the mark than the rest of us.'

'Looks like she crashed and burned with them though.' They were passing out of earshot, not having noticed their eavesdropper behind the potted cheese plant.

'Leaves the field clear for the rest of us, doesn't it? So, what do you think about the rumours about her? True?'

Raven didn't get to hear the answer but it was horrible to know that even girls she had once thought of as friends were questioning her character. She didn't have long to brood as the two new boys emerged from the hall. Yep, her first impressions had been right: they were both gorgeous. Joe was more instantly appealing, perhaps, but there was something about Kieran that made her want to look at him again. And again. She lifted the paper higher.

'So how would you do it?' Joe was asking. 'Dispose of the evidence?'

'It's harder than you think.'

'I get that.'

'And you'll only find out if I decide you have a need to know.'

'Like when you are using it on me?'

'Correct. So tread carefully, my friend.'

Joe shook his head. 'I think it's too late for that. I'd better make a will.'

Odd conversation. Raven put down the paper and watched them walk away. The view was mighty fine. It was like spotting two big cats prowling a jungle, moving sinuously through the undergrowth. *OK, OK, Raven, enough hanging about eyeing up the new guys.* Kieran had already demonstrated in a fairly insulting manner that he only looked at her twice to dissect her character and habits. She would be better off working out how to beat down the rumours about her stealing rather than languishing after him. Her past made her shy around boys;

27

she usually dealt with her attraction to guys by turning her sassy attitude on full. Best to put a distance between herself and Kieran so she didn't embarrass herself. That shouldn't be too hard; she couldn't imagine they'd share any classes. Kieran didn't seem the type to go for arts.

'As you know by now, most of your marks will go on the assessment of your final dance piece and your written inter-pretation.' Miss Hollis, the dance teacher, flexed her arms above her head, rolling her neck muscles to loosen up.

Raven couldn't believe it: Kieran was in her class. He had come in late and sat on the floor near her, stretching long legs crossed at the ankles before him. He studiously ignored the excited whispers of the girls around him, looking as if he would prefer to be anywhere else than here.

'The exams are coming up fast and we have a new member of our AS set to fit in. Girls, this is Kieran Storm whose been doing the subject at his old school. We'll need to reorganize our groups. So, Kieran, what style do you prefer? Ballet, jazz or modern?'

Did he really just mutter: I'd prefer to be sticking sharp objects in my eyeballs? Raven gave him a querying look. What on earth was he doing here? He was the most reluctant convert to dance she had ever seen.

'Kieran?' repeated Miss Hollis.

'Modern.'

'OK, we have two groups doing that. Liza, Mairi and Rachel, and Gina and Raven.' The teacher glanced round the twenty girls gathered at the front of the room. 'Raven, where's Gina?'

'She's not back yet, miss.' Phew: bullet dodged. She wouldn't have Kieran dumped on her.

Miss Hollis turned to the other group. 'How's your routine shaping up? Would you be able to fit him in?'

'Oh yes, miss,' gushed Mairi. 'I'd be really happy to have him—in our group, I mean.' The rest of the class giggled as Mairi blushed an amazing shade of red. Liza whispered 'Hottie McTottie' so Mairi could hear, making the girl's embarrassment even deeper.

But then teacher turned back to Raven. *Go away, go away!* 'But if Gina is missing, perhaps we should put him with you, Raven?'

Kieran's crystal green eyes latched onto her, producing that same tingle down the spine she had felt last night.

No, no: she had resolved to keep her distance and this would ruin that plan. 'Without Gina, it will be hard to know what to do with him, miss.'

'I know exactly what I'd do with him,' whispered Liza.

Miss Hollis shot a reproving look at Liza then fixed Raven with her gaze. 'But you are one of my most experienced dancers, Raven; I'm sure you can adapt to having a boy in your group better than most.'

The teacher's expectation was clear. 'I guess we'll sort something out.'

'Thank you, Raven. And if Gina doesn't come back for any reason, then you can simply slip Kieran into her role.'

'That'd be hard as we were working to the theme of birth—we'd gone for mother and child—Gina being the mother.'

A couple of girls giggled. Kieran frowned at the ceiling.

Mrs Hollis tapped her fingers on her crossed forearms. 'Well, some of the best dances come from being forced to radically rethink our preconceptions.'

'If you say so.' How had her avoidance tactics been defeated so quickly?

That issue settled to her satisfaction, Miss Hollis clapped

her hands. 'OK, girls—and Kieran, of course: let's warm up. We'll do some neck isolations, then some hip swings.'

Kieran placed himself at the back of the group just behind Raven. She didn't like him there; she had the distinct feeling he was following her rather than the teacher and that made the normally innocent exercises uncomfortable. She wished she had put on trackies rather than a leotard and leggings.

Miss Hollis signalled the end to the warm-up. 'OK, now work in your groups. Start with some trust exercises. I'll go round and see each group individually.'

Raven turned. He stood right behind her, hands on hips, confident half-smile on his face, lord of all he surveyed. Apparently he was not shaken by being the only male in the room. This was the first time they'd stood eye-to-eye and she was struck at how tall he was. Elf and hobbit—that's how he made her feel. She reached for her usual sass to counter the height difference. 'So, Sudoku, how would you like to do this?'

He pushed a lock of hair off his face. 'Trust exercises—what are they?'

She gave him a querying look. 'You don't know?'

'Obviously not as I just asked you.'

'You know: falling back and trusting your partner will catch you. That kind of thing.'

'What is the point of doing that? I already know I'll catch you and if you try and catch me we will both end up on the floor.'

She rolled her eyes. 'Ya think?'

'I know.'

'OK, Sudoku, give it a go.'

'I am not falling on you.'

'See, you don't trust me.'

'No, I don't.'

30

She leant closer and prodded his chest. 'That was the point of the exercise. You've just failed.'

Challenge issued, he responded. 'All right, Miss Stone, catch me.' Spinning round, he let himself fall back. She made a good attempt at grabbing him as he fell, but gravity won and they ended up on the floor, her under him.

'Geez Louise, give me some warning next time!' huffed Raven, shoving him. She tried not to give away her intense awareness of her body plastered against his spine.

He cleared his throat and sat up. 'See, I'm too big for you to support my weight.'

Raven rolled out from under him and sprang to her feet. 'Let's try that one more time, Ace, with fair warning.' Kieran didn't answer, his gaze snagged on her hair. Her hands flew to it: as usual it was misbehaving, waving around her head in disarray. 'Are you listening to me, Kieran?'

'Possibly not. Have you got anything sensible to say?'

Her hand itched for something to throw at him. Nothing available, she settled for a put-upon sigh. 'Gina never gave me any of this trouble. I can't wait for her to get back.'

'Maybe the two of you would be enough to catch me.' He got to his feet. 'When do you think she'll get here?' Kieran rolled his shoulders.

'I don't know. She should've been here already. It's just like Johnny and Siobhan—they've been gone months—Hedda last term and, I don't know, a bunch of others.'

Kieran's attention focused abruptly, smile vanishing. 'What do you mean, just like Johnny and Siobhan?'

Raven shrugged, wondering why he cared. 'You know, people saying they were going to come back then not showing up for ages—or not at all. Gina was totally, like, fired up for this term when I last saw her before Easter. I expect she just missed her flight or something.'

31

'You don't know?'

'She might've texted me.'

'But your phone's out of action.'

She crossed her arms, not liking the reminder of the fight. 'As you noticed last night.'

Kieran dug in his sports bag. 'Want to contact her on mine?'

His offer surprised Raven. They were strangers, after all. 'You sure?'

He held it out to her.

Casting a quick glance over at Miss Hollis—she was busy with one of the Jazz groups—Raven checked her planner for a number and tapped it in. When she'd finished, she handed the phone back to Kieran, much happier.

'Thanks. I hate not knowing.'

'OK, guys, what've you come up with?' Miss Hollis appeared at their side; she excelled at teacher stealth attacks to pick on slackers.

Kieran tucked the phone away quickly. 'We're just batting some preliminary ideas between us.'

'You'd better not spend too long doing that. We've only got a few weeks to put this together.'

'It's OK, miss: we'll get there,' said Raven.

'How are you approaching it?'

'We're working the kinks out of a few trust issues,' said Kieran smoothly. 'I think Raven isn't sure about me yet.'

Raven looked daggers in his direction.

'Really? Can I help with that?' Mrs Hollis looked between them expectantly.

'Oh no, miss,' Raven said sweetly—then cast her arms wide and collapsed into Kieran's arms, lifting one leg to point a toe. She had to admit his reactions were good: he caught her. She used the momentum of the catch to bounce up and do a free spin, ending with her arms in a curving shape pointing back to him. That made the score about even, she would say.

'Excellent.' Miss Hollis applauded. 'I can see that putting you with a male partner, Raven, is allowing you to use his power as a springboard for your natural gymnastic ability.'

'What?' Kieran scowled. She got the message he did not consider himself anyone's springboard.

'The man in a dance is expected to lead, help, and support his partner.' Mrs Hollis patted Kieran on the back. 'I'm hoping you'll put those muscles of yours to good purpose, Kieran. Carry on.'

Chapter 3

'Call yourself my friend?' Kieran threw his sweaty sports kit at Joe's head.

Joe sat up from his computer on the desk in their shared room and brushed the trackies to the floor. 'How's your plié?'

Kieran told him succinctly what he could do with himself.

'I'll take that under advisement.'

'Not a complete waste of time though.' Kieran dropped his art folder on his bed and went to his plant research on the window sill. They needed more space. He pushed Joe's books off the shelf and onto the floor.

'Do you have to do that?' Joe groaned as Kieran began distributing the pitcher plants, lobster-pot, snap and flypaper traps around the room, chucking things out of his way.

'This is important.'

Joe went to move a flowerpot off his bedside table.

'Don't touch!' Kieran said with a snap in his own voice.

'Why not?'

'It's in a carefully calibrated position. I'm going to release the bluebottles.' He got the container out of the cupboard where he had been storing the flies bought from a pet shop. Intended for lizards, they would do just as well for his purposes.

'You are not letting them out while I'm in here—that's gross.' Joe picked up some oranges from the bowl beside his computer and began to juggle—he liked to keep his skill sharpened.

'Not gross. It is scientific. I want to see which plant is most successful predator and how long it takes to digest the flies.'

'Can't you read about that in a book?' Joe let the fruit fall back into the bowl, throwing the last from behind his back.

Kieran gave Joe a 'do-I-look-like-someone-who-relies-on-second-hand-information?' stare.

Joe cast his eyes to the ceiling, seeking patience. 'Are you going to explain why exactly you are turning our bedroom into a haven for flesh-eating plants?'

'It is important in an old case I was reviewing.' He tapped the flies awake.

Joe snatched them from him. 'You can do that later. Think about this case for the moment. Tell me why Dance was not a complete waste of time.'

'I was paired with Raven Stone.'

Joe sat back in his chair, wheels rolling him away from the desk, removing the flies from Kieran's reach. 'You should be thanking me, man!'

'I'll grant you one thing: I repent of every bad word I ever said about leotards. But, Joe, I'm trying to tell you something. Her roommate hasn't come back from the spring holiday. Raven went on to say that other students have also gone missing for odd periods and the names all correlated with the parents we are investigating: Hedda, Johnny—I'm guessing his surname is Minter as there's only two Johnnys in the school; Siobhan Green, and others I didn't get her to list.'

'What's the name of her friend?'

'Gina Carr.'

Joe entered the information into their mission files. 'Daughter of American diplomat currently posted to London. Military attaché.'

'Another high flyer.'

'Parents of most of these students are, but it does fit the pattern. We've nothing on him yet.'

'Then maybe we're in at the start of the process for Carr. We should check if there's any hint of ransoms being demanded or blackmail—they could be extorting favours from the parents in return for the safety of the children.'

'I guess. But why leave the children in the school when they are released? Hedda is strutting around the place, no sign she was the victim of some ransom plot. You would've thought the first thing a parent would do is take the kid and run a mile in the opposite direction once they were free.'

Kieran had to agree with Joe: it didn't make sense and strayed beyond the bounds of the original mission they had been given. A concerned government official, very senior in her field, had called in YDA to investigate. She told Isaac, chief of their agency, that she thought something serious was going on. Strange decisions were being made. A Siberian gas pipeline had been rerouted against all expectations. A senior government official of a Middle Eastern country had been made president of the national bank with no previous hints that he was up for the position. Telecoms contracts had been sold at below the market price. The only link she could find was that all the people who had the final say on the decisions had children who were students in the Union of International Schools. He and Joe had enrolled expecting to find some net-working happening via school events and friendship circles, deals done in backrooms on Sports Day, not this more sinister turn of events involving the kids themselves.

'Let me look again at the list of pupils and see if I can identify from school records those that have gone missing. I'll keep in the ones who've come back but highlight their names.'

Joe knew better than to refuse Kieran when he was in puzzle-solving mode. 'Coming right up.'

'I'll cross-reference them with the parents involved in corrupt practices—I'm sure the answer must lie between the two. And I'll text Isaac to tell him to put eyes on Carr—see if he reveals anything.'

'Here you go.' Joe dropped the printout of names on his desk. 'I'll leave you to it. Got Biology next.'

'Rub it in, why don't you.' Kieran shot him a look from under his brows. 'You don't happen to know any good sources on dance—a handbook or something?'

'Just so happens I'm an expert, though street dance is more my thing.' So why wasn't Joe doing the AS? Oh yeah, because this was about humiliating him. 'What kind of dance, Key?'

'The teacher called it "Modern".' Kieran tapped at his keyboard, starting to run a trace on Gina's phone. Having so many tasks to do made his brain purr with pleasure: finally a challenge worthy of him.

'We thought you might need help so I put a few DVDs in my suitcase.' Joe threw him some recent dance movies which Kieran plucked out of the air without looking up. 'Watch and learn, my friend.'

Today was tanking. It had started with another envelope under the door—same picture but this time with her head in a noose. Being paired with Kieran had been the cherry on the already very stale iced bun of a morning, torn as she was between attraction and irritation when dealing with him. Wanting to offload her angst on some friendly ears, Raven checked in at the school office to see if they'd heard from Gina or her parents. She found her grandfather chatting to the secretary.

'Hey, granddad, how's your day so far?' She adored him so much; every time she saw him shuffling about the school in his baggy blue boiler suit, she felt a little surge of warmth. She didn't care what the others thought of his job. She could just imagine Mr Arrogant Storm looking down his nose at her granddad. So what? Granddad was her only close family left and she was determined to appreciate every second of his company. He, however, was stuck in the notion that she preferred her school friends and made sure he kept out of her way no matter how many times she told him different.

'I'm fine, love. How about you? Settled into your routine?'

Raven shrugged. She didn't want to burden him with the foul atmosphere between her and the other girls in her year and the stupid notes; he already worried enough about her and his health was touch-and-go at the best of times.

He bent a little closer, noticing her attempts to hide her bruise with make-up. 'How did you hurt your eye, Raven?'

'Accident. S'OK. Gina's not back yet though. I was wondering if Mrs Marshall has had a message.'

'You must be missing your partner in crime.' At least Granddad understood.

'Yes, I am.'

The secretary leafed through her phone calls. 'Nothing, dear. Don't worry; she'll turn up soon.'

'Has the school contacted her parents?'

'I'm afraid I can't share that information with you.' Her smile was brittle, setting off alarm bells.

'Do you mean they have and that something's wrong at home?' Unlike other students, Raven knew to expect bad news. The phone call at two in the morning. The car returning from the hospital with only one occupant.

Mrs Marshall turned away, moving the late register to a different table. 'Don't jump to conclusions, Raven.'

'I'm her best friend, Mrs Marshall. She wouldn't mind me knowing.' Desperation made her voice catch.

'School policy. Haven't you got a lesson you should be in?'

Her grandfather put his hand on her arm. 'Raven.' His calming tone was enough. She knew she had a tendency to fly off the handle; he was skilled at reeling her back in.

'Sorry.' *Deep breath.* 'Yes, I've French next. See you later.'

Raven hurried to class. She couldn't get past the niggling worry that something had happened to Gina.

Entering French last, Raven took the seat next to Kieran's friend.

'Hi, Joe, how're you doing?' She brushed away a bluebottle that had landed on the desk.

'Much better now you're here.' He winked, but Raven sensed his flirty manner was reflex rather than personal; something a wise girl enjoyed and didn't take too seriously.

'Why thank you.' She got out her folder.

'Heard you were paired with Kieran this morning.'

'Uh-huh.'

'How'd he do?'

Was Joe smirking? Raven wasn't so keen on anyone who made fun of Dance; it was her hardest AS level by far. 'He did OK.'

'Really?'

'Surely you know he's a good dancer? He did it at your old school.' Hang on: Joe had said they were expelled for blowing up the lab. If Kieran was doing arts subjects, why was he playing with chemicals? 'He did do Dance, right? You're not trying something on here?'

Joe frowned. 'What, us? No! Why would we? Yeah, he's a good dancer—good at everything.'

'You see I wouldn't be exactly thrilled to find I'm caught up in some joke.'

'No joke—trust me.' Joe swivelled to Adewale on his other side. 'Hey, nice to meet you: I'm Joe.'

Ignore me, why don't you, but I'm on to your game. Raven decided it was worth pushing Kieran a little harder on his dance credentials. If school was going to be in the sucks-out-loud zone socially, then at least her work shouldn't suffer.

She eavesdropped on Joe's conversation with his neighbour. 'What do your parents do, Adewale?'

'My father works in the City. Banking. Yours?'

'Mom's in rehab; Dad's in prison.' Joe drew a cat's face in the margin of his empty pad.

Adewale laughed. 'You're kidding me?'

'Nope.'

Adewale swallowed his chuckles. 'Hey, I'm sorry, man.'

'No problem. Gotta laugh or I'd cry. My godfather swooped in and rescued me, which is why I'm here.'

'And who's your godfather?'

'He's a colonel in the British Ministry of Defence.' Joe revved up his smile another gear. 'And at least good old dad's not a banker. Talk about unpopular.'

The Nigerian grinned back, put at ease by Joe's joke. 'I find it hard to live that down, I can tell you. My mother's a nurse—how's that?'

'Now you can hold your head up with pride.' Joe turned to Raven. 'See, he's a good guy really.'

'I knew that already. Hey, Adewale—did you have a good holiday?' asked Raven.

'Not bad, thanks. I don't suppose my watch turned up over the break, did it? Your granddad said he'd look.'

'He didn't mention it so I guess not. Sorry.'

'I'll have to tell Dad then and get him to contact the insurers. He won't be pleased. It was a Cartier. Looks like it was stolen rather than just lost.'

'That's rough.' Joe grimaced in sympathy. 'I'd better keep my Rolex locked up if there's a thief here.'

The teacher called their attention to the white board where she was running through a movie version of their set text, *Le Malade Imaginaire*. Raven began to take notes but she couldn't forget the conversation she had overheard. Joe's dad in prison? Really? And how did he end up with a British godfather paying for his education? And what about Kieran's parents? Were they also in trouble? Was that what brought the boys together? She could hardly ask as Joe hadn't been talking to her. That'd be rude.

'It's OK,' Joe said in a low voice.

'What do you mean?'

He put a body and tail on his cat, and then started on an owl. 'I know you heard what I said. I've not got a problem with it. What my parents have done is nothing to me now. And my godfather's really great.'

'When does he get out?'

'Dad?'

She nodded.

'Never, I hope.'

That meant he'd done something very bad. 'I'm sorry.'

'Don't be. It was good that he was caught. I owe NYPD my life.'

New York Police Department. 'I'm still sorry—has to be tough.'

'Thanks.'

'And your godfather—does he make a point of helping boys with no parents to support them?'

Joe gave the owl a miserable expression. Was that a beatbox he was perching on? 'Sometimes, yeah. That's how he found me. But he's also a good friend of Kieran's family.'

'Kieran's family?'

'Oh yeah. I've met them. Grand house, classy ancestors– they've got the full English upper crust vibe going on. Kieran can't bear it. He thinks you should get by on brain power and refuses to use his background to get ahead.'

'Wow, does he have a title?'

'Let's just say, his parents are welcome in the Ascot Royal Enclosure any time, but if you mention it, he'd hit you with one of his demolition jobs on the class system of this country and freeze you out of his life for all eternity.'

Raven didn't quite get Kieran's attitude as she thought that, if she had a posh family, she'd be tempted to make the most of it. 'OK, got it.'

Joe drew a circle round the owl then made it into a moat. 'Funny thing is, he's more ashamed of his privilege than I am of my tough start in life.'

'Are you two quite finished?' asked Mrs Gordenstone, the teacher, flapping a copy of the play in front of them. 'Or shall I put this class on pause while you get better acquainted?'

'I apologize,' Joe bathed the teacher in one of his smiles. Her prickly posture relaxed a little. 'Raven was just helping me catch up.'

'That's all very well, Mr Masters, but now is the time to concentrate on today's lesson.'

'*Bien sûr, madame.*'

Reprimand skilfully diverted, Joe settled back in his seat. He checked his watch.

'Late for a hot date?' teased Raven when he checked it again a minute later.

'But, sugar, I ain't asked you yet.'

Raven laughed at his hickabilly tone.

'I'm just expecting a phone call,' Joe explained. 'I'm gonna have to cut class early. Cover for me?'

'And say what?'

'I've come down with an imaginary illness?'

'Yeah, like that'd work in this class seeing what we're studying.'

'Migraine. Migraine is a good one. Impossible to disprove.'

'Expert at this, are you? OK, I'll cover for you.'

Joe slid his books back in his bag and left his seat, making his excuses to the teacher with a very convincing act. He was out of the class two minutes before twelve.

For a couple of newcomers, supposedly good at all their subjects, Kieran and Joe weren't that interested in taking their classes. Come to think of it, they were here because they had got themselves expelled from their last school. Looked like they might be on the same track.

Isaac's face came on screen in the Skype box. Brush cut blond hair and laser blue eyes, he had the look of a man who had been round the block a few times, but at a hundred miles an hour, tyres screaming, before taking down a few scumbags.

'Hey, guys, how's it going?' Isaac was fiercely protective of his trainees. If they messed up, he would shout at them, then take the rap. There was not a hint of a politician about him: the buck stopped with him every time.

'Good, thanks, Isaac.' Joe took a seat in front of the monitor, first moving a Venus flytrap off the chair. Kieran quickly transferred it to a similar spot so the results wouldn't be ruined. 'Key's turned up something weird—students here are disappearing during the school term with no explanation, and there's a link to the parents we're investigating.'

'More than a link—the correlation is ninety-five per cent,' added Kieran. 'The one aberration was a case of meningitis so I think that's a genuine exception.'

'Latest is a girl called Gina Carr; dad is in the American embassy in London. Key's done a report. We'd like you to put a tail on Carr—see if he starts acting against his country's interests.'

'Yes, I'll do that and I look forward to reading the report. Good work. I guess you are exploring the obvious explanations for this—blackmail and the rest?'

'Of course, but nothing is clicking just yet,' admitted Joe.

'Early days. You've made more progress than I expected.' Isaac's eyes lifted to the left of Joe to fix on Kieran standing behind his chair. 'How's it going?' Isaac knew that, like most Owls, Kieran did not suffer fools gladly and was less adept at slotting in to a new environment than Joe.

'I'm doing fine, sir.' Kieran decided not to rat on his mate about the dance thing. 'Got one more lead handed us—we were given Gina Carr's number, the girl who has gone missing over Easter. I fed the details in to our tracking programme and the phone is reading as being pretty much on our doorstep, at that fancy annex owned by the Union of International Schools.'

Isaac drummed his fingers on his desk. 'You mean the manor?'

'Yes. They call it a sport and leisure facility to house students who don't want to go home during vacations when the school is closed.'

'Interesting. That place needs a closer look.'

'It's supposed to be off-limits to us during term time as they use it for conferences, due to open again in the summer to run courses for the students. It's about five miles from here—the other side of the farm that also belongs to the UIS. The website suggests it is more like an exclusive hotel spa than a school camp. I've looked at satellite imagery and it seems to be all leisure-related—pools, golf course, tennis courts—nothing to spark suspicion. Very luxurious.'

'Yeah, we can't expect the little darlings of the rich and privileged to rough it in their playtime,' drawled Joe.

'Gina might've left her phone behind for some reason but maybe she's still there. She could, of course, be ill or having an exam meltdown—nothing to do with the case we're investigating. But even if that's true, the school knows what's up and is hiding the truth from everyone here, including her best friend.' Kieran kept Raven's name back on purpose, though he wasn't exactly sure why. Some instinct to keep her out of this.

Isaac frowned, extra lines appearing on his forehead and bracketing his mouth. 'OK, I'll send in a team to see if they can discover anything. People employed at the manor must know more about what goes on there. If the girl's still on site, there'll be staff aware of the fact.'

'I think, sir, Joe and I should put in an application to go to the manor at the end of this term with the other students who spend their holidays there. We can pull out if it's a dead end but I'm interested to get a look inside myself.'

Isaac chewed that over for a moment. 'OK. Do it. Fact-finding only though, Kieran.'

'Of course, sir.'

'I'll add our names to the list.' Joe made a note. 'Is there anything else for us?'

'Not at this stage. Just keep out of trouble; don't do anything to raise suspicions about your interest in the parents we've identified.' Isaac rubbed the bend in his nose—sign of an old break. 'And don't take risks. I've other guys I've trained for that.'

'Sure.' Joe grinned, giving the Cheshire Cat a run for his money. 'Cats and Owls are supposed to stick to evidence collection.'

'That's right. OK, back to the grindstone. I'll check in again soon.'

'Over and out.' Joe cut the connection. 'Do you think he was pleased with our progress?'

'Hard to say with Isaac. He's quicker to say when things are off track.'

Joe closed down the computer. 'I meant to tell you: Raven was lapping up the information on our background I gave her. Obviously she wants to get even after your little party trick on the first evening.'

'It is not a trick; it's deduction.'

'Whatever. She was the one to introduce your name into the conversation about families.'

Kieran went cold. 'What did you tell her?'

'Usual cover story.' Joe flipped a ball of paper into the bin. 'Nothing touching on the truth.'

That was OK then. 'You didn't embroider, did you?' Joe was liable to get too much in to his cover stories.

'Only a little. I kept it vague. Said you were upper class. Parents good friends with royalty.'

Kieran groaned. 'Did you have to do that to me?'

'She wouldn't believe the truth and it fits. You are the most aristocratic poor boy I've ever met.'

'False advertising and you know it. So what about you?'

'I tuned up my story a little after our last job—this time I hinted my dad was a murderer and my mom a druggie.'

'Joe, Isaac will kill you if he gets wind of that.' Kieran loved Joe's parents, two of the nicest people on the planet. They had unofficially adopted Kieran as a son when they discovered his own were such bad news. 'Why are you taking risks with our cover?'

Joe looked a bit sheepish. 'I like watching their reactions, see if I can sell them the story.'

Kieran shook his head. Joe enjoyed the role playing on missions and if he had one weakness it was to indulge his imagination too much.

'Look, Key, I tell people what I think they want to hear;

46

they believe it quicker that way. Having a dad in prison fits the media image of African American youth.'

Too late to pull Joe back now—the stories were out and doing the rounds. 'OK, it's done. Let's move on.'

'What's next, Key?'

Kieran picked up a DVD. 'Thanks to you, I'm going to study this. You go sweet talk that red-haired girl—that should be punishment enough for doing this to me.' He waved the dance movie at his friend.

'OK, off to do penance over the lunch table. See you later.'

Chapter 4

At the end of the week, and after a vivid nightmare where she dreamt Gina and Kieran were dancing the foxtrot in the cemetery where her parents were buried, Raven had to take action.

'You're through to the American Embassy. How can I help you?'

'Oh, hello. May I speak to Mr Carr? The military attaché.' Raven felt awkward asking. She had the impression, from the few times they had met, that Mr Carr did not approve of her. Even so, she was risking it as Kieran had assured her that her text to Gina had received no answer.

'Who's calling, please?'

'My name's Raven Stone. I'm a friend of his daughter, Gina.'

'I'll see if he is available to take your call, Miss Stone.'

Raven twiddled the cord of the pay phone in the school lobby as hold music tinkled down the line. The flex slithered through her fingers. She had a row of twenty pence pieces on the ledge but this call was eating them like a gannet swallowing silver fish. *Come on, come on.* She fed another into the slot. '*Summertime and the living is easy,*' sang Ella Fitzgerald in a tinny voice. No, it wasn't—not with your best friend still missing and a week of school already over.

'Thank you for holding, Miss Stone. I'm afraid Mr Carr is unable to take your call at this time but if you would like to leave a message, I'll make sure he gets it.'

'OK, thanks. Can you tell him that Raven called and

wanted to know if Gina was all right. She's not come back to school and I'm worried about her.'

'Do you have a number where he can contact you?'

'Could he leave a message for me on the school's main line?' Raven read off the number.

'Got it.' The receptionist read it back to her. 'Can I help you with anything else?'

Sorting out her life? Solving her money problems? 'No, thank you.'

'You have a nice day now.'

Unlikely. 'Thanks.' Raven put the phone back on the hook and heard the money tumble into the machine. No change in the slot for her to claim. The call had cost her over three pounds thanks to being on hold for so long.

'What are you doing out of class, Raven?' The head teacher paused on her way through the lobby, a party of parents of prospective pupils in tow.

'It's my free period so I was calling Gina's father, Mrs Bain.' Another note had arrived; this time they'd gone for a gravestone with her name on it and Raven had been desperate to ask Gina's advice what to do. Stupid thing had been responsible for her nightmare. She hated feeling scared in a place that had once seemed a perfect refuge.

The head teacher did not look thrilled by this news but with strangers at her side could not make an issue of it. She turned to them, like a defence barrister using Raven as her exhibit A. 'We like our students to be able to keep in close contact with family and friends. Mobiles are allowed, naturally, but this phone is also available for their use.'

One of the fathers stepped forward, a cheerful man with a crop of straw-like hair. 'How do you like the school, if you don't mind me asking?'

Raven glanced over at the stony face of Mrs Bain. Just at

the moment she loathed Westron but it would be suicidal to say that in front of the head teacher. 'It's fine.' If you don't mind attacks in the girls' changing rooms and threatening anonymous letters.

'Friendly? My Georgina is a little shy. I'm looking for a school where she will fit in.'

'As you'll see in the prospectus, we can offer many extra character building courses at our annex to help with problems like that,' said Mrs Bain, holding up a glossy folder.

'I don't see shyness as a problem,' the father said stiffly. 'I just want to know if she'll be happy here.' Raven wanted to give him a cheer. 'Will she enjoy it?'

'She'll do OK.' Raven couldn't say something she didn't believe—she hated lying. She looked to the head teacher for permission to leave.

Mrs Bain scowled at her cool endorsement. 'Hurry along, Raven. The bell for the next lesson is about to ring.' Mrs Bain turned her back but continued in a loud voice. 'Raven is one of our scholarship pupils. We have bursaries for a number of special cases. We see it as part of our giving back to the community. The vast majority of our students, however, come from the very best backgrounds. We think that this is one of the principal considerations for many parents who send their children here. We can guarantee that they will mix with others from the very highest echelons of society.'

Snob. Raven walked quickly down the corridor out of sight and checked her timetable. Dance next. She wondered what excuse Kieran would give today for not doing any actual dancing. He was going to mess up her assessment and she had been hoping to take it for A level. That was going to stop. In the mood she was in, either he produced the goods or danced solo.

All business, Raven launched her plan at the beginning of the class. 'Miss Hollis, Gina's still not back. I think Kieran and I will have to choreograph a new routine. Can we use one of the music practice rooms if they're free?' The music block had a number of large, sound-proofed rooms for orchestral practice. Raven was determined to pin Kieran down and she preferred to do it somewhere private.

'Good idea, Raven. Got your music?'

Raven held up the CD.

'Off you go then. I'll pop over in fifteen minutes and see how you are getting on.'

'C'mon, Sudoku.' She held the door open for him.

'You're very assertive today.' Kieran picked up his bag. It was bulging open with heavy tomes on—Raven read the titles—number theory and astronomy, as well as a pad with closely written but beautifully accurate handwriting. Her scrawl would look laughable next to his. 'I thought I was supposed to lead in dance.'

Not if he was leading them into a blind alley.

'I don't see the point of time wasting when you can cut straight to the chase.' Raven poked her head round one door in the music block. 'Good—this one's available.' She switched on the CD player and slid in the disk, nervous about what she was about to do now the moment had arrived. He had already detected that her surface confidence had cracks, one of the many reasons he disturbed her. 'OK, now let me lay my cards on the table. I want to know if you can dance or if you've been messing about since you arrived.'

His eyes went to the door.

'Uh-huh, no escape—not today.' Was she really being this bold? Go her. 'I'm counting on getting a good mark in this exam so I can do this course next year. If you rain on my parade I'll not be happy.'

'*Your* parade?'

I will not fold, I will not fold. 'Ours, if you pull your weight.'

'I can't see that being a problem. It's only Dance.' Kieran did some stretches and abdominal crunches. Raven had to remind herself not to get sidetracked from her aim. 'You're treating this class, Raven, like it's rocket science.'

She saw the trap before she fell in; he was baiting her to say 'it's not rocket science' so he could give her one of his supercilious looks. 'Fine, if you don't want to be here, just leave.' She waved at the door.

'I never said that.'

'No, you just behave as if all this is beneath you. You're really irritating me.'

'I never would have guessed.' He was smirking now.

She bunched her hair back in frustration, his eyes following her hands again in that unnerving way of his. 'What can you do, Ace? It's clear we have to start again on this routine anyway so we might as well play to your strengths.'

'My strengths?'

'You do have some, right? I saw you do a Sudoku puzzle in seconds flat so you clearly have quite a brain. Dancers need to be quick thinking, understand patterns, so that's good.'

'I'm glad you think I have some strengths.' He sounded so superior she wanted to kick him.

'Being the genius that you are, I'm sure you already appreciate that music is like Maths.'

'Yes, in many important respects.'

'Do you play an instrument?'

'Piano.'

She could imagine that—he had the long artistic fingers. She shoved away the thought that she had always found people with a musical skill incredibly attractive. 'That's good. The piece is "Shake it out": do you know it?'

He wandered over to the grand piano at the far end of the room and played a melody—something by Mozart, she thought, though she didn't know its name. 'I don't listen to much contemporary music.'

Why was that not a surprise? 'It's got great lyrics. Let's listen together and see what strikes you.'

Kieran closed his eyes for the duration of the song, looking like a person deep in meditation. She let the track play to the end. 'So? What do you think?'

Kieran proceeded to give an analysis of the key signature, the structure, and even the sound engineering. Raven dropped her head on her hands.

'What about the gutsy singing, the ballad building to an explosion of sound, the emotional content?'

Kieran shrugged.

'What kind of emotion do you think the song is trying to convey?' Raven would have found his ducking of any feeling-related language fascinating if it weren't inconvenient. 'OK, look, she's singing about being in a bad relationship—a romance that breaks her down, one she has to shake free—a kind of rebirth.' Raven's mind darted through the possibilities. 'Yep, that's good—that's strong. You can be the emotionally repressed guy; I can be the girl who gets away.'

'I'm the what?' He did not look pleased by her casting.

'The guy who is like the devil on her back, weighing her down. Now, let's put some moves together that convey that— like our motif in this piece.' She shook her arms and legs to loosen the muscles. 'OK, what do you think of this move?' Humming the chorus, she did a combination of back arch moving into a slow walkover handstand, going into a pirouette.

Kieran's eyes glistened with what might have been appreciation. 'You're very athletic.'

'I've enjoyed doing gymnastics since I was little.' Her skin prickled with awareness of him; she had to admit he had a surprisingly well toned body for a genius—biceps, triceps, and six-pack all visible under his tight black T-shirt. She wasn't going to look at them—she wasn't. 'Maybe that's why I like dance. Got a problem with that? Have a go.'

'OK, I will. It looks easy enough.' With a put-upon sigh, he attacked the floor, springing over, failing to spot as he turned and ending up with a wobbly stance. He looked taken aback that it hadn't gone well.

Raven folded her arms. 'Don't tell me, big guy: you have no sense of balance?'

'I understand balance.' He put his hands on his hips, running over the move he had just made, perplexed. 'It's supposed to be easy.'

'Easy?' Raven had never seen such incompetence from someone doing Dance—he clearly hadn't even done the basics. He had to be doing this as a joke—messing with her future. She forgot about being shy with him. 'You don't know the first thing about how to move, do you? You've been lying to me!'

'Obviously I don't yet understand it. Not your kind of dance, at least.'

'So what kind of dance is your kind of dance then?'

Annoyed too, he folded his arms and stared over her head, eyes fixed on a poster displaying the various parts of an orchestra.

'Hey! Are you listening to me?' She knew she was getting too confrontational with him but his remoteness was infuriating. 'I need you to work with me here. You can't be completely useless at everything; you must be able to move a little!'

He clutched his fingers on his elbows, looking as remote as Mars.

'Please, give me something to go on. Ballroom, maybe? Isn't that what you posh kids learn? Or . . . or Latin?' Hell, no. He had no passion for that. 'Hip-hop?' That too sounded ridiculous so she committed the fatal error of laughing.

His expression became even more distant. 'Do your own dance, Raven. Tell the teacher, I quit.' He picked up his bag.

No! She didn't want to be the only one doing a solo. 'What? You're giving up, just like that?'

He walked out—an answer of sorts.

'Aargh!' Raven stood in the middle of the empty room, wishing she had something handy to throw. She kicked the piano stool. She really shouldn't have lost her temper like that; she now felt about an inch high. The annoying thing was she probably even owed him an apology and saying sorry to Mr Arrogant was about as attractive as eating bush tucker. One thing she had learnt was that he didn't take failing at something well; she shouldn't have rubbed it in.

Zapping the music back on with the remote, she worked off her temper by dancing alone.

Joe burst into the room. 'Are you OK, Key? Raven told the teacher you felt ill—left class early. Everyone in the Sixth Form Common Room is asking me what's wrong.' He glanced at the screen in front of Kieran. 'What's that? You've got access to the academic results of all the students. You find something?'

Kieran tapped a few keys, temper seething.

'Key, you're worrying me, bro. Say something.'

'There's a sequence.' Kieran strove for cool and rational; if he kept talking maybe he wouldn't have to face up to failing. 'The students that we've noted as absent—when they come back, they all improve in their performance.'

'So, what are you saying? Whatever is happening to them while they are away does not harm, but helps? Like they are getting extra tuition or something?'

'I cannot support that conclusion at this time; I'm simply giving you the facts. Denzil Hardcastle—crashed out of his

GCSEs, thanks to a preference for joyriding rather than studying. Left with all A*s in his A levels. Talented but volatile footballer, Mohammed Khan, went from police caution for violent disorder to school team captain. Anger issues solved, he was headhunted by Chelsea to play for their junior team. Jenny-May Parker caught in possession of Class A drugs, came back with a squeaky clean attitude and is now at Harvard studying Law.' Kieran called their profiles up in rapid succession, jabbing the keyboard with restless fingers. 'They are the most obvious examples but all of the students show some level of improvement in one or more areas of their school record. All their parents are down on our list.'

'That's interesting.' Joe was looking at him strangely, like Kieran was an unexploded bomb he was working out how to defuse.

'Cross referenced to our mission data, you'll find that all of them connect to some recent corrupt behaviour from their parents—a contract granted when others in the field had the edge, a political decision that swayed against expectations, a promotion that seemed out of context.'

'So the students start acting normally and their parents are the ones freaking out?'

'I'll have to keep digging but I don't think anyone is acting within usual parameters.'

'Agreed.' Joe hovered beside him, trying to see his face. 'Key, what's up?'

'Nothing.'

'Now that's just not true, bro.'

'I walked out of Dance, OK? I wasn't ill.'

'Walked out? But you never give up on anything!'

'Then your joke misfired.' Kieran erased his search history and closed down the computer. 'I'm not some dancing bear to be tormented for your kicks and giggles.'

'Key, we never meant it like that. It was supposed to be . . . well, funny. You're so perfect all the time, so sure of yourself, that we thought you'd stumble along and look . . . ' Joe shrugged. 'You know.'

'Like a total prat. I do, so "ha-ha". You guys just crease me up with your sense of humour.' He'd been made to look an idiot—and in front of Raven. The corrosive power of his rage ate at his usual control. 'I'm going out. Don't follow me.'

Joe held up his hands. 'OK, OK. Where are you going?'

'That is none of your business.'

'When will you be back?'

'Who says I'm coming back?'

Kieran felt good slamming the door on Joe. It wasn't rational but he enjoyed the vicious drama of the moment. He turned into the school gardens, taking rapid, even strides down the yew hedge walk. OK, OK, enough. He needed his control or he couldn't think straight. He had to regain his grip, deny that Raven had got under his skin. He reached for his mental retreat to calm down, thinking through the collection of newly discovered mathematical equations he had read on the University of Cambridge website. He immediately felt much better. Once calm, he would work out how he had come to fail at something for the first time in his life.

Raven tapped on the door of Kieran's room. Rules stated that she wasn't supposed to be in the boys' wing this late but, feeling a complete heel for chewing him out over dancing, she didn't want to leave matters where they were till morning. She knew too well what it felt like to be picked on and made to feel a failure—that's how she felt most of the time outside of dance classes. She knocked again and this time the door opened.

'Raven? Something the matter?' Joe stood in the entrance, blocking a clear view of the room beyond.

'Is Kieran in?'

Joe stepped back to show her the empty chamber. 'No. He went out and hasn't come back yet.'

A screen saver whirled on a computer screen, strands of DNA linking and unlinking. She guessed that was Kieran's from the piles of worthy tomes and paperclip tower surrounding it. Was that a dance movie DVD on the top of the books? The desk next to it had Mickey Mouse ears on the monitor which suggested Joe was the owner. Every spare ledge was crammed with plants; each pot had squared sheet stuck to it, a graph wriggling its way across the grid. Was Joe doing a biology experiment in his room? Perhaps Kieran wasn't the only one who was eccentric.

She looked back at Joe. 'Was Kieran OK?'

Joe grimaced. 'Not really.'

Raven squeezed her hands together. 'Look, that's my fault. He wasn't ill in class. I pushed him too far in Dance. Embarrassed him, I guess.'

Glancing down the corridor, Joe took her arm and gently led her into the room. 'That wasn't your fault. And it was me who pissed him off, not you.'

'How do you figure that? I was the one who shouted at him for screwing up his first dance move. Tell him I'm sorry, will you?'

'I will. When he comes back.'

'How long's he been gone?'

'Six hours.'

'What!'

'Kieran doesn't often lose his temper but, when he does, it's a while before he calms down and this was a big deal for him. I've never known him get anything wrong ever. I was about to go look for him.'

'Can I help? I kinda feel responsible.'

'Sure. I think he went outside.' Joe grabbed a flashlight from his bag. He picked up an apple from a bowl on the table, rolled it down his forearm and flipped it from his elbow to catch it. 'He's missed supper so he'll be hungry. Brain like his takes lots of calories.'

Raven zipped up her hoodie. 'He's extremely clever, isn't he?'

'The most intelligent guy I know.'

'So why's he doing Dance and other arts subjects rather than advanced Maths and Science? They seem more his thing.'

Joe closed the door behind them. 'Because he's already taken his A levels in them. Our godfather wanted him to broaden his focus before going to uni and he's the one signing the cheques.'

They jogged down the stairs to the nearest exit. 'Hate to break it to you but he doesn't seem very comfortable with that choice.'

'Yeah, you're right. I had hoped it would be good experience for him but I'm not so sure now.'

Even with Joe and the flashlight for company, the garden was a spooky place after dark. The clipped hedges cast moon shadows across the path, making the familiar strange. A musty odour of old leaves stirred underfoot seemed more intense at the night, reminding Raven unhelpfully of mouldering graveyards. The castle itself had turned into something sinister—lighted windows gouging holes in the black walls, crenellations pressed against the sky. Its history of war, plague, and murder crept out from where it had been hiding all day under bright notice boards and learning goals. Raven shivered, wanting to get this over with as quickly as possible.

'Any idea where he would have gone? Has he got a favourite place already?'

'I'm not sure if he's been out and about much. Your guess will be as good as mine.'

'What about ringing him?'

'Already have. His phone is switched off.'

'OK, then we do it the old-fashioned way.' She cupped her hands around her mouth. 'Kieran! Where are you?' She paused. No reply.

Joe shouted his friend's name. Nothing.

'Do you think he's gone "out" out? Out of school, I mean?' Raven rubbed her arms, feeling the chill.

'Anything is possible with him. But let's look around here first. We'll do the normal search pattern. Quarter the grounds and take each section in turn. Start at twelve o'clock.' Joe pointed straight ahead with the torch and gestured a ninety degree sweep.

Raven was amused by his military language. 'Normal search pattern? You do a lot of this, then?'

'Boy scout training.' His explanation seemed a little too quick.

'Can't see you as a boy scout somehow. I thought you grew up in a dysfunctional family.'

'So the scouts were my salvation.'

'Are you joking?'

'Could be.'

In his own way, Joe was as annoyingly elusive as his room-mate. He said more but she came away with very little, and there was nothing she disliked more than people hiding the truth from her.

They stepped out of the yew walk on to the croquet pitch in front of the orangery. A dark shape caught her eye. 'What's that on the lawn there?'

'He's doing it again,' groaned Joe, spotlighting Kieran with the torch.

They hurried over to where Kieran was on his back by the sign for the fire muster point. He was staring straight up at the stars.

'Doing what exactly? Sleeping outside?'

'Nope. Counting the visible constellations. Little mental game of his. It can go on for hours. He has very good night-sight.'

'Geez, he needs to stay *in* more.'

Joe chuckled. 'Sorry but he's one of a kind.' He bent down and shook his friend's shoulder. 'Time to stop, Key.'

Kieran rose gracefully to his feet, fluid like a bolt of silk unrolling. Now why couldn't he move like that in class? 'Hi.' He took the apple Joe offered him.

'Better now?'

Kieran nodded then frowned when he noticed her. 'Why are you out here with Raven, Joe?'

'Looking for you. We were worried.'

Kieran's expression lightened, but he still looked puzzled. 'Worried about what?'

'About you.'

'Why?'

Joe rolled his eyes. 'Because we argued, remember?'

Raven felt she had better make her apology now before they got too far off the point. 'Kieran, I just wanted to say that I apologize for pushing you in class and making you uncomfortable.'

'You did?' Kieran looked surprised by her admission. Of course, World of Kieran probably hadn't noticed her little show of temper.

'You walked out on me.'

'Yes, I did. But I've worked it through while lying on the grass.' Calmly, he did a backwards walkover. 'Was that what you meant?'

Joe laughed. 'That's neat, Key.'

61

Raven wasn't sure what had come over him. A little bubble of excitement expanded in her chest. Perhaps this could work after all? 'Yes, it was. First part anyway. How did you learn to do that so quickly?'

'I did the maths.' He smiled but she wasn't sure if he was serious or not.

Joe passed her the flashlight. 'Here, you two sort out your dance issues. I've got an essay to finish.'

'We won't be long.' Kieran picked up his jacket and shook off the grass.

'Take all the time you need. Bye, Raven. Thanks for coming over.' Joe jogged back to the castle.

She was suddenly very aware of being with Kieran, in the dark with little chance of being interrupted. She shivered.

'Here.' He wrapped the jacket around her shoulders, swamping her. 'Better?'

'Yes.' It was official: she had just fallen in love with a large size leather jacket. She didn't want to let it go: it smelt so wonderful and was as good as a hug as it settled around her.

'It's a bit big on you.'

'I think it's a perfect size for keeping me warm.' There was a definite tension between them and she suspected it wasn't just because they irritated the hell out of each other.

'Suits you.' He smiled at her and her heart did a ridiculous flip in her chest. Raven folded her arms, wondering if she should turn off the torch. The dark would be easier; it helped hide her dumb reactions to him at least.

'So we're good now, are we, Kieran?'

Kieran took a step towards her. 'Yes. We're good.'

'I'm impressed by your progress.' She gestured to the spot where he had executed his backwards walkover. Where was her normal sassy self? She seemed to have gone back to the castle with Joe.

'It wasn't so hard once I'd broken it down to its constituent parts. Perhaps you could teach me that spin move next?'

'Does that mean, as long as you have time, you can do the same thing to the routine we put together—put it together piece by piece?'

'I think so. It wasn't so hard after all.'

'Doing one move is not dancing, Kieran.' She frowned at him. It hadn't taken him long to get his confidence back. 'There's far more to it than that.'

'Is there now?' He was standing very close.

Her voice went all husky. She was ashamed of her hopeless weakness around him and decided to deal with it by just ignoring it. *Remember, he hasn't noticed you as a girl; don't embarrass yourself.* 'So you'll stick with Dance then?'

'Yes.'

That was a huge relief. She'd not wanted to be the only one without a partner. 'Great. I'll try to jettison the bad attitude and I promise not to shout at you again.'

'You probably will.' Even in this poor light, she could see that his smile was wry. 'I seem to provoke people to do just that. Even Joe, who has the most long-suffering nature of anyone I know.'

'I won't.' Without meaning to, Raven swayed a little towards him, near enough to scent his mixture of faded aftershave and damp fleece sweater. She found the combination very appealing. Then Kieran reached out and touched her cheek with his fingertips, like a moth coming down to rest briefly. Hardly there, this slight point of contact still felt unnervingly intimate. Warmth spread through her, a sense of peace settled inside. His touch untied some of the ugly knots in her core, ones that had twisted and tightened as anxiety mounted with every passing day of this school term. She closed her eyes, allowing herself to succumb to the magic.

His fingers skated down to her neck, touching the sensitive hollow of her throat.

Then as suddenly as the spell was cast, he broke it. Fingers lifted, taking something with it. 'You had grass caught in your hair from my jacket. I'll walk you back to the castle.'

She opened her eyes, mortified that this moment had been all one sided. His face gave nothing away. 'Oh, OK. Thanks.'

'Shall I take the torch?'

'Sure.' Confused as to what had just happened, she let him lead the way back inside.

Chapter 5

It was close to eleven when Raven finally made it back to her room. Reliving the memory of his touch on her cheek, she took a moment to realize that something had changed. The second bed in the room was occupied.

'Gina?' She quickly switched off the main light she had turned on, so as not to dazzle her friend. She groped for her bedside lamp instead.

Gina turned over, her dark blonde head buried under the covers. Raven couldn't bring herself to wake her. What if Gina's lateness had been because she had been ill? Curiosity wasn't enough to justify disturbing Gina when she was fast asleep.

Glancing around the room, Raven took in the other changes. Gina's possessions were neatly lined up on her side of the dresser, jewellery already hanging from a pretty ornamental stand, nothing tangled or heaped up. Raven noticed her ankle bracelet among the gold chains—Gina must have borrowed it last term. Raven thought she'd lost it—she'd tease her about that in the morning.

Opening the wardrobe to hang up her sweater, she saw Gina's clothes were folded on the shelves or on hangers. Her shoes were in a regimental row under her bed. Someone else must have unpacked for her because her friend was constitutionally messy. That supported the idea that Gina was still convalescing and needed lots of TLC.

Looking forward to a morning catch-up session, Raven kicked off her sneakers, threw the rest of her clothes on the upright chair and tugged on her favourite pyjamas decorated with faded cartoon moose; they'd been her mom's, once-upon-a-time.

'It's so good to have you back, Gina,' she whispered to the darkness, happy to hear the sound of regular breathing from across the room. 'I've got to tell you about this gorgeous but totally dementing guy who's joined us this term—he's got this blue-blood air and is way too handsome for his own good so I shouldn't really like him, should I?' She ran her fingers over the spot he had touched. 'I'm sure you'll have a lot to say on the subject of Kieran Storm. I don't know if I want to kick him or kiss him: how mixed up is that? You know me—unsure of my moves around boys. Well, he has that effect on me times ten.'

Gina murmured something and turned over.

'Speak in the morning.' Raven pulled the duvet over her shoulders. Now things would start to go right; she was sure of it.

Light spilt into the room from the open curtains. A bird cawed. Raven groggily opened her eyes and saw a shape moving across the sunbeams.

'Gina? What time is it?'

'Six-thirty.'

'Geez. Is this revenge for disturbing you last night?'

'Don't be silly, Raven. It's just time to wake up.'

Like hell it was. Raven pushed up from her pillow. Gina was already dressed, her hair curled up in a French twist, make-up applied. She was wearing what Raven could only call a sober suit. She looked like someone's PA, not in the least like the normal casually-clothed Gina.

'Got an interview?' teased Raven. 'I've never seen you so smart.'

Gina gave her a cool look and bent over to make her bed.

Raven put her hands under her head, elbows spread on the pillow, grinning at her friend. 'Where've you been, Gina? I was really worried about you.'

'My course overran. My absence was cleared with the head teacher.'

So she had been fretting about nothing. 'Why did no one tell me?'

'Why should they have told you?' Gina wasn't meeting her eyes.

'Because I'm your best friend, duh. Us screw-ups have to stick together—remember the pledge?'

Gina stood up, back stiff. 'I see. Well, I'm afraid we can't be this term.' She fiddled with the thin gold chain around her neck, running the pearl droplet to and fro.

A heavy weight settled in Raven's stomach. 'Can't be what?'

'I'm sorry but I can't be your friend again—not like we were. I've asked that you move rooms today.'

Raven sat up. 'Whoa. Gina? Are you joking? You've had me kicked out of our room?'

'You have to understand: I can't keep my eyes closed to your little problem, can't live with the stress—it's not good for me.'

'My little problem? What the heck are you talking about?'

'You know what you do. Toni told me last night about what happened in the changing rooms. If you carry on you'll end up in trouble with the police. I don't want to see it happen.'

'You what? You don't believe the rumours about the bag, do you? That's rich coming from you, seeing you're always borrowing stuff without asking!'

Gina frowned, the comment not hitting home. She looked like she had never heard of such a thing. 'I've worked hard on the course to get myself into a good place. No offence,

Raven, but my course tutor showed me that you're a negative influence. I must surround myself with only positives if I'm to succeed. Mrs Bain agrees. I must stick to my new resolutions so the good work isn't undone.'

'What kind of negative influence?' Raven felt sickened. It was happening again: her foundations crumbling from under her.

'To succeed in life, you must seek the best, emulate the most worthy examples, strive for excellence.'

'What is this crap? Who's got you believing lies about me?'

'And avoid all displays of low behaviour, like swearing.' Gina did up the buttons of her jacket. 'I know it's hard—hard for us both—we were so close before it all came out, but if you just pack your things and go without a fuss, your grandfather will move them to your new room this morning during classes. Mrs Bain thinks it best if you have a room on your own. She's moving Hedda in with me.'

'Do you even realize you what you are saying? You don't even like Hedda!' Raven pushed back the covers and grabbed Gina's arm to shake her. 'It's me—Raven. I am your friend. You are my friend. That has to mean something, surely?'

Gina's eyes skated away. She wasn't enjoying this confrontation any more than Raven but was determined to see it to the end.

Raven began to feel frightened as she grasped that Gina wasn't going to stop wrecking their friendship. 'Remember how I was there for you when you split up with Nathaniel?'

'That was stupid of me to get so upset. Relationships that divert energy away from the goal of personal success are also a mistake.'

'Stop talking like that. It didn't feel like a mistake at the time—you said it felt like the end of the world. You cried. I cried for you.'

'Indulging in emotional displays over minor adolescent dramas is selfish and detracts from the positive drive forward.'

'I hope this is some sick joke of yours. If it is, Gina, I'm gonna kick your ass for this!' Raven sounded fierce, but she hurt.

Something flashed in Gina's eyes. Raven had the weird impression that her friend—ex-friend—was scared of her. 'If you attempt any physical abuse, you'll be immediately reported to the school authorities. Now, I have a meeting to go to. I hope you can be packed up before breakfast?'

'A meeting? At this time?'

Gina walked out without replying. Raven stared after her, stunned. Cold. Had that been real or was she dreaming? How had the wheels just come off that relationship so spectacularly?

There came a soft tap on the door. It would be Gina. She'd come back in and say 'Fooled you!' or something like that. Raven would hit her with a pillow until she made an apology and they'd be OK again.

'Yes?'

Her grandfather poked his head round the door. 'Sorry to disturb you so early, Raven, but I've been asked to take your things to a room in D corridor. Can you box them up for me?'

Tears rushed to Raven's eyes. She brushed them away, reaching for anger to help her through this. So it wasn't a joke; someone had poisoned Gina against her. 'Granddad, what the heck did I do wrong? I don't get it: why doesn't Gina like me any more?'

He looked down. 'I'm sure it's not your fault, sweetheart. How can anyone not think you are wonderful?'

She couldn't worry him; he was supposed to avoid stress in case it brought on another heart attack. 'And you're not biased?' She smiled sourly.

'Exactly. Come here. I need a hug even if you don't.'

She got out of bed and dashed into the sanctuary of his embrace.

He patted her back affectionately. 'You know girls of your age, Raven—mood swings, petty squabbles—all part of growing up. Gina's just got a bee in her bonnet today and Mrs Bain thinks it best to separate you. It seems a big deal now but in a year or so you'll laugh about it. Do you want a hand packing?'

Raven reminded herself that he was in an awkward spot, being both grandfather and employee obeying orders. Bottom line was she knew he was on her side. She leant back and tapped his chest to show she was OK. He could let go. 'I'm fine. It won't take long. And if Gina doesn't want me, I sure don't want to be near her.' Act brave and maybe the feelings inside would match one day: that was her motto.

He nodded. 'That's the spirit. Foolish female will see sense soon enough. She'll be apologizing tomorrow.'

She switched on her sass. 'Abjectly? On her knees?' How could Gina think she was a thief?

'Naturally.'

'Love you, Granddad.'

'You too, sweetheart.' He picked up her fist and knocked his knuckles against hers. 'Don't let the blighters get you down.'

Her mouth wrinkled up at the corners. 'Thanks. I won't.'

'It's too late, you know.' Hedda shoved her tray in Raven's back as they lined up by the cereals.

Raven took a deep breath and decided to ignore her. Cornflakes or muesli? Choices, choices.

'We all know you stole them.'

OK, so maybe she couldn't pretend she hadn't heard. 'What have I stolen this time? Do tell. I so enjoy your little fantasies.'

70

Hedda put her tray down, hands on hips in a commanding gesture. She made sure she had the attention of everyone in earshot. 'All those things you stole last term? They turned up in reception this morning with a note saying you wanted to return them to their owners and were very sorry for having taken them.'

Adewale barged past, making her stagger. 'I thought you were OK, Raven, but it turns out you're a dirty little thief. You knew how much that watch meant to me.'

'Hey!' Raven called after him. He'd always been her friend before. A nightmare—she was stuck in a daytime nightmare. 'I didn't steal anything!'

Hedda gave a vicious smile of satisfaction. 'See, everyone knows now that you stole from them.'

'Impossible—as I didn't take anything from anyone. Your logic is way off, Hedda.'

'Pretend all you like, but we know the truth.' Hedda picked up her tray and stalked past. 'No wonder even Gina doesn't want to share a room with you.'

'It wasn't me,' she called after her.

The little crowd around her broke up, no one meeting her eyes. She stood staring at the cereals, reeling from Adewale's hurtful accusation. She felt horribly alone. It was like reliving how she felt being dumped in a new school after her dad's death, battling the rumours put about by her foster brother that she had the morals of a drugs slut. It had taken months of fighting to kill off that gossip; would she have to do the same here?

'I think muesli is the healthier option.' Kieran put a packet on her tray, steering her on to the next counter. 'What was that about?' He looked past her to where Joe was putting his tray next to Hedda at the table over which she presided. Adewale was sitting with Gina.

'Your friend gone over to the dark side too?' Raven asked bitterly.

'No, Joe just likes to get on with everyone.'

'Good luck to him then.' She searched for a spot where she would receive a welcome.

'I like this place here.' Kieran nudged her towards a small table half hidden by a cutlery stand. He watched her toy with her packet. 'Not feeling hungry?'

'No.' She felt sick—sick of everything.

'You need to eat.' He opened her muesli for her and tipped it in the bowl. She said nothing to stop him so he then sliced half his banana on top and poured on some milk, his jade green eyes flicking over to glance at her. 'There: the perfect breakfast. Nutritionally balanced. Eat.'

'My friend, Gina, is back,' she blurted out, much to her own surprise. Something about his refusal to probe helped free her up to speak.

'And how is she?' A strand of his chestnut hair swung on to his forehead as he dipped his head to concentrate on stirring his mug of tea. He brushed it back irritably, expression now fixed on his drink as if he was reading the secrets of the universe in the surface.

'All right—if you think "complete bitch" is acceptable. She's had me kicked out of our room on the top corridor.'

'I see.' He extracted the teaspoon, tapping it on the edge with two precise knocks to shake off the drops. His carefulness in table manners was that of a scientist at a workbench, each movement calculated.

'You might but I don't. Maybe she bought into Hedda's mad accusations that I'm a thief—that was what that little scene was about just now.'

He replaced the banana peel on his tray, making the edges match so it looked as if it had never been opened. That could have been annoying but oddly this morning she found it reassuring. She had the crazy idea that if she spent long enough with him he would sort things out and make the messy parts of her life as neat and tidy. She still didn't know why he paid her any attention: maybe he saw her like one of his puzzles that needed solving?

'I'm not, you know. Not a thief.'

'Of course not.' His calm acceptance was a huge help. 'Tell me what Gina said.'

'Do I have to?'

He shrugged. 'Only if you want to.'

'She wasn't her old self at all—kind of like an evil twin had taken her place, one that believed every bad thing about me.' Raven frowned, reviewing what she remembered. 'It is her, isn't it?'

'I don't know—I've not met her yet.'

'It has to be her—physically at least. But it's like she's had her personality removed. She's suddenly become a neat freak and using words that don't seem her own. She spouted some nonsense about having to separate herself from negative influences. That would be me, apparently.'

'And she's never acted like this before?'

'Never. She was always so funny. We dubbed ourselves "Westron's screw-ups", you know, like, one for all and all for one, the messed-up musketeers. She even gave me a jewellery box with that inscribed on the lid.'

Kieran smiled.

Encouraged, she continued. 'We would get into trouble together and she'd laugh about it—in fact, she was the one who caused most of it. She was always, always untidy, scatterbrained, would swear like the rest of us. This morning she was Miss Prim, butter-wouldn't-melt-in-her-mouth.'

'Why are you the one having to move if she's had a change of mind about sharing with you?'

'Good question but the answer's simple. Mrs Bain has never really liked me and if one of her paying pupils has a problem, the scholarship student has to give way.'

'Interesting.'

She scooped up a mouthful of cereal, plucking up the courage to ask. 'Can I hang with you today, Kieran? You and Joe, I mean?'

'Why would you want to do that?'

O-K. Not a very flattering response. Kieran seemed perplexed by the request, not gushingly pleased as she would be if he had said the same to her. She wished she hadn't asked, as she had just revealed that she needed someone: weakness always invited a kick in the teeth. 'Forget I asked.'

'No, explain.' He trapped her hand under his large palm, long fingers stilling her attempt to leave the table, then quickly pulled back. It was like brushing against an electric fence, the tingle shooting up her arm.

'It's just that I . . . er . . . I seem to be rather short of allies at the moment.'

'I see. And having allies is important to you?'

She almost smiled. 'Kieran, most people like to surround themselves with friends. You know, Woody and Buzz, Frodo and Sam, Batman and Robin?' Why was she languishing after a guy who didn't get the basic need for companions? It was like a fish longing for a giraffe: a relationship doomed from the start.

'I've always found people to be very unreliable.'

'I'm with you there, Ace, but that's the chance you take.'

'If you don't mind risking it, then of course you can "hang" with us—though I find that phrase a bit unfortunate, recalling the fate of partners in crime on the scaffold.' His eyes twinkled with amusement.

'Don't agree if it'd be a bore.'

'No problem. I'd say having you "hanging" with us would be entirely our pleasure.'

Mine too, she thought.

After breakfast, Kieran snagged Joe's arm before they went their separate ways for class. He gave him the quick headlines of Raven's news.

Joe rubbed his newly shorn hair—he'd met with one of Isaac's colleagues at the barber in town at the weekend to collect his car keys and was still getting used to the cut. 'So she thinks her friend's acting like a different person?'

'There's definite change, like in the other cases I mentioned. With Gina, it's from messy to neat with the added twist of turning against her old friend. I guess she's also going to apply herself to her studies more than she has in the past. I'm wondering just how they're getting the students to change and why.' Kieran glanced at his own hair in a window, wondering if he should ask Joe if he needed a haircut too. He rarely thought about such things but he didn't want Raven to think him scruffy. 'Let's find a quiet corner—I don't want to be overheard.'

'I know just the place.'

Joe took him through a little used back door. They sat side by side on a bench by the old servants' entrance. Two ducks waddled over the gravel towards the wet patch under a black iron pump.

'What did you get from Hedda?' asked Kieran.

'Other than a stomach ache?'

Kieran smiled. Yes, eating with that girl would do that to anyone with any sense.

'Oh, she is on some personal vendetta to assassinate Raven's character. It seems as though she's a hot button for

75

Hedda. Other students are joining in, including Adewale who I had down as a good guy. But I think Raven's greatest sin is that she is perceived as being "not one of us".'

'Why? It can't be a prejudice thing—they are from all sorts of nationalities—Hedda's Swedish, Toni is Angolan, Adewale Nigerian and there's at least one Chinese, two from the Indian subcontinent and an American in the group.'

'I think it's social status. Class and money—that's what they have in common. I pass thanks to my mega-rich god-father showering me with Rolexes and funding my education. That speaks of serious connections.' Joe's watch had actually come as a reward from a jeweller in Switzerland when they had foiled a plot to rob the vault two months before. Kieran had one too. He had noticed other students checking out his wrist but hadn't realized until now the watch was treated as proof of good credentials. 'They like you, thanks to my little rumour about your classy family.'

'I wish you hadn't started that.'

'You rarely tell any of us the truth about yourself so you shouldn't have a problem concealing it from an outsider.'

True, he did not share his private life with many, only those in the YDA with a need to know. Joe had been told some of it but even he hadn't heard the full ugly story. 'The class thing though: it just makes matters complicated with Raven.'

'But don't get too hung up on the girl, Key. Odds are we'll be shifted to another mission in a couple of months. This won't go anywhere and you can't have a serious relationship on a job, you know that. Flirting is OK; falling in love, majorly bad.'

'I've said she can spend time with us.'

'And that fits with our mission how exactly?'

Kieran knew he was acting out of character; he didn't need Joe's bemused look to tell him that. 'Not when we're talking to Isaac, obviously. Just she's being victimized and I don't like it.' It offended his sense of justice; that was the only reason he would acknowledge.

'Kieran Storm, the caped crusader, flying to the maiden's rescue.' Joe clapped his chest in a mock 'you're-my-hero' gesture. 'I am so going to have to put this on the Yoda message board.'

'You will not. Anyone would have said the same to her.'

'But you wouldn't have—not before meeting Raven. You would have looked straight through her and told her to toughen up. Your ratings with the girls will rocket when they realize you have developed a soft spot for one of them.'

Kieran gave a dismissive snort.

'Face it, Kieran. You are attracted to her and you'll have to admit it sooner or later. But remember, my friend, as you just pointed out yourself, everything she knows about you is false. If she discovers that, she might not forgive you. That's part of the reason we are told not to have serious relationships on a mission—too much damage all round.'

'I'm not going to make a hash of it. I'll keep my . . . my relationship with Raven in one compartment and the mission in another. I won't get serious.'

Joe shrugged. 'Your funeral, pal. Don't say I didn't warn you.' He headed off to lessons leaving Kieran in sole occupation of the bench.

Kieran closed his eyes, enjoying a brief break in the sunshine. The last few years, since dating had begun in earnest, he had watched his friends turn into total idiots over the girls they fancied; he had been a little smug about it, always believing himself above such illogical behaviour. He never argued with the girls he'd dated, hadn't felt that burning urge as he did with Raven: every other conversation with her ended up in a blazing row; the other half resulted in an overwhelming desire to kiss her.

She was distracting him. He should be thinking about the patterns, not about the fact that he was taking a step into the unknown with her. *Focus on your mission, Storm. Concentrate.*

Making a big effort he forced himself to review the progress of the mission to date. So what did he know? Relatives of these students were making bent decisions of global importance. If it wasn't stopped, one of these decisions would cause a catastrophe. Their job as agents of the YDA was to choke it off at the source; it was the only hope of diverting disaster down the road.

He had quickly latched on to the fact that the majority of these people had children whose behaviour had noticeably changed; the most likely cause was the courses they attended at the manor. Some kind of extreme pressure had to have been applied to make such rapid character alterations in the pupils. The word 'brainwashing' was dancing around in his mind. But why? With the correlation between parent and child behaviour, it couldn't just be to benefit the school by giving them more obedient pupils. There had to be a link back to the parents' actions, some payback.

Not all the missing students had returned yet but there had been no protest on the school's database from the parents for their prolonged absence, no phone calls or angry emails. What conclusions could be drawn from that? Either the parents didn't know the truth about what was happening to their offspring, happy with the explanations they had been given, or they were complicit. What had the pupils at the school been told? He would have to ask Raven. She had been in the dark about Gina but maybe there had been excuses given for the others who had gone missing for longer.

Sunshine pouring down on him, Kieran took a moment to enjoy the sense that he was assembling a case point by point. It was of sufficient complexity to be a challenge; he wouldn't have liked it if the answer was too obvious, his talents wasted. He had, for example, searched through the decisions of the relatives, but he could find no clear link between the things they had done, no single person or entity benefitting. How, for example, did granting a diamond concession in Sierra Leone to a mining company ahead of their more respected competitors link to the promotion of a junior state department official to a more senior rank? And those blueprints for a new palm print-activated gun for the US military that had got into the hands of the Chinese: who had been at either end of that deal? It had the stench of major corruption, favouritism granted without a clear connection between the parties, like someone was bartering favours: *you do X in return for Y then Z will do A.*

Kieran let the idea run through his mind like an equation but the result was not understandable in arithmetic terms. There had to be an unknown in the mix, something integrating it all.

A clearing house. The solution came to him once he thought of the favours like currency. Was the school—not just this one but the whole network of the Union of International Schools—acting as the central bank with its various branches managing the flow of favours? If so, it was a clever system as the links were so tenuous no one could claim that diplomat A or businessman B had any reason to privilege the other, having no known relationship. There was next to no chance of a charge under international anti-bribery legislation that a backhander had been passed, as nothing was visible.

The clearing house was a good working hypothesis. What Kieran could not yet see was where the mind-altered students fitted in this scheme and what the people behind the school got out of it. They would be the next two elements to puzzle out.

Chapter·6

After lunch, Joe and Kieran returned to their room to work on their assignments. Kieran was also running a scan of Westron's communications with parents, looking for key terms, another on an analysis of links between diamond mining and trustees sitting on the school's board, and two little personal ones, tracking NASA's Mars programme and the CERN's hunt for the Higgs. The space left over in his brain was devoted to writing an essay on *Pride and Prejudice* for English.

Joe pressed print on his French assignment. 'You know, Key, you never did explain about those bluebottles. What case was it?'

'A Victorian one in the old papers—murder in the greenhouse. The solution hinged on how long the body had been lying there next to the carnivorous plants.'

'Gruesome. I like it.'

'They found flies decomposing in the plants but the little greenhouse had been sealed from the outside and carbon monoxide pumped in. I was looking at how long it took the plants to attract the flies in a confined space, timing each species, and then noted how long the bodies take to be digested. I have established a range for the carnivorous plants available to a Victorian collector and my preliminary data suggests they hanged the wrong man. It couldn't have been the gardener. Someone else had been in there later, which also fits the most likely time of death as well as they could fix that in those days. My money's on the brother who inherited.'

'Tell me again why you are doing this?' Joe rolled his eyes.

'Because no one else has. It is a puzzle to be solved. An injustice to be righted.' An itch he had to scratch, but he didn't add that last. Joe already knew that he was attracted to mysteries like a bear to a picnic basket.

The computer screen pinged as Isaac's number came up. Joe clicked the answer button.

'Hey, Isaac, we weren't expecting you to check in. Everything OK?'

Clearly not, as Isaac's expression was icy. 'Is Kieran with you?'

'Yes.' Kieran moved so the webcam caught him.

'Are you all right?'

'Er, yes. I think so.' He glanced at Joe.

'Kieran, the school rang me.'

'Uh-oh,' murmured Joe.

'They said you had left a lesson yesterday without seeing the teacher first and had refused offers to go to the nurse about your illness. They implied you were either skiving—which I know is impossible for you, Kieran, where learning is involved—or that you were hiding your symptoms. They were concerned, seeing you are new to the school.'

Kieran winced. He wished that particular incident could now be filed in the category of finished business. 'I'm fine now, thanks. Back on track.'

'What really interested me was that they said the lesson in question was Dance. I thought they were joking. They were surprised when I laughed. Did I not even know what subjects my godson was taking? I had to admit I did not—which was a major humiliation. Consider my shock when I discovered that you were doing Dance, Art, Drama, and English.'

'It was a shock to me too.'

Isaac did not respond to Kieran's drily amused tone. 'I then followed back the paper trail and realized that certain of your friends had taken care of that part of your enrolment. Joe, have you anything to say?'

'Damn,' Joe said in a low voice. 'I'm sorry, Isaac.'

'Why?' Isaac was curt, a sign he was really angry. Isaac's fury was like a sandstorm—searing and gritty. Anyone with any sense took cover.

'We thought it would be a laugh. You know how good Kieran is at everything else. This mission was judged low risk and isn't due to take long; a few weeks of arts were supposed to be a new experience for him, I guess.'

'I put aside what you've done to your partner for the moment, but I can't understand why you've jeopardized the job to have . . . what? A joke at Kieran's expense?'

'Isaac, I'm really sorry. We were jerks.'

Isaac leant forward on his desk. 'More than jerks. Unprofessional. I don't think you yet grasp the gravity of your offence. You have put your mission and your personal safety at risk by throwing in an unstable element. That I cannot accept.'

Kieran wanted to protest that he wasn't unstable, but Isaac was on a roll. 'Disciplinary action will be taken, Masters. If you wish to graduate from the YDA and earn your scholarship to university, you cannot afford to have something like this on your record. This was explained to you when you signed on.'

Kieran fiddled with his phone, disliking intensely that he was present for Joe's reprimand. He hadn't appreciated the joke but he didn't consider it a matter worth fouling up Joe's future.

'Kieran was supposed to fit in. You could have slipped him into some science classes with no one noticing anything but an extremely gifted pupil. Instead you chose to dump him somewhere he was most likely to do something, well, Kieranish. Do I make myself clear?'

Since when had 'Kieranish' become an English word?

'Yes, Isaac.' Joe sounded chastened.

'I don't suppose you'll tell me who else was in on this little joke of yours?'

Joe shook his head.

'At least you don't add snitch to jerk. I can guess. I'll be having words with Nat and Daimon. I think you can all three safely count on being recalled and put on probation.'

Kieran had had enough. He really did not want his best friends at the YDA to end up on report because he had failed to handle their joke well. Before he could express this thought, Isaac turned to him.

'Kieran, are you really OK with Dance? I can ask the school to change your option if you think your idiotic friends have tossed you such a curve ball that you won't be able to bat this one out.'

'No, Isaac, I'm fine.'

'Really?'

Kieran arched a brow. 'Do you doubt me?'

'Of course not. OK, then I'll send in another of our students to assist you in the completion of this mission, someone who will help and not hinder. Masters, pack your bag.'

Out of sight of the webcam, Joe kicked the rubbish bin.

No, no, no, this couldn't happen, not to Joe. Wrong result.

Kieran knew he had to do something but it meant forfeiting some of his pride. He never talked to Isaac or his other mentors on subjects other than strict mission business. He didn't *do* emotional appeals. 'Isaac, can I butt in here?'

'You want to report on your progress?'

'Yes, but that wasn't what I wanted to talk about first. I wanted to ask you to let Joe off this time.'

He heard his friend stop moving about the room. No one ever got Isaac to change his mind: he was famous for his ruthless verdicts on his students. Tough love, he called it, saying it was better to fail them than take them into a career to which they were not suited. Kieran wasn't encouraged by Isaac's stony expression. He had to give it a whirl anyway. He mentally sacrificed his pride on the altar of friendship.

'I was mad at Joe at first when I found out what I was studying, but after reflection on my skill set, I decided he could have a point.'

'A point? What kind of point?'

Kieran looked down at the worn patch on his jeans. 'I need to be able to handle arts as well as sciences to be a better investigator. With the greatest respect, you and the other mentors were allowing me to duck the issue.'

'You actually want to do arts now?' Isaac was clearly unconvinced.

'I'm finding my own way through. English I can manage as I am extremely well read.'

Isaac smiled wryly. 'I know. I wasn't concerned about that. You killed my team at the last quiz evening on the Dickens round.'

Kieran carried on, piling up the evidence in the case for the defence. 'In Art, the teacher said she found my levels of craftsmanship and restrained expression very promising. She thinks I draw like Leonardo da Vinci.' Which wasn't surprising as he had studied the master in great depth. 'In Drama, I am taking options for light and sound design where possible. With so many performers, someone who likes the backstage work is welcome. I've already sorted out a glitch in the PA system in the auditorium.'

'Yeah, I saw a note from Mr Partington on your file that you are an asset to the class. But what about Dance?'

Kieran refused to look at Joe, who he knew was hanging on

his every word. 'I admit that that class is my biggest challenge.' Well, actually she was only five foot three. 'I'm finding a way through that too.'

'What sort of way?'

'His classmate is being very helpful,' Joe chipped in, some of his usual ebullience restored. 'A certain Miss Raven Stone is taking good care of him.'

'Yes, well,' muttered Kieran, adding a clip to his tower.

'Kieran, are you embarrassed?' Isaac's voice defrosted a little.

Kieran ignored that. 'My dance partner is being of assistance both with the subject and to our enquiry.'

'I see.' Isaac arched his fingers together. 'And you think your teachers here at the YDA were remiss in letting this part of your training slide?'

'Frankly, yes.'

'I see. That's a lot to take in.' Isaac glanced off camera. Kieran realized that their boss wasn't alone in the room. 'What do you think?'

Kieran couldn't hear the answer of the unseen person. He deduced it was the mentor for A stream, Dr Waterburn, brought in on the emergency consultation.

'Yes, I agree. Kieran's blending better than I expected. Exposure to arts subjects won't kill him.' Isaac turned back to them. 'OK, Joe, for taking unapproved chances with a mission, you lose a life but you're not out of the game yet. No more second chances.'

'Actually, Isaac, that doesn't make sense because logically another chance would be a third chance, wouldn't it?' Kieran argued reasonably. He had to correct such unscientific figures of speech; they rubbed him up the wrong way.

Joe hit him round the back of the head with a rolled-up essay.

Isaac looked to Joe, his ice age rapidly thawing. 'OK, we get why you did it, Joe.'

Joe snorted. 'I'm trying to wean him off saying stuff like that but it's tough.'

'I'll not let it affect the job, I promise,' said Kieran.

'You don't have to excel, just fit in so no one starts asking questions about you.'

'I understand.' Though he had never done anything but excel at any subject he had taken in the past and had no intention of not doing so here. 'I have a new theory to send you, Isaac.'

Isaac rubbed his hands. 'Excellent. I didn't think you'd let me down, Kieran.'

'It is only a theory,' he cautioned. 'Something that might start to link what's going on at the school with the bigger picture.'

'Yeah, but a theory from you is worth gold. Joe, consider your butt well and truly kicked and we'll put this away. Agreed?'

Joe sat down beside Kieran. 'Thanks, Isaac.'

'But it is your last warning. Anything like this again and you'll find yourself out of the YDA.'

'Understood.'

'I'll see you both at the exeat weekend coming up. I'll send a car to bring you home. Over and out.'

The connection closed.

'Phew.' Joe bumped shoulders with Kieran. 'Thanks. I owe you big time.'

Kieran returned to *Pride and Prejudice*. 'Yes, you do. Don't expect me to make a habit of it.'

Joe grabbed the book and scrambled out of reach as Kieran tried to get it back. 'It is a truth universally acknowledged . . . ' He jumped over the bed, knocking over a pitcher plant. Kieran dived and saved it just in time. 'That a single guy in possession of a dangerous sense of humour . . . ' Kieran feinted right then rugby tackled Joe to the ground, pinning his legs down. Joe threw the book over to the other side of the room. It fell in the bin with a clang. 'Must be in want of a friend who can blag him out of trouble. The end.'

Kieran flopped sideways to lie on his back beside Joe. He began to laugh, everything so much funnier thanks to relief that Isaac had not ended their partnership. His mood was infectious. Joe caught it and lay shaking next to him.

'Stop laughing!' gasped Kieran.

'Can't.'

There came a soft tap on the door. Raven peeked in.

'Are you two OK? I heard . . . um . . . noises.'

'No,' groaned Joe. 'He's killing me—with laughter. Arrest him.'

She gave a weak smile. 'Oh. I see.'

Raven was distressed about something. The thought sobered Kieran quickly. He sat up. 'You can come in, Raven. What's the matter?'

'Oh, nothing.' She stepped into the room, twisting the tie on her jacket uneasily. 'Just dropping round the CD for Dance. So you can rehearse.' She glanced over her shoulder.

'Don't give us that. Something's upset you.' Like Kieran, Joe was quick to sense all was not well. He stood up and closed the door behind her. 'You can tell us.'

She clenched her fists then dropped them by her sides in despair. 'It's just that I've been called before Mrs Bain for stealing. Granddad too. I don't care about me—I don't even like it here—but I think they're trying to get him sacked.'

Kieran wanted to give her a hug but was rooted to the spot. Joe gave him a significant look as if to say 'go on' and, when he didn't move, took over.

'Hey, hey.' Joe wrapped his arms around Raven so easily.

Why could *he* not do that? 'They won't fire him or kick you out. There's no evidence.'

'That's not true. Gina said she saw the gold watch in our room the night she returned—the one that belonged to Adewale. It turned up with the other stolen stuff in reception so now it's all linked to me. But I didn't take any of it—I didn't. I keep telling everyone but it's like . . . like I'm just mouthing the words with no one hearing. And people are sending me horrible letters just to twist the knife. I'm so angry but I don't know what to do.'

OK. Enough. Kieran wasn't going to let his friend do his job. He tapped Joe on the shoulder. With a pointed look, Joe handed Raven over. Ah, that felt better immediately. She nestled against his chest, a hot bundle of hurt feelings. His arms were at first stiff, and then he relaxed, rocking her gently.

'We'll sort it out, Raven,' he promised, letting his face drop to the crown of her head, catching the scent that was hers alone.

'But everyone hates me now.' Her voice was lost against his shirt buttons.

Hardly. He wouldn't describe what he was feeling for her anywhere near that end of the emotional spectrum. '*We* don't—and I'm sure lots of your other friends feel the same.'

'Yeah, Raven, just because Gina's setting you up, don't mean it's gonna work out the way she thinks,' added Joe.

'Setting me up?' squeaked Raven.

'Joe's right. The watch had to come from somewhere. How better to disguise your own crime by accusing another?'

'Oh my gosh, you're right!' Raven pushed away from his chest and gazed up at him. 'I'm such an idiot! How could she do that to me?'

Anger was better than tears even if it did mean losing the hug. 'But don't do anything drastic.' He knew her well enough to realize she didn't always think her reactions through.

'Why not? I'm going to murder her.'

'No, you are going to outwit her.'

'Huh?'

'Listen to my man, Raven,' Joe said. 'You'll only end up in worse trouble if you burst in and accuse her. She'll say you're lying to cover up what you've done.'

'But that's not fair!'

They had to deter her from doing anything rash or she might upset the investigation. If things worked out, she'd get her payback when they took down the scheme. 'No, it's not. But haven't you heard that revenge is a dish best served cold? Put yours in the deep freezer.'

'You want me to find some self-control? I don't have much of that,' Raven said grumpily.

'It seems we are all fated to learn new things today.' Joe grinned at Kieran. 'Aren't we?'

Thefts—accusations—and now blaming Raven, who was convenient because she had neither power nor influence: Kieran knew they had to be watching the early stages in the process of reeling in Gina's connections. Both he and Joe were eager to find out exactly how that was done so they could understand more of the scheme they were investigating. Once Raven had gone back to her new room in the infirmary wing, they went in search of her ex-best friend and found her standing on the edge of the crowd that circulated around Hedda and Toni, a humble new planet in their binary solar system. The gang hung out in the sixth form common room, occupying the best sofas by the huge Tudor fireplace, its gothic cast iron grate keeping the logs in check, no flames in the hearth at this time of year.

'How do you want to play this?' Kieran asked Joe as they approached.

'Good cop/bad cop works for me. You needle her; see what you can provoke her to say . . . '

'My pleasure.'

'And I'll then rush in all sympathetic, defending her from you. It'll help convince them I'm on their side.'

'Joe!' cried Hedda, treating his appearance as if she'd caused it. She held out her hand, pearl-pink polished nails beckoning him closer. 'We were just talking about the prom. Are you planning to go?'

'I guess so. How's it going, guys?' Joe included the rest of the crowd in his greeting. 'Gina, isn't it? Welcome back.' He took a seat beside her.

Gina preened under his attention. 'Thanks. You have to be Joe Masters.'

'So my reputation precedes me. Don't believe anything anyone has said. Whatever it was, I wasn't there and even if I was, I couldn't possibly have done it.'

She laughed, smoothing a neat hairstyle that needed no tidying. Kieran only knew about fashion from the pages he scanned past in the newspapers, but he thought he recognized some of the latest designer trends worn by thirty-year-old executives, not sixth formers. Now he gave it some thought he realized all the girls in the group around Hedda and Toni were displaying similar tastes.

'You won't have met my friend Kieran.' Joe waved towards him.

'He's the one who got stuck with Raven in Dance,' said Hedda. 'Poor guy. Be nice to him.'

Gina nodded towards him. 'Hi, Kieran. I hear you walked out on her. We don't blame you. I've moved group too.'

'Actually, she's been great. We're still working together in that class.'

'Isn't he cute! He's too nice to say a bad word about anyone, even if they earned it.' Hedda patted the seat beside her. 'Come and sit with me, Kieran. You need to hear the latest. It'll change your mind about the Crow.'

'I doubt that.' But he sat down.

Hedda placed a finger on his wrist. He moved his hand. 'You know Raven's got a problem with stealing.'

'No, I don't know that. You are making a supposition based on no empirical evidence that would stand up in court.'

His flat tone appeared to wrong foot her, as it did not fall into the usual script. He suspected she too often set the agenda of the conversations around her. 'Oh. Well, she has. Everyone else knows. Anyway,' she turned to Joe, thinking to find a more sympathetic audience, 'Mrs Bain has finally taken action. I wouldn't be surprised if Raven isn't suspended by the end of the day.'

'Yeah, flap away, Crow,' Toni added with relish.

'So how did you find out she's been stealing?' Joe asked, giving no hint he disliked their attitude. That was why he always got to play good cop.

'We all suspected, naturally, what with Raven envying all the rest of us for our wealth, but Gina provided the proof.' Hedda flicked her brown eyes at Kieran. 'Evidence that even a court would not be able to question.'

'You've got that wrong. It's the job of a court to test evidence.' Bad cop strode out to throw his weight around. 'Gina has made an assertion. Why take her word over Raven's? Is she a reliable witness?'

Gina gasped. 'Of course I am—I swear it. I found that watch

91

in our room. She'd had the nerve to hide it among my things. I was shocked—I thought we were friends!' Odd—Gina was displaying none of the usual signs of the liar, no flicker in her expression. He wished he could take her pulse and test her skin temperature to check what was going on as she spoke. Even better, wire her up to a lie detector.

'So you concluded it had to be her—why?'

'Because she's my roommate, duh. Or was. I asked for her to be moved.' Gina folded her arms. 'She needs help; I'm hoping the school with take action.'

'What about you? Couldn't you have put it there?'

Gina gave a strained laugh. 'And then what? Forgotten about it?'

'You tell me.'

Joe shook his head. 'Hey, Kieran, lighten up. Gina wouldn't do that to a friend. I mean, that would be way beyond cruel.'

Gina nodded eagerly. 'That's right—I don't do that kind of thing. And I . . . and I've only just got back and Hedda's tote had gone missing and I wasn't even here!'

'But the bag turned up almost immediately. It hadn't been stolen, had it?' Kieran trapped her gaze. She was grasping.

'That was Raven's story,' sneered Hedda.

Good cop breezed in to defuse the tension. 'But the good thing is that everything's gone back to its owners. Let's not fall out over it, especially as we've only just got to meet Gina.'

Kieran shrugged, pretending he didn't care one way or the other. 'Just saying.'

'So, Gina, you came back late.' Joe gave her a warm smile. 'What kept you away from meeting me earlier, hey?'

'My course overran.'

'I'm so pleased you're here now. What course was that?'

'Personal development.' She did not seem very forth-coming with the details, even with Joe fixing her with his flirt-o-dar beam.

'Oh? Maybe I need some of that. What d'ya think? Would I like it?' Joe put his ankle on his other knee, arm lightly draped behind her.

Gina shrugged. 'I guess. I found it really useful.'

'So where was it held? What kind of things did you get up to?'

'At the manor. We did all sorts of things.'

'Neat. Like what?' He risked giving it a final push but Kieran sensed they had hit a wall.

Hedda cleared her throat. 'I'm sure it was all the usual boring stuff. I think we'd better get to class. Gina, are you coming? See you later, Joe.'

'Yeah, later.' Joe got up with the others and, accidentally-on-purpose, bumped into Gina, dropping his pencil case and text books. 'My bad. Sorry.'

The group helped him pick up his belongings. Kieran noted that Gina handed Joe the plastic pencil case. Excellent. They had the fingerprints they had agreed to harvest. They were going to check them against the jewellery box Gina had given Raven before Gina underwent her personality change. While it was far-fetched to think someone else—what Raven had called the 'evil twin'—had returned in the place of the real Gina, they could at least eliminate that possibility.

'Talk later, OK?' Joe called to Gina and Hedda.

'Don't forget: stay away from Raven,' Hedda called back. 'She's bad news.'

'If you're seen with her, people here won't like it,' added Toni.

The girls walked off, kitten heels clicking.

'Was that a threat?' Kieran murmured as Joe tucked the

pencil case in a plastic bag at the bottom of his backpack to preserve the prints.

'Yeah, Key, I think it was.'

'Excellent. I like threats. It means we're getting close to something they don't want us to know.'

Chapter· 7

Raven set out her belongings on the shelf in the box room she had been allocated. It had until recently served as overflow accommodation for the sick bay to isolate contagious cases. She hadn't missed the implication that she was being treated like a disease.

It was so unjust. The more she thought about it, the likelier it seemed that Gina had been behind the thefts from the start, even in the time when they had been friends. Looking back, Gina had hinted she was getting tied up in knots dealing with her bossy father. Nothing was ever good enough for him. Towards the end of last term, she'd started behaving recklessly, telling Raven that if she couldn't please she might as well annoy her dad. Swinging from mood to mood, she had 'borrowed' stuff from Raven without asking but Raven had assumed this was a best-friends thing and made no fuss, not wanting to upset her. It brought her up short to realize she had probably never really understood Gina, not realizing her behaviour was the cry for help. And now it was too late. Gina had found another way. She'd divorced her old self and everything that had gone with it, including Raven. But why turn so viciously against her?

And it wasn't just Gina. Another of those poisonous notes had been left for her to see on arrival in her new room. She hadn't bothered to open this one but chucked it straight in the bin. It appeared she had a talent for making enemies.

Raven spread her duvet on the bed, trying the thin

mattress. The room felt like a prison cell. It even had bars on the window, some hangover from the days when they feared feverish students would throw themselves out. She found everything about it depressing.

There came a gentle tap on the door and Kieran put his head round. Boy, was he a sight for sore eyes: earnest jade green gaze, ruffled hair and strong arms that had held her so kindly earlier. She shouldn't like so much the way his body moved but, hands up, yes, she had noticed. It was just as well he couldn't hear her thoughts.

'Settled in?' His eyes swept the room and he frowned.

'Yeah, I know: it looks like a nineteenth-century lunatic hospital.'

He came in and shut the door. 'Actually, Victorian asylums in the main were quite progressive institutions, replacing the torment of the old Bedlams with good diet, fresh air, and gentle exercise.'

'Good to know.' Raven felt better having him in here; he was her breath of fresh air. 'All I need are a few posters and maybe this place will be passable. Did you need something?'

'I just called back to say I can't rehearse this weekend. Joe and I are going home.'

'Oh. OK.'

'We're back Sunday evening.'

'Have fun.' She watched as he examined the things on her dresser top. He paused at a photo of her with her parents.

'This is a nice picture.'

'One of my favourites. That was the last holiday before . . . our last time together.'

'Let me guess: that's Cape Cod.'

'That's right. Do you know it?'

'I've never been, but I recognize the lighthouse. I've made a study of them.'

She laughed at his geekiness. 'As one does. Dad adored the coastline. I expect your family holiday on private Caribbean islands.'

His mouth turned down at the corners. Wherever they had gone, he hadn't appreciated it. 'Something like that.'

'Do you have brothers and sisters?'

His hand paused on the frame containing a picture of her granddad. She hadn't noticed any family pictures in his room; neither he nor Joe put their backgrounds on display, which was unusual. Nearly everyone had a picture of someone somewhere in their bedroom. 'Yes. A sister. I mean I did. She died seven years ago.'

'Oh, Kieran, I'm so sorry.' Maybe that was why he had no photos: painful memories.

'So am I. Sorry for you about your mum and dad.'

'How did she die, your sister?' Raven appreciated the fact that finally he was opening up to her even if the subject was so sad.

'It was heart failure when she was fifteen.'

'So young? That's terrible.'

'She had Downs but they didn't pick up on the heart problem until too late.' His expression tightened.

That was scandalous. Raven thought that his posh parents should've been able to afford the best doctors in the country, but she didn't want to state the obvious. She could imagine the parental guilt of realizing you had missed something so vital.

He turned. 'But you'd've liked Hannah. Everyone loved Hannah—you couldn't help it.'

'Then I'm really sad not to have had the chance to meet her.'

Kieran made a visible effort to drag his thoughts away from his loss. 'So, no brothers and sisters then?'

'No, I was the only one. Mom couldn't have more kids.

I would have liked more family. With just my granddad, it doesn't feel enough somehow.'

'There's no one else?'

'No. I never expected to end up this way. My parents, they didn't tell me, you see. Pretended everything was fine, that Mom was just having treatment for something routine. I was too young to know the difference. When she died, I realized I had been the only one not to know, not to be prepared.'

'Maybe they lied because they thought it best for you?'

'I'm sure they did, but they were wrong. Nothing is worse than a life based on lies.' She rubbed her arms, trying to drive away the chill of memory. 'Then Dad went off to war. Told me he'd be fine. I knew by then not to trust that kind of promise. He couldn't keep it. I was dumped with family friends, the Boltons, while they worked out what to do with me. That was . . . not good.' Understatement of the year.

'That's tough—to lose everything familiar all at once.'

'Yeah, it was. Life with the Boltons was hell too. The boy picked on me, spread rumours at school—stupid lies about me being on drugs.'

'Which you weren't.'

'Absolutely not. He was the one with the problem, it turned out. Then Granddad came to the rescue.' She unpacked a few more toiletries for her dressing table. 'Odd to think there's barely anything left of my parents.' She smiled sourly. 'I suppose this all sounds weird to you, seeing how you live.'

'It doesn't sound weird in the least.' He gestured to her jewellery box. 'May I borrow this?'

Raven began to regret her outpouring; would he want to distance himself now she'd told him all that ugly stuff? 'Of course—but what do you want it for?'

'A still life for Art. I like the shell decorations.'

'Yeah, take it.' Raven tipped out her earrings. 'I've gone

off it anyway, seeing how the giver has turned out to be a heartless liar.'

He held out his book bag. 'Can you put it in there please? I don't want to knock off one of the shells.'

She dropped it in. 'It's not that special. I wouldn't care if you did.'

'Thanks, Raven. I'll look forward to seeing you when I get back.'

'Just don't change on me, OK?' She was getting anxious now when anyone went away, having seen what happened to Gina.

He smiled with his usual confidence. 'I won't.'

The flimsy lock gave way with a crack. Raven jolted from sleep, hazily grasping that her bedroom had been invaded.

'What the heck are you doing?' She rolled to take a defensive position, crouched on the bed.

Six students dressed in black surrounded her, white pillow cases over their heads so that she could not see their faces. Last time she'd witnessed this was when she first joined the school—part of the initiation rite for a newcomer. Some of her alarm subsided.

'Geez, guys. Piss off and annoy a first year, why don't you?' These rites were frowned on but those that did still go on at school were supposed by tradition only to involve new kids. She reached for the light to chase them away but before she could, the nearest one made a grab her. She broke his hold on her ankle with a kick to his stomach. He bent over, clutching himself, breath whistling between his teeth. Oops—not his stomach then.

'Get her!' gasped the one she had just emasculated.

Three boys dived and managed to catch her arms and legs.

Wriggling, she was lifted her off the bed. 'Put me down, you jerks!' She was angry more than scared. The last week had been bad enough without these idiots putting the seal on it this Saturday night.

'Raven Stone, you're not wanted here,' said in the leader in a hoarse voice. She didn't recognize it: male, purposely speaking low to disguise his tones, or maybe because he was still recovering. From the silhouettes, some of the gang were girls, the majority boys. They carried her through the doorway and out into the corridor.

'Cut it out. This isn't funny.' Raven struggled, managing to get one arm free and elbowed the nearest pillowcase in the face, following through with a heel of the palm shove to the region of the nose of a second. They dropped her. She sprang up and raced down the corridor, bare feet thudding on the lino.

'She's getting away!' shouted a boy.

Heart pounding, Raven headed for the door to the outside, planning to take refuge in her grandfather's cottage the other side of the gardens. Even with nothing on her feet and shorter legs than them, she was moving ahead. Thanks to Jimmy Bolton, she knew how to run. She began to hope she'd get away. The fire door was only metres away across the foyer. All she had to do was crash into the bar and she'd be out.

Then someone flew out of a room by the back door, rugby tackled her and took her down to the tiles. 'No you don't, bitch.'

Feet thundered behind. 'Have you got her?'

'Yeah.' There were so many of them—far more than the six who had come in to her room.

'Don't let her see your face!' A hand pinning her down on the floor, a pillowcase was pulled over her head. Before she could do anything to free herself, her wrists were tied behind her and then her ankles bound together with stretchy material—bandages from the medical room.

'Prisoner secured.' The guy who had squashed her was breathing heavily down her neck.

'Let me go!'

A rag was stuffed in her mouth.

Now she was scared. She couldn't see, could hardly breathe past the gag. Claustrophobia was a secret weakness and this was pushing all the buttons. One person hoisted her up, this time in a fireman's lift, and hurried through the exterior door. She could hear others following but now had no idea how many or where they were going. It was freezing outside dressed only in her pyjamas. She was going to kill them, each and every one, once she got free. That's if they didn't go and accidently kill her with this stunt first. *Fricking idiots.*

After five minutes being carried upside down, they entered a building of some sort and she was dumped on a cold concrete floor, adding a bruise to her tailbone. Now she could guess where they were: the old cricket pavilion out by the pitch. No one used them except to shelter from rain if caught on the far field during PE.

'Go away, Stone!' the first voice chanted. His voice was picked up by the others. 'Go away, Stone! Go away, Stone!'

She curled up, head to her knees, trying to make a gap for her nose in the baggy material. Not a panic attack; not now.

A wheel squeaked and cold water hit her back. They'd put her under the ancient shower head. She couldn't help a choked shriek. The flow was cut off.

'We hate thieves!'

The water turned on again. She tried to edge out of the spray but was prodded back in place by a broom. Her tormentors weren't going to risk getting wet. Hatred for them boiled inside her but she didn't even know who they were, couldn't touch them with her hands bound. Water off.

'You don't belong here.'

Water on.

Now Raven had a new crisis. The material of the pillowcase was wet and clinging to her nose and mouth. She tried to spit out the gag, but there was no shifting it. Oh God, she was going to suffocate! Using her knees, she scuffed at the hem, pushing it up so her chin and nose were free.

Water off.

'No more warnings. Leave our school.' A girl's voice that time.

Gina? Surely it couldn't be?

'Yeah we don't want no skanks here,' another girl said.

Water on.

She was freezing but all she could do was endure. She wasn't going to give them anything, not a word, not a shiver. The water went on and off for what seemed like hours. They were playing with her—giving her hope that they'd stopped only to switch it back on again.

'I think she's had enough,' the first boy said. The spray dripped to nothing. This time it wasn't false. She could hear footsteps and a door banging. They'd gone. Now she shivered. Squirming with her knees, she managed to pinch the pillow-case off and dislodge the gag, not that that helped much as the showers were pitch dark. She pushed herself up the wall then realized it was easier to go across the floor to the door. Reluctantly she slid back down and rolled through the icy puddle of water still draining through the iron grate. She told herself not to think about the spiders and cockroaches that had taken over the changing rooms when the humans abandoned them. The door to the communal shower was closed but she could just wriggle underneath through the gap. That

102

got her as far as the locker room. Drifts of leaves had gathered in one corner. The air smelt of mildewed sheds and forgotten places. She was so cold now the only thing that kept her moving was pure rage, running through her bloodstream like jet engine fuel. Her way was blocked by a jumble of benches so she pushed up to her feet and jumped across the room, navigating by the faint moonlight coming through a thick glass window high up.

The door did not budge. Bolted from the outside.

So they weren't finished. Her torment was supposed to include a night tied up as well, was it? She was going to scream with fury.

No. She refused to give them that much. Screw them! Using her flexibility, she stepped over her bound hands, bringing them to the front. The relief on her shoulders was instant. Bringing the bandages up to her teeth, she sat in a pile of dry leaves and began to chew the knots.

Chapter 8

The Young Detective Agency had its London headquarters in Clink Street on the south bank of the Thames. The street, named after an infamous prison, ran between the Globe Theatre and Sir Francis Drake's pirate ship, the *Golden Hinde*. This placed the YDA's converted warehouse in what had been for centuries the most disreputable part of the city. Even though developers had given the area a facelift, its shady past wasn't forgotten, and that suited the agents just fine.

A history lesson outdoors, there was nothing dated about the inside of the building. Conceived as an elite international training college for young people showing an aptitude for all aspects of crime detection, it housed about eighty students; bedrooms and living areas at the western end of the complex, working areas to the east. The laboratories and seminar rooms were kitted out to the highest specifications, matching any-thing belonging to the FBI or Scotland Yard. Kieran had made sure of that when Isaac left him in charge of equipping the place after the last remodelling.

At his favourite bench in the forensic lab, with a view across the river to St Paul's Cathedral, Kieran sat on a high stool examining the pencil case and the jewellery box for prints. The aqueous component had of course evaporated almost completely from the box, making dusting inefficient, so he was using fluorescence to pick up the traces. Discarding Raven's marks, he had isolated two nice prints on the box and was now matching them to the ones on Joe's case. He could already see that there was enough similarity in the ridges to make them from a single hand.

Joe came in with a mug of Earl Grey for Kieran and a four-pack of Coke. 'So?'

'Gina is the same girl. No doubt about it. Thanks.' He took a sip, noticing now that he was really thirsty. He had been so caught up in work he had forgotten to stop for meals. He got up to stretch, taking up his bullwhip and making a few preliminary cracks to get back in the habit. That circus skills course had been one of the best things he had done last year at the YDA. Billed as summer relaxation, they had all got far more from it than they expected. Joe had come out of it an accomplished juggler, but Kieran preferred the distance and precision of the whip.

'I suppose that simplifies matters. I was beginning to think alien abduction.' Joe wiggled his fingers in mock spookery.

'This isn't an episode of *Scooby-Doo*.'

Joe pulled up a stool. 'Was that like a joke referencing pop culture post-1950? Who are you and what have you done with Kieran Storm?'

Kieran tried not to smile.

'Raven is having one majorly good influence on you. I could almost kiss her myself, but I'll leave that to you.'

Kieran snapped the whip against the targets he had set out earlier along the window ledge. A paper flower fluttered into two parts. He did not like this talk that lifted the lid on something private.

'What?' Joe leant back on his stool. 'Don't tell me, you haven't kissed her yet? Man, I left you with the best opportunity the other night. Don't say you blew it?'

'I didn't blow it.' Flick—a second target met a paper death on the floor.

'So did you kiss her?'

'And that's your business how exactly, Joe?'

Joe grinned. 'It's not. I'm just curious to see the kind of girl that can thaw Kieran Iceman's control. Though I admit I take my life in my hands when you're in one of your Indiana Jones phases.'

'The forces involved in the manipulation of the single tail of the bullwhip are fascinating. It reaches the speed of sound and makes a small sonic boom.'

'Keep telling yourself it's just science; the rest of us know you're really into it because it's cool.'

The door to the lab swung open and a trolley crashed through.

'Joe, you can be a pain in the neck, did you know that?' Kieran put the whip down to greet his friends, Nat and Daimon, who were responsible for the interruption. 'I thought you'd be along eventually.'

'Key!' Nat, the blond one of the pair, squeezed him in a punishing hug. 'You are the man.'

'Yeah,' Daimon high fived him. 'You saved our *cojones* from a roasting. We are in your debt.'

Nat greeted Joe then pulled up a stool. 'Seriously, Key, if you hadn't headed Isaac off his warpath we wouldn't still be here, so thanks. We aren't exactly his favourite students at the moment.'

'Uh-oh, what else have you done?' asked Joe.

Daimon smiled at the memory. 'Let's just say the girls are going to take some time to forgive us.'

'This sounds good.'

'Remember Key invented that dye for camouflaging skin? The one that passed as normal body wash so we could take it on a mission without anyone being any the wiser?'

'Yep. Sure do.'

'One of my more interesting experiments but I only got as far as primary colours,' noted Kieran. 'I hadn't finished blending it before we were sent on a mission.'

'Exactly. So we tested it.'

'I know it's safe.' He wouldn't make a stupid error like that.

'No, I mean we tested if it would pass inspection by the most suspicious minds on the planet.'

'And?' asked Joe.

'We discovered that if you put a bottle of it in a bathroom, it works like a dream.'

Kieran knew exactly how that would turn out, having devised the formula himself. 'But—'

'Yup. Pretty blue girls—and I'm not talking mood.' Daimon winked.

'No, I'd say that their mood was more a shade of red. I've not seen Greta so angry before.' Nat rubbed his hands.

'It wasn't meant for . . . ' Still, the picture was irresistible. He wished he'd been there.

'I really liked her with blue hair,' added Daimon.

'And skin. The skin was good. Like a Smurf.'

Joe started laughing.

'Funny thing was that while she was away reporting it, Samira was already in the shower.'

'Izzie and Nel too. Tragically, they then stopped using the body wash, realizing that it had been tampered with.'

'I hope you took photos.' Joe regarded them with great pride. The competition between the boys and the girls of the YDA was an ongoing war of wits. Practical jokes were regarded by the students as a form of benign warfare, allowing them to hone their skills.

'We wouldn't invade the privacy of their bathrooms while they were occupied.' Nat looked angelic.

Daimon gave a wicked grin. 'Even we have our limits.'

'But we did manage to take a few pictures of them gathered to complain outside Isaac's office in their bathrobes.'

'But you were caught?' asked Kieran.

'We were *celebrated*,' corrected Nat, 'by the other boys.'

'Then given a bollocking by Isaac. Bathroom-cleaning duty for a month. The girls come and crow every time to see us wearing Marigolds.' Daimon held up his hands.

'Still, it was worth it.' Nat sighed dramatically.

'We're just waiting for their revenge. It's going to be ugly. There are some mean minds among the girls and I think Isaac has given them free reign to design a suitable payback.'

'I thought Cobras like you lived for danger,' said Kieran. Daimon was in B stream with the other agents who showed aptitude for handling high risks.

'Which is why I know when it's time to retreat. And our boy here,' he slapped Nat on the back, 'prefers not to be tracked down by his own kind. You know what they're like when they're let off their leash.' D stream, the Wolves, were merciless hunters, especially the She-Wolves.

Joe rubbed the back of his neck. 'I'm pleased we're well out of it then. I'll send flowers to your funeral.'

Nat peered over Kieran's shoulder to check his results on the prints. 'By the way, Key, they know you formulated the soap. Sorry about that.'

Kieran frowned. 'You mean they think I was part of it?'

'Maybe.' Daimon shrugged and helped himself to a spare Coke.

'Probably.' Nat grimaced apologetically.

'I'm going to emigrate.' Kieran was only half-joking.

'They'll still hunt you down. These are Yoda girls we are talking about. You can run but you can't hide.'

Joe nudged him. 'Buy them chocolate and disassociate yourself from these morons.'

'That might do it,' Nat agreed.

Opening a new browser window, Kieran put in an order for a huge delivery with Fortnum and Mason. 'I'm charging this to your account,' he told Daimon.

'Fair enough.' Daimon made his allowance multiply each month teaching poker to the other students. Then he realized. 'Hey, how do you know my bank details?'

Nat slapped him round the head. 'It's Key we're talking about here. He could break in to the Pentagon; I don't think your current account is going to be much of a challenge. So, guys, how's the mission going?' He pushed the trolley laden with snacks nearer so Kieran and Joe could help themselves.

'It's coming together.' Joe chose a sandwich and rocked back on his stool. 'We've found a link between the students and the parents—the pupils are being sent on character building courses and coming back changed. Kieran thinks there has to be something happening to them when they go away—some kind of brainwashing or maybe bribery or threats to reform their behaviour.'

'Or a combination of all three,' added Kieran.

'Bribed to be good kids?' asked Nat.

'I'm not sure about good. One of them came back totally poisonous.'

'Surely they wouldn't crumble so easily, so quickly?' Daimon had great faith in his own strength of mind and assumed everyone else was the same.

'Minds are clay not diamonds, Daimon.'

Daimon's expression hardened. 'So, not knowing the details, you think the students are being manipulated?'

'Something along those lines. We need more evidence before we know for sure.'

'There's nothing like that going on at the school, so it's got to be happening at the manor,' said Joe.

'The manor?' asked Nat.

'The school has this plush annex—a kind of health club which they use for training courses and vacation camps.'

'Already I'm suspicious. "Plush" and "school" sound weird together,' said Daimon.

Joe nodded. 'Yeah, you're right. During term, old boys and girls of the UIS network come there for conferences, bringing their colleagues from their places of work and their money. I thought it was a kind of fundraising wing, exploiting the contacts the school's graduates make, but there has to be something more. All the students who have gone through the personality change have been there.'

'And not everyone has come back,' Kieran pointed out. 'Some may still be there.'

'And that might just be the key to this puzzle. We'll have to get in.'

'What is less obvious is how the scheme at the manor relates to the wider problem that brought us into the case in the first place. I'm trying to find a pattern but nothing has leapt out so far. I suppose it'll end up as a game of hunt the money.'

'They give you money for doing them a favour, or you pay them money for brainwashing your kids?' Nat asked shrewdly.

'Not sure yet. I'm thinking it's not a one-way street. This much is clear: it all goes through the Union of International Schools and is nearly undetectable.'

'But not for Kieran Storm.'

'No, not for me. If the trail's there, I'll find it.'

'Cool.' Daimon took a pack of cards from his pocket. 'Game?'

'You finished here, Key?' asked Joe, gesturing to the work bench.

'Yes. I've sent in our report.'

Daimon shuffled, arcing cards from hand to hand. The

circus skill he had picked was magic tricks and sleight of hand—not that he had needed much help in that department, being a natural at deception.

'So we're off duty. Perfect.' Joe closed down the mission file on the screen. 'Where do you want do this?'

'The common room isn't safe right now,' admitted Nat, glancing over his shoulder.

'I thought here would be good.' Daimon cut the pack. 'That's why we brought food.'

'Don't tell me: the girls have kicked you out? They have, haven't they?'

Daimon nodded.

'They've really got you worried, haven't they?' Joe stretched his arms above his head, revelling in his friends' discomfort. 'OK, let's stay here. I wonder if you can beat Kieran this time, Daimon?'

'We're about even so far in our encounters. He's the toughest of the tough—his computer of a brain versus my cunning and all-round cheating mind.' Daimon fanned the cards on the counter.

Joe rolled his eyes at Nat. 'That kinda makes us the cannon fodder in this battle, doesn't it?'

Nat rubbed his palms together. 'But I always live in the hope that I can sneak past both while they are engaged in the clash of the Titans.'

'Hey, Nat, good plan.' Joe slapped him on the arm approvingly. 'Deal the cards.'

The YDA's driver dropped the two boys off at reception late Sunday afternoon. Joe looked up at the castle then across at Kieran. 'Ready?'

Kieran's answer was to walk in. Both of them had

111

returned energized by their weekend away. Isaac had spent a lot of time with them talking over their findings, helped them fine-tune their goals for the next few days. Kieran couldn't wait to get started, but first there was something he had to do.

'I'm just going to check on someone.'

'Raven, by any chance?' Joe was smirking.

Kieran gave him a stony look. 'Just returning the jewellery box.'

'Yeah, yeah. Keep hiding the truth from yourself, bro, but you are so lost. You need to be very careful you don't break mission rules. I'll take your bag to our room.' Joe spied the bullwhip. 'Really? This for driving the enemy off or lassoing Raven nearer?'

Now there was a picture to savour.

'Just take my bags, Jeeves.'

'Yeah, yeah—tugging my forelock right now, sir.' Joe opted for another, less respectful hand gesture. Kieran grinned and took out the jewellery box.

When Kieran reached the infirmary wing, he was surprised to find the door of her room standing wide open.

'Raven?' Kieran ventured inside, but she wasn't there. He stood in the corridor and listened, wondering if she had nipped out to the bathroom or kitchenette, but it was silent. Instinct tugged him back inside. His gaze swept the scene. This was not right. The bedding was dragged off the mattress and on to the floor, a rubbish bin kicked over. He counted the pairs of shoes: he knew how many she had—four—and they were all here, including her slippers, just how they'd been when he'd called round to say goodbye. She had left the room unwillingly and barefoot.

Possibilities tumbled through his mind. Her grandfather. He was most likely to know where she was. Kieran pushed past the students on the stairs and dashed outside, long strides eating up the path. He hoped Mr Bates was at home.

Fortunately, when he tapped on the front door of the caretaker's cottage, Raven's granddad answered immediately. The television burbled in the background and Kieran could smell shepherd's pie in the oven.

'Yes? Oh, hello. Kieran, isn't it?'

'That's right, Mr Bates. I just called by to ask if you've seen Raven?'

'No. I actually thought she was with you when I didn't see her about this weekend.'

'With me?'

Mr Bates looked down. 'Well, she did tell me she was spending a lot of time with you and I thought that maybe . . . '

'I've been away. She isn't in her room.'

'Ah, I see. She won't have left the grounds as she has to have my permission to do that, but I haven't seen her since yesterday dinnertime.'

'OK, thanks. I'll search for her around the school then.'

The fact that Kieran thought something might be wrong reached Mr Bates. 'Let me know the instant you find her or I'll have to go looking myself.'

'Of course. I'll track her down—don't worry, sir.'

Kieran sprinted back to his room. His partner was lying on his bed, head buried in *Forbes*, reading up on the quartet of rich men who were the school trustees. 'Joe, we've a problem.'

Joe threw his magazine aside, all business. 'What kind?'

'Raven's missing. There are signs of a struggle in her room. No shoes taken so she went unwillingly—I'm discounting sleepwalking as she would've turned up by now. Spread of the bedding and disturbance on the carpet suggest she was carried by at least four people. That kind of scene doesn't go unnoticed in daylight so I'm guessing it was likely to be at night.'

'Last sighting?'

Kieran paced, running his hands through his hair. 'Her grandfather mentioned he saw her Saturday supper. He assumed she was spending the day with me so didn't think it odd when she missed lunch.'

'Dammit.' Joe shoved his feet into his trainers. 'We should've guessed something might happen; things were getting so ugly last week.'

'And she mentioned threatening notes too—I should've listened harder.'

Joe checked his set of lock picks as Kieran retrieved a pencil flashlight from his bag. 'Where should we search first?' Joe asked.

'Outbuildings. Not within earshot of the school and you are less likely to meet staff there, especially at the weekend.'

Joe grabbed a blanket off the bed. Kieran took some thick socks from his drawer.

'I've a really bad feeling about this,' Kieran admitted. 'Let's go.'

Chapter 9

So cold. Raven huddled in the leaves, unable to believe that she had been left for so long. Her mind had stopped functioning properly, stuck on bewilderment. Why was no one coming for her? Had they not noticed she was missing? She had managed to get out of the knots on the wet bandages, sacrificing the skin of her wrists to do so, but that hadn't got her much further. Her shouts and thumps on the door had not been heard—or if they had, had been ignored. She had dropped to sleep a few times but was worried that she would slip into hypothermia. She guessed she only avoided this fate thanks to the warm spring day taking the chill from the changing block. She dreaded what would happen overnight if she was still here. She had made a flag of the bandages and stuffed it out of the barred window, hoping the flutter would attract someone to rescue her, but so far her hook had caught no fish.

'Raven?'

She heard scraping at the door. It took a moment to realize it was her name being called. She tried to speak but nothing came out. *Don't go away—please, don't give up!*

'The door's padlocked. Can you pick the lock, Joe?' *Kieran.*

'I'm on it.'

'Raven, if you're in there, we're coming. We've seen your sign. You saved us hours of searching.'

Never had she been more grateful to hear Kieran's voice. She began to shake. Perfect—she was cracking up after having held it together for so long.

Light poured into the room.

'Is she still in there?'

A torch beam swept the corners of the room, passed her then reversed. 'Yes.' Kieran crossed the floor, expression thunderous. 'Blanket!'

Raven held out her hands. Kieran took them and rubbed them vigorously in his. 'She's freezing. Bastards.'

Joe wrapped a blanket round her shoulders. Kieran picked her up. 'I'm sorry, Raven.'

It felt so wonderful to be warming up again, but painful too as blood began to move about her extremities. He sat, cradling her on his lap.

'Sorry?' She sneezed. 'Why you sorry?'

'Sorry this happened to you. We'll make them pay.'

She let her head drop on his chest. 'I don't even know who "they" were.'

'First task, get you warmed up. Second, report this.' Joe, equally terse, tucked the blanket more tightly around her. Both boys were wearing very formidable expressions. Her avenging angels.

'What's the best treatment for suspected hypothermia? Do we need to take her to hospital?' Joe asked Kieran.

'I'm OK.'

But they weren't listening. 'We'll put her in bed in dry clothes and use body heat—that's the quickest way.' Kieran rapped his words out like a commanding officer. 'Find a hot water bottle from somewhere. I've not noticed one in the stores but Mr Bates is likely to have one—right age demographic.'

'Still here you know.'

Kieran rubbed her arm. 'I know—and thank God you are.'

The two were unstoppable. Joe ran off to get a hot water bottle. Kieran carried Raven to his room, past the whispering groups of students enjoying their Sunday evening. If looks

116

could kill, there would have been mass murder as Kieran glared at them. He helped her out of her damp night clothes (Kieran's eyes kept shut throughout that particular manoeuvre). The T-shirt he lent her (slogan *Sure it works in practice, but does it work in theory?*) hung to her knees. Hurrying her into the bed, Raven was a little shocked when he then got under the duvet with her and hugged her to his chest. She hadn't anticipated that.

'Sorry—no choice.' Like her, he clearly felt awkward at the sudden ramping up of the contact between them. 'You need to warm up quickly.'

'You could get expelled for doing this,' she said through chattering teeth, hands pressed flat against the furnace of his rib cage. She could feel the steady thump of his heart.

'Don't care. This is the most reliable way of restoring your core temperature.'

'My feet are the worst.'

Dipping out of the covers, he whipped a pair of socks out of his pocket and pulled them over her frozen toes, rubbing her soles briskly as he did so. He then went back to full body contact, his warm chest and long legs pressed against her.

'Why me?' she asked quietly.

He knew what she meant. 'Because they're sick and twisted. For some insane reason they've decided to pick on you and feel they can get away with it.'

'I'm not going to let them get away with it.'

Kieran smiled. 'That's my girl: don't get angry, get even.'

'I'm spitting mad too.'

''Course you are. But tomorrow—you can go after them then. Just now you need to rest.'

Her shivering subsided and she burrowed closer to his warmth. She hadn't felt this cared for in ages. With Kieran there, gently stroking her back, she fell into an exhausted sleep.

Kieran slid out of the bed when Joe returned with a hot water bottle already prepared. He tucked it in a jumper so it wouldn't be too hot for her, and then put it in the space he had occupied.

'Is she OK?' Joe asked in a low voice.

'Physically she's fine now. But she's upset.'

'Who wouldn't be?'

'What did you tell her grandfather?'

'That it was some prank that went wrong. I said we'd report it. He was all set to come over here but I suggested he wait until the morning when she had had a chance to sleep. He took some persuading but he eventually agreed for her sake.'

Kieran twitched the duvet making sure her feet were tucked in. 'Raven might want to see him.'

'Yes, but he was *really* angry—not his usual mild self at all.'

'Now we know where she gets her temper from.' Kieran sat down on the desk chair. Seeing that his bedside table was covered in plants, he got up and swept them off to make space for a glass of water for her. Sod the data collection: he didn't want her inconvenienced by his experiment.

Joe looked at the ceiling with a perceptive smile but made no comment. 'I thought it would be doing them both no favours if he said things to the school that he might then regret. From what I understand from Raven, he needs the job.'

'So what do we do with her now? I don't think we can put her back in that room—I don't trust anyone under this roof but you and her.'

'I told Mr Bates to wait until tomorrow but I didn't say we would. I think we should go to Mrs Bain now.'

'Won't we be drawing attention to ourselves?'

'Maybe, but I was thinking her reaction would tell us more about what's really going on here.'

Was that a twinge of conscience he was feeling? 'You see using what happened to Raven as a way of advancing our mission?'

Joe's expression was steely. 'Key, she is part of the mission, someone we will only be with for as long as it lasts. You are remembering that, aren't you?'

Kieran looked over at the wildly curling hair scattered over his pillow. 'Yes, of course, I know that.'

'You know we can't do serious relationships. The rule's been inflexible since Kate Pearl and that disaster in Indonesia. It's a red line for Isaac. Kate did blow the entire mission.'

'Yeah I know.' He did, but it was different facing it himself. He now felt acute sympathy for Kate Pearl.

'We'll lock the door; leave her to sleep,' suggested Joe. 'I doubt anyone will try get to her in here.'

'And we'll know if they do.' One of the first things Kieran had done was set alarms around the windows and entrance to their room to guard the privacy of their computers and other personal items.

'OK then. Let's go find Mrs Bain.'

The head teacher was not difficult to track down as she was holding a meeting in her study.

'Meeting on a Sunday? Dedicated to her work, isn't she?' whispered Joe as he lurked with Kieran in the shrubbery out-side her window. She sat at the head of a mahogany table, a pair of black-framed glasses perched on her nose. Four men they had only seen in pictures before sat two on each side. They formed the board of trustees for the Union of International Schools.

119

'Key, what can you tell me about them?' asked Joe.

Facing the window was an older man with white swept-back hair wearing a double-breasted jacket.

'Old guy who looks like a polar bear in a suit? That's Anatol Kolnikov, chair of the trustees, former Russian Minister of Education. From the dagger and star insignia on the tie, he's also former Russian KGB, though that didn't get into his wiki entry. He's one of the rehabilitated politicians of the post-Soviet era. Drinking habit. Smoker—cigars not cigarettes. Cheats on his wife.'

'An all-round nice guy then.'

'On his left, the guy who looks like he's been dug up from his ancestral vault? That's Tony Burnham, British industrialist. Normally wears frameless specs, five eleven, suit hand-stitched, Savile Row. No telltale tie as he's wearing a bow but I'll take that as evidence of bad taste, or maybe he's colour blind.'

'Yeah, he should be locked up for that as the least of his sins.'

'The other two with their backs to the window—that stout man with dyed black hair and tanned skin—that's Ramon Velazquez, Mexican telecommunications king. Has got through three marriages. Latest wife is related to a major player in a drugs cartel but he's trying to keep that quiet. Can't see much from the back but I'm thinking he has a heart condition—there are signs which suggest mild pain, what with the clubbed fingers and chest rubbing.'

'Remind me to put the ambulance on speed dial for him.'

'Last man, that's John Paul Garret, American oil and gas man. Remarkable for being unremarkable; he slips past everyone's notice so easily, which I think it part of his mode of operation—ghosting, being places but leaving no trace. I think you know more about him as you were reading up on him in *Forbes*.'

'Yeah, billionaire with no flair. He didn't make much of

120

a story but maybe we're about to find out that boring hides something much more interesting. Why are they here, do you think?'

Kieran quickly read the dynamics in the room. Though Mrs Bain was chairing the meeting, she was deferential to the men, giving that overly eager-to-please smile of someone reporting to their boss.

'My guess is that this is a report back meeting. She's their link between the parents and their kids. If we could hear what was being said I bet quite a few of our questions would be answered.'

'So, do we wait or interrupt?'

'Let's give it a minute.'

Mrs Bain was presenting something to the men—they couldn't hear what but she was going through a pile of files one by one, reading the covering page then making comments.

'Interesting that she doesn't have her secretary in attendance,' mused Joe as they watched Mrs Bain get up to refill the coffee cups.

'Perhaps she doesn't want her to eavesdrop on what's really going on, so holds the meetings on a Sunday. Ready to go in and see if we can overhear what they're saying?'

'Let's do it.'

The boys re-entered the building and headed for the head teacher's suite of rooms. This had been the gun room of the old castle, now converted into a luxurious set of offices. The outer room was dark, but as they entered Mrs Bain walked into her secretary's office to refill the coffee pot. Rumbled.

'What are you boys doing here?' she asked sharply.

Joe was quick to adapt to the new circumstances. 'Mrs Bain, we apologize for disturbing you.'

'As you can see, I'm in a meeting.' She gestured to the men in the room beyond.

'I'm sorry, but we wanted to report a grave breakdown in school discipline.' Kieran loved the way Joe said that: so respectful but with a hint of disdain only he could hear.

Mrs Bain put the coffee pot down. Kieran guessed Joe's formal mode of expression, taken from the school's rules and procedures, had flummoxed her and it took her a moment to sort through what he was really saying. Then she smiled and cocked her head winningly to one side, making light of it for the benefit of her guests.

'Grave breakdown? Forgive me, Mr Masters, but I can't hear the sound of rioting students so I'm at a loss to what you're referring.'

The Russian stood up. 'I think we've concluded our business here. We'll leave you to sort this matter out.'

Embarrassed, Mrs Bain fluttered around them, handing over coats and briefing papers. 'I'm sure it's nothing.'

'Absolutely, Mrs Bain. Tight ship you run here, we know that.' The skeletal one gave her a shark smile. Kieran added Harley Street cosmetic dentist to his list of facts about the man. 'We've more to discuss. We'll take it over to the other place.'

Mrs Bain gave the location of that away by an instinctive glance out of the window. The 'other place' had to be the manor. 'Yes, of course. I wish you a very pleasant stay.'

'Until the autumn, then.' Burnham shook hands with her and led the party out of the room.

Mrs Bain could not hide her irritation at the interruption. Kieran deduced that these private meetings with the trustees were her pat on the back for good work and he and Joe had just denied her a treat. Excellent. 'So, Mr Masters, what crisis drives you to my door on a Sunday night?'

Kieran left the talking to Joe and occupied himself examining the room's contents. They'd already been through it once, at night, but he was looking to see if anything had changed.

122

Mrs Bain leant on the table, fingers resting on a pile of folders that he hadn't seen in any of the cabinets or the safe behind the painting over the mantelpiece. Reading upside down he saw that the top file had Gina Carr's name on it, bracketed with her father's.

'I'm talking about Raven Stone,' said Joe.

'Oh?' Mrs Bain's expression darkened. 'What has she done now?'

'Not what she's done but what's been done to her. She was the victim of a serious bullying incident. She was taken from her room in the early hours of the morning by masked students, tied up, put under the showers in the old cricket pavilion, soaked to the skin for a prolonged period of time, then left all day to freeze.'

'Hardly to freeze. It has been exceptionally warm this weekend.' Mrs Bain picked up the files, moved to her desk and looked down at her computer screen. 'Twenty-four degrees on average.'

'Mrs Bain, we are reporting the water torture of a fellow pupil and you only comment on the weather?'

Putting the folders away in her top drawer, Mrs Bain walked out from behind her desk and gestured to the two boys to take a seat on the sofa at the far side of the room. Remaining standing, she was exercising basic psychology, taking the dominant position; both Joe and Kieran had been trained to recognize it.

'Mr Masters, you are from the States, yes?'

Joe nodded. 'Yes, ma'am.'

'You may think I sound harsh but you probably aren't familiar with the traditions of public schools in this country. There is a certain—how do you say?—allowance for rough justice, regrettable though that is. Miss Stone was caught steal-ing from the pupil body but my respect for her grandfather meant I did not expel her as I would any other student. This may have struck her victims as unfair and they meted out their own punishment. On the plus side, I think this will have lanced the boil. Miss Stone will have learnt a hard lesson but it should mean that the school returns to business as usual tomorrow, with accounts being settled.'

The woman had the compassion of a Lucretia Borgia.

'You describe the people who tormented her as victims; surely the truth is Raven was theirs?' Joe said reasonably. 'You've proved nothing against Raven, but this attack is a flagrant breach of your own rules. Are you not going to punish them for what they did?'

'But you said they were masked. I will, of course, talk to Miss Stone about it and see if she can identify them. I will also have a word with the whole school making clear that such behaviour is not condoned by me. What more can I do?'

Launch an inquiry. Question the most likely suspects who had been vocal in their dislike of Raven. Stand up for the one who had been hurt, not make feeble excuses for the bullies. With difficulty, Kieran held his tongue. Joe was right: it was what she was not doing or saying that was interesting. This school was one twisted institution.

'Aren't you curious to hear how Raven is?' Joe asked, keeping his tone even, though Kieran could see he was riled by her answers.

'I assume she's fine or you would've said so.' Mrs Bain moved towards the door.

'We took her to our room and warmed her up, thank you for asking. If we hadn't found her when we did, we would've been taking her to ER.'

Mrs Bain stopped trying to usher them out and folded her arms. 'Is she still there?'

'Yes. May seem weird to you but once she was OK, we

124

didn't immediately kick her out to go back to a room where she was terrorized last night.'

'Well, we can't have that. Girls are not allowed in the boys' dormitories.' Mrs Bain pressed a button on her desk phone. 'Gillian, can you go to the medical room please. We've a case for you.'

'She's staying where she is.' Kieran spoke up for the first time.

'She most certainly is not, Mr Storm. She'll be looked after in the medical room. Mrs Jones will see to her. Please ensure that Miss Stone gets there—or do I have to send someone to fetch her?'

'But . . . !' Kieran stopped his protest when Joe tapped his foot against his.

'OK, will do.' Joe's wide smile held no warmth. 'Thanks. This has been most illuminating.'

'And thank you for coming to report it.' Her tone was equally icy; both of them were saying the opposite of the surface message. 'My door is always open to students.'

Except to Raven, thought Kieran. It was bizarre. The head teacher was complicit in the attempt to make Raven the school pariah.

Joe motioned to him to say nothing as they walked away but Kieran was ready to explode.

'Vile woman!'

'Kieran,' Joe warned.

He tugged Joe in to an empty classroom, unable to wait to vent his feelings. 'She knew.'

'That's what the smart money is on.'

'She's not only allowing it; she's probably behind it!'

'I agree, but that makes no sense, does it? If she really wanted to hurt Raven, she would've expelled her when she had the chance.'

'Whatever made her decide to keep her here, it won't be out of the kindness of her heart. She doesn't have one.' He pictured a shrivelled up lump of jerky in the place of what had once been a living organ.

'Do you think she really believes Raven stole those things?'

'Not really relevant, is it? The head teacher is supposed to protect her pupils, even the ones she doesn't like, not throw them to the wolves.'

'But do you? We know Raven's innocent; does she?'

Kieran's rage was beginning to pass, allowing his mind to clear. 'It would be very curious if she did.' He rubbed his chin, searching his memory for matches for this kind of behaviour. 'There's a long tradition of societies finding a scapegoat. It's not about the faults of the individual but about the dynamics of those using them. I'm guessing that, as the closest to Gina, Raven became a very handy target when they decided to recruit her friend, a plausible way of explaining away Gina's problem with stealing—they may even have given Raven the scholarship thinking a day would come when they could make use of her like that. Keep piling the stuff on the scapegoat that no one cares about and then get rid of her when you're ready, leaving everyone else with a clean record.'

'You think they'd go that far?'

'It's not beyond the bounds of possibility. I'm beginning to see there must be some exchange between the parents and the trustees: something along the lines of "you clear my little darling of all accusations and I'll owe you". Raven is being blamed for Gina's crimes. And maybe not just her: I think we should start to be a bit more worried for the ones that haven't come back.'

Joe dug his hands in his pockets. 'What've we let ourselves in for? And how are we going to keep Raven out of harm's way?'

Kieran struggled to remain rational. No one had been

harmed yet as far as they knew; maybe they were overreacting? Still, the school definitely did not feel safe for any of them. 'Ousting into the cold would be seriously bad news. Raven and her grandfather have nowhere else to go.'

'So in your theory they're prepping her as some kind of fall guy?'

'Yes. And if she wasn't here, I think they'd pick on someone else. As far as that goes, it isn't personal.'

'So are we taking her to sick bay or not?'

'I think we have to.' Kieran didn't like that idea at all.

'You know what, Key, you're not looking too good yourself.'

'What?'

'I think you might be coming down with stomach pains, grumbling appendix.'

'And I need someone to monitor me overnight?'

'You're catching on, bro.'

Raven had a fuzzy recollection of being woken out of a deep sleep. She didn't want to move: the bed had smelt like Kieran and being under his duvet was almost as good as having him next to her. Yawning, she was bundled in to a dressing gown, hustled to the medical room and handed over to the matron who put her between cold sheets. Waking up properly thanks to that, she felt a spike of alarm to be back on this wing of the castle—that was until she realized Kieran was staying with her, having taken over the bed next to hers. He handed the nurse a care sheet of symptoms to watch for in case his suspected appendicitis flared up in the night. He sat propped up on the pillows, consulting a medical dictionary, with an 'I-will-not-be-moved' expression on his face.

'I want my temperature taken every four hours,' he instructed Mrs Jones. 'You will also note down my description of my abdominal pain. It's very important to construct a history if I need to take this to hospital.'

The nurse walked away to fetch some painkillers, muttering something about hypochondria. When her back was turned, Raven stretched a hand out to him. 'Oh, Kieran, I'm sorry. I didn't realize you were ill—and you carried me all that way. Did that set it off?'

'Set what off?' He touched his fingers to hers, giving them a light caress that sent a shiver down her arm.

'Your appendicitis.'

'I don't have an appendix. It was taken out two years ago.'

'Oh.'

'I'm your guard. You can go to sleep without worrying about any repeats of last night's attack.'

Raven was about to protest that she didn't need babysitting but changed her mind. She tucked her hand back under the covers as the nurse returned. 'Thank you.'

'There you are, Kieran.' Mrs Jones placed a little cup with two pills in front of him. 'Take these and try to sleep.'

'Aren't you going to check on Raven?' he asked, palming the unwanted pills so she would think he had swallowed them.

'Miss Stone, how do you feel?' Mrs Jones had the bedside manner of an anaconda.

'OK now, thanks.' Raven pulled up the blankets and lay on her side peeking across at Kieran. He winked at her.

'I'll be in my office.' The nurse had a bed there where she could sleep in-between rounds. 'Just press the buzzer on your table, Kieran, if you need anything or the pain gets worse. I should warn you we have CCTV in here so I can monitor my patients. No shenanigans from either of you.'

'Marvellous.' Kieran smiled at her innocently, ignoring the implication that they both better stay in their own beds. 'No one dare disturb Raven again if there is a digital witness.'

Mrs Jones walked off without a comment.

'I think I'm going to sue this school,' murmured Raven. 'Neglect.'

Kieran punched his pillow to make it more comfortable. 'Spoken like a true American.'

'You don't approve?'

'Oh, I approve one hundred per cent.'

'Shame I don't have the money for legal representation.'

'Or proof.'

'Or proof.' Yeah, there was that. She'd only thought that one of the girls sounded a bit like Gina but now she recalled the incident she had begun to doubt even that—it was all a jumble. But why waste time thinking about such creatures when she had Kieran's company for the night, with him lying only a few feet away so she could hear his breathing and take comfort that he was keeping vigil? His presence next to her was like the warm glow of fire on a winter day, thawing out the hurt of the last twenty-four hours. He wouldn't let anyone harm her—a promise she could take to the bank.

'Goodnight, Raven.' He lay down on his side to face her.

'Goodnight, Kieran. And thank you.' She fell asleep with his green eyes watching her across the gap between the beds.

Chapter 10

The morning after the night in the medical room Raven moved out to her grandfather's cottage, refusing to stay on her own under the castle roof. Granddad fully supported her decision, staring down Mrs Bain when she had protested that he was breaking the rules on the use of school property. Raven unpacked her stuff in his second bedroom and decorated the plain white walls with the posters Kieran had thought to bring back for her from his weekend away. They were a great selection from old dance movies—*West Side Story*, *Singin' in the Rain*, and *Billy Elliot*. He had handed them over casually, saying he'd just come across them but she wondered—and speculated—and wondered some more. They were a very thoughtful gift from a guy who was just a friend.

On Thursday morning, as she had an early breakfast with her grandfather, Raven broached the subject that had been on her mind. 'I've been thinking about September.'

He poured himself a cup of strong black tea. 'I'm a year off retirement, sweetheart, so the chances of finding another position aren't good.'

'That's OK, Granddad. You stick it out here. But when I've done my exams, I'm going to transfer to the local sixth form college. I've got the forms if you will help me fill them in.'

'Of course I will, but are you sure? Graduating from Westron usually guarantees you a place at a good university—sets you up for life. The network of past pupils gives you a huge advantage in the wider world. And there's your scholarship—that's a lot of money you're turning your back on.'

Raven stirred the milk in her cereal bowl, oat flakes drowning in the white. 'I hate it here.'

'I don't blame you. I'm not too keen on this place myself.' Her grandfather had complained vociferously to Mrs Bain about the attack but no action had been taken. Both had been depressed and further disillusioned by the outcome. 'And I think you are right to pursue other options.'

'I think I'd do better with ordinary kids—ones who don't automatically look down on me. I want just, you know, to fit in. I now get why some of the other scholarship students threw in the towel—we're not really welcome here.' She'd work out a way of carrying on seeing Kieran if she could—and if he was interested.

'I see. In that case, I'll see if I can persuade them to let you continue to live with me here.'

'Is that going to be a problem?'

'Technically I'm not supposed to have anyone else here. Mrs Bain only allowed you to move in when I said it was the only way we would both stay on at Westron, notice period be damned.'

'Aw, thanks, Granddad.'

'And I can't see what harm it would do. There's a spare bedroom and I'm your only family. The thing is they are very determined to keep Westron for Westron students and staff only; you'd be seen as an intruder if you're no longer a pupil here.'

'Afraid I'll spill their dark secrets?' The school was getting weirder by the day, a strange atmosphere among the students, a fierce silent battle of who was in and who was out.

'They're somewhat paranoid. I think it's because so many of the youngsters are from celebrity backgrounds. The prospectus does promise complete confidentiality.'

'Tell them not to worry about me—I couldn't be less interested in them.' Raven got up and took her dance kit off the dryer hanging over the Aga.

'We'll see. So, what've you got today?'

'Final rehearsal for our performance piece. Kieran promised he'd have learnt it by now.'

As her granddad got up, his knees clicked. 'Leaving it a little late, isn't he? The assessment is tomorrow.' He put his hand to the small of his back, rubbing the base of his spine. Raven swallowed her remark about taking it easy; he couldn't afford the luxury of putting his feet up if he wanted to keep his job.

She kissed him on the cheek. 'You're telling me. See you later.'

Hugging her bag to her chest, Raven crossed the lawn from the cottage to the main building, sneakers getting wet with dew. Though she passed several groups heading for their lessons, no one said hello to her. She had got used to being ignored by the other students; in fact she told herself she preferred it that way. She tried not to think about the old days, when Gina and she had been a team. Could you be a team of one? If so, that was her now. Even the teachers, with the honourable exception of her dance tutor, paid her the minimal notice. Her work wasn't being marked when she handed it in, and if the students ever had to divide into groups she was always mysteriously left out and no one did anything about it, unless she happened to be in class with Joe or Kieran. Kieran had told her to treat it as a chance for sociological observation, a learning experience of crowd behaviour.

Yeah right.

She decided to treat it as a chance to separate herself from the school emotionally and imagine her life beyond its walls. Every time they acted like jerks she waved a mental two fingers at them, keeping her real thoughts hidden behind a bland expression. She couldn't wait to leave. But the worst part—the thing she hadn't shared with anyone—was that it felt like she was reliving the bleak months after her father's death. Whispers behind her back; cruel comments in the corridors; the feeling of having nowhere safe to go; enemies around every corner; being made to believe she was worthless. The scars that had begun to heal over the last few years had split open again and grief for her parents seeped out. None of this would have happened if they hadn't died. The fact that Westron was making her feel this way only added to her fury.

Kieran was already in the practice room they had booked. He had put it under his name because whenever she put hers down she got bumped by one of the other groups. She hovered outside looking in through the glass panel. He was standing in a shaft of light, doing some stretches and shoulder rolls. The dark mood lifted a little. Now that was something to cheer a girl up when nothing else could. He could move like a dream, but he was missing the most important aspect of dance: you had to perform and not just go through the motions. She still hadn't managed to get through to him on that.

'Hi, how are you?' she called brightly, coming in and throwing her bag in a corner.

'I'm fine, thanks.' He smiled at her as she took off her trackies and sweat shirt. 'You?'

'OK. But I'll be as happy as a clam if you learnt it all the way through.'

'Are clams happy?'

'They are in America. So did you?'

'I did.'

'You mean we're actually going to put this together and not just run through the various moves?'

He nodded.

'You've got spotting sorted?' They'd had quite a few sessions together trying to get that right.

'Sorted.'

'You mean Kieran Storm is going to dance?'

He nodded once again.

'Great. I've been waiting for this.'

Slotting his iPod in the speaker dock, she tapped on the music.

The Dance exam was scheduled for the morning, with all the performances running one after the other, no breaks. Nervous, Kieran and Raven walked side by side to find out when they were on. Raven looked at the list. 'We're last.'

'Is that good?'

Raven noted that Gina had found a place with the other Modern group who had tried to have Kieran on their team. She had got the better part of the bargain, even if Kieran was still not quite ready to perform in front of an audience. 'I don't suppose it matters. At least the examiner is from outside the school; we'll get a fair assessment. Let's get seats at the back.'

Kieran sat beside her in the dance studio. She could see he was mentally running through his moves. Raven nudged him with her shoulder. 'Don't over-think it. We'll be fine.'

In a pause between dances, Joe slid into the chair beside him. 'How's he doing?' he asked Raven, ignoring Kieran. 'Is he like Robot-Kieran or Gotta-Dance-Kieran?' Joe did jazz hands.

'I think right now he would prefer to be facing a pride of ravening lions.' She brushed the back of Kieran's hand in sympathy.

'Yeah, I can see that.' Joe looked a little concerned.

Kieran suddenly straightened. 'You know what? We are going to be great.'

She smiled in surprise. 'I know—I've been telling you that for weeks.'

'No, I mean it this time.'

'And I didn't?'

'You were just being kind.'

The musical intro to the second-to-last dance began. Kieran raised a brow at Raven.

'Yep. Time to go backstage.'

Joe slapped his back. 'Break a leg.'

Kieran punched him in the stomach—not too hard. 'Thanks, pal.'

Raven dragged Kieran into the wings before Joe could hit him back. She smoothed down the front of his costume where she had rumpled the black short-sleeve top. 'Ready?'

'It's going be good, Raven.'

'Hmm.' She was a little sceptical but thought it sweet of him to say so. The repeated experiments had only shown his unwillingness to perform before an audience. What happened in the practice room stayed in the practice room; he was always holding back. 'You're playing the role of someone who is quite self-absorbed, cold even, so it's OK.'

'But you want me to perform, bring the emotion out.'

'Yes, but the main thing is you dance it all the way through.'

'And you're supposed to be showing some regret leaving me.'

'That's what I'm trying for, yes.'

The other dance had about a minute left. Kieran took a step closer. 'Then I want to try an experiment. I've been thinking about it for weeks.'

'What's that?' She couldn't look away from his tiger-intent gaze.

'This.' He lifted her up and backed her against the wall as his lips closed the distance to capture hers. She'd wondered—known they were circling something—but now his move had arrived when she least expected it. He wasn't just kissing her—he was devouring her. He seemed to pour everything into it—their mutual fire that only burned hotter when they argued, laughed and danced together. He held her up with one hand on the back of her thighs, her legs around his waist; the other hand stroking her neck, shoulders and hair—everywhere he could reach. At first she was shocked that he was pouring out his passion for her in a public place, but then she was driven past thought and melted in his arms, matching kiss for kiss, stroke for stroke.

They didn't hear the cough behind them. It took a tap on the shoulder from Miss Hollis to break them apart.

'I hope that was just for luck,' she said, amused.

'We were . . . um . . . ' Raven struggled to find her words.

'Just getting into our roles,' Kieran finished. 'Finding a spark.'

'Is that why . . . ?' Raven blushed. She sincerely hoped it was more than just an aid to performance. It had certainly felt more than that. 'Yes, exactly.'

Miss Hollis checked the music was cued up correctly. 'So I take it you're ready? I've not seen this all the way through so I'll be interested to see what you've done with the piece.'

'No one has,' muttered Raven, bunching back the hair that Kieran had dislodged during the kiss. Had Kieran finally declared himself or was she jumping to the wrong conclusion?

'OK. Starting positions, please.'

In contrast to her confusion, Kieran appeared fired up after the kiss. He walked on to the stage showing no nerves.

OK, Stone, put that aside for later. The show must go on. She moved to her opening spot.

Chapter 11

Raven did not know what had come over Kieran. When the music started, he began moving as if he had been possessed by the dance. Technically he had shown he had the routine memorized, but she had doubted he could bring his performance to the stage as he was so closed off emotionally in public. Now he injected what she could only call alpha-male attitude into the moves—they may have broken off the kiss but the dance became its extension. The chemistry between the two parts, the female dancer shaking off the bad relationship and the man trying to keep her, went from tentative to combustible. Raven found her own performance improving to meet the raised bar like high jumper making a new personal best. It was the most incredible dance experience of her life and she didn't want it to end. He folded her into his arms so tenderly, with such yearning, that she had to remember the choreography asked her to spin away and reject him. Her reluctance was not feigned. His resulting anger was explosive—vital. He dominated the stage, moving with a gymnast's ease through the more ambitious steps. She forgot about the examiner, the audience: all she could see was him.

As the last chord faded, the audience were silent. Then the applause started—reluctant from the anti-Raven brigade, but enthusiastic from many in the room. A piercing whistle echoed from the back row. Had to be Joe.

Miss Hollis came on stage, smiling broadly. She squeezed Raven's hand and then gave Kieran a hug. 'Now I know why your marks were predicted to be so good! You've been teasing me, Mr Storm, hiding your lamp under a bushel,' she said in a low voice.

Raven thought it more a case of finding the match to light it.

'Thanks.' Kieran looked extremely pleased with himself—and for once he had earned it. He had moved well out of his comfort zone for her.

Miss Hollis faced the audience. 'And on that exhilarating note, we conclude our performances. Thank you so much for coming to support your year group. Please head back to normal lessons.'

Trying not to watch the examiner finalizing her notes in the centre of the front row, Raven let Kieran take her hand and they left the stage together. She hadn't yet said anything to him, but maybe they had done their talking in their dancing? He dropped her palm but only so he could put his arm around her shoulders, pulling her closer to his side.

She decided to make light of it so as not to humiliate herself. 'Wow, Ace, that was a revelation.' She stopped by the girls' changing rooms, not wanting to leave him and go in to face the hostile gang inside. She didn't do well in changing rooms.

His eyes shining with post-performance pleasure, he lifted her hand to his lips and kissed it—old-fashioned gallantry. 'Thank you.'

'It's me who has to thank you. Kieran, I underestimated you. You really know how to pull out the stops when you have to. That was some act.'

'I had the right incentive—and it wasn't an act. That was the answer—I just had to mean it.' His gaze went to her lips. She couldn't help but dart out her tongue and lick them, just in case. Much to her regret, he didn't take the opportunity as other dancers were approaching. Oh joy. It was her ex-best friend. Gina could add poor timing to all round bitchiness.

'Kieran, you were fantastic!' gushed Gina. 'None of us knew you could dance like that!'

'Thank you. But it's down to Raven. She's an excellent partner.'

Gina ignored that comment. 'But the height on that handspring! You're an amazing gymnast.'

'So's Raven.'

She nudged him in the side. There was no point him continuing to defend her, not when Gina and her crew had determined to deny her existence, and she was planning to leave anyway.

'What did you think of our performance?' Gina asked, fishing for compliments.

'I don't know much about dance,' he said with magisterial disdain, tone implying it was a subject that had failed to interest him sufficiently.

'It was great—very impressive,' said Raven, deciding she would be the bigger person and give credit where it was due.

Gina looked briefly at her, a flash of doubt in her eyes. Raven's heart squeezed—it was almost as though the old Gina had peeked out at her for a moment. 'Thank you,' Gina said stiffly. 'Kind of you to say so. We'd better get changed.' This remark was addressed to the rest in her group. They went in past Raven, not inviting her to join them.

'You'll be OK in there?' Kieran nodded at the door.

'I'm going to grab my things and go back to the cottage for lunch. I can change there.'

'Good plan.'

They stood for a second, poised. Both were aware the rules had altered but neither was sure what the new game was called.

Kieran took the lead. 'Raven, how about we celebrate? I've got to go home again tomorrow but I'd like to take you out to a show, whatever you want really. I'm not happy leaving you here after last time.'

He was asking her on a real date? Time alone with him was just what she wanted. 'You want me to come with you to London? OK, I'll ask Granddad.'

'I've some things to do at home first in the morning but should be free by the afternoon. I thought I'd get us tickets for the play at the Globe, if you'd like that.'

'Cool: I've always wanted to go.'

'You can either come up with Joe and me and do some shopping or whatever in the morning, or come up later: your choice.'

Raven registered that he wasn't inviting her to meet his family, which hurt a little but then it was just a first date. She wondered if he was ashamed of her humble background. Still, he was asking her out, which had to make up for that. 'I'll ask Granddad to drop me at the station and come up later.'

'Just buy your ticket one way. Joe will drive us back in the evening.'

'Joe can drive?'

'Yeah. He had his car brought up. It's stashed at the far end of the staff car park. Not entirely within the rules but no one's noticed it yet.'

'That's so cool.'

'Well, that's Joe for you.' Kieran seemed a little put out by her admiration for his friend.

She leant towards him. 'But not as cool as you, Kieran Storm. You blew us all out of the water with that performance.'

'I did?' He rubbed the back of his neck. 'Yeah, I did, didn't I?'

'Arrogant much?' teased Raven.

140

He grinned. 'But it was all down to my extraordinarily gifted partner. Thank you, Raven.' Bending his head, he kissed her gently, rubbing his fingers through her hair as if he couldn't bear to let go. He ended by resting his forehead against hers. 'See you later.' He didn't release her.

'Haven't you forgotten something?'

'Don't think so.'

'This is the part where you're supposed to let go of me.'

'Why would I want to do that?'

Actually, now he mentioned it, she couldn't think of a single reason why either.

In the boardroom of the YDA overlooking the Thames, Isaac was reading the profiles of the four trustees that Kieran and Joe had assembled. Joe was chatting to his mentor from C Stream, Jan Hardy, a retired Scotland Yard commander who had the art of blending nailed: she could pass for anything from unthreatening pensioner to flamboyant diva, depending on the requirements of the mission. Dr Waterburn, Kieran's own mentor, was tapping away on her computer; she kept her relationship with her charges to factual exchange, as they preferred. At least, as he had once thought he preferred. Kieran wouldn't have minded someone a little removed from the mission to talk through the complicating emotional issues. He shouldn't be going anywhere near Raven but he'd stood in the middle of a corridor for fifteen minutes kissing her and hadn't wanted to let go—why was that? But his mentor was totally the wrong person to confide in: such a conversation would be excruciatingly embarrassing for both sides and only get him in deep trouble.

'So, guys, lay this out for me.' Isaac leant back and pushed the files away. 'We have people exchanging favours through what Kieran calls the clearing house of the school—I see that. I imagine some of those favours must benefit the trustees, otherwise what are they getting out of it?'

'That's right. The strongest lead I've found so far is that Kolnikov's last gas contract was signed by one of the parents of an Angolan pupil,' said Kieran.

'OK. Let's take it as read that there are many other examples. How did it come about? Any theories?'

'There's one interesting point of contact: the trustees all had a child go through the school in the same year.'

'And then what?'

Kieran laced his fingers together. 'This is speculation.'

'Go on.'

'What if, when Kolnikov Junior and the other trustee kids were there, their fathers realized they had joined a herd just waiting to be milked? Wealthy, influential parents; captive audience of young people; total control thanks to the boarding system.'

'But what part does the manor play in all this? My people who got in as part of a day conference say that it appears completely normal. They didn't have access all areas but there were no signs of anyone being held there against their will, nothing to raise any red flags. Staff members were charming but stuck to their script. The only thing they could fault was that it was too faultless.'

'Even so, something's happening there and it has to be seen as necessary—these kind of men don't offer to reform problem kids without a reason,' said Mrs Hardy.

'I think it's part of the hold over the participants in the favour exchange,' explained Kieran. 'What's to stop one of the parties getting cold feet and spilling the secret to a government or employer? The students who've been on the course had all got into difficulties with the school authorities. I'm wondering if, as we get nearer the time of the course, Mrs Bain might not come up with some evidence of our misdemeanours that a concerned parent or guardian would not want to have made public. They might even engineer the problems in the first place for the ones they want in their scheme.'

'Funny you should say that: she has already suggested you enrol on a personality development course and promised me a detailed report on you both.' Isaac smiled. 'I look forward to reading it.'

Joe shook his head. 'And I hadn't even put our names down yet.'

'She wants to smooth your rough edges.'

'Geez, keep her away from me!' joked Joe. 'I'm thinking she is keener on getting favours out of you, Isaac: our impressive godfather, Colonel Isaac Hampton, *frightfully* senior in the Ministry of Defence.'

'Yes, I've a notional desk in Procurement.' The senior ranks of the MoD were supportive of Isaac's college and allowed him an official cover with them as he was former military. 'You can do the course if you think it'll move the investigation along, but I promise you I'll kick you from here to Canberra if either of you change one iota as a result.'

Kieran weighed up the offer. 'I think this contact with you will develop into a form of blackmail. Your kid is broken: I'll fix him but on the understanding you stay on our side. If you take what you know to anyone else, both you and your kid will suffer.'

'And they are doing more than fixing,' added Joe. 'They're making accusations go away by framing someone else for the most visible crimes.'

'That's an intriguing twist of nastiness. How are they managing that?' asked Jan.

'There's this girl with a stealing problem—it got to a stage

143

where other students were noticing things going missing. They "cured" her by making her believe it wasn't her behind the thefts and gave her someone to blame—her former best friend, Raven Stone, the caretaker's granddaughter. A complete rehabilitation—everyone, including the girl, thinks she's innocent and the only one to suffer is someone no one needs care about because Raven has no useful connections or powerful parents.'

'I think it's not just this case where Raven has been made a scapegoat,' said Kieran, reminding himself not to get angry—this wasn't the place. 'The school is using her as a convenient target for many of the so-called reformed students. She helps consolidate their group identity—a shared enemy.'

'Fascinating.' Jan loved delving into the murky depths of criminal behaviour. 'I'm jealous you've got to spend all this time in a hotbed of intrigue.'

'It's not so much fun. There are victims.' Kieran rolled his pen between his fingers.

Jan's gaze settled on his face with a thoughtful expression. 'Crime always has victims, Kieran; that's why we're here.'

In fact, Kieran had to admit she was wrong about him: he had been attracted to it by the chance to solve puzzles; only now was he seeing it from the point of view of those involved.

'Still, it's ugly to witness it in action.' Joe saved Kieran from having to reply. 'The girl they are picking on is a friend now; we want to make sure nothing bad happens to her. Don't we, Kieran?'

Kieran would have kicked Joe under the table if he could have reached.

'Just remember your focus is on your mission, not playing knights in shining armour.' Isaac had caught the byplay between them and Kieran feared he was drawing the right conclusion. Not much got past Isaac.

'I think we aren't seeing the whole picture yet, sir.' Kieran dragged his thoughts back to his job. Damn, it was getting more difficult to do so; he kept worrying about Raven.

'Why do you say that?'

'We've possibly spotted the set-up but not what makes the whole thing hold together as a scheme.'

'Well, once you've done one favour for the network, they've got that to hold over you. The temptation would be to keep your head down and do what's asked.'

'That's the problem—it doesn't look to me as if it works like that. It's more than silent grudging consent—it's active participation. I don't get the feeling that blackmail is the main motive. Self-interest and something else.'

'Yeah, Key's right.' Joe poured himself a glass of water and topped up Jan's drink with his usual thoughtfulness. 'From what we've seen of the parents, they're acting more like they're part of one of those secret societies, Freemasonry, that kind of thing. They probably have funny handshakes—I bet they go the whole nine yards.'

'Carry on investigating the dynamics of this group, but we now need to move to evidence gathering if we are to take it down.' Isaac gestured to the files. 'We've got a pattern but it would be next to impossible to prove this in a court, as it's easily denied.'

Jan nodded. 'But just as Al Capone was sent to jail for tax evasion and not murder, our boys have to find the loose thread that we can pull—something that'll get them arrested.'

'Yeah, good point. I don't mind what the crime is as long as we can make the charge stick. These guys are dangerous, but take out the kingpins—the trustees—and I think the network will collapse.' Isaac looked over at Dr Waterburn. 'Have you anything to add, Naomi?'

Her fingers hovered over the keyboard as she paused in

her typing. 'Isn't that rather a job suited for B or D stream students?'

Kieran frowned at his fingers. Logically, his mentor was right but Kieran did not want to hand Raven's future over to one of the smooth-talking Cobras like Daimon, or even a hunter Wolf like Nat.

'Kieran, do you assess this situation to have gone beyond your capabilities?' asked Isaac.

He meant had it moved from the deduction phase to action? 'No, I think there's still a role for Joe and me. Besides we're embedded in the school. A new team would have difficulty taking over this late.'

'So the level of danger is acceptable?'

'Yes.'

'Joe?'

'I'm cool with staying.' Joe glanced over at Kieran. 'There're lots of loose ends that still need tying.'

'All right. Tie them up for me; get the evidence; then get out: those are your orders. I'll handle the take down of the trustees but any tip-off when they are next in one place would be useful.' He gathered the files and tapped them straight on the table top. 'I think we're done here. Enjoy your free afternoon.'

Joe snagged Kieran's elbow as they left the meeting.

'What?'

'In a hurry to meet Raven?'

'No.' *Yes*.

'I want to talk to you about the prom.'

'About what?' Sometimes Kieran couldn't find a logical thread to Joe's conversation. 'Correct me if I'm wrong but aren't we in the middle of a complex operation here? What has the prom got to do with anything?'

'You can't keep up the cover if you miss the details, my

friend. You must have noticed that almost everyone is going on about it. Hedda has been dropping heavy hints she expects me to ask her.'

Kieran grinned. Finally: payback for Joe's sins enrolling him in arts. 'Are you going to take one for the team and do it?'

Joe's lips curled in disgust. 'I suppose so—it would keep me on the inside track of her clique. But have you asked Raven yet?'

'I don't think she wants to go.' He had given himself a pass on the prom thinking they would both prefer to remain at home that night. He'd been thinking pizza, a sofa, a couple of DVDs she liked and a little together time.

Joe sighed. 'And I thought you'd made such progress on female psychology, but you're still on course 101. Yes, she hates the school prom but also it would be worse to have no one ask her. She would enjoy shocking everyone's expectations and turning up looking amazing on your arm. Think of it as her giving the finger to all those who have tormented her.'

This female brain stuff was far more complex that Kieran had guessed. 'So she hates them all but still wants to spend the evening with them?'

'Yes.'

'With me?'

'Yes.' Joe nodded encouragingly.

'That's not logical. And I thought you told me not to get too serious about her—to keep some distance as the rules demand? Isn't the prom something of a declaration, you know, that we're dating.'

'Key, you *are* dating—your brain hasn't caught up yet with your subconscious. I'm not asking you to get serious, just to make sure she's OK for the big night. Ask her.'

Kieran suddenly felt very worried. 'What if she turns me down?'

'That, my friend, is the problem of being the boy in a relationship. Even in these days of sexual equality, you are still expected to stick your neck out.'

'That's not fair.'

'Welcome to my world, Key.'

Raven perched on the wall outside the Globe, people-watching—one of her favourite pastimes. She wondered what the party of Chinese tourists would make of the play they'd booked to see. She sometimes had to find a translation for Shakespeare, so imagine making sense of him from another language. Four skateboarders rolled by—a single file cavalry charge, scattering people out of their path. A woman fed the pigeons and seagulls, a lumpy collection of bottles in a plastic bag at her feet. She moved off, taking the flock with her, birds wheeling over the choppy grey waters of the Thames.

Then someone pounced and put his hands over her eyes. 'Guess who?'

As if that woodsy smell of his aftershave wouldn't give him away? 'Um, the Mayor of London?'

'Nope. Try again?'

'Prince Harry.'

'Sorry, no.' He lifted his hands away and dug them in his pockets. Who needed a prince when she had Kieran standing in front of her?

She swung her legs over the edge of the wall so she could stand and face him. 'Then it must be Kieran Storm.' She went up on tiptoe to brush a kiss on his cheek. 'And that'll do nicely.'

'It will?' He smiled down into her eyes. 'Well then.' He dipped his head and kissed her lightly on the lips, her lids closing as she savoured the sensation.

When she opened them again, he was smiling down at her, green eyes no longer distant but very present. 'Hello, Kieran.'

'You got here OK?'

She grinned. 'Obviously I did because I'm standing right in front of you.'

A little frown line appeared between his dark brows. 'Yeah, I suppose that was a stupid question.'

It was sweet to find that he wasn't his usual arrogant self with her. Both of them were fumbling to find a new way of relating now they had shifted up a level to more than friends, and it was reassuring that he wasn't too confident with his moves. She tucked her thumbs in her jeans, unconsciously mirroring his stance. 'You're never stupid. It's not possible.'

'Thanks. I'm glad you think so.' He brushed the backs of his fingers over her cheek, letting them drift to tuck a strand of hair behind her ear. It recalled the moment in the garden when he had first touched her in that way. She held his gaze.

'Did I really have grass on me?'

He knew exactly what she was talking about. His eyes skated away for a second to rest on the flags flapping on the poles along the edge of the Globe site. 'You could've.'

'But I didn't, did I?'

'No.'

Thoroughly pleased by his answer, she linked her arm with his and tugged him towards the theatre. 'I'm glad.'

'Glad?'

'Yes. I thought I imagined the moment, that I'd stood there like a chump dreaming up a special tingle between us when all the while you'd just been thinking practical thoughts about getting me tidy.'

149

He shifted from holding her elbow to putting his arm around her shoulders, bringing her to his side. 'I wasn't thinking *practical* thoughts, I promise you.'

She laughed. It was so perfect to be with him she wanted to do something foolish like sing at the top of her voice. Not wanting to embarrass him, she settled for more conversation.

'How was home?'

'Fine.'

'Mum, Dad?'

Kieran's eyes flickered over the crowds on the South Bank. He rolled his shoulders, relieving some tension he had stored up since the day before. 'Same as usual. Asking what I'm doing, how the exams are going—you know the kind of thing. They liked the sound of the dance we did—said they wished they could've come.'

'Why didn't they?'

'Oh, they would've but were too busy with their jobs. Do you want to hire a cushion?'

'No, I'm OK. So we are sitting, not standing in the pit?'

'Maybe another time we can be groundlings. I thought I'd treat you on our first date.'

First date: that sounded wonderful. 'And so you should, Ace. What've you done with Joe?'

'He's meeting us later. He's seeing friends.'

They passed the lady checking tickets at the door and climbed up the wooden staircase that wound inside the circular walls of the Globe. Built to match the original Elizabethan theatre that had stood near this site, the Globe was a unique acting space, open to the elements just as it would have been in Shakespeare's day. Raven was really excited to see it: the pictures on the web didn't do it justice.

'Oh, it's so pretty!' She leant over the railing. 'I didn't

150

know the canopy above the stage was painted—wow—there are stars and zodiac creatures. And the thatched roof: that's just so amazing.'

'They made it as accurate as they could. A bit daft really considering the number of days of rain we get in London.'

'But it's only the groundlings who get wet and who cares about them?' joked Raven.

'Not us, not today, as we are in the posh seats.'

'What are we seeing?'

'*The Winter's Tale*. Raging jealousy and women pretending to be statues. And there's a great bear scene.'

'Yeah, my all-time favourite stage direction.'

Despite knowing about that, Raven had never read the play so wasn't aware how it all unfolded. It was rather fun watching a Shakespeare play without foreknowledge of how it ended—fresher somehow. The acting was riveting, helping her over the more boring stretches; the intimate space of the wooden O involved every member of the audience with the cast. The only thing that annoyed her was the insipid heroine of the second half, Perdita. The play could've done with someone who was less of a doormat.

After the prolonged applause at the curtain call, they rose to go, the rumbling thunder of audience feet descending the wooden staircases rolling through the acting space.

'Verdict?' asked Kieran.

'Great show but I wanted to shake Perdita.' She buttoned up her jacket.

'Why? She's supposed to be sweet and naive.'

'Yeah, but she believed that guy was a shepherd when he was really a prince. I mean, c'mon, he was called Florizel! That should have been a warning. No girl can possibly fall in love with someone with such a stupid name.'

Kieran smiled. 'I think Shakespeare was referring to the

Jacobean love of Arcadian poetry. These weren't smelly peasants but idealized classical figures.'

'But strip away the silly names and you get a guy lying to a sappy girl.'

'He does tell her the truth eventually.'

'Yeah, but only after she's fallen in love with him.'

'Well, I enjoyed it,' Kieran said briskly as they walked out into the sunshine.

'So did I—I can't help getting involved. Just ignore me.'

'I'd never ignore you, Raven. You have my full attention.'

A flock of pigeons scattered in front of them, the downdraft of their wings wafting her hair. Crowds massed in the pavement under the blue summer sky; language students all wearing the same orange backpacks occupied the South Bank taking photos of the theatre, so that Londoners had a struggle to get through them. The city had surrendered to the invaders without putting up a fight.

'The acting was first class.' Kieran tucked her hand in his.

'I agree.'

'Amazing: you agree with me on something!' He tapped her nose. 'Is that a first?'

'Don't push it, pal. I'm not going to be making a habit of it.'

He sighed and shook his head. 'What am I going to do with you?'

She raised one eyebrow. 'Kiss me again, maybe?'

He put his finger under her chin to tip her head up. 'That's an excellent suggestion and a second point of agreement.'

'Kieran? Kieran? Is that you?'

Startled, Raven took a step back. Kieran froze, his eyes screwed shut. The pigeon woman from earlier pushed through the Italian school party and dumped her shopping bag of booze by his feet. She did not look like someone Kieran would know:

152

her mass of badly dyed black hair tumbled from a red scarf, her lids were heavily rimmed with kohl, her skin slathered with too much foundation so that it had caught in the lines around her eyes and mouth. As for her clothes, if the black skirt was any shorter she would be arrested.

'Hey, baby, it's me. I've been dying to see you but Isaac wouldn't tell me where you are. I've been coming to the YDA every day hoping to run in to you.' Her voice was hoarse, like she'd gargled pebbles.

Kieran moved to put himself between Raven and the woman.

'I'm sorry but I can't speak now. I'm with someone.'

'I can see, baby. I won't keep you long.' The woman peered round Kieran's shoulder. 'She looks very sweet. Works for Isaac too does she—one of your students of crime at your college?' The woman held out her hand to Raven, each finger weighed down with rings. 'Hi, honey. I'm Gloria, Kieran's mum.'

His mother? Automatically, Raven shook her hand.

'Mother. Please.' Kieran sounded desperate.

Raven didn't know what to think: she'd expected him to deny it but it seemed Pigeon Lady was what she said. How had that happened?

Gloria smiled at Raven, swaying slightly. From the smell coming from her breath, she had begun her drinking early, or maybe never stopped. 'He's ashamed of me, poor baby. Doesn't like to be seen with his mum.' Her eyes filled with tears. 'But he's my only one left to me—the only one who loves me since his shit of a father ran out on us.' She gave a half-hiccup, half-sob. 'Don't turn your back on me too, baby—I couldn't bear that.'

Raven glanced up at Kieran. He looked cold, completely unmoved by his mother's pleas. She was so pathetic; Raven didn't know why he wasn't rushing to help her, but he probably had his reasons. Clearly, a very complicated history here and she'd just been dropped right in the middle of it.

'This isn't the place for this.' His voice was clipped, allowing no emotion to seep through.

'It's OK, Kieran, if you need time with her, I can . . . um . . . go to a coffee bar or something,' Raven offered.

'I don't need time with her.'

Raven winced at his cruel tone. This wasn't a Kieran she knew. In fact, she had been brought slap up against the reality that she didn't know him at all.

Gloria gripped his forearm with her chipped multicoloured nails. 'I won't spoil your evening. You go have fun—that's all I ever wanted you know—for you to be OK. The YDA is your big chance—I understand. But . . . but I'm short again, baby. Can you give me the fare home?'

'How much this time?' Kieran took out his wallet.

'I know Isaac pays you well for your work for him,' she wheedled, eyes on the notes he had in the pocket. 'Fifty quid?'

He took out all his money and thrust three twenties at her. As she flicked through the notes to check the amount, he began walking towards the nearest underground station, towing Raven along with him.

'Love you, baby,' Gloria called. 'See you again soon?'

As Kieran didn't reply, Raven turned to give her an apologetic wave for her son's abrupt departure. Gloria was watching him with agonizing longing on her face.

'Don't,' snarled Kieran.

'What?'

'Don't look at her.'

'But she's your mother!'

'She's nothing to me.' He swiped his ticket at the barrier with the desperation of someone fleeing a fire.

'That can't be true.'

'Just . . . just drop it, Raven. I can't talk about this.'

She stood beside him on the platform, no longer touching, anger burning down the gunpowder trail to a keg of explosive emotion. It didn't take a genius to know that his relationship with his mother was a broken one, but how did that square with Kieran's spiel about his parents being too busy with their jobs to visit Westron, and Joe's claim that Kieran came from a posh family? Gloria's accent suggested pure London, no aristocratic upbringing, and she was a highly unlikely candidate for employment. Who did that make his father?

Another of Gloria's comments came to mind.

'Kieran, who's Isaac? Is he your dad?' Maybe he would redeem himself by setting the record straight for her?

Kieran watched the train announcement board count down to the arrival of their service. 'Forget she mentioned him. Forget everything she said. It's not important.'

But it was. 'I only asked if he was your father.'

'No, he's not my father. He's my friend.'

'A friend you work for. Doing what? What's the YDA and why did she say you studied crime?' No reply. She tried to piece together what he had told her about himself. 'Was that the school you got expelled from?'

Kieran turned on her, his hands were shaking. 'Can't you just leave it alone, Raven? Must you stick your nose in to my private business? That woman is my biological mother but she lost the chance to be anything more a long time ago. I have nothing to do with her. If you want to be with me, then you won't mention her again.'

That hurt. She thought she had been given a right to know his personal business, but it seemed she was just a date to him. Practically a stranger. 'Fine. Let's pretend that didn't happen. Let's pretend I'm not going out with a guy who has lied to me about the most basic things about him—about his family, about the fact that he's doing some kind of job he won't explain to me.'

'Just . . . just leave it.' He scraped his fingers through his hair as if his head was paining him. But if he sucker punched her like that, throwing her concern back in her face, then she was damn well going to keep up her own shields. He wanted her to back off? Then she would—permanently—if he didn't give her a straight answer.

'Leave it?' she said with mock consideration, finger on chin. 'Erm, no, I don't think I can do that. I won't leave it because, A, you have lied to me and, erm, let me see, B, you've lied to me.'

Fury rolled through him, his green eyes blazing as he spat out the facts. 'Fine. You want the truth? Well, you've just seen it. I'm not the sodding posh boy of Joe's invention, OK? I come from that woman and maybe you can see why I don't like to advertise the fact.'

'You've had weeks to set me right, so why didn't you?'

'Because I didn't want to!' he roared. 'Damn it, Raven, can't you understand that?'

She wasn't about to let him make this her fault. 'I warned you I hated lies. OK, maybe I can see why Gloria's not exactly the first thing you want to tell me about, but what about this job she mentioned? What the heck are you involved in?'

He said nothing, too angry to speak.

'I can't forgive someone systematically lying to me.'

His silence was worse than angry defence. She took it as a sign he didn't care enough to tell her the truth.

'You and Joe made it all up, didn't you—your posh family, your big house in London, your sister? Geez, that was low, using that story to play on my sympathy. You probably even lied to your mother to hide the fact you were expelled from college. No wonder she hasn't been able to find you. But I won't put up with it—I can't. You'd better start telling me the truth about yourself and what you're doing or I'm outta here.'

He dug in his pocket and took out his wallet. Seeing it was empty, he gave a horrible hollow laugh. 'I was going to give you the cash to get yourself back to Westron but, guess what, my vampire mother has sucked it all away.'

'You were sending me back on my own?' That felt like a knife in the guts. She'd wanted to be the one to walk away from him, head held high, but he'd got there first and added a slap to the blow, trying to pay her off.

'I can't be with you right now.'

'No need to flash your cash, Kieran. I'm perfectly able to get myself to Paddington on my own.'

'I'll refund you the money.'

'I don't want your fricking money, OK?' Her skirt began to flap in the breeze running ahead of the approaching train. Raven hated the fact that she was perilously close to tears—hated him for doing this to her. 'You know what? You can just . . . just go to hell, Kieran.'

She got on the train and kept her back to him until the doors closed, taking deep breaths to stop her sobs in their tracks. OK, a final glance to show him she didn't care, that she was tough, that he hadn't beaten her down. But when she looked round, he had already gone.

Chapter 12

Raven surfaced from her tenth length of the pool. One of her favourite places at Westron, the old orangery had been transformed in the 1920s into a swimming bath but they had wisely kept the pale stone columns and high glass windows, maintaining a wonderful air of elegance. The setting reminded her of *Great Gatsby*-style cocktail parties, flappers dancing at the edge of a pool to a gramophone and sipping gin slings, whatever they were. This evening she found it particularly easy to indulge those fantasies, as the oblique shafts of the sun bathed the surface in golden light. She swept her fingers through the liquid gilt, letting the droplets fall into the water.

She needed something nice to compensate for the awful break-up with Kieran. That relationship had nosedived before it had even got properly underway. She should have known he wasn't as perfect for her as he had seemed: people lied the whole time. Sometimes they did it because they thought it best for you, like her dad about her mom's condition; others just because they were spiteful, like Jimmy Bolton, who had made her life at home and school one long torment. But strip away the motives, it all came down to screwing her over with a lie, leading her out blindfold on to a ledge, swearing she was safe, then disappearing and leaving her stuck.

It was the one thing she asked of relationships, that they be based on truth: the one thing that Kieran had not given her.

The outer door banged and her heart sank. In retreat mode after the horrible return journey, she had thought she would have the pool to herself. Saturday night was party time for the school; only social outcasts came here at this hour. Now her sanctuary had been invaded: Joe was standing at the far end, towel draped round his neck.

As the only two people here she could hardly ignore him, so she swam towards him.

'Hi, Joe.'

'Hey, Raven.' He sat on the edge of the pool, dangling his legs in the water. 'How was London?'

'The play was OK.'

'And?'

'And what?'

'Did you turn him down?'

'Turn him down for what?'

Joe cast his eyes to the ceiling where the golden light danced. 'I can't believe it. I've just seen Kieran and he's not talking to me—or anyone. I thought you must have done it, but you're saying he didn't ask you?'

'Ask me what, Joe?'

'To the prom.'

Such a regular school matter seemed laughable in the face of the giant meltdown. 'Er, no. I don't think that was on his mind—we kinda broke up.'

'So what did you do to upset him?'

It was her fault how exactly? She heaved herself out of the pool and grabbed her towel. 'Me? I did nothing.'

'He's gone into one of his dark moods. Something must have happened.'

Raven wondered if she should say anything but Kieran had asked her to forget Gloria. It was annoying that she still felt some residual loyalty to him when he didn't deserve it. She at least did what she promised. 'You'd best ask him.'

'OK, I will.'

She patted her hair dry. Kieran had shut her out; maybe Joe would be able to help her understand why he valued his secrecy more than he did their relationship. 'Who's Isaac, Joe?'

Joe's eyes rounded in surprise. 'Isaac? No one. He's no one.'

'You're so full of it—both of you are.' Raven felt hurt that they never gave her anything, not a straight answer, not a little bit of their trust. 'He's someone special to Kieran. You work for him. Is he the godfather you mentioned? Does he pay for your education with some kind of employment deal in exchange?'

Joe's face hardened, irritation bracketing his mouth. 'Please leave it alone.'

'You're not going to tell me, are you? I just don't get it: what's the big secret? I just asked who this guy Isaac was, not for your pin code!' Raven was tired of trying and trying with no answers, no real support. Back to being on her team of one after dreaming she'd found a double act to which she could belong. 'Some friend you turned out to be.'

Joe tried the cool guy/hysterical girl approach, holding out a hand to calm her down. 'Raven, be reasonable.' Big mistake.

'Like you are, you mean? You know what, Joe? It's not reasonable to expect me to trust you when you don't tell me anything real about yourselves. That's not friendship.'

'Don't over-react.'

Fuel on flame. 'Don't you dare patronize me, Joe Masters!' She squeezed the towel in clenched fists, wishing she could wring his neck. 'I thought you two were OK, but you are just . . . just shells of people pretending to be my friends. When it comes to anything that matters—that reveals who you really are—then pfft! You're gone. I'm surrounded by . . . by fake people. This place makes me sick.'

'Raven—'

'You know what? Both you and Kieran can go take a running jump off a very tall cliff for all I care.'

'Geez, Raven . . .'

She held out a hand to warn him off. 'Who's Isaac, Joe?'

Joe swore under his breath then looked back at her, expression set. 'No one, Raven.'

'OK. Fine. I know where I stand then.' She pulled on her trackies and sweatshirt, ignoring the fact she was still wearing a wet costume. Arm went down the wrong hole first time, further infuriating her. If it hadn't been the only thing she had with her, she would have ripped it apart. 'The pool is yours, Joe. Knock yourself out.' Slamming the door behind her, she headed back to her cottage, the only place that held a person whose words she could believe.

Safe in his room, Kieran stared at the data streaming across the computer screen, burying his scream in the numbers. Raven had consigned him to hell; no need: he had already been there, done that and got the sodding T-shirt when he was ten, thanks to Gloria.

Knowing that he couldn't ignore the day's events, Kieran sent an email to Isaac informing him of his meeting with Gloria. He received a reply back instantly on the YDA live messenger service. Isaac must have set up an alert for his communications, proof he was concerned.

I should have warned you. Jan said she'd seen Gloria hanging about the South Bank. I'll talk to Gloria again, impress on her that she should leave you alone. I've told her before that her stipend from us is reliant on keeping her distance as long as you request it. Do you want me to cut off the money?

Isaac had been bribing Gloria for years to allow Kieran a chance to have a solid education and stable home at the

YDA. When Kieran had been under sixteen, she had repeatedly threatened to take him away when she went on one of her drunken road trips with the latest boyfriend; mercifully, Isaac had managed to persuade her otherwise. It was easier now Kieran was old enough for his opinion to count; Gloria had stopped threatening this nuclear option and was left with wheedling more money out of them. Just knowing she was out there, though, where any of the YDA students might see her with him, made Kieran feel sick to his stomach. Isaac told Kieran he did not mind dealing with his family baggage; he had even said he felt desperately sorry for the woman, a victim herself who had never had the strength to straighten out despite many chances over the years. Kieran couldn't even manage that much.

He turned away from the screen and leant back in his chair, seeking help from the ceiling. When he thought of Gloria, he felt . . . empty. He certainly didn't share Isaac's pity. He supposed that a person could give an addict only so many chances before they tired of the cycle of hope and disappointment. At some point she had to be responsible for her actions. She had to want to break the circle and while she was stuck in it she did untold damage to herself and to her children. His mother was guilty of neglecting Hannah, leading to his sister's premature death—he couldn't forgive that. Hannah had had a different father to him, but that man hadn't stuck around after she was born. No denying Gloria had had it tough. Kieran's father also ignored his child, leaving before the birth to take up his post at a particle research facility, his brief relationship with Gloria (they had met at the college bar where she had worked for a time) an embarrassing secret left firmly in the past and no parental responsibility enforced or claimed. Gloria had a hundred per cent record of picking the wrong man.

Kieran's life had been a mess—no regular meals, no clean clothes, cold bedsits—until Isaac's talent scouts had spotted him at a maths competition and Isaac had taken the trouble to ask after him. When he discovered how fragile Kieran's home situation was, Isaac had stepped in and become the father to him that he had never known. Kieran would pay any price to keep Gloria's toxic presence out of his life. He had his answer.

Leave her the money. She would be worse without it.

Kieran brushed his fingertips over the keys, wondering if he should confess. Yes, he owed it to Isaac.

There's another problem: Raven Stone was with me and Gloria mentioned you and that I was studying crime detection. Joe's cover story about me was that I'm from a posh family and I went along with it. Raven knows we've been lying to her. She knows you employ me in some way and that Gloria is my mother.

He pressed 'enter'.

The computer was quiet a moment, then the reply came back.

That is unfortunate but Miss Stone, as you mentioned, is unlikely to be able to do any damage with this knowledge, having no friends or powerful connections at the school. Your mission comes first.

Damage? That had been the other way round—he had hurt Raven by his stonewalling of her questions. Could he explain that to Isaac? As much as he admired his mentor, he no more wanted to discuss feelings than stand naked in Piccadilly Circus.

Kieran? Did you get my last message?

Isaac knew he was still online.

Yes, sir.

And?

I'd like to tell her part of the truth, about me I mean. Not you.

Why?

Because I've fallen for her. *Because I promised to be her friend and she feels betrayed.*

You are YDA. You can't be her friend. You will be leaving there at the end of the mission and any loose ends have to be cut off. You know the drill.

Kieran's fingers wanted to type out something drastic—his resignation, a string of swear words—but he held himself back. He relied on the YDA for everything—food, clothing, a roof over his head, a scholarship for his future studies. He loved the work and the friends he had made there—the intellectual challenge of excelling in detective work. Outside the agency, he would be in a bedsit with Gloria. He didn't have the luxury of choice.

OK. He pressed send, feeling like this was the real end of his hopes for a relationship with Raven, even if she gave him another hearing. He was choosing the YDA over her. That felt wrong, like he was committing emotional hara-kiri. *But what if I work out a way to see her again after this mission ends? She's trustworthy.*

There was a brief pause. He could imagine Isaac sitting in his desk chair, tapping his mouth as was his habit when considering a tricky decision.

I think it fairer to you if I just say 'no' now. Even a genius like you can't square the circle of our need for secrecy and yours to be open with a girlfriend. Every YDA operative faces the same choice at some point. I can't change the rules for you. It's a red line issue, Kieran.

The cursor pulsed in time with Kieran's heartbeat. He couldn't think of the words for his reply. Isaac came back first.

Kieran, I'm genuinely sorry. I'll see what I can do when this all unravels to make sure Raven and her grandfather emerge OK in the aftermath. I give you my word.

And Isaac's word was gold.

Thank you. Signing off now. He had all the concessions he was going to get from Isaac tonight.

Goodnight, Kieran. Say hi to Joe for me.

Kieran turned off the monitor, erasing the message history. He had just deleted his chances with Raven. He hated himself with a passion he usually reserved for his mother. He picked up one of his plant experiments and threw it out of the window, watching it arc in the air and then smash on the flagstones of the terrace. That felt good. He took another—and another—until the path below was littered with dying carnivorous plants. Who the hell cared about his oh so clever tests to clear some dead gardener's name? He certainly didn't.

Joe came back in, still damp from his post-swim shower. 'You OK now?'

Far from it. He remained staring out the window, breathing fast. Focus on the mission. 'Isaac says hello.'

'So you reported in. Are you going to tell me what you said because I'm mighty confused just at the moment.' Joe chucked his trunks at the laundry basket.

'Confused?' He couldn't deal with Joe being angry. He'd had more than he could handle in one day. 'Why the hell are you confused?'

Joe noticed the plant carnage outside. 'What are you doing? No, second thoughts: don't answer that. I've got something to tell you. Ran into Raven at the pool. She is pissed at us both.'

Kieran kept silent. He would feel that way too if he'd been led up the garden path to a relationship with someone and then they'd turned out not to be who he thought. She wouldn't want to have anything to do with Gloria's son—and she'd be right.

'She was asking about Isaac and crime detection.'

'I see.'

Joe tugged the towel round his neck backward and forward uneasily. 'Why did you tell her about him? That's a massive breach of security, Key.'

'You think I'd sell us out?' He felt a surge of outrage: here he was sacrificing his relationship for the mission and Joe was accusing him of doing the opposite!

'I just don't know. You're different since you met her.'

'And what if I did? What would you do about it?'

Joe rubbed his hands over his scalp. 'I'm not sure. I guess we'd have to . . . to handle it. Damage limitation. Look, I'll explain to Isaac. Tell him what pressure you've been under . . . '

His friend's willingness to cover for him released a little of the fury he had been battling. 'It's OK, Joe. I didn't. I was just telling Isaac.'

Joe's face brightened with relief. At least he hadn't been put in the impossible position of having to rat on his friend. 'So how . . . ?'

'Gloria. We met my mother in London today.'

'You, Key, are one unlucky guy. The chances of that must be minuscule.'

'Not so small. Isaac forgot to warn me that she'd been bugging him at HQ for the past few days trying to scrounge off me.'

'Still.' Joe gave a sympathetic shrug.

'I've told Isaac. He's going to speak to her.'

'What about Raven? It must've been a shock—you know how Gloria seems to other people.'

'Tell me about it.' Kieran had died with shame the day two years ago when Joe had seen him with Gloria and Isaac at HQ for their sixth-monthly meeting—something Isaac insisted on to keep the family link going. Joe had never mentioned it again after Kieran had reluctantly explained who she was.

'Now I understand why she's upset that we've been lying

to her. I laid it on thick when we first spoke about your posh background.'

Kieran felt suddenly very tired. 'Can't do anything. She's collateral damage of the mission.'

'That's harsh.'

'Isaac's orders. Red line. No personal relationships. He says he'll make sure she's OK at the end.'

'But you really like that girl, Key. And she's good for you. Her straightforwardness kind of balances your complicated brain. She makes you happy.'

Kieran buried his head in his hands. 'Don't you think I realize that? I don't make her happy so she's ended it. I can't even explain why I lied so she's never going to forgive me.'

'Never? She doesn't seem the kind to hold a grudge for long.'

'But she'd demand an explanation and you know how things are for me. I can't break cover and I can't throw in the YDA. It wasn't just going out a few times to make each other happy—it was getting, you know, deep. I see Isaac's logic.'

Joe sat on the bed. 'That's not good. I hadn't realized.'

'And we shouldn't forget that something dangerously sick is happening here—people are at risk. I can't jeopardize all that by exposing myself as an agent, even if I know Raven would prefer to have her fingernails pulled out than tell anyone.'

'She's not the kind to go running her mouth off.'

'Yes, but we have some training to withstand pressure. Who knows what they might try to do to her next? They've already tortured her once. If I let her into the secret—against Isaac's orders—and she spilt it under pressure, then we're all stuffed and I'd've done something much worse than just put distance between us.'

Joe grimaced in agreement.

Kieran felt a little better now he saw that, even if she let him, there were so many good reasons why he shouldn't get back with her. 'I believe that whatever lies behind this scheme here involves big money and seriously bad people. Swatting us out of existence would be nothing to them. I don't want to risk Raven. She's already a target.'

'But we really don't want her to talk about the split in case she says something by mistake to the wrong person.'

'Who will she talk to? She only had us.'

'Yeah, true.' Joe rubbed his chin. 'I think we should go on being friendly to her, keep her with us where we know what she's doing.'

Kieran gave a dry laugh. 'Good luck with that. Last time I spoke to her she consigned me to hell.'

'Don't underestimate my charm or her forgiving nature.'

It sounded like Joe was just going to prolong Kieran's agony, making him see her when he knew he shouldn't for his own sake. Still, he didn't really believe even Joe could persuade her to put up with that. 'OK, fine, whatever.'

Joe took the hint he wanted to move the conversation on from heartache. 'So what do you think they're doing to the students to make them turn on her?'

Kieran dug out of the back of his cupboard six books he had read on brainwashing since he had become interested in the theory of mind alteration. 'This. Over at the manor, they call it character development, counselling, training for success, but I think they're just doing what people have done for centuries: they're manipulating minds.'

'You believe that is possible?'

'It is not a belief; it's a fact. You should read Hunter on brainwashing, Lifton's *Thought Reform and the Psychology of* —'

Joe threw a cushion at him. 'Stop geeking out on me. I've got my able sidekick—aka you—to read that stuff.'

'Is that what I am?'

Joe smiled. 'I dunno. Maybe I'm your Watson. In any case, what I mean is, I accept it's real but how can they do it so quickly to these students?'

'That we will only find out by experience.' Kieran put the books back in the cupboard inside a locked holdall. It wouldn't do for any of the school staff to get interested in his reading. He closed the door. 'Joe, do you think Raven's going to be OK?'

Joe paused in the process of selecting a T-shirt from his drawer. 'Are *you* OK?'

'No. No, I'm not, Joe.'

'Then I guess that's your answer.'

Chapter 13

Raven hid in the cottage all Sunday, and used the time to study. She stayed in her pyjamas and pretended the world beyond the house did not exist. The teachers had piled on the homework and she told her granddad part of the truth when she said that she was simply catching up. As the next few weeks were devoted to exams he accepted her explanation. The real reason she had gone into hibernation mode was that she couldn't bear to see Kieran. Every glimpse was agony, like the fox in the fable looking at the grapes. Everything she wanted was just out of reach. She longed to be with him, but what was the point when the Kieran she was with was mostly a stranger? It didn't help that one of the tasks she had to do was the write-up of the dance piece they had performed together. Sitting there, remembering every step of the routine, how it had come together, the kiss, did nothing to blunt her emotions.

On Monday morning, Raven knew she had to pull herself together and face school again. She only shared Dance with Kieran and all that remained of that course was the final written paper on Tuesday, so at least she did not have to deal with the torment of sitting with him in class. He was in the other English set from her so that was safe. The only lesson that would prove a problem was French, as she normally sat next to Joe, and that was first thing. OK, so it had to be faced. Raven had never backed down from the difficult. She wasn't going to make a big statement by not sitting with him; she'd just show she was still angry and hope he did something to allow the gap to close. An apology and an explanation would make a good start.

She slid into the seat next to Joe. 'Hi.'

He looked up. 'Hi, Raven. How was your day yesterday?'

'Fine.' She could do polite.

'Ready for the exams?' He was making small talk as if nothing had happened.

'As I'll ever be.'

He waited, probably expecting her to ask about him or Kieran, but she wasn't moving from her resolution to keep the distance between them until they told her the truth. He read her cool expression correctly. 'I see. You're still angry with us. You should consider the possibility that it might not be our fault.'

She felt a twinge of guilt as he turned to talk to his other neighbour leaving her the space she had established. It was supposed to be a tactic to force Joe to cross over, make the first move to being real friends to her, but instead it just left her more isolated.

Own goal, that one. She sighed and propped her chin on her hand, her head feeling so heavy with depression that she wanted to curl in a ball and give up. You broke up with Kieran, you fool; what do you expect? A marching band welcome from Joe?

The teacher's voice cut through her gloom. 'Now, Lower Sixth, today we are going to do essay plans under exam conditions. No talking.'

What joy. Raven recalled that she'd been told once that these were the best years of her life. Whoever said that must have forgotten what it felt like to face an endless series of exams while undergoing heartbreak.

At the end of the test, Joe waited for her to pack her bag. She deliberately took a long time but he wasn't to be shaken off.

'Are you coming to lunch? Key and I will protect you from the others. He'll want to see you.'

She hadn't been in the dining room for days. 'Thanks but no. I'd prefer to eat at home.'

'I know you guys broke up but he'll wonder if you are OK if you avoid him. He'll worry.'

She had rather thought it was Kieran avoiding her. There were more ways than one of not being there for someone. Though he was there physically, the real him had always been absent.

Except when he kissed her. She wouldn't let that not be real.

'I'm not feeling very hungry, Joe.'

Joe picked up her bag, refusing to release it. 'Come have a drink with us then while we eat. They're serving fruit shakes this lunchtime. You like those, don't you?'

'Joe . . . ' She tried to protest but he just grabbed her hand and tugged her to follow him.

'Yeah, I know you're pissed at us but let's at least carry on going through the motions of being friends. Key's doing the best he can. You won't see us again after the end of term so let's at least do the last few weeks as kind-of-friends.'

But kind-of-friends hurt. 'Please, Joe. I can't.'

He stopped and turned to face her, showing the hint of steel beneath his charm. 'It's me who's begging here, Raven. Not for you, not for me, but for Key. We can't explain everything to you but I bet you've made a few deductions of your own about Kieran's family. He's had a rough weekend and it's made worse by knowing he hurt you.'

'He did.'

'He knows that—but it wasn't on purpose. Gloria always messes him up. She's like radioactive waste—the briefest contact making him sick. I'm just asking for a little kindness towards him. Can't you do kind?'

Raven wanted to kick him. It wasn't fair. She was the one that had been failed but Joe made it sound as if it was partly her fault, and that she had let Kieran down in some way. Her shoulders slumped.

'I tell you, Raven: Key's never felt like this about a girl before. You've been good for him. I'm really sorry that romance hit the buffers so early on with the trust issue, but at least can we make the let-down easier on the guy, or he'll retreat permanently into his mind ice age and never risk showing interest in a girl again.'

Raven closed her eyes for a moment. 'Joe, are you asking me to forget what happened so I can patch Kieran up and send him on to other girlfriends?'

'Putting it bluntly, yes.'

She wanted to scream. Kieran was hers, not some other girl's. Joe was asking far too much. 'You're crazy.'

'But you're strong. You care about him enough to know I'm right. Just don't hurt him any more, please. He's had enough kicks in the teeth already.'

She folded her arms. 'And I haven't?' Even though she felt Joe was being unfair to her, asking her do to something beyond what she could bear just now, she appreciated that he was fighting his friend's corner. It would've been nice to have someone in hers. In the past she would've gone to Gina; now there was no one. She pictured the boxing ring—Joe slapping Kieran on the back, mopping his brow with iced water, pushing him back to face . . . what? Her shivering alone in her little corner.

Not much of an opponent.

OK, Raven, suck it up. She didn't do self-pity; there was no point. 'I'll come to lunch with you.'

'Thanks, Raven. I owe you.'

Kieran was already at the table, a sandwich and an apple sitting untouched on his tray. Joe had persuaded Raven to choose a baguette, fruit shake, and juice and then carried her tray to put it beside Kieran's.

'I'll just get my lunch,' he muttered, hurrying back to the canteen.

Kieran looked at her once then back at his meal. If he was surprised to see her, he wasn't showing it. Sub-zero in Kieranland.

'Hi.' She toyed with her apple juice, struggling to release the straw from the fiddly wrapper.

Long fingers took the carton from her and efficiently snapped the plastic and pierced the seal. He held it out by the edges. As she reached to take it, he said:

'Don't press the middle. It'll spill from the straw.'

Always so careful. She wished he had been as cautious with her feelings. Raven took the juice by the top edge, her fingers touching his briefly. The tingle was still there. 'Thanks.' To be fair, he could do concern. She remembered how gentle he had been with her on the morning after Gina's return. Joe was right: it shouldn't be so hard to be kind in return now. 'How are you, Kieran?'

'I'm OK. You?'

She shrugged. 'Fine.' His hands were only a few inches from hers but she could not bridge the gap. What was the point? He wasn't going to tell her the truth and she wasn't going to be his pushover girlfriend.

'Just so you know: I don't blame you for hating me. I'd feel

174

the same in your shoes. And I didn't lie about Hannah. That was true. I told you, I think, because I wanted to give you something real about me.'

Oh Kieran. 'I can be what Joe calls a kind-of-friend, but trust is important to me. I told you that too. If I don't know someone, how can I really be their friend?' Let alone their girlfriend, but she knew better than to drop that bomb of a word into the conversation.

He spun the apple on its axis, holding the stalk. 'I just want you to know that if I could do any of this differently, I would, but I'm under . . . ' he frowned, searching for an appropriate word, '. . . obligations, important ones that I can't break without doing more damage.'

Raven couldn't think what those could possibly be but Joe's response at the pool told her it was futile to ask. The boys were involved in something to do with this Isaac guy, their godfather, provider of suits and school fees. She intended to see if the internet held any answers, but her search for YDA had led to nothing remotely like a college. That was the wall between them; Kieran kept on adding the bricks and mortar and didn't help her attempts to climb. Still, she could make peace from her side.

'It's fine. I don't understand, but it's fine.'

He gestured to her tray. 'Are you going to eat that?'

She looked down at her baguette. 'I guess. What about you?' She picked it up.

'Haven't felt hungry.'

'Neither have I.'

They shared a fleeting moment of understanding. 'A bite each?' suggested Kieran.

'OK.'

Joe returned with a clatter of a heavily-laden tray. He smiled at Raven, mouthing 'thanks' behind Kieran's back. 'So, guys, what do you want to do tonight?'

Raven swallowed her mouthful. 'I've got revision for my Dance written exam tomorrow.'

'That means Key has too. Come study with us. No more holing up in the cottage, at least not as long as we're around to keep an eye on you.'

'Or you could come over for supper with Granddad and me. I vowed I'd spend as little time as possible here.'

'Do you have the fixings for peanut butter and jelly sandwiches?'

'Sure do.'

'Count me in.'

Kieran muttered something about revolting American habits.

'I expect Granddad has marmite.'

'Thank God you live with someone civilized.'

'Then it's settled. Supper and study at your house.' Joe beamed round at them both. Raven realized he was genuinely happy to have his little school family semi-repaired. He had begged on behalf of Kieran but he couldn't be content either, knowing all was not well. Though it was costing her, she had to admit it was better to settle for half a friendship than nothing at all.

When Raven left them to go to English, Kieran collared Joe.

'How the heck did you persuade her to sit with us? I thought she'd cast us off.'

'I told you how I'd do it: a little charm and an appeal to her forgiving character. It should've been harder after what we've put that girl through but she changed her mind when I went down on my knees and begged.' Joe sorted out his rubbish for the recycling and dumped his tray. 'I'm not suggesting you get back together but we need to keep the mission running. She's a target; we can't protect her if she's not near us. She's also a source of information.'

'She's not just those things.'

'Understood. But Raven likes us and I still want to be her friend even if we can't do it free and clear. She's too nice to be hard on us, even if we deserve it.'

Kieran wasn't used to being liked. He deposited his apple core in the compost bin. 'I see.'

'Just be gentle with her feelings, OK? I've negotiated a truce; don't go risking that, and definitely no serious stuff.'

'OK.' Joe had no idea how hard that would be. Kieran wasn't sure he could do it.

'See you later.'

Joe sauntered off to his class, hooking up with Hedda and her crew as they passed. They seemed to give him a chilly reception but he soon charmed his way back into their favour. Kieran's next lesson was English and, just to crown an already difficult day, he found Adewale and Gina leaning on the wall outside the classroom, heads together. Giving them a cool nod, he took out his folder to read the notes he had made on the set poetry texts.

A hand splayed across the page, pushing the folder down so it tumbled to the floor. The ring binder sprang open, scattering his notes across the corridor.

'We saw you sitting with Raven.' Adewale said it like an accusation. Gina stood behind him, backing him up.

Kieran surfed on a wave of anger. Having no desire to scrabble at their feet, he left the papers where they were. They'd picked the wrong person to bully, particularly one who was already spoiling for a fight. 'That's right.'

'But you should know by now that no one goes near her.'

Kieran pushed his hand away. 'What's your opinion to me? I do what I like.'

'Look, Kieran, I've nothing against you personally. But you should wake up to the fact that there are some people you just don't hang with. Thieves aren't welcome here.'

'Raven is not a thief.'

Adewale swiped his hand angrily through the air, dismissing his assertion. 'Bullshit. She took my watch.'

'No, Gina said she did. You have no case.'

Gina tugged Adewale's sleeve. 'He's already told me: he thinks I'm guilty.'

'Sweetheart, that's just wrong.' Adewale put his arm around her shoulders. 'He doesn't know you like I do.'

'I don't see how you can reach that conclusion.' Kieran scowled, irritated by Adewale's illogical deductions. 'Gina's the only one who saw that watch.'

'Are you saying Gina's the thief?' Putting Gina behind him, Adewale was now getting into Kieran's space.

'Finally, you are getting something right. Back off.' Kieran looked down, distracted by the damage Adewale's trainers were doing to his notes. Otherwise he would have noticed the fist coming for his face.

Pain exploded in his cheek bone. He reeled into the wall, but his training kicked in. Using the momentum to spin him around, he launched a counter-strike. Blow to the diaphragm, kick to the back of the knees, hand twisted up behind back to neutralize the assailant. A text-book defence.

He ignored Gina's shrieks. 'What was that you were saying, Adewale?'

'Let go, man!' Adewale's face was pointing at the ground, blood rushing to his head. Their classmates scrabbled for position around them.

'Not until you agree that you guys will back off and leave us alone. Say it!'

'Yeah, yeah, she's welcome to you, you nutter.'

Kieran lifted Adewale's arm up slightly, just to make his point, not because he was annoyed of course.

He locked his anger deep inside, logic clicking back in

control. 'I think I know now who joined in the attack in the cricket pavilion. It was you, wasn't it?'

'She stole my watch!'

'I thought we'd been through that. She did not. Gina said she had but Gina is lying. Not that that excuses what you did to Raven, you fricking coward. You'll leave Raven alone in future or, I promise you, I'll do to you what you did to her, but I won't stop until you're crawling on your knees for her forgiveness. Understand me?'

'Yes! Now let go: you're breaking my arm.'

'Incorrect. I'm merely applying pressure to catch your attention. If I wanted to break it you'd know that by now.' He gave Adewale a final shove. 'Pick up my papers, both of you.' He clicked his fingers down at the file contents.

They looked at each other, uncertain, neither wanting the humiliation.

'You made me drop them so you pick them up.'

Silence.

'Pick. Them. Up.' Kieran gave them a smile that had them on their knees and bundling A4 sheets together.

Gina shoved them in the ring binder making no attempt to straighten them. Kieran let that pass. 'Here you are.' Her lashes dipped over her blue eyes. 'And you're wrong about her.'

Again he had the strange conviction she believed her version of events, the truth erased from her memory, as her expression seemed so free of guile. He felt a flash of pity for her. 'I'm not wrong, Gina, but I tell you this much: I'm very sorry you are.'

Kieran walked into the classroom and took a seat on his own. It was no surprise when no one chose to sit near him.

The confrontation with Adewale was the big news of the afternoon. Even Raven, outside most gossip circles, got to hear about it thanks to Hedda's loud voice as she passed through the common room to the sixth form library. They didn't see her, as she was behind a shelf of newspapers and reference books, so she paused to eavesdrop.

'He went crazy, can you believe it? Attacked Adewale because he told him the truth about Crow.'

Raven wondered who she was talking about. She couldn't imagine anyone fighting to defend her.

'Actually, Ade did throw the first punch,' muttered Gina.

'But he was out of control. Almost broke Adewale's arm. He's dangerous.'

'What did Joe say?' asked Toni.

'He laughed. Said Adewale had it coming for underestimating Kieran.'

Kieran? He was the one who had fought for her? It was not big of her, Raven knew that, but she couldn't help a little flip of pleasure to hear that someone had stood up for her. Her corner no longer looked so lonely. But Kieran? She imagined he'd be playing it cool after they broke up—not rushing to defend her honour. And was he OK?

'Joe doesn't take our warnings seriously,' complained Hedda. 'He has such potential but he doesn't see how harmful Raven and her kind are.'

Her kind? What was that? Those poor enough to need a scholarship? There was a lot of her kind if that was what Hedda meant. Outside the privileged walls of Westron, Hedda would struggle to find someone who didn't offend her. One of Raven's small revenges had been to imagine Hedda coping in her last high school—she'd be eaten alive by the sharks in five minutes flat.

'Kieran's worse. Not one of us,' said Toni.

Uh-oh. Sounded like the boys were soon going to be joining her in reject zone.

'Don't worry—Mrs Bain said she has plans to straighten them out. They just need to be taught the right way to see things. They're fundamentally sound and I think a few weeks at the manor will do the trick.' Hedda patted Gina's arm. 'It helped sort you out, didn't it?'

'Yes, I was really lucky to get the chance.' Gina sounded breathy, like a beauty contest winner simpering to camera. 'I feel so much better about myself now—got my priorities straight. I had the first, you know, *nice* conversation I'd ever had with my dad. He says I'm now the daughter he always wanted.'

'Aw, sweet!' cooed the other girls.

Ugh, horrible, fumed Raven. Unable to listen to any more of this, she came out of hiding and marched up to the group on the sofas. 'Hey, Gina?'

Her ex-friend looked up warily. 'What do you want?'

'I just wanted to say that before you had your brain transplant I thought you were great. Sure, you had a few issues, but you were basically a good laugh and a good friend. You were interesting and had your own opinions. Your father should've accepted you for what you were, not try to squeeze you into a mould of his choosing. Think about that, won't you?'

Gina brushed the material of her pencil skirt nervously, pretending not to listen.

'What would you know about parental expectations?' sneered Hedda. 'I seem to recall you don't have any.'

Her insult was so sharp some of the girls had the decency to look shocked.

'That's not fair, Hedda,' Gina muttered.

Raven swallowed the lump of hurt that had formed in her throat. 'My father died serving his country, so you can just shove your big foot in that foul mouth of yours and shut up about him.'

Hedda did not back down. 'You are nothing but a

parasite—living off the wealth of others. It's our fees that pay for your scholarship.'

'It's my father's life that pays for your freedom. Without men like him defending your countries, you'd not be sitting here looking down on me. But do you know what? I don't care what you think of me. If there are any parasites in the room, it's you with your false sense of entitlement just because—woo-hoo—you stand to inherit your wealth.' She waved her hand mockingly. 'Good for you. If any of you had actually done anything to earn my respect, then I'd give it. But all I see is a coven of bitchy rich girls who wouldn't last five seconds in the real world. Suck on that, why don't you?'

Leaving quickly so she had the last word, Raven strode out of the common room. She'd already burnt her boats with the girls from her year a few weeks back but it felt good to dance around the smouldering fire after putting up with so much. And as for Kieran—actions speak louder than words, surely?

Chapter·14

The smell of cake greeted Kieran and Joe as they knocked on the back door of Raven's cottage. When she opened it, they saw she had a striped apron over her clothes, a dab of flour on the end of her nose.

'Hello. I'm so glad to see you guys. I've baked.'

Joe grinned. 'Great detectives that we are, we can tell. What's the big occasion?' He walked in past her, patting her on the shoulder.

Sorting through the scents, Kieran could smell dark chocolate and walnuts. She'd cooked his favourite brownies.

'My version of a hero's welcome.' Raven wrapped her arms around Kieran's waist and hugged. Taken aback, his hands hovered for a second before crushing her to his chest. 'Thanks, Kieran.'

'What are you thanking me for?' Where was a red line when he needed it?

Joe cleared his throat. 'I'll just go and see how the cakes are getting on then.' He pointed to the kitchen. 'Your grand-dad here?'

'Not yet. He's setting up for dinner at the castle.'

'Yeah, of course he is.' Joe gave Kieran the nod. 'Looks like you won't be interrupted then.' He hurried into the kitchen and closed the door.

'So what's this for?' Kieran repeated. He began to hope that maybe she'd give him a hearing—that yesterday's row wasn't as final as it had felt. He shouldn't want that but he did.

'I'm thanking you for what you did for me.'

Kieran ran his hands up her arms to cup her face, thumbs brushing her cheekbones. 'I'm not supposed to kiss you now.'

She frowned. 'Who says?'

'I thought we broke up and have only declared a truce. Sort-of-friends don't do kissing.' And he had promised Isaac. It turned out his word was no stronger than an ice sculpture in a heated room.

'Heroes who defend their sort-of-friend deserve one though.' She went up and touched her lips to his. He gave a little groan and let go of his restraint. One hand supported her back, drawing her higher, the other cradled her head. This was what they both needed, the soft press of lips, shared breath, his gentle strokes along her spine, delicious thrill of her fingers running over his chest. He was spun out of the everyday, where nothing added up, to a world of pure, magical numbers, where every equation was resolved, all difficulties untangled. She was the answer to his 'find x' in every emotional algebra problem he had been set. He had been a fool to think even for a second that the YDA mattered more than this.

Finally, Raven had to take a break and drop back on her heels. She didn't let go but nestled her head to his chest. 'You're too tall.'

He smiled. 'Sorry, but couldn't that be that you're too short?'

She drew a square over his heart. 'Maybe I could get a box to stand on.'

'Ever practical. Or I could sit with you on my lap. I like solution that better.'

'Now I know why they call you a genius.' She leant back to look up at his face. 'Did Adewale hurt you?'

He touched the bruise forming on his cheek. 'No.'

184

'Hah, liar.'

'It was nothing. I put an end to it before it really started.'

'I'm shocked it was him—he's always been a nice guy.'

'He probably still is under it all, but your enemies have all been persuaded you are a threat to them and they're going after you like white cells after a virus.'

'Watch out they don't go for you. I think you and Joe are suffering in the popularity stakes for remaining loyal to me.'

'We can look after ourselves.'

'I know. But next time, let me be your back-up.'

He rubbed the flour from her nose. 'I might let you hold my jacket.'

'OK. I love that jacket.'

He smiled. 'And I'll leave the girls to you—I don't fight girls.'

'Yeah, I'm all over those bitches, never you worry about them. They can't fight for toffee.'

She looked adorable with her face all screwed up with her determination to defend him. 'Fierce, aren't you, tiger?'

'My father taught me some neat self-defence moves. I'll show you if you like, in case Adewale comes after you again.'

Kieran had already undergone a course of advanced self defence taught by a former marine, but the idea of Raven showing him her moves sounded very appealing. 'I'd like that. And, um, Raven?'

'Hmm?'

Red lines crossed, trampled, smashed through—boy, was he in trouble in so many ways, but logic had taken a holiday. 'There's the prom coming up. Do you want to go?'

'Come again?'

He raised his eyes to the ceiling light. 'You're going to make me suffer, aren't you?'

'Absolutely. If you're doing what I think you're doing, you've got to ask properly or not at all, my mom used to say.'

He met her eyes. 'Raven Stone, would you do me the honour of being my date for the prom?' He kissed her fingertips.

'Kieran Storm, it would be my pleasure.'

'Thank you.'

'But what about after—you and me? Will you tell me the truth?'

He bent his forehead to rest against hers. 'Don't worry—I'm working on it.'

'You are?'

'I promise.'

There was a crash in the kitchen and an oath from Joe. Raven giggled. 'I think Joe just found out that the tin is still hot.'

'Sneaking my hero brownies are you?' shouted Kieran.

'Yeah.' Joe sounded completely unrepentant. 'If I don't get to make up in the hall, at least I should get a treat in here.'

Raven took Kieran's hand, her slim fingers wrapped around his. 'Let's go have some before he eats them all.'

'I'll follow you anywhere,' he said, only half joking.

After leaving Raven with her granddad, Kieran returned with Joe to the main building. He didn't follow Joe to their room but took a left towards a different flight of stairs.

'You OK?' Joe asked when he realized Kieran wasn't following.

'Yes, fine. I'm just going to take a look about the place.'

'See you back at base then. I'll do a report for Isaac.'

'Great. Thanks.'

'You did all right with Raven—took a nice line, friendly but not too intense. Letting her down gently.'

Joe didn't know about the kiss in the hall then. Kieran guessed Joe wouldn't be so impressed if he knew how many rules Kieran had broken, and intended to go on breaking. Kieran's career at the YDA would be toast if that came out.

Kieran waited for Joe to turn the corner then carried on up to his favourite spot in the castle, the battlement walk. Students weren't supposed to go here but lock picking was one of the first skills taught at the YDA, and he needed somewhere to think without interruption. Easing through the arched door, he disturbed the pigeons occupying the slates. They flew off over his head in a shudder of wings. He knew not to duck. Pigeons' eyesight ran at the equivalent of about two hundred and fifty frames per second; a normal film that ran at a tenth of that speed would seem like clicking through a slide show to them. The upshot of that fact was that they would move out of your way even if you thought they were on a collision course.

He leant on the crumbly parapet. Sandstone, heavily weathered. Some lichen—*Caloplaca flavenscens* if he wasn't mistaken—that had taken at least two hundred years to spread its orange stain over the stonework. He took a breath, settling his brain for a good think in the twilight.

All right then. Facts established, now he could deal with the emotions.

He had known since his conversation with Isaac that he had taken a wrong turn. Isaac had said even Kieran couldn't square the circle of his loyalty to the YDA and his attachment to Raven, but what was the point of having a brain like his if he didn't use it on something really important for once? If anyone could do the impossible, it would be him—that wasn't arrogance but awareness that he did have the edge over others in this at least.

He tapped the balustrade. Applying his brainpower to the problem, he could see that he mustn't tell Raven about his mission until it was over in order to ensure her safety. But surely new rules kicked in when that was done? He had another year at the YDA then university. YDA students at college were given more freedom, as backgrounds were under less of a microscope in the loose mixed community of a university. He just had to convince Raven to hang on in there for a while until he reached that stage.

But a year seemed too much. If she went to sixth form college, some guy would snap her up and push him out of the picture. He couldn't bear it if he lost the right to be the one to kiss her.

Of course. Kieran slapped his forehead, berating himself for his slowness. The conclusion was obvious. He couldn't believe he hadn't thought of it earlier. He just needed to pull off a few miracles and hope she really was the forgiving sort. But that was for later. His job now was to keep her safe so they could get to that point.

It would start with one very difficult conversation with Isaac; he was going to be annoyed Kieran had ignored his orders.

Weighing that up, with the possibility of serious consequences as Isaac hit the roof, Kieran decided it was worth the risk. Isaac also repeatedly told them that they weren't his pawns. Kieran was going to find out just how sincerely Isaac meant that by making some gambits of his own. If anyone was going to walk away from the relationship, it wouldn't be him. In fact, he was damned if he'd let Raven chuck in the towel over his lies to her without doing his utmost to change her mind.

Kieran decided that by far his favourite moments of the exam weeks were those when Raven took it upon herself to teach him her self-defence techniques. He enjoyed playing dumb as she clearly got so much pleasure from instructing him. It also gave him plenty of excuses to let her put her hands on him, which they both liked more than they let on.

'Now this evening I'm going to show you how to leverage your weight.' They were in the gym at dinnertime so had the place to themselves, crash mats out as Raven had warned they were going to get serious after the easy lessons on going for vulnerable spots—eyes, nose, groin, etc.

'I thought leverage of weight was something hedge funds did for their assets by using sugar derivatives.'

'Come again?'

OK. So Raven didn't do financial sector jokes. 'Nothing.'

She rolled her eyes. 'OK, Mr Storm, stop making incomprehensible remarks that go over the head of mere mortals and get your butt here.'

He grinned, loving it when she got bossy with him.

She frowned at him, sensing he wasn't in a serious mood. 'Now try going for me—any way you like.'

'But I don't want to hurt you.'

'You won't.'

He made a fairly obvious attempt to grab her arm. She used a neat jujitsu move to defeat him, lunging down and bending her elbow towards him so he had to let go of her wrist. 'And now I'd run.' She mimed a dash for safety. 'You try it. Pretend I'm Adewale grabbing you.'

He'd let her grab him anytime she felt so moved. 'Do your worst.'

She darted forward and gripped his wrist. 'Now lunge and break my hold.'

Where was the fun in that? Instead he pounced on her waist and lifted her off her feet. 'Give up?'

'Put me down! You're supposed to be trying to get away!'

Not a chance. He spun her in a circle. 'I am in your power.'

She batted him over the head. 'Idiot! I'm in your power.'

189

'Say that again.' He kissed her chin.

'No, never!'

'Ah, a challenge!' He dropped her on her back on the crash mat and began tickling.

She wriggled. 'Stop it, no fair!'

'Say it!'

She tried another jujitsu move, hooking his wrist, holding his elbow, trapping his foot, which was the first part of the manoeuvre to reverse positions, but her laughter stopped her following through. He started peppering kisses over her face. 'Say it!'

'All right, all right—I am in your power, you great heffalump.'

He stopped tickling her and stared down into the depths of her eyes. Nutmeg with dark chocolate streaks. 'And I am in yours.'

Her smile wobbled a little. 'Really?'

He twisted to bring her on top and on to his lap. 'Yes. I just want you to put up with me for a few more weeks.'

She drew back. 'I can't just be a temporary amusement and you won't explain what's really going on so I'm worried we're . . . screwed. I kinda thought the prom date was a goodbye—a sweet ending.'

That was what Joe thought too but Kieran wasn't satisfied with that: he'd found his girl and no way was he letting her go. 'I don't mean it like that. I'm asking you to put up with me not being straight with you. Not telling the truth. In the summer holidays, when we meet up, I'll explain anything you want to know.'

Her eyes sparkled with curiosity but an even heavier dose of doubt. 'You mean about Isaac?'

He nodded.

'And the YDA—and Gloria?'

190

'Yes, the whole sad saga if you've got patience to hear it.' He just hoped she wouldn't walk away when she learned the details of his disastrous background. But Raven wouldn't care about ancestry—he was fairly confident of that. One thing he decided he could straighten out right now. 'The posh thing— that was just Joe pulling your leg.'

'I have to admit I didn't think Gloria looked like someone from the upper classes.'

'Joe has an active imagination.'

She wrinkled her nose, smelling a rat. 'And his druggie mom and imprisoned dad?'

That was for Joe to explain. Poor old Mr and Mrs Masters were the sweetest couple in Manhattan and Carol wouldn't know her aspirin from her crack cocaine. Her expertise was quilting and pot roasts. 'Can we leave that until August?'

Raven looked at his face for a long time, scrutinizing his expression. Somewhere along the way, she had learnt not to trust and he had unintentionally reinforced the lesson. She took a breath, coming to a decision. 'OK, my man of mystery, I'll reserve judgement. You're making me act against my instincts, you know?'

'But I'm worth it?'

'Yes, you're worth it.' Raven twirled a lock of hair. 'I'm in your lap.'

'Yes, that's right.' He thought that was obvious.

'No, Kieran, I am in *your lap*.'

'Oh yeah.' He got it now. 'And I was right about my deduction: our height issue is cancelled in this position.'

'So what are you going to do about it?' She looked up at him through her lashes.

'I'll show you one of my self-defence techniques.'

'You mean aside from tickling?

'Yes. This one is called distraction. If you are still thinking about attacking me when I've finished then I'm not doing a good job of it.'

'And does it go something like this?' She leant forward and kissed him.

'What? You know this one too?' He pretended surprise.

'I do. But I don't think I'm very good at it yet.'

'Ah. I beg to differ. But they do say practice makes perfect so I think we'd better try for perfection.' He closed the distance between them.

Kieran found Joe studying hard when he got back to their room.

'How was self defence?' Joe asked.

'Perfect.' Kieran smiled into the depths of his cupboard as he put away his sports bag. He didn't like keeping his renewed relationship with Raven from Joe but, if he told his friend, then he would be asking him to hide it from Isaac, introducing a conflict into Joe's loyalties. Kieran had every intention of telling Isaac himself. Eventually. When he had got his miracle in place.

'Don't want to be a buzz kill but Isaac has told us to call as soon as you get back.'

A few days ago Kieran had asked for Isaac to consider his proposal on miracle-making. Isaac had said he would think about it and put the phone down on him. Kieran wondered if this was the reason for the unscheduled call now. 'Let's get it over with then.'

Joe put through the call. Isaac's face filled the screen. Kieran knew he wasn't the most astute at reading expressions but even he could see that their boss was beyond angry. He hadn't somehow found out about the resumption of his relationship with Raven, had he?

'Hey, Isaac, it's us.' Joe tugged a chair alongside his so Kieran could share the screen.

'Boys.' Isaac gave them a nod. 'I received an email from the head teacher today with that promised report on you two.'

Relief swooped through Kieran. So it wasn't about Raven—not yet.

'What have we done wrong now?' asked Joe in a resigned tone.

'As far as I'm concerned, nothing. No, it's her who has really wound me up. She sent me a letter about your forthcoming enrolment in the personal development course.' Isaac shook out the pages he had printed off. 'She wanted to make sure it was crafted to my specific requirements. There follows a detailed character assassination—sorry, *analysis*—of each of you with suggestions of areas in which you might improve. You mentioned the possibility of them fabricating evidence for blackmail, Kieran—well, we've just hit jackpot.'

'Sweet!' Joe cracked his knuckles. 'OK, what's wrong with me?'

Isaac smiled sourly. 'She was complimentary about most aspects of your character—good team player, cheerful disposition, intelligent—but you lack, and I quote, "suitable deference for authority" and "will to succeed". Here's the killer: you also drink and drive.'

'Do not.'

'I know—but here's the police report, all typed up and official looking. You took one of the school buses for a spin apparently. If I thought there was a shred of truth in it, I, as your concerned and corruptible godfather, would be eager to keep that off your criminal record.'

Isaac chucked the page aside. 'I could've told her about your lack of deference myself. She asked me for any additional suggestions so they could be included in your personalized training programme.'

'I hope you told her you couldn't improve on something that was flawless.'

Isaac laughed darkly and turned to a second, much bigger printout. 'Kieran, I'm afraid Mrs Bain isn't a fan of yours.'

Kieran folded his arms. 'I take that as a compliment.'

'She suggested that you might need a longer and more intensive treatment.' Isaac leafed through the six pages listing his defects. 'Odd. Here she praises your academic achievements, especially in Dance. What's this?'

'Yeah. Turns out I'm not bad.' Kieran rubbed the back of his neck, feeling the skin heat with embarrassment.

'He's the Fred Astaire of the twenty-first century, Isaac,' Joe chipped in. 'You should've been there.'

'With this girl he likes?' Isaac's laser gaze was uncomfortable.

'Yes, with cute Miss Stone. They made a great team.'

'Hmm. That's behind you, right, Kieran?'

Kieran rearranged his paperclip tower. 'I know about your red line, Isaac.' Truth—just not the whole truth that he was bopping on the wrong side of it.

Isaac tapped his fingers on the papers. 'As I was saying, Mrs Bain finds more to censure than to praise. She told me you were caught pirating videos and music—a plausible lie—but she added hacking into the US military to get me really worried.'

Kieran frowned. 'It's possible but I don't think I've done that yet.'

'I hope not. I would sign off on this intensive course she recommends to find out what they do, but I'm worried that might leave you open to mistreatment. Their techniques have to be pretty heavy duty to get kids to change so quickly. I don't want to put either of you at risk. What's your judgement, Key?'

'Going in armed with the knowledge they're going to

attempt to brainwash us means that neither Joe nor I would make susceptible subjects.'

'Is what they're doing illegal?' asked Joe.

'Tricky.' Kieran had wondered this same thing. 'If the students agree to be there and the parents request it, unless they hold us against our will, it might be completely above board.'

'Ethically, it sucks,' said Joe.

'Yes, but bruised ethics aren't enough for a conviction. The exchange of favours if we could prove it—now that would be illegal as it is a form of corruption. And the missing students—Johnny Minter and Siobhan Green—I'm wondering if they aren't being held against their will. They may have turned out too difficult to influence.'

'And I guess once they pass a certain point, the trustees wouldn't accept failures as it risks the whole scheme coming to light. Isaac, Key's right as usual. We've really got to find that pair and we can only do that from inside the manor.'

'OK, I give my permission for you to try this. The case against them is building so just don't mess it up. No heroics. Call for extraction at the first hint of anything that puts either of you in danger.'

'Understood.' Joe's hand hovered over the mouse, ready to end the conversation.

Isaac's gaze dipped back to Kieran. 'Oh, and Kieran, we'll be expecting a repeat performance here when you get back to base.'

'I'm not the kind to dance solo.' Kieran hoped Isaac got the message.

'I'm still thinking about that. Goodnight.'

Joe closed the window on the screen. 'What was that last part about?'

'I made Isaac a suggestion.'

'What kind?'

'Oh, just about making sure Raven's OK at the end of this.'

'That'd be nice. But you know the rules—you can't be part of her life.'

'I'm not talking about breaking rules,' though he was already doing that, risking his YDA place if found out, 'more expanding them.'

Joe chucked a pen at him. 'Did you know that speaking in riddles is an annoying habit?'

'I'm achieving the impossible, Joe. Just another day in the office for Kieran Storm.'

'And when did you get so arrogant? Oh, I forgot: you were born this way.'

Kieran smirked.

'I just hope this big head of yours isn't going to mean we've underestimated what they'll do to us at the manor.'

Kieran stopped smiling. 'Yes, you're right. But we've got to make a breakthrough and this is our best hope. Watch my back?'

'Do you need to ask?'

'No. And I've got yours.' They bumped knuckles.

'Six pages.' Joe started laughing.

'I'd be more worried that Mrs Bain rather likes you.'

That comment led to a pillow fight. After tipping over the coffee table, knocking over Kieran's paper clip tower and bursting the seams of the cushions, they reduced the room to chaos.

Joe blew the feathers from his mouth as they settled like snow on his head. 'Hope you've got a genius way of clearing this up?'

'Naturally.'

Joe perked up.

'It involves the creation of a vacuum in a specially designed device.'

Joe flopped back on his bed and groaned.

Raven's last exam was an English literature paper on the set poetry text. Kieran also took it in the hall with her, only a seat away thanks to the alphabet. Never one to shine academically, she felt it went well, as being near him settled her jitters and helped her concentrate. Maybe he was sending her clever vibes or something. Nice if his intelligence was catching. More likely he just made her feel happier. After their papers were collected in, she got up, hoping to walk out with him. He started moving towards her.

'Mr Storm, could you come here please?' Mrs Bain was waving to him from the front of the hall.

'Uh-oh, bad luck.' Raven narrowed her eyes at her nemesis.

'And I was hoping to celebrate end of the exams.' Kieran brushed a kiss over her cheek. 'Catch you later.'

'OK. I'll be at the cottage.'

She didn't have long to wait. Kieran rushed in, a backpack in one hand. 'I'm sorry, Raven, but the course my godfather wants Joe and I to go on has been brought forward. It starts today. The minibus leaves,' he checked his watch, 'five minutes ago. But I told them they had to wait. I couldn't go without saying goodbye.'

'You're going on a course?' Raven felt a heavy sensation in her stomach: dread. Not him, please—not when she and Kieran had just been getting back on track. 'Where?'

'The manor. For two weeks.'

She swore under her breath. 'Please, don't go. That's where Gina went. People change there—in bad ways.'

He ran his fingers over the tense muscles of her neck. 'Sssh, it's OK. Really it is. I won't change. I'm too pig-headed. Joe and I will look after each other.'

'No, listen to me. That place isn't normal—it can't be if they come back good girl and boy zombies.'

197

Kieran sniffed in disdain. 'I wouldn't call them good.'

'You know what I mean—good from their parents' viewpoint.'

'Now that would be interesting—coming back in a form Gloria would approve.' He smiled wryly. 'When I get bored, I'll think about what that might be.'

'Kieran, please, listen to me: you'll go in as a prince and they'll turn you into a frog.'

'I always thought the guy in the story was more interesting as the frog.'

'That's not what I mean and you know it! Please take this seriously.'

'Don't worry about me.'

'I can't help it.' She buried her head in his jacket, just wishing she could wave a magic wand and stop him going. 'I'm afraid for you.'

'No need to be. Trust me.' He soothed her by running his palm gently up and down her back. 'I'm your Frog Prince, am I?'

'Maybe.' She hadn't meant to admit that. She didn't want him to distract her from the warning she was trying to give.

'Interesting. In that case, I know that I get a kiss from the princess—it's in the small print.'

'But . . . !'

'Ah-uh. Kiss first.'

He was trying to tease her out of her worry and, foolish though it was, she couldn't resist him. 'You want a kiss? Where? Nose?'

He pretended to frown. 'Nope. Frogs don't have noses.'

'Webbed toes? I'll tell you now, pal, I don't kiss anyone's feet.'

'Not my webbed toes.' He pointed to his big smiling mouth. 'Here.'

She moved forward, then stopped. 'No, I can't.'

'Yes, you can.'

'No, I mean, what if you change?'

'Then you'll just have to kiss me again to change me back. Problem solved.'

She hesitated.

'Ri-bik.'

She smiled.

'Ri-bik.'

'Are you going to keep croaking until I kiss you?'

His eyes twinkled. 'Ri-bik.'

'OK, OK, two kisses—just to be safe.' She closed the gap. Somehow the kisses merged into each other—there could have been four or fourteen, she was no longer counting. The teasing game was forgotten and it became a heated exchange, an exploration of mouths as first his tongue caressed hers and then she reciprocated. For a moment it felt as if they were one person, almost sharing the same skin. Finally, he let her go.

She took a moment to recover. How did you come back from that? Sass was her usual answer.

'So, frog or man?'

'You tell me.' He pressed a kiss to the tender spot below her ear, sending renewed shivers down her spine.

'You're still Kieran.' *My Kieran*, she added to herself.

'That's right.' He tucked her hair behind her ear and met her eyes, expression solemn. 'Please don't worry about me. I promise I'll be back for the prom. If anything really serious crops up before then, I'm giving you this.' He pressed a piece of paper in her hand.

'What is it?'

'Don't open it unless you have to. It's Isaac's number. For emergencies when I'm not around.'

'You're giving me Isaac's number?' She clenched her fist

around the paper. 'You really do trust me, don't you?'

'One hundred per cent. I've never lied to you about that.'

She had to say it. If he was going to change, she had to say this now, before anyone got hold of him. 'I'm falling in love with you, Kieran Storm.'

He wrapped his hand around her fist. 'So am I.' He frowned. 'Not the Kieran bit—Kieran is a fool sometimes—especially when it comes to his girl.'

'Kieran,' she said gently.

'I'm being too pedantic?'

She nodded.

'OK, second attempt. What I mean is I think I'm falling for you too. How was that?'

Of course thinking would have to be part of the deal; he wouldn't be Kieran without that. 'Much better.' They hugged for a long minute until a hooting outside the cottage disturbed their privacy.

'That's them. I'll be back before you know it.' He pushed something else in her hand before leaving.

'What's this?'

'A present!' he called, jumping into the back of the minibus and sliding the door closed.

She waited for the bus to wind out of sight then opened the parcel. A phone dropped out of the package and on to her palm. A nice one—not too flashy to attract attention but top specifications. It came with a note.

No point giving you a number without something to call it on. Elementary logic so you can't refuse. Kieran xxx.

Chapter · 15

A full moon rose over the trees of the deer park, turning the view to greyscale lawns and silhouetted oaks. This was Kieran's first in-the-flesh sight of the manor. He had studied the satellite imagery so knew the layout but it was more impressive than he had expected. He had been shown to a room on his own, Joe billeted on a different floor. The noble family that owned Westron had abandoned the old-fashioned Tudor castle and moved a few miles to a new site in favour of living surrounded by the best the eighteenth century could offer. What they had built was a Palladian gem of a country house, architecture by Vanbrugh and gardens designed by Capability Brown.

Joe slid into the room. 'Nice digs.'

'Not bad.' Kieran unpacked his shaving stuff and put it in the en suite bathroom cleverly built into the corner of the room. No external windows, the extractor fan hummed loud enough to kill any hopes of overhearing them. He nodded to Joe, giving him the signal it was safe to talk.

'Mine's one floor down, two over. The Cavalier's Chamber. I see they put you in the Pagoda Bedroom.' Joe perched on the edge of the bath.

'The Chinese pattern on the wallpaper is hand painted. Worth a fortune. The housekeeper told me not to touch it.'

'So a game of darts is nixed then. Why do you think they brought the course forward? I thought this place was dedicated to conferences during term.'

'Perhaps they had a cancellation.' Kieran let his scepticism seep into his tone.

'Or?'

'Maybe they didn't like us sticking by Raven.'

'I can't see why that should worry them.'

'I agree it doesn't make a lot of sense. So I've been thinking. Maybe we were wrong to assume Raven is their chief target? At least, I'm wondering now if they aren't also aiming for Robert Bates.'

'Her granddad? Why?'

'I'm thinking they're easing him out—him and other staff members who wouldn't go along with this system. When Raven leaves, they'll make him choose: his job or his granddaughter. He'll have to go and they'll have got away with bullying her into quitting and forcing him to resign. And the dance teacher, Miss Hollis, told me after our exam that this was her last term teaching at Westron. Her contract hadn't been renewed.'

'Yeah, I get it. And the caretaker goes everywhere, knows everything happening in a school—he'd soon notice a pattern if all these kids keep coming back changed.'

'I predict the next move, if they've not already done it, is that he will be told he can't continue to house her. His job means he has to live on site. They are making it so he has to choose between his position and his granddaughter.'

'And he'll choose Raven.'

'Of course. They may offer him early retirement to sweeten the pill but it has to look to the world that they aren't kicking out a man with thirty years' service. He has to choose to go.' Kieran took his bull whip out of his backpack and threaded it through the loops of his jeans so it went round his waist several times. An odd belt, but unless you looked very carefully it would pass inspection.

Joe just arched a brow.

'You never know.'

'True. I can see this scheme could add up to big business. So how do you think they are getting their results?'

'That, my friend, is what we are going to find out.'

Joe stood up. 'OK. Orientation meeting is in a few minutes in the Music Room. Ready?'

'Let's go catch ourselves some crooks.'

Kieran did not recognize the couple introducing the course to the six students. The man—'call me Heath'—was fresh-faced, casually dressed in jeans and polo shirt, recalling a children's TV presenter in his enthusiasm. His partner, Namrata Varma, took a more serious approach. Her long dark brown hair was beautifully groomed and she wore a spotless white suit. Kieran now understood who had given the girls at Westron their style notes.

'Over the next weeks while we are together, we are going to have lots of fun.' Heath bounced around at the front as if he had springs in his ankles. 'This course is designed to strengthen those elements of your character which are most helpful to your personal development and to weed out the harmful. We'll be giving feedback on a daily basis in our one-to-ones so you each have something tailored exactly to your needs.'

He stepped back and Namrata took over. 'Now, as you will know, your parents or guardian have put your name forward for this course. We are sure you do not want to disappoint them by failing to give it one hundred and ten per cent of your attention.'

Kieran raised his hand.

'Yes, Kieran?'

'It is not possible to give one hundred and ten per cent of a self-contained resource such as attention. A hundred is the maximum mathematically achievable.'

'I see.' She did not look too happy at the correction.

'And also, as a mammal, part of our attention will always have to be devoted to our survival instincts—our security, hunger, thirst, and so on. I would think that the real level any of us can give you is more likely to feature in the high seventies, and then only for short bursts.'

Kieran could feel Joe shaking with laughter beside him, hand covering his mouth. He enjoyed the small victory of bursting the bubble of their management-speak by deconstructing it in this way.

'Thank you for sharing your wisdom with us.' Namrata sounded like she was sucking on lemons. 'I'll expect seventy nine per cent from you then, Mr Literal-minded. The rest of you, I think you understand what I'm driving at.'

Heath popped back into the conversation. 'Let's crack on, shall we? A healthy body, guys, is part of the secret of success so we want all of you to take care to sleep well, eat well, and play well.' He shook his hand, making a concealed bottle rattle. 'We've got some vitamins here—again we've asked a nutritionist to advise us on a personally devised regime for each of you, engineered for teenage metabolisms. Take these now and we'll give you the next dose with your breakfast.'

Joe raised a brow to Kieran. They had already agreed that they wouldn't take anything suspect.

'If those are just vitamins then I'm Santa Claus,' murmured Kieran. He had considered the possibility that drugs to increase suggestibility might be involved. He was looking forward to analysing the pills.

The pair wittered on about their plans; Kieran listened only for the truth underlying the surface spin. He deduced that the students were going to be isolated from each other for most of the time but there was precious little detail on the actual content in the solo sessions.

'And now I expect you are all anxious to get to your beds.

Before you go, come and fetch your vitamins and the folder of your schedule.' Heath pointed to a table where Namrata was laying out cups of water and little trays of drugs, one set on top of each folder.

'Distraction?' suggested Joe.

Kieran nodded.

Joe led the way, picked up his pills and shook them in Heath's eyeline. 'These mine?'

'That's right, Joe, healthy body!' Heath passed him a cup of water.

While Joe messed around, palming the pills as he pretended to toss them back with the water, Kieran made a less flamboyant grab for his. He turned his shoulder to Namrata, only wetting his lips and not drinking.

'Everything all right with your schedule?' she asked, coming too close. Her eyes were on his cup, not his file.

'Yes, thank you.'

'We're going to work on that literalness of yours, Kieran. You must realize that it gets in the way of normal relationships.'

Kieran thought of Raven, how she laughed when he went a little off track with his remarks. She enjoyed his logical flourishes. 'I don't think of it quite like that.'

'Your godfather doesn't share your view, but let's see how you feel about this in a day or two, OK?'

Interesting. There was a huge emphasis on pleasing people whom the students should be eager to impress. After years of falling short of expectations, the course was promising instant repair of poor family relationships. It was a huge incentive to buckle under their pressure. It was good they didn't know how far he'd go to please Raven; that was one gap in his armour he didn't want exposed.

'You want to make friends, don't you? I have you down here as a social misfit, uneasy in large gatherings of your peers, always saying the wrong thing. No offence, but I think you demonstrated the truth of that tonight.'

'Miss Varma?' Kieran dug his hands in his jeans pockets, pushing the tablets deeper.

'Yes?'

'As you say, I take things more literally than they are meant, so please explain something to me.'

She foolishly took this as a sign that he was recognizing he had a problem. 'Go ahead.'

'Why is it that before someone says something insulting they tack on "no offence"? You were aware what you said was going to offend me so the phrase was a lie.'

She gave him a snake of a smile. 'I see we have a lot of work to do, Kieran.' She turned away to find a more tractable student.

Back in his room, Kieran left the reporting in to Joe as he quickly analysed the tablets with the tiny kit he had brought in his wash bag. Setting out a mini lab on the vanity unit, he only had the basics, but the preliminary results surprised him.

'Joe, looks like I'll have to change my name to Santa as these *are* vitamins—the usual cocktail: A, B3, C, D—I haven't got time to test for everything but I can't see that the pills have been adulterated in any way.'

No answer. He stuck his head round the door of the bathroom to find Joe fast asleep on his face, phone still clutched in his hand. He decided the results could wait for the morning.

'Hey, my friend, time you went back to your room.'

Joe yawned. 'Yeah. I'm tired. That was fun, wasn't it?'

If you like baiting the brainwashers. 'Need help finding your room?'

'No, I'm good.'

Kieran offered him a hand and helped him to the exit. 'Did you report in?'

206

'Um, don't think so.' Joe rubbed his eyes. 'Sorry. Dropped off to sleep the moment I lay down to do it.'

'It's OK—I'll make the call. I'll come by and get you in the morning in case you oversleep.'

'Yeah. Appreciate it. I'm gonna sleep so well tonight.' Joe stumbled off.

Kieran found Joe's yawns catching. He splashed water on his face to wake up. They had been studying hard for the exams as well as working on their mission, not to mention the recent emotional upheaval, so both were running on fumes. He rang Isaac's number.

'Everything OK, Kieran?'

'So far. We're both here and had our orientation meeting. They handed out tablets and I got excited about the possibility of drugs, but it turns out they were just vitamins.'

'Shame. Would have been a convenient piece of evidence. Other impressions?'

'Sounds like a training course so far. Tutors plausible.'

'Joe OK?'

'Yes. He just went to bed. We're both really whacked. Exams only ended today.'

Isaac chuckled. 'I keep forgetting you have that stuff to do. Did they go OK?'

'I believe so.'

'From you that means you got an A. You are quite something, Kieran. Always surprising the hell out of me.'

Kieran walked to the window, looking out towards Westron Castle. It was out of sight but he could sense where Raven was like a compass pointing to the north. 'Have you given my suggestion any thought?'

'Working on it. But I must tell you I'm not convinced.'

'I promise you it will work. You don't know her.'

'Let's talk after this is over.'

'That's the kind of thing people say when they are going to say no.'

Isaac did not give an inch—not that Kieran expected him to. 'Mission first, talk later. Keep in touch, OK?'

'Of course. Either Joe or I will check in tomorrow.'

Kieran ended the call. His screen returned to the photo of Raven he had taken a few days ago and selected as his wallpaper. Was it too late to contact her? He decided on a text in case she was already asleep.

Everything OK here. I'm still the same old me. Miss you. See you at the prom if not before. Frog Prince.

Not the most eloquent message but it would have to do. He pressed send. His screen flashed up with a reply almost instantaneously.

Glad to hear you r OK. Missing you too. Thanks for the phone. It means so much. Love Raven. xx

Love. And two kisses so he would turn back to a prince. Kieran's thumbs hovered as he wondered if he should send something a little more poetic, more charming. Joe would do that—flatter her with lyrics and clever little comments. But then she wouldn't believe it was him if he started acting so out of character.

I wish I did charm but in the absence of that, I just want to say I think about you all the time.

There was a pause.

Even when you are employing that formidable brain of yours on working out the Theory of Everything? ;)

If the theory did not contain you somewhere in it then it would be useless to me. Goodnight.

Aw, thanks. Goodnight. P.S. You don't do so bad in the charm department. I now have your texts as evidence.

Kieran went to sleep with a smile on his face.

*

Raven cradled the phone to her chest. Confused, that was how Kieran made her feel. In love and confused. Still, at least they were warm feelings, rather than the cold slice of hurt and loneliness she had experienced after the Gloria incident. What got at her most was that she didn't know where the two of them were going. Kieran had promised a big revelation after the end of term, but what if he just disappeared on her? She had no home address for him, no way of preventing him walking out on her as easily as he had walked in. When she was with him, it felt like he fitted her, like a jigsaw piece slotting perfectly in place, but when he was away, all her old fears rushed back and she wondered if their relationship wasn't going to be dumped back in the box and jiggled around, any emerging picture reduced to random fragments.

Some of her happy feelings fizzled out. Dad had walked out with his kit bag on his shoulder. Mom had gone with a suitcase in the car. Neither had been able to return. When good intentions met harsh reality, harsh reality won every time.

It came as no surprise when she drifted into the dream. Walking down a white corridor at Junior High, gun metal grey lockers either side. Everything bigger and longer than she remembered. Ahead she could see her parents, arm-in-arm, laughing with heads close together. If she could just run fast enough, maybe she'd catch up.

Dealer kid steps out in her path. *Hey, girl.*

She shakes her head. Ignore him. Step around.

Don't turn your back on me. Do you a special deal if you do me one.

Not in this lifetime. Running now. But her parents are getting further away and she's going nowhere, like running on a moving walkway in the wrong direction.

Now the entire school football team are standing in her

way, padded and helmeted. *Told you were easy. Wanna play?* calls the Quarterback.

So not going there. But she has no power of speech, only this weird running without getting away. She looks down. Her foster brother, Jimmy Bolton, is lying on the floor, hands round her ankles, smug smile on his choirboy face. *Warned you I'd get even.*

She tries to shake him off but her parents are fading, stepping out of the doors at the end into bright, blinding daylight. Someone else is with them. Kieran? The footballers are getting closer, like she's the opponent they're about to tackle, or maybe the ball they're going to kick. A ring of boys with pillowcase heads joins them.

Go away, Stone!

Water pours from the sprinklers. She throws her arms up to protect her head, knuckles crack on her headboard.

The real pain woke her from the imagined one. Heart thumping with the surge of adrenaline, she lay back on the pillow, nursing her hand. Far better to be awake and hurting than still stuck in that dumb dream. Ghosts of her past unleashed by fears in the present—yeah, she got it. She didn't need a shrink to get her on his couch to explain that to her.

She took the phone from her bedside table and checked the time. 02:28. She scrolled through the last message from Kieran. He was OK. Not changed. She had his phone number even if she didn't have his address; he couldn't just vanish on her. She'd text him in the morning. For now, she would just have to trust him to look after himself.

Shaking off a mild headache, Kieran hurried down the stairs to wake Joe. He had overslept himself and there was only five minutes to go before breakfast.

No answer. Opening the door, Kieran found the room empty. The bed had been slept in but Joe must have done better at getting up than him. Then again, Joe hadn't stayed up text-messaging his girlfriend.

The breakfast room was bathed in sunlight. Healthy food options were spread out on a long table—no bacon and eggs here. Kieran waved at Joe who was already digging in to his grapefruit. He grabbed a packet of muesli and a banana and went to find his place. Each student had a name tag by their seat, a little cup of vitamins by their name. He noticed his had two extra tablets than everyone else.

Heath came in, sleeves rolled up, thumbs tucked in his belt loops. 'Hi, guys. Everyone sleep well?'

'You bet!' called a boy from Year 9. 'Magic pills those.'

'Please take your vitamins with your food—they can be rough on an empty stomach.' Heath turned to select his breakfast.

Kieran slipped his in the empty banana skin. He noticed Joe actually took his.

'Hey, Joe, I know they're probably only vitamins, but best to be safe than sorry,' he said softly.

Joe swallowed his gulp of water. 'Huh, what's that, Key?' Joe reached out to refill his cup but his movements were clumsy.

'Are you still tired?' Kieran felt the tick-tick of apprehension in his stomach. Joe wasn't acting like his normal self. Quickly checking the room, he realized that all the students in the room appeared hyper—talking and laughing too loudly, movements a little uncoordinated.

'Never been better. Woke up so relaxed, man, you wouldn't believe it. Isn't this place cool? Got a great programme.' He waved his folder, pages falling out between their chairs. 'Oops.' He began to laugh, looking down at his feet as if he couldn't think what to do about the things he had dropped. 'I get to do fitness training this morning—weights, pool, running machine. I'll be one buff guy when I leave.' He leant down to pick up the schedule but misjudged the distance between his fingers and the floor. 'Would you look at that? Did you get me drunk?'

Alarmed, Kieran quickly picked up the fallen sheets. 'You didn't take the pills last night, did you?'

'No—at least, I don't think so.' Joe frowned. 'It's all kinda fuzzy.'

But he'd drunk the water. The pills had been OK but Kieran remembered Joe gulping down the water they'd been given with it—a carefully measured dose, just like this morning.

'Don't drink that.' He took what remained in the cup from Joe. How long would it take for the drug to work its way out of his friend's system?

'Anything you say, my friend.' Joe smiled blearily at him. 'You know, Key, I love you, man. You are my best pal.'

'Yeah, best pals.' Kieran did not want to hear drunken confessions.

'Really sorry you had to split with Raven. That was rough. I feel for you, you know?' Joe was emotionally bleeding out— eyes tearing, mouth spouting words without editing. Normally he was demonstrative but in carefully judged ways.

'Yeah, I know, but perhaps we should not talk about that now? You need to sober up.'

'You mean I'm drunk?' Joe peered into his orange juice. 'Did you spike my drink?'

'No, I didn't. These people have.' Kieran looked down at his bowl. Was anything here safe to eat? The banana maybe. If he could get Joe to eat something that might mean less of the drug was metabolized. Grapefruit was out for a start, as it had the opposite effect, making chemical absorption faster. He moved it out of Joe's reach.

'But these are nice guys. Didn't you think they were nice?

212

I was just talking to Namrata and she's OK, you know? And there's so much to do here—it's like one long, looong vacation.'

The signs were unmistakeable: the already talkative Joe was even more loquacious than usual; he seemed to have forgotten they weren't here to be cooperative. Thiopental maybe? That drug was used in the cocktail for a truth serum, lowering the subject's defences, making them pliable and open to suggestions. 'Don't eat or drink anything else they give you, Joe. Only eat what I give you. You've got something in your system already.' Kieran was going to have to send an alert to Isaac and get Joe out of here. If he could take a sample of the water, so much the better, but maybe a blood test would provide the evidence of drugging? He should never have said there was little danger: that was his desire to stick in the school with Raven speaking, not his dispassionate assessment of the situation. If he had been thinking only about the mission he would have recommended handing this over to another team with more experience.

Joe leant forward, pupils dilated. 'Key, my man, you need to lighten up. The food here is great.'

Kieran was tempted to slap him to shake him out of his daze but that wouldn't help, not while the drug had a grip. 'Listen to me carefully, Joe: you're endangering us. You have to remember why we are here.'

Joe began to laugh. 'Oh yeah, I remember now! We're detectives, undercover—hey everyone, we're here to spy on you!' This caused a few heads to turn.

The boy from Year 9 joined in the laughter. 'Cool.'

Kieran had to act fast. 'We're not playing that game, Joe, remember? That was at the murder mystery weekend last term. This is the "How to Succeed" course.'

'Ah. I get you. Ssssh!' Joe tapped his nose but missed so scratched his cheek instead. 'I've a secret.'

Kieran brought his ear close to Joe's lips. 'What is it?'

'I feel drunk.'

'You're drugged, not drunk. You've got to snap out of it, Joe.' This conversation was going nowhere, just circling.

Joe frowned then swayed upright. 'Listen up, everyone, Kieran thinks they've drugged us.' He looked down at the empty cup. 'And do you know something, I think maybe he's right. He's one clever dude.'

Now he had done it. While the other students took the shout as all part of the hilarious breakfast they were having, Heath and Namrata zeroed in on Kieran. She got out her phone and made a call as Heath crossed to take Kieran's elbow.

'Kieran, I'm very disappointed that you're making trouble so early on. That's not the spirit at all.'

Joe beamed at Heath. 'Such a nice guy,' he said to no one in particular. 'Have you tried the orange? It's freshly squeezed.'

Two large men in dark suits came in to the room and went to Namrata for orders. She pointed to Kieran.

Heath smiled tolerantly at Joe. 'Yes, I have. Great isn't it? But I'm afraid we'll have to take another approach with your friend—a little adjustment to his programme.'

The suits crossed the floor to stand either side.

'Come with us, sir,' one said.

'I'd prefer to stay here, thanks.' Kieran weighed up his chances to getting out. Joe couldn't be relied on at the moment, nor could any of the other students. Not good.

'I wasn't giving you a choice, sir.' The heavy seized his wrist and pulled him up out of his chair.

Kieran lunged and broke the grip, Raven-style. He backed away. 'I'm resigning from the course.'

'Hey, no need for that! That's Key—he's a great guy,' said Joe. He tried to get up but Heath pushed his shoulders so he collapsed back into this chair.

'Resignation is not an option,' said Namrata, ignoring Joe's protests. 'Your guardian has signed you over to our care. Take him away, please.'

The two men charged, driving Kieran against the wall. He hadn't anticipated such a quick transition to violence. One had him in a headlock and the other cuffed his hands behind his back, before he could execute any further defensive moves.

'Get off me! Joe!'

Joe rubbed his hands over his face in confusion. 'What's going on? That don't look fair. That's my man, Kieran.' He got up to intervene.

'Don't worry, Joe, Kieran just needs to lie down for a little.' Heath guided Joe firmly back into his seat again. 'He's not feeling very well either. Are you feeling woozy?'

Joe nodded. 'Everything's so loud. I don't understand.'

Heath got out a syringe and put a shot directly in Joe's arm. 'You'll both be fine. You just need a rest.'

'Joe, don't listen to him. Get out of here!' Kieran was dragged backwards out of the room. His last glimpse of Joe was his friend slumped, head in his hands. He could only hope that Joe remembered his emergency alert when he came out of the drug-induced fog and got out of there. If not, things were looking grim for both of them.

Chapter·16

Raven was a little unnerved when her texts to Kieran over the next two days received no answer. Already haunted by the scenes in her dream, she messaged Joe instead.

No worries, Raven. All peachy. Joe had texted back.

That didn't sound like Joe. *Can you ask him to contact me?*

Sure. When I next see him.

I thought you were on the course together?

There was a long pause before she got a reply.

We're on separate schedules. Heath says he's fine but busy.

Who is Heath?

Great guy. Our tutor. He says I'll see Key later.

Westron was really quiet over those first few days after Kieran and Joe had left, lawns empty despite the June sunshine tempting everyone outside. The GCSE and A level students were still taking exams; the younger pupils busy with course work, only the lower sixth had free time on their hands. Taking advantage of the fact, students in her year were either on courses or work experience. Raven was the odd one out again as her week in the workplace at a local dance studio had mysteriously 'fallen through' according to Mrs Bain. And Raven was ·born yesterday. Her punishment for imagined wrongs continued. At Junior High she had suffered from an unearned reputation of being the local slut, here she was regarded as the thieving bitch. She just couldn't get the breaks, could she? Raven knew that she could do nothing about what other people thought about her, only control what she thought about herself. She deserved none of this and should ignore it as far as humanly possible. Sticking to that resolution, she spent the week keeping busy, altering a second-hand gown for prom and worrying about Kieran.

He didn't text. Neither did Joe. If this carried on, she would go over to the manor and demand to see them.

On Friday afternoon, her granddad caught her checking out her dress in the mirror.

'Well, well, well!' he exclaimed. 'Where did you get that?'

She swished the long skirt of the one shoulder, tight-fitting red taffeta dress. 'I got it second-hand on a charity website. Do you think it works?'

'It's beautiful, darling.' He hung his coat up on the peg just inside the door. 'Did you want a contribution to the cost?'

'It was only twenty-five pounds, thanks to a stain on the hem that I managed to cut out when I reduced the length. I had the money saved up so I'm good, thanks. Cup of tea?' She draped the dress over the back of a chair and moved to the kettle.

'Please. What about shoes and whatnot?' Granddad was so sweet when he tried to talk girl-clothes.

'I've got some that'll do. It's just a school dance.' Though she was ridiculously excited to be going with Kieran. She had imagined sweeping in on his arm so many times, smiling serenely at her enemies. 'So how was your day?'

He sat down with a sigh. 'Not good to be honest with you, Raven. I had another long talk with Mrs Bain today.'

'And?' Her hand shook as she poured milk into two mugs.

'She is adamant that you can't stay here after the end of term.'

'Oh, OK. I ... OK, we'll have to deal with that then.' Raven leant on the counter. What could she do? Rent a room near the sixth form college? Could they afford that? She'd need a part time job.

'So, naturally, I said that I would hand in my resignation.'

'You said what?' The kettle clicked off but she made no move to pour the water in the tea pot.

'My dear, there is no need to sound so scandalized. You are my priority. Where you live is where I will live. I'm sure I can get something to tide me over until I can draw my pension. It's only another year after all. Mrs Bain said something about seeing if she can swing early retirement for me. She's being very helpful.'

'Apart from the fact that she is completely unreasonable about me living here!'

'We can't bite the hand that feeds us, darling.'

'You can't, but frankly I feel like chewing it right off!' She threw a tea bag in the pot and drowned it in the boiled water. 'What harm do I do occupying the spare bedroom?'

'I think she feels it is the thin end of the wedge. If she lets you stay with me here, then other members of staff would ask for the same privileges and the confidentiality of the school would be compromised. A single story leaked to the press about one of the children here and the school's reputation would be ruined.'

Raven could hear the echo of Mrs Bain's words in her grandfather's explanation. 'That is totally mental. Do you believe her?'

He grimaced. 'To be honest, I don't think it makes a lot of sense. She is overreacting. It wasn't like this under the old head, Mr Grimshore, and we had some VIP children here then too. This new company who took over the school for their network have some very odd ideas. I won't be too sad to say goodbye.'

'But this cottage has been your home for decades.'

'No, love: you are my home. This is just bricks and mortar.'

Raven swallowed against the lump in her throat. She

poured the tea and put the cup down in front of her granddad. 'Thanks.'

He patted her hand as it rested on his shoulder. 'No need to thank me. You bring this old man so much happiness. I miss your mother—and your grandmother. With you here, I have both you and the memory of them to keep me company. They would have been very proud of you. Your mother was very like you, you know?'

He didn't often talk about Raven's mother; it was painfully sweet to hear the reminiscences. 'What? Impossible to live with?'

He laughed. 'No. She had very firm opinions. Your father did too. I bet the sparks flew when they butted heads.'

Yes they had, but her parents had always managed to find more they agreed on than put them at odds. Rather like her and Kieran. 'I'll get a job—help with the finances.'

'Get a job if you like but only so you can save for college. You, my dear, are going places and I will be cheering you on.'

She wrapped her arms around his neck and hugged. 'Thank you, Granddad.'

'You are so very welcome, Raven.'

Kieran could not remember the last time he had slept. Each time his eyes closed, he was shaken awake or had water splashed in his face by his monitor of the moment—Namrata, Heath, or a nameless third person who was on duty at night.

'You impress no one. You believe you're cleverer than us but you're wrong.'

He shook his head, trying to clear his thoughts. The recording had been playing constantly since he was dragged out of the breakfast room he didn't know how long ago. From the number of bathroom breaks and meals he estimated at least forty-eight hours had passed. The pretence at being civilized had continued in a fashion, in that he wasn't in a bare cell or anything as obviously barbaric as that, but a small seminar room. He had been handcuffed, wrists behind his back, to a chair at a desk facing a screen where his personalized reform programme played on a loop. Fifteen minutes long, it was a montage of clips of students in his year pointing out his defects. He knew every beat, every frame, and was sick of looking at himself through other people's lenses. As if he cared what others thought of him; that had never featured high on his list of important things to do. He needed no persuasion he was not likely to win any popularity contests. Tell him something he didn't know.

'Kieran is gorgeous to look at, until he opens his mouth,' said Toni to the interviewer.

'He needs to work on his social skills. He just doesn't get it, does he?' added Hedda. 'No attempt to fit in.'

For the first twenty-four hours of this, Kieran had distracted himself by translating their words into every language he knew. Next he had thought of various options for encoding it. Finally, he had become too tired to think at all and just endured.

His forehead hit the desk again and the door opened. Heath stepped in and clicked off the presentation. Baring Kieran's arm, he gave him another shot of the drug to ensure cooperation. With sickening care, he dabbed off the bead of blood and tapped cotton wool over the area. Kieran no longer resisted, as he had the bruises from his previous futile attempts when the two enforcers had held him down.

'Ready to talk, Kieran?'

'I'm ready to sleep.' The injection made his brain woozy but he refused to buckle. *I'm too bloody stubborn for that.*

'I'll let you sleep in a while. Just let's make some progress first.'

'How's Joe?'

'Do you want to see your friend?'

Warily, Kieran nodded, his head feeling too heavy for his neck.

'He wants to see you too. If you are good I'll arrange it. But you need to earn it.'

Stuff that. Kieran pressed his lips together. He knew what Heath wanted. He had been asking for the same thing over and over: he wanted Kieran to confess his 'faults' and admit that he wanted to be like everyone else. *The first step to straightening yourself out is to recognize that you have a problem and that we have the solutions.*

'I'm trying to help you, Kieran. You've taken a wrong turn and developed some very damaging personality traits.'

'Damaging personality traits? Take a good look at us both. I'm not the one brainwashing teenagers.'

Heath took a seat across the table from Kieran. 'You think this is brainwashing?'

'You call it reprogramming, but that's just another name for the same thing.' Kieran realized he probably shouldn't be so blunt but the drug had the effect of loosening his tongue, not to the extent it did on Joe, but enough so that he said more than he wanted. 'Thiopental, isn't it?'

Heath smiled. 'Oh very good, Kieran. You are the first one to identify our little helper.'

'It is illegal to administer drugs to an unwilling subject.' He licked his lips, desperate for a drink but that too came at a price.

'You forget, Colonel Hampton signed off on us using all reasonable and necessary means to achieve your transformation. Thiopental is very necessary.'

'My godfather would never agree if he knew.'

'But he did—he signed the paperwork. He thinks you need

reformation—and that's what we are doing here, though it might seem harsh to you at the moment.'

'Show me.'

'Now, now, Kieran, who is in charge here? I believe that would be me. You have to give me something first before I make any concessions.'

'Showing me the permission form is not a concession—it is a challenge to the legality of what you are doing.'

'So eloquent and so misguided. I'm sure we can make something of you if only you just bend a little.'

Kieran told Heath what he could do with himself in coarse Anglo-Saxon terms.

'Oh dear. Looks like you need to be in here a little longer. Such a shame as the others are enjoying our facilities—the tennis courts, pool, weights room, games room. Would you like to enjoy those? Be with your friends?'

'All I want to do is sleep.' And get out of here. Isaac surely had to be worried by now?

'And you can—when you admit you need our help.'

'I admit you are a sociopath.'

'Me?' Heath looked surprised by the charge.

'One who exhibits extreme antisocial attitudes, like, er, let me think, handcuffing a student to a desk maybe? Add to that a complete lack of conscience.'

'But I'm trying to help you. You are an intelligent young man by all accounts—surely you understand? We've found the subject must first be broken down to be rebuilt. It will be so much better in the long run.'

'Do you actually believe what you're saying?'

'You'll see, Kieran, once you submit to the process. Just think how pleased Colonel Hampton will be when he sees you navigate the tricky waters of society with the ease of an experienced pilot. Take your place in the UIS network and you'll never regret it, I promise you.'

Kieran had had enough. 'Look at me!'

Heath smiled sympathetically. 'I am, Kieran. You have my full attention.'

'I've been cuffed to this bloody chair for days. In what way is this reasonable or necessary?'

'Trust me: it gets results. I'll be back to see how you are getting along. A few more hours and then you might like to trade a concession for a chance to go to bed, eh?'

Heath clicked the presentation back on. Kieran set his features to blank. If he closed his eyes, they got physical with him so it was better to submerge his thoughts behind a neutral face.

'See you later, Kieran.'

He grunted, and raised his eyes to watch the screen. They had made a mistake, these manipulators. They had forgotten to edit their own material closely. Yep—there she was. That was the second of screen time that made the rest bearable, a brief glimpse of Raven passing through the back of the picture. How many times now? One hundred and eighty two.

He dropped his gaze. He'd have to wait another fifteen minutes to see her once more.

'Oh, it's you.' Raven came face to face with Gina in the yew walk. For once, Gina was alone, not surrounded by her usual gaggle of friends. 'Where's the coven?'

Gina bit her lip, a big white florist's box in her arms preventing her making a run for it. 'If you are referring to my friends, they are getting ready for the prom. I'm on my way to join them.'

Raven checked the time on her new phone. It was only four in the afternoon. 'Wow, you must have some major work to do on yourselves if you need three hours.'

223

'Hedda and Toni have brought in a masseuse, make-up artist, and hairdresser. Three hours will barely be enough. Now, if you will excuse me.'

Raven stepped aside, shoulder brushing against the spiders' webs netting the yew. 'Gina, why did you do it?'

Gina hesitated. 'Do what?'

'Lie about me. Do your best to make my life a misery. I was your friend once.'

'I didn't lie.' Gina spun round and glared at her. 'Stop saying that!'

'Oh give it a break: we both know you had a problem with stealing things before Easter. What about my ankle bracelet? You've still got that I think.'

Gina swallowed, eyes revealing her confusion. 'You . . . you gave it to me.'

'No, I did not. Think! You took it and I let you because I . . . I thought you just wanted to share my things as a friend.' It hurt to remember the fun times they had had together, the late night chats and laughing over stupid stuff. She missed having another girl on her side.

Gina's eyes darted up the path towards the castle. 'I'll give it back then.'

'I don't care about the ankle bracelet—I care that you ruined my reputation to protect your own. What the heck happened to you at the manor?' And what was happening to Kieran and Joe right now? It was days since she had heard from either of them. She was getting frantic with worry. If they turned up at the prom having had a great week, she was liable to slap them both silly.

The mention of the manor seemed to snap something back in place inside Gina. 'You are purposely trying to confuse me. I know the truth. You steal because you envy us. We are no longer friends so we shouldn't be talking. I have to go.'

Raven sighed. Her brief hope that she was getting through was dashed. 'OK, fine, rewrite history if you must. I don't think I can summon up the energy to care. You weren't much of a friend to me, were you?'

Gina's back stiffened but she marched on.

Raven's much shorter beauty regime saw her ready in an hour. She checked her reflection in the mirror, deciding that the colour really suited her. She was looking as good as she could look. The single shoulder cut made a necklace impossible so she accessorized with big gold hoop earrings and chunky bracelet—both cheap costume jewellery rather than the real thing. All she need now was her escort. Where was he?

Her granddad had been busy all day directing the outside caterers and making sure the band set up in the right place. He hurried back briefly half an hour before the event started to give her a gift. At least *he* remembered.

'By rights, this should be what your young man does but as he's been away all week and doesn't know the colour of your frock, I thought I'd treat you.' He handed her a wrist corsage of red roses tied with a black glittery ribbon to a gold bangle.

'Oh my gosh, that's just the finishing touch!' She slipped it on eagerly.

'And something for your hair.' He tucked a few spare blossoms into the upswept style she had pinned. 'What a beautiful young lady—the belle of the ball—and I'm not biased.'

She kissed his cheek. 'Of course you aren't, Granddad.'

'Have a lovely time. I'll keep an eye out for you.' He looked at his watch. 'Shouldn't your young man be here by now? The minibus came in from the manor an hour ago.'

It had? 'Maybe he's getting changed?'

'That'll be it. I'll see you over there then. The hall looks wonderful even if I do say so myself.'

Raven didn't know what to do while she waited—patience was never her strong suit. She'd paid her last visit to the bathroom, had all her things for the evening packed in her little clutch purse, and had her shoes on. She sat by the window, watching the path. No one approached the cottage.

She checked her phone for a message. Nothing. She tried ringing Kieran but the phone clicked to voicemail. She checked the time. The dinner was due to start any moment now.

'This is ridiculous!' she exploded. She couldn't sit here any longer—she had to go and haul Kieran out of his shower or whatever he was doing. He might have forgotten—become distracted by some super extreme Sudoku puzzle and lost track of the time. He was probably still sitting there in jeans and T-shirt. If Joe was taking one of the other girls, he might not be around to kick him out of their room.

Looping her skirt over her wrist, Raven strode out of the house, heading for the castle. The place looked like something out of a fairy tale, lights strung in the trees and over the door. Everywhere she looked she could see couples strolling on the paths and lawns, enjoying the warm evening. She spotted Joe easily. He was standing with Hedda on one arm and Toni on the other. Wonderful: her two favourite people guarding the boy with the answers. Raven was sure they would love to know she had been forgotten by her date. Swallowing her pride, she approached them just as the dinner gong sounded.

'Hi, Joe, have you seen Kieran?'

Joe took a moment to turn then smiled blearily at her. 'Raven isn't it?'

'Of course it's Raven. I'm looking for Kieran.'

Hedda tugged at Joe's arm. 'Come on, Joe, we have to go in.'

'Joe!' Raven's voice cracked with desperation. 'Please!'

'Raven, the crow. Just a moment, Hedda.' Joe swayed. 'No, no. Friend. Not crow. That's the others.'

A new suspicion crossed Raven's mind. 'Are you drunk?'

Joe shook his head. 'No, I'm just a little tired right now. Kinda floating. Stuff going round and round in my head, you know? Kieran, you say?'

'Yes, Kieran. Your best friend.'

'He's my date,' said Toni quickly. 'I'm meeting him inside. He just went to get me a drink.'

'Is this true?' Raven couldn't believe it, but why lie in front of Joe when it could so easily be proved wrong?

Joe frowned. 'Has there been a mix up? I thought Key was taking Raven.'

'Oh no, he changed his mind.' Toni held out a white rose corsage on her wrist that matched her short white dress. 'Look: he gave me this.'

'I don't believe you.' Raven pushed past Toni determined to find Kieran. The corsage was a step too far. Until that point she just might have believed that Kieran had been manoeuvred into taking another girl to the prom and standing her up, but she had noticed that Hedda was wearing a similar corsage arrangement and she doubted very much Kieran would have thought of it. She would bet her bottom dollar that these had also come with the prom makeover crew; they'd probably been in the box Gina had been carrying. Toni was just trying to hurt her feelings—not a difficult task, she had to admit.

'Raven?' Joe called.

She swung round.

He appeared to be having a moment of clarity. 'I don't think he's here.'

'What?'

Joe dropped Hedda's arm and sank down on a stone step. 'I'm not feeling great. I'm confused. He said something to me last time we met but . . . '

Hedda hauled Joe back to his feet. 'C'mon Joe. You need to get inside. You weren't ready to come back so soon. You've hardly started the treatment—you need more help. When I was on the course I remember feeling happy and relaxed in the first week, not like this.'

'Joe, where's Kieran?'

'Ignore her—she's just white noise, remember? Block her out.' Hedda managed to get Joe to stumble a few steps.

'Minute. Something wrong. Yeah.' A memory flickered across his face. 'No wait, what . . . he's not good, Raven.'

'That's enough, Joe. You've had too much to drink.'

Hard to do as alcohol was banned. 'Let him speak, Hedda.'

'He's said enough. Joe, you're going inside.'

'Get away from him.' Raven tugged Hedda's arm, squashing her corsage.

Hedda swung her purse at Raven. 'Leave him alone. Why are you always making trouble?'

'There will be if you don't let him talk to me!'

'Is there a problem here, ladies?' Mrs Bain arrived in time to see Raven snatch Hedda's evening bag and throw it in the bushes.

'You've got to do something about her, Mrs Bain. She's out of control!' Hedda pointed an accusing finger at Raven. 'She just stole my bag!'

'I only want to speak with Joe!' said Raven.

'Joe's not feeling well. He doesn't know what he's saying.' Hedda circled Joe's waist. 'Hey, Joe, lean on me. We understand you're not feeling yourself.'

'Not myself,' echoed Joe.

'Take Mr Masters inside, Hedda.'

Toni ducked under Joe's other arm and helped Hedda lead him in. Raven tried to follow.

'Oh no, you don't.' Mrs Bain stood in her path.

'But I have a ticket.'

'And I have just rescinded that ticket. You are not to set foot inside.'

If Raven thought she could get away with tackling the head teacher, she would have been delighted to give it a go. 'I have a date.'

'With whom? I'll tell him you are unable to come.'

'Kieran Storm.'

'That's all right then. Mr Storm is unwell. He isn't here.'

'Toni said he was.' Raven wanted to scream. She tried to see past Mrs Bain but she couldn't spot Kieran anywhere in the crowds gathering to watch their confrontation.

'She was mistaken.'

'And Joe's "unwell" too. Don't you find that strange?'

'There must be something going around the manor.'

Raven wondered if she could sprint past the head teacher and go ask Joe a few more questions. She tensed, ready to make a try.

Mrs Bain blocked the path. 'Don't even think of it. Go back to the cottage and pack your bags. I don't want to see you on my school premises ever again, Miss Stone. Your behaviour is a disgrace—picking a fight with other girls, stealing from them, bag snatching. You were a poor bet when I graciously took you on after your last school threw you out.' That wasn't how it had gone down but Mrs Bain was clearly OK with rewriting history too. 'You're lucky I'm not calling the police.'

Raven folded her arms to stop her from shivering. 'I wish you would.'

'Would what?'

'Call the police. I think something really sick is going on and you know what it is.'

'You have until tomorrow morning to get off Westron land. I'll tell your grandfather he must find somewhere else for you immediately.'

'You're all heart, Mrs Bain. I'm sure the local paper would love to hear about this. I think I'll send them a photo—the dress,' she picked up the skirt, 'that'd make a good image. Old hag headmistress chucks out orphan for trying to go to the ball. I can see them running with that.'

Mrs Bain took a step towards her and grabbed her upper arm. 'If you so much as breathe a word to anyone, then I will make it my priority to destroy both you and your grandfather. He can kiss goodbye to his pension and you your future in any place of education. All I have to do is share your school record and you'd be sunk—drugs, sexual misconduct, thieving—yes, I think that covers it.'

Raven curled her nails into her palms. 'You can't do that. None of it's true.'

'Just watch me. Now get out of here before I call my security team.' Mrs Bain pointed Raven firmly towards the cottage. 'I don't want to see either you or that trashy red dress again.'

Chapter · 17

Raven put the corsage in the fridge to preserve the roses, stripped off the red dress and put it back on the hanger. It hadn't been trashy; it had been fabulous. But without Kieran to see her in it, what was the point? Needing comfort clothes, she pulled on a pair of black leggings and a long jumper. Maybe Mrs Bain was doing her a favour stopping her going to the prom? She would have been a wallflower all evening without her date. Not that stupid things like that mattered when Joe was acting really weird and Kieran was a no show.

OK, Raven, what now? She paced the kitchen, unable to decide the most effective course of action. She had her marching orders but she didn't care about that. Mrs Bain could kick her out tomorrow, broadcast the lies about her, but tonight, Raven had to get to the bottom of what had happened to Kieran. Her future didn't matter if his was in jeopardy. Joe was incoherent and barricaded in by her enemies; Kieran wasn't answering any texts or calls. That left the mysterious Isaac. Kieran had given her instructions to phone him only in an emergency. He had meant if she was in trouble, but Raven was more than happy to reinterpret the orders to apply to the situation she now faced.

She took out her phone and selected the contact. Her thumb hovered. It felt strange calling a complete stranger, but still . . . She pressed the green button.

'Hampton here. Who is this?'

'Is that Isaac?' Feeling really awkward, Raven stirred the crumbs by the toaster that sat on the kitchen counter.

'Isaac Hampton, yes. Who is this and how did you get my number?'

'Mr Hampton, my name is Raven Stone.'

'Let me guess: Kieran gave you my mobile number.'

'Yes.'

She thought she heard him sigh. 'What can I do for you, Miss Stone?'

'You are some kind of guardian to Kieran, is that right? His godfather.'

'Correct, but I'm afraid I can't share any personal details about him if that is why you are calling.'

'No, no, it's just that I'm really worried about him—and Joe.'

'Why would that be? I've heard from Joe regularly this week. He and Kieran have been on a course. I thought you would know that, even if Kieran has cut contact with you since you and he split up.'

'Yes but . . . but we didn't really split for long. It's kinda confusing but we were in touch at the beginning of the week—in touch a lot. You know, texting, that sort of thing.'

'He didn't end his relationship with you?' Isaac's tone was ice.

'We made up. He was sending me texts then nothing. And Joe's not OK either. You wouldn't say he was if you'd seen him tonight, sir. Joe's really weird. It's like he's drunk or ill.'

'He's at Westron?'

'Yes, he's come back for the prom. And Kieran was supposed to be here too but he didn't show up. He didn't send word and I was his date.'

'I see.' She could hear a pen tapping in the background. No prizes for guessing the Isaac really didn't approve of her.

'Are you near Joe at the moment, Miss Stone, so I can have a word?' Clearly he didn't trust her.

'I'm afraid not. I've been chucked off school premises. Mrs Bain is keeping me away from the other students. Look, sir, I don't know what Joe told you but I think he hasn't seen Kieran for days. He was upset when I pressed him for details and seemed to remember something and he said Kieran was "not good".'

'Thank you, Miss Stone. You've been really helpful.'

Raven clenched her fist on the counter. 'Is that it? Aren't you going to do something? I think this situation's out of control.'

'I hear you.'

'But you're not listening. Can't you understand? I'm trying to tell you I think Kieran might be in danger. I know there's some arrangement between you—some job he's doing for you. It's gone wrong and I'm worried.'

'Contrary to your assertion, I do understand.' His voice was like a whip crack warning her she had gone too far with the sass. 'But your part in this is over. I'll take it from here.'

'With respect, sir, screw that. I'm going over to the manor and demand to see Kieran. I can't go to bed trusting that you'll fix it. I don't even know you and it was you who sent him on that course.'

She was certain he sighed this time. 'You're committed to this course of action, are you?'

'Yes. I'm heading out right now. I was just phoning you as a courtesy.'

'And how are you going to get there?'

'Bike.'

'Motorbike?'

'No, bicycle.' She felt foolish announcing she was going off on her rescue mission under pedal power. So lame, but she was hardly James Bond.

'Then all I ask is that you wait for me by the entrance to

233

the manor. I can be there in forty-five minutes. Is that accept-able to you?'

'You're close by?'

'I have a helicopter at my disposal.'

She gave a hollow laugh. 'Of course you do.'

'I'll see you in forty-five minutes. Do not go in on your own. I'll call when I land. I'll put down nearby and make my way from there. Do you give me your word you will follow my instructions?'

Raven frowned. 'And if I don't?'

'I'll tell Mrs Bain what you are planning to do. I'd prefer to know that you are out of the way, not running blind into danger, even if it's her doing the restraining.'

'Mr Hampton, you are a pain in the butt.'

'If we're working together, it's Isaac. Or Colonel Hampton if you prefer.'

She was reserving judgement about how friendly she was going to be towards him until she met him. 'I give my word, Colonel Hampton.'

'Thank you. Wear black.' He ended the call.

What kind of man has a helicopter? A useful one. Raven dug out a black denim jacket from the back of her wardrobe. Finding a set of lights for her bike, she started the long ride to the manor. It was much closer as the crow flies but she had to go round by the roads, not much fun in the long June twilight. The slog up Windmill Hill gave her plenty of op-portunity to wonder if she was doing the right thing. She felt a bit more positive as she freewheeled down the other side. Kieran seemed to trust Isaac implicitly. She just had to hope this wasn't another trap and that Isaac wasn't involved in the madness going on at the manor and Westron.

Pedalling the last mile to the entrance, Raven thought how different she had imagined this evening was going to be. She had had dreams of whirling around the dance floor

234

with Kieran, amazing all those who despised her with their elegance. No chance of that now.

By the gates to the manor, Raven stashed her bike under a bush just off the verge. She sat down to wait, watching the road. There was very little traffic. No one came or went to the manor and the other cars sped by without noticing her. She checked the time. Thirty-five minutes had passed since the call. She thought she had heard the throb of a helicopter a few minutes ago but had seen nothing overhead. Her impulsive side was shouting at her to get going, stop hanging around, and go find Kieran. Only the fact that she had given her word kept her seated.

The touch on her shoulder made her almost jump out of her skin.

'Miss Stone?' Isaac was standing a few feet behind her. He had come out of the darkness without a sound. 'Sorry to startle you.'

Raven got up and brushed off the seat of her leggings. 'No you're not.' She held out her hand. 'I imagine you make a habit of it.'

'Tough cookie, aren't you?' He shook her hand with a firm grip.

'Try to be.'

'Military father?'

How did he know that? 'And one iron lady of a mother.'

He smiled at that. 'OK. Let's do this.' He pulled on a pair of black gloves.

'Do what?'

'I thought you'd already decided to break in.'

'But with you as Kieran's godfather, can't we just walk up and knock?'

'I agree with your analysis that something sinister's happening. If we declare our hand like that, I believe we won't get to see him. I am not minded to ask.'

'I'm with you there.'

'The manor has surveillance but there're gaps we can use. We're going in over the fence a hundred metres that way and then I want you to follow me closely, doing everything I do.' He began walking away from the gates.

'How do you know this?'

'We've studied this place for some time.'

'We?'

'My team. Kieran and Joe are inside because we believe there is something criminal happening here. They were collecting evidence for me.'

'I was right then. You send your own boys to do your dirty work?' She was rapidly deciding she didn't like this man very much at all. 'Why not do it yourself?'

'It's their job, Miss Stone. They work for me. There was not supposed to be any significant danger involved in this task.'

'Got that wrong, didn't you?'

'I completely agree with you, Miss Stone. I'll apologize to my boys when I've got them back safe and sound—and after Kieran explains why he disobeyed his orders concerning you.'

'What orders?'

'You're not supposed to be part of this. He's in deep trouble for that. I hope we will find him OK so I can haul him before a disciplinary board and tell him that.'

'Good luck telling Kieran anything he doesn't want to hear. He's got a wide streak of stubborn.'

'Noticed, have you? Here we are.' Isaac stopped by the wall topped with barbed wire. 'I'll go first then pull you up.'

She watched as he scaled the wall and snipped the wire with cutters. He was scarily prepared, which made her question just what kind of organization he represented. Government? Military? He had to be one of the good guys, didn't he?

'Ready?' Isaac held out his hand.

She took a run and leapt, catching him around the wrist. He used her momentum to pull her up. They both then jumped down, landing catlike on the woodland floor below.

'Very good,' he murmured. 'Now keep low and follow me. No sound sensors but nearer the building, no talking. If you need to stop, just tug the back of my jacket. Ready?'

Raven found it odd how easily she fell into his plan. He had a manner to him that instilled confidence, like a good platoon leader. You didn't have to like him; you just had to follow. 'Lead the way.'

Kieran woke with a start in a completely dark space. Where was he? The memory trickled back—he had finally been allowed back to his bedroom at the manor, despite not giving an inch on any of the demands they had made of him. There were blackout curtains at the window and they had been pulled ever since he had been brought back to his bed. Deprived of sunlight, he had no way of telling how much time had passed. Groggily, he stumbled to his feet and groped his way to the bathroom. His personal effects had been taken, so he couldn't even brush his teeth. He settled for splashing water on his face.

The door opened and Namrata came in with the two enforcers. There had to be an infrared camera somewhere in the room, or a motion sensor. He never got more than a few seconds to himself.

'Feeling better, Kieran?'

He rubbed his face in the towel, saying nothing.

'If you are feeling more alert, perhaps you'd like to explain this?' She held up the drug testing kit that had been in his wash bag.

He ignored her, pulling on a clean T-shirt, the same one he

had lent Raven and was now his favourite. He liked to think the fabric still kept a little of her scent, a kind of force field against the bad guys. He could guess where the questions were leading—to another round of personality reform.

'You see, finding this made us wonder if you came here in good faith. Frankly, we have been very disappointed with you so far. You've not shown any sign of improvement or willingness to listen to what we have to offer. Instead, you have been suspicious from the start. Why did you feel the need to test what we were giving you?'

A good question. Where to start? Because they were a bunch of sadists? Yeah, that's what he'd start with if he was going to reply, which he wasn't.

'Everything we are giving you is there to help you. With your stubbornness, you are showing no loyalty to your friends, your school or even the wishes of your guardian.'

But Isaac would be proud of him. Encouraged by that thought, Kieran walked towards the window. They were on the third floor but he might be able to pull the blackout curtains down at least and see what time of day it was.

'Please keep away from the window, Kieran. You have not earned the right to look out.'

He turned. 'And when since did looking out of a window constitute a privilege?'

'Since I said.'

Heath entered the room. 'How's he doing?'

'Intractable,' she said succinctly.

'Did he explain the kit?'

'Not yet.'

'I like chemistry. Never go anywhere without it.' Kieran glanced round the room for a weapon. His head was clearing. They hadn't given him an injection for a while. He might not get a better chance.

'What's your recommendation, Namrata?' asked Heath.

'You know, I really don't think we're going to make any headway with this one. I fear we're wasting our time.'

Kieran decided the bedside light had a fairly hefty base. It could take out one of the enforcers if his throwing arm wasn't out. The other might be blinded by the potpourri—it looked gritty and dusty.

'Shall we put him with the other two?'

Kieran's hand stopped moving towards the lamp. This might be a chance to find the missing students. He had begun to fear the two kids might have been taken out of the country, or worse, but it sounded like they were here somewhere.

'Yes, I think so. Let us see if together they can make the right decision.'

'You could just wash your hands of us. Let us go.' Kieran straightened up. 'Their parents and my godfather will want to see us. You can't keep us hidden permanently.'

'We have no intention of doing that.' Heath gestured to the enforcers. 'Take this boy to join our guests in the basement.'

'Why don't you just call it a cell?'

Heath ignored his comment. 'I'm sorry we couldn't help you, Kieran. Our methods rarely fail and I apologize that we let you down.'

Kieran would have found Heath's version of what was happening here fascinating if he had the luxury to reflect on it in safety. Taking careful note of escape routes, he let the two men escort him downstairs.

Isaac led Raven without any hesitation through the woodland, across the nine-hole golf course, right up to the windows of one wing of the manor. She fell into step with him, learning to duck when he did, step around hazards, or slide under fences. They approached the house itself by going down on their stomachs and wriggling through the shrubbery. The last time she had seen this kind of manoeuvre it had been army recruits under cargo netting, so she was veering towards thinking his organization was military. They took people at seventeen, didn't they, so that made sense. The jarring note was that she didn't see Kieran attracted to a life in khaki. At the edge of the flower bed, Isaac motioned her to come up alongside him. The curtains were open and they could see a cleaner vacuuming the library while a woman placed flower arrangements on the tables between the sofas and armchairs. No sign of panic. No hint that anything out of the ordinary was happening inside.

Raven tapped Isaac on the shoulder, eager to move on. He held up a hand, a 'just wait' signal. His patience was rewarded when two dark-suited men walked in and took seats in the chairs either side of the fire. A waiter came in and put two beers on the side tables and left, beckoning the cleaner to follow him. The men kicked back and relaxed, taking swigs straight from the bottles. Who were they? They looked like club bouncers, not participants in a training course. Then one took off his jacket, revealing a shoulder holster for a gun. So that answered that question. They were looking at the security detail. But weren't there all sorts of permits needed for that kind of thing in England? Since leaving America, Raven had rarely seen an armed man, so why here in the middle of the countryside where the only threatening things were the occasional bull in a field or an over-enthusiastic farm dog?

Having seen enough from this angle, Isaac beckoned her to follow him. He slipped back deeper into the bushes and headed for the far end of the manor to the kitchen entrance. Once on the other side of the shrubs, he got back on his feet and started running. Raven had to work hard, her shorter legs making it difficult to keep up, but she had the feeling he would leave her behind if he felt she were a weak link. His next stopping place was between two huge bins. The cloying smell of rotten food hit. Raven put her hand over her nose, breathing through her mouth.

Isaac leant to her ear. 'OK, here's the plan. I'm going to slip in through the door there and signal if it's an all-clear. Wait here until I give the sign.'

'What's the signal?'

'I'll come to the entrance. As soon as you see me, run across this courtyard as quickly as possible. This part is on the CCTV so it's vital you do it fast. You'll only be in sight of the camera for a second so unless you're really unlucky, no one is likely to notice. Don't be surprised when the lights come on—they're motion activated—but I imagine these bins are a favourite with the local foxes so that won't be seen as unusual. Know what you have to do?'

'Wait here then act like a fox.'

Isaac smiled. 'Exactly.'

'And if you don't come back?'

'Run—and call this number. I'll put it in your phone now.' He took her handset and quickly entered the details. 'It's under Yoda.'

'OK. Run and ring, my young apprentice. I've got that.'

He watched to see she put the phone away. 'Good. You are doing well. Just one question.'

'Hmm?'

'Did you know you have roses in your hair?' He gave her a wink and slid out of their hiding spot.

Raven touched the back of her head and realized she had forgotten about her prom hairdo and make-up. He must have thought her strangely overdressed for a break-in.

Even though Raven was watching him, she still found it hard to track his movements. Isaac had a way of blending into the background, using every shadow to his advantage. He was inside, door closed, before she had taken six breaths.

OK, Raven: that's how you do it when your turn comes. She just wished he had picked a less stomach churning place to wait. Inspiration struck. She plucked one of the scented roses from her hair and put it to her nose: an unexpected bonus of an otherwise wasted prom outfit.

Kieran was marched past the wine racks then pushed inside an underground room lit by a weak bulb. From the lingering smell of carbolic soap, he deduced it had once been a laundry, now converted to a dormitory for the manor's less pliable guests. The two people already inside stood up as he entered, backing together against a wall. They only relaxed when the door closed, leaving just Kieran.

The boy glanced up at the light, his scalp shining through his shaved dark hair. When the bulb remained lit, he gave his companion a brief smile. 'Good. I thought for sure they'd turn it out to piss us off.' He waved sardonically to Kieran. 'Hi, I'm Johnny Minter. I can guess why you're here. Your mini-break taken a turn for the worse?'

'You could say that. Kieran Storm. And you must be Siobhan?'

The girl, a nervous-looking brunette, nodded and moved closer to Johnny. 'See,' she whispered, 'our absence has been noticed. I told you it was only a matter of time.'

Johnny waved to the bunk beds set up around the room. 'Take your pick. That one's mine and Siobhan's is over there. Best find it before lights out. Our luxurious en suite is through that door there.'

Kieran chose the one nearest the door, best placed to protect the other two but also affording the greatest chance of escape. He sat down on it, studying the walls for signs of cameras or listening devices.

'Yeah, the room's wired,' said Johnny. He slid to the floor, putting his arm around Siobhan's shoulders as she sat beside him.

'How long you been here?'

'Weeks. First it was just me, and then they added Siobhan. Now you.'

'Do you get out?'

'Oh yeah. We get taken out for exercise and re-education sessions but we're not allowed to see anyone else. Not sure why they let us stay together.'

'They want one of us to crack and persuade the other to follow,' Siobhan said softly.

'But I'm a West Ham supporter—can't get more bloody minded than one of those suffering the torment of relegation and promotion every effing season. And Siobhan here is Irish—need I say more.' He gave her an approving grin. 'Up the Rebels, yeah? What about you?'

Kieran shrugged. 'There was just something about me that rubbed Namrata up the wrong way. They gave up on me after about a week.'

Johnny whistled. 'Cool. You get the record. It took at least a month before they decided I wasn't going to break. She's a cow, isn't she? But I think Heath is worse as he still pretends to be our friend.'

The light flicked out.

'Thanks, Heath. We love you too!' shouted Johnny.

'I think they're just tired of us now—wish we'd crumble so they could get on with business.' Siobhan sounded resigned.

'Don't put it like that—like we owe them anything. We are

beating their system—the more fed up with us they are, the better. Eventually they'll just wash their hands of us and let us go.'

Looking at these two dropouts and comparing them to the ones who had returned to Westron, the last element of the mystery fell into place. 'They're forming disciples, aren't they?' This wasn't just about straightening out bad behaviour; it was crafting future members of the network, more finely tuned to the needs of the trustees and the others in the network. The parents were useful in their own way but a new cadre of supporters, well trained, loyal only to other UIS graduates, was being propagated for planting in international business and government. That's why no one was acting like they were being forced: they were all too happy join the gang, being part of the 'in' and not the 'out' crowd.

'That makes us heretics in their cult of the beautiful people,' said Johnny happily.

As Kieran's eyes adjusted he realized there was a faint light in the bathroom. 'What's that?'

'Old laundry chute. Connects to the linen room above but it's barred. This place is a health and safety nightmare.'

Siobhan snorted. 'Like that's their first consideration. Hi, Mr Inspector, we're worried about the fire escapes in our torture chambers.'

'So how do you pass the time?' Kieran tested the bed frame. It was bolted to the floor.

'Talking mostly. I think I've bored Siobhan with every memory of my fairly depressing childhood.'

'You aren't boring, Johnny.'

'She knows lots of songs, so that's been good.'

'Do they drug you?' asked Kieran. It was odd to have a clear head again after a week of fog.

'Nah, gave up on that after the first two weeks. I think they don't quite know what to do with us. The others changed really quickly—like they were ready to see the error of their ways and hurry into the fold of being good little boys and girls. You should've seen them in their confession sessions, all crying to be let into the clique of perfect people. But I didn't. I blew through the first week in a rage—the drug just made me really foul mouthed. I cursed my father every way I could imagine for not thinking me good enough.'

Kieran found that very interesting. He had read that the most resistant minds to brainwashing often had some passion or belief that acted as a counterweight to the pressure to conform. 'What didn't your father like about you?'

Johnny laughed. 'You should ask "what did he like?". That would be the quicker conversation. I've not changed a bit. His main gripe was my politics. He found out I was a member of an activist environmental group and he's an oil man. Big embarrassment if I chained myself to one of his drilling platforms in the Arctic as I was planning. And that's where I'm heading the moment I get out of this place—after I've launched my court case against them of course. False imprisonment and torture—and that's just the start. I'm going to use my damages setting up an eco-camp outside my dad's office.'

'Johnny spends a lot of time devising his brief for his barrister.' Siobhan's tone was warm but gently teasing.

'What about you, Siobhan? Why have you stuck it out?' asked Kieran.

'I guess it's because there's a part of me that they can't touch no matter what they do to me.'

'She's a saint, this one. I've never met a proper Christian before and I have to say I'm impressed. She even prays for me, which is kind because I'm not on speaking terms with any fathers, including the one on a cloud.'

'He isn't on a cloud, Johnny. I wish you'd stop with the Victorian stereotypes.'

'She says a lot of things like that but she knows I'm only pulling her saintly leg.' Johnny gave an affectionate chuckle.

'So why have you been put on the course?' asked Kieran. He couldn't imagine why any parent would complain about a well behaved, devout daughter.

'I want to train as a medical missionary—midwifery.'

'What could possibly be wrong with that?'

'My parents are raving atheists and think I should aim either to marry a rich man or enter the family business. They think my faith is all pie in the sky when you die.'

'What's the family business?'

'Military supplies.'

'Her dad's Ireland's best-known gun runner. Name a nasty conflict anywhere on the globe and Mr Green will be there with his kit to make it worse. What about you, Kieran? How did you manage to get kicked down here so quickly?'

Bearing in mind they were being monitored, Kieran couldn't explain his real role at the manor. He would have liked to give them hope that they would soon be released when the YDA turned up to bust the operation. 'I think I pushed a few red buttons. I like chemistry so I had a look at those pills they were giving us—vitamins by the way, the drug was in soluble form the first night, injections after that. Thiopental. Supposed to make us cooperate. But I didn't agree with their description of what was wrong with me. Said the wrong thing a few too many times. Told them they were trying to brainwash us—which is an abuse of our human rights.'

'Good for you. Welcome to the reject zone.'

'Thanks. Proud to be here. It's the best accolade they could give me.'

Chapter 18

Time crawled while waiting. Pins and needles had set in from holding still. Raven was beginning to think that something had gone wrong. She had almost screamed when a cat walked across the courtyard, triggering the lights. The comforting thing was that there had been no response from any security guards. Isaac had been right: the automatic lights no longer meant an intruder to those inside.

A shadow appeared in the entrance and beckoned. Finally: Isaac had come back for her. Trying to emulate his way of moving, she hurried across the paving, inside at the same moment the lamp flicked on. The floodlight went off again immediately. She guessed it was better not to say anything. Doors would be monitored so they had to get out of the danger zone as quickly as possible. Isaac moved down the corridor towards the kitchens and ducked inside below the counter level. The room was empty, surfaces cleaned for the night, light from the blue fluorescent bulb over the larder bathing the steel tops in fake moon-glow. A tap dripped with a little thud into the deep sink by the industrial washer.

'We're safe to talk,' Isaac said, getting out his phone and texting in a report. 'I've checked the lower floors and aside from the two guys we saw the place seems quiet. I think any other security operatives must have gone with the course participants to the prom. What time does that end?'

Sitting with her knees hugged to her chest, Raven gripped her ankles. 'Eleven.'

'So Joe should be back by half past. I want to extract both cleanly, without anyone noticing, OK?'

'I was hoping you were going to kick butts and take names.'

He smiled and tucked the phone back in his jacket. 'That comes later, when my boys are safe.'

'What do you think goes on here?'

Isaac studied her face. Raven got the impression he was weighing her every reaction. 'Raven, Kieran has been worried all the way through that if you know too much you'll be put at risk.'

Nice to know there was a good reason for his secrets, but that had to stop. 'Colonel Hampton . . .'

'Isaac. I'm always on first name terms with people I take burgling.'

It was her turn to smile. 'OK, Isaac, it is. I've just broken in to a private house and intend to do much more than that. Do you really believe a bit of information is going to put me at any more risk?'

'Good point. OK, here's what we think is going on. The school is part of a network of favour-exchange—corruption to you and me. The parents are first lured in by the guys here getting hold of their kids, setting them up and persuading the parents it is better to cooperate, do the odd favour or three, than have their children's lives ruined. In return, the guys here "straighten" the kids out, just as the parents would prefer, adding gratitude to arm twisting. Kieran's theory is that they are using some heavy duty pressure to brainwash the kids here to parental specifications, squashing rebellion and normal teenage behaviour into approved moulds.'

'Well, that explains Gina. What about Joe?'

'It sounds like they are using inhibition-reducing drugs to break down their victims in the initial period of their retraining. It can't have gone far with Joe yet as he's only been here five days. I'm hoping that under that haze you saw, the drip feed of misinformation won't have taken root. Both boys were under strict instructions not to take anything like that, but they must've been tricked.'

She believed him but it seemed so bizarre—to use powerful drugs on perfectly well young people. Not bizarre—criminal. 'I think you're right that it's not working that well on Joe yet.'

'How do you know that?'

'He's still being nice to me. Everyone else who graduated from this course comes back thinking I'm the spawn of the devil.'

He grinned at the sarcasm in her tone. 'Ah, yes, brainwashers need an enemy to make their subjects scared and group-focused—to create what's called a bunker mentality.'

'But me? What threat do I pose?'

'It's you for the moment but there'll have been others before you.'

She realized he was right. A couple of other scholarship students in the years above her had dropped out early, making no secret of how they disliked the snobbery in the school.

'It's what you represent, rather than you yourself. Confidence, sassy, self-made . . . '

'Don't forget poor and blue-collar.'

'That too. You and the others in your position have been used to make these insecure rich kids fear that they will be found out as inadequate as they are all about inherited privilege and unearned wealth.'

'That's stupid.'

'I know, but people have been brainwashed to believe far more ridiculous things, like the Heaven's Gate community who thought they were going to be boarding a spaceship trailing the Hale-Bopp comet.'

'What happened?'

'It was in 1997; thirty-eight people and their guru killed themselves to catch a lift.'

Raven found it hard to credit that anyone could be that misguided. 'Were they crazy?'

'Absolutely—but only because they had fallen for the brainwashing techniques of a madman. Real life is weirder than anything you'll read in fiction. Brains do buckle under the wrong pressures. Given enough time, most people can be made to believe black is white.'

She rubbed her shins. 'Do you think Kieran's OK? He won't have changed?'

'The science suggests people with ingrained beliefs resist the best. Kieran believes strongly in logic and reason. I'd like to see the man who could make him do anything that doesn't satisfy those measures.'

Yet he'd learnt to dance for her, hadn't he? That hadn't been rational.

A crunch of gravel outside broke the quiet. 'That's the minibus parking up out the back. They must've dropped the students at the front already. We'll give them a few minutes to clear the foyer, then we'll go in search of the boys. Joe told me the name of their rooms—Cavalier and Pagoda, on the first and second floor respectively. We'll fetch Joe first, then go up and get Kieran.'

'What if the boys haven't got the evidence you need to shut this place down?'

'Raven, I'm not leaving them here. Their safety comes first.'

It was a huge relief to hear they weren't to be sacrificed for the job they were doing. 'How are we getting them out?'

'I've got a team assembling at the perimeter. If we get the boys that far, then my men will take over. I can bring the team in if there's an emergency, but I want to try this first, going under the radar. The safety of the other young people has to be considered. Armed men storming the place might produce casualties. I don't want to risk the innocent.'

It had to be asked. 'Who are you, Isaac?'

He grinned. 'I'm on the side of the angels, Raven.'

She sincerely hoped so or she was screwed.

The light flicked on, slowly illuminating. Ironic that Heath and Co. had put a power-saving bulb in their cell: torment teenagers and save the environment at the same time. Kieran readied himself, noticing that the other two did so, slipping out of their beds and standing with their backs to the wall.

The door opened and Heath strode in, accompanied by Mrs Bain and the Russian trustee, Kolnikov. That wasn't good. He had expected these two to keep their distance from the actual dirty work at the manor.

Mrs Bain pointed at Kieran. 'There he is.'

Kolnikov rolled on the balls of his feet, bar-room brawler stance. 'What is Colonel Hampton to you?'

'He's my godfather.' Kieran licked his lips, remembering he hadn't had anything to drink for quite some time. He was trying not to give in to fear that help would not arrive in time.

'How did you meet him?'

'At a maths competition.' Truth.

'What do you do for him?'

'I don't do anything. He's sponsoring my education.'

Kolnikov closed the distance and used his muscular hand to pin Kieran to the wall by the neck. They stood eye to eye as the Russian examined his face. 'He's lying. He knows more than he's saying.' He dropped his grip and stepped back.

Mrs Bain folded her arms, her fingers playing an anxious tune on her sleeves. 'I'm so sorry, sir. The boy was vetted, as all my students are. His sponsor, Hampton, came up clean.'

251

'Of course he did. So would I if you did the same process on me. It is only because I called in a favour that I know all is not as it seems.'

'How did you find out?'

Kieran did not like the fact that they were discussing this freely in front of them. It meant they didn't think it mattered what the three of them heard.

Kolnikov took a cigar out of a pocket and lit up. 'Our new recruit, the American Defence attaché, Carr, was negotiating in favour of my company in the Ministry of Defence today.' He blew a plume of smoke in Kieran's face. 'I'd asked him to find out how useful Hampton might be to that contract; instead, being well trusted by the Brits, he discovered that Hampton was not even a civil servant.'

'What is he?'

'My contact didn't know. Said it smelt like special ops to him but no one was saying any more.'

'Do you think this boy's part of it, or is it just a coincidence?'

Kolnikov turned away, dismissing Kieran. 'I have been successful in my career taking the attitude that there is no such thing as coincidence.'

'Do you recommend we move to Plan Beta?'

Kolnikov stubbed out the cigar on Kieran's bedpost. 'That is exactly why we put you in charge, Meryl. You always see one step ahead. Yes. We close down this branch of the operation until we've dealt with Hampton.'

'But sir, we've guests already in the system. We've only done the first of two weeks!' Heath protested.

Kolnikov raised an eyebrow and Heath shut up. 'They will have to be seen to at a later date. You will be redeployed to Los Angeles. The programme there is going well. Make the arrangements, Meryl.'

'Of course, sir. What do we do about these three and the other boy?'

Kolnikov gave a roll of his shoulders. 'Remind me of the parents. Hampton we can discount.'

'Green and Minter.'

'No one we need worry too much about. Good. Arrange something plausible.'

Mrs Bain rubbed her throat. 'Are you authorizing me to use . . . to dispose of the evidence?'

'That's exactly what I'm doing.'

Once Raven and Isaac left the kitchen, she sensed that there were more people in the house than before. It wasn't that she could see them, but the building just sounded fuller—doors closing, voices at a distance. Fortunately, they didn't encounter anyone and got to Joe's room with no problem. Isaac tried the handle. It wasn't locked. They slipped inside, closing the door softly behind them.

Joe was lying face down on the bed. He'd not managed to change, only remove his shoes, dinner jacket and tie. He was asleep.

Isaac shook him by the shoulder. 'Hey, Joe, time to go.'

'Wha—?' Joe stirred.

'Find his shoes, Raven.'

While Isaac levered Joe upright, she scrabbled under the bed to retrieve some trainers. She hadn't realized how difficult it was to get footwear on an uncooperative person until she tried to wrestle his floppy feet inside them.

'We're getting you and Kieran out of here.' Isaac threw Joe's arm over his shoulder and heaved him to his feet.

'Key's . . . trouble, man,' Joe slurred.

'Yeah, we get it. Come on, Joe, time to wake up.'

'How're we going to get both of them out of here if Kieran's as bad?' asked Raven, propping Joe up on the other side.

'That's a question that you won't have to answer.' Mrs Bain stood in the doorway flanked by four security guards. 'Well, well, this is a surprise. Colonel Hampton, I presume?'

A square-jawed man with white hair walked in behind her. 'Is this him?' He spoke with the rolling vowels of a Russian accent.

Isaac lowered Joe to the bed and readied himself to fight.

'So it would seem, sir.' Mrs Bain gestured to the security men to fan out, guns pointed at Isaac.

'The girl?'

'Another of my students. Nobody of any importance.'

'Good. Secure him.'

Isaac's eyes flicked from man to man, assessing the weaknesses, his hand going to an inside pocket.

Swearing sharply in Russian, the large man brushed past his guards and grabbed Raven, pulling a handgun on her. A moment too late, she tried to twist free but he held the muzzle to her temple. 'Stay very still or I will shoot.'

She froze.

'You can't fight your way out of this, Hampton, you can see you are outnumbered.'

Isaac's gaze turned briefly to Raven. She stood still, heart pounding in her chest. The muzzle of the gun pressed against her skin like a cold fingertip.

Isaac slowly raised his hands.

'Search them.' Her captor shoved Raven in the direction of the nearest guard. He quickly patted her down, removing her phone. She wasn't carrying anything else. Isaac's pockets yielded a larger haul: his phone, wallet, gun, and lock picks. The big man flipped through the contents, discarding the cash and checking for ID. Raven swallowed against her brewing panic.

She looked to Isaac to see if he had any ideas. He had been waiting for her to meet his eyes. He looked at the door and gave a tiny nod. She mirrored the gesture. He nodded again. He wanted her to run if she got a chance. No one thought her a threat; all their attention was concentrated on Isaac. If she got clear, she could raise the alarm.

'Who are you, Hampton?' asked the man.

'I thought you knew everything in the KGB, Kolnikov. Don't you have a file on me?'

The Russian looked up from checking Isaac's phone. 'I've not worked for that organization for some time.'

'No, you prefer serving your own interests to your country's. I wonder what your president would say if he knew?'

'I count him a friend.' He tucked the phone in his pocket.

'I imagine his feelings might change if he knew about that gas pipeline deal you manipulated.'

Kolnikov's expression darkened. He crossed to where Isaac was standing and rammed a fist in his stomach. Isaac bent double and staggered forward, knocking the Russian into the guard behind. Joe, lying on the bed, surprised them all by surging up and flopping into the legs of the two nearest him. The guys had created a distraction for her. She had to act fast. Raven broke her guard's grip and rolled across the floor. Mrs Bain stood between her and the exit. Raven rose up and scissor-kicked the head teacher. Mrs Bain ricocheted into the wall, leaving the doorway open. Raven took her chance, bullets hitting the lintel as she sprinted through.

They were shooting at her! Until that point she hadn't quite 'got' how deadly serious this was.

She had to get out of sight. Racing down the corridor she pushed through the swing door to the stairwell. There were more voices below, alerted by the gunshots. Up it was. She tore up the stairs. Kieran's room had been on this floor. He could still be here. She ran lightly down the corridor until she saw the label 'Pagoda Room'. Sliding inside, she closed the door, praying no one had seen her. An alarm began ringing in the building, feet thumped down the hallways. Raven stood with her back to the door, panting. It was clear that the room was empty, bed stripped. He had been here though: she could smell his aftershave lingering in the air. He was so close—she just wished she could hold him. He had to be all right. Had to.

No time to think about that now. What to do? First priority: don't get caught. Second: get help. They'd taken her phone so she didn't know how to contact Isaac's team. He hadn't said exactly where they were other than outside. She didn't like the idea of stumbling round in the dark looking for them. It could take hours and she had the distinct impression that the people here would deal with Isaac and Joe in much less time than that.

Call the police? But the local constabulary would be unprepared for such a situation. The good guys who looked bad, thanks to the break-in, and bad guys looked good thanks to their prestigious positions.

Think, Raven.

She froze as she heard people approaching. They were searching each room as they went. She had to hide. The wardrobe and under the bed were too obvious, as was behind the curtains.

The bathroom.

For once being small played to her advantage. She kicked up the shelf in the vanity unit under the sink, stuffed it in the back and then squeezed in, folded double, and pulled the door closed not a moment too soon. The Pagoda Room was invaded by a team. They tossed the bed, opened the wardrobe and then one searcher came into the bathroom. Raven held her breath.

'Clear!' he shouted, having given the bath a cursory inspection, not even considering the little unit.

'OK, let's check if she's gone down to try free the others.'

'My guess is she's run for it.'

'If that's so, the dogs will get her. Come on.'

The footsteps retreated. Raven waited a few more minutes, just in case it was a trap, and then eased out of her hiding place. At least she knew where the others were and that any attempt to go for help would have meant encountering the dog patrol. Fine, so she would give the search team time to look downstairs, and then she would make use of their helpful hint; because, if she didn't know how to summon help, then she would find someone who did. She was going for Kieran.

Chapter 19

Kieran knew they didn't have long to think of a plan before the men returned to dispose of them. He guessed they would want to make the plausible accident happen off site, as three dead students would not be great advertising for the school or the manor.

'Did I get that right—they're going to . . .' Siobhan clutched Johnny's hand.

'They're getting rid of us,' confirmed Johnny.

'They're working out how to make our deaths look an accident.' Kieran didn't have time to soften the blow.

Siobhan took a sharp intake of breath and started to shake. 'No, no.'

'But we're not going to let them,' he continued quickly.

Johnny gripped her shoulders. 'Listen to the guy, Siobhan. He's right. We need to make this as hard for them as possible. It's the only way we'll get out of this.'

'But, Sweet Jesus, help us. Johnny . . .'

Johnny kissed her fiercely. 'No cracking up allowed.'

She clenched her fists. 'I know. Sorry. What can we do?'

He hugged her in approval. 'That's my girl. Let's make them wish they never started this.'

'I'm totally on board with that.'

Three distant pops were followed by an alarm ringing throughout the building.

'What was that?' asked Johnny.

'Gunshots.' Kieran rubbed his hand over his face, deeply

afraid that Joe had done something to provoke them. 'Let's take it as a good sign. We may not be alone here.'

'But no one knows where we are,' said Siobhan, her expression losing some of its hard-won ferocity and veering back to desolate.

'That's not true, Siobhan. I've got friends who are watching. I didn't think they'd realize there was a problem so soon, but maybe someone called them in. Any idea what day it is?'

'I think it's Friday. Why?'

Kieran tugged the bed. It didn't move an inch. 'Great, I missed the prom.'

'That's good news, how?' asked Siobhan, confused by his sudden change of topic.

'I stood up my girlfriend. She'll know something's wrong.'

'But won't she just get angry at you?'

'Not Raven.' And she wouldn't, he knew that. Her astute instincts would tell her the situation was heading downhill. With any luck, she may even have called Isaac.

'You're going out with Raven Stone?'

'Trying to—if we can get past the little detail of people trying to kill us.' Kieran smiled to reassure Siobhan. 'Look, now there's a chance we've got help somewhere nearby, we need to make sure people know something is up and give them the chance to react. Delay, make a fuss, do anything to bring attention to yourselves.' He studied their cell, an idea coming to him. 'I'm going to try—'

He didn't have time to finish his sentence as the door opened again and three men came in. Two kept their rifles on the occupants, while the third approached Johnny with handcuffs. He was a gorilla of a guy with short red hair and a mean set of lines clipping his mouth.

'Don't make this harder than it need be or we'll shoot the girl,' said the man.

Anger blazing in his eyes, Johnny held out his wrists. The handcuffs clipped on. Kieran watched closely as the man checked the fit and slipped the key in his back pocket.

He turned to Siobhan. 'You next, honey.'

Siobhan used very un-missionary-like language to tell him what he could do with his endearment. The man wasn't annoyed but rather amused by her spirit. 'Sorry, honey, but I've got orders. Wrists.'

Johnny gave her a nudge and she held up her hands to have a second set of cuffs put on her. One pair still dangled from the man's belt. Kieran thought through the moves he would have to make and shifted to the headboard of his bed.

'No moving!' barked one of the gunmen.

Kieran froze mid pace, foot off the ground, pretending this was a dark game of musical statues.

'Cut it out,' growled the guard.

'You told me not to move. See, I'm being a good little soldier.'

The man with the cuffs approached. 'I'll deal with him.'

As the big guy got into reach, Kieran wobbled on one leg, making out he was losing his balance. He fell against the man, one hand dipping into the back pocket the other taking the cuffs from his belt. Before the guard knew what he was intending, Kieran cuffed his own wrist and put the other end around his bedpost. They wouldn't be able to move him so easily now, thanks to the bolts in the ground anchoring the bed.

'Think you're smart, do you?' The man reached for his back pocket. 'Where the hell is the key?'

'He's taken it,' said the gunman. 'Picked your pocket.'

Kieran made a dramatic gulp. 'Actually, I've just swallowed it.'

The man's face went puce with rage. He drew back a fist and punched Kieran in the stomach. Pain shot through his midriff. Tethered by the cuff, Kieran was spun into the bed-head and slithered to the floor. He curled up, slipped the key in his mouth and took the two kicks to his body.

'Search him,' ordered the gunman. 'He could be lying.'

The red-haired guard roughly checked Kieran over, too stupid or too much in a hurry to think to check his mouth. 'Nothing. He must've swallowed it like he said.'

'Leave him; we're running out of time. Where's the spare?'

'In the security office.'

'Let's take these two to the garage and then come back for this joker. I'd enjoy a little time with him. I think a couple more bruises won't be noticed where he's going.'

With a parting kick, the guards hurried Siobhan and Johnny out of the room, shutting the door behind them.

Idiots. Kieran spat the key out and unlocked the cuffs. He tucked them in his jeans waistband. You never knew when they might come in useful. Just in case their stupidity had stretched to leaving the door open, he tried the exit. Locked from the outside, as he had expected. He had heard the rattle of someone entering a number on a key pad each time the door had been opened so it was no good trying to get out that way. There was only one option left open to him. He went into the bathroom and put down the lid of the toilet. Standing on it, his head just about reached the dark channel of the old laundry chute. He could see from here that it was barred at the top, leaving a wriggle space of about three metres, something like a chimney flue but much cleaner. Braced against the walls, how long could he hold himself in it?

As long as necessary, he decided grimly.

Undoing the leather whip he had threaded like a belt through his jeans loops and tucking it down the front of his T-shirt, he stepped on to the cistern. He swung himself up and started the tricky business of wedging himself in the gap. It became a little easier when he got to the top as he had the bars to hold on to, giving his screaming muscles a break. He looped the thin end of the whip around the iron grating, making a kind of cradle for him to sit in, and steadied himself by holding the bars. Now all he had to do was wait.

Ducking behind a rack of coats in the foyer, Raven watched as two men escorted Johnny and Siobhan out of the front door. They looked terrified—hardly a surprise as they had cuffs on their wrists and their two-man team had weapons drawn. Siobhan tried dragging her feet but a guard solved that by hoisting her over his shoulder. No sign of Kieran. Had he been taken out already or was he left behind? With two of the guards outside for the moment it was too good a chance to find him if he was still in the building. Johnny and Siobhan had come from the kitchen wing so Raven headed in that direction, looking for somewhere people could be secured. She already knew the kitchen was clear so didn't waste time there. Hadn't Isaac said he'd checked the lower floor already? She would bet on him being a thorough man, so it was likely the room was out of the way, a forgotten corner of the building on another floor that had not been on their route, an entrance to a cellar maybe, or storeroom.

She opened a number of cupboards but they all proved empty. Then she came to one at the end of the corridor—a linen store, bigger than most. She went in and looked behind the racks to check for further doors. Nothing like another exit was visible in any of the walls.

Turning on the spot, she stepped on something soft. There was no sound but she sensed it was an animal, and one in pain. She forced herself to look down, fearing to see a squashed mouse; instead, she saw fingers gripping the grate below her feet and the glint of eyes gazing upwards.

'Kieran! Oh God, I'm sorry!' She jumped back and crouched over the grill, rubbing at his offended fingers.

'Sssh!' he cautioned.

Pausing to listen, she could hear sounds in the room below them. A door banged against a wall. A man shouted in alarm.

'He's not here!'

'Impossible!'

Kieran's knuckles tightened. She could see the strain on his face as he held his body up against the grate. She did the only thing she could think of to help him: she spread herself across the grid to cut out any light that would give away his position, taking care not to press on his fingers.

'The girl must have got down here while we were outside. She must have seen us punch in the code.'

'Search the lower floors again—and do it properly this time!' That was the Russian—the one who had held the gun to her head.

Footsteps retreated from the room below, heading upstairs at the double. Heading for her position.

'Hide!' whispered Kieran.

'No shit, Sherlock,' she muttered, jumping to her feet.

'I think they've left the door open. I'll come to you.'

She heard him drop lightly to the floor. Where could she conceal herself? There was a stack of laundry bags by the door from a delivery of clean sheets. She took out a pile of the starched and ironed linen and put it neatly on the shelf, guessing that any disturbance would be noticed. Having made sufficient space, she climbed inside. Realizing a saggy, human-shaped bundle would be a dead giveaway, she stuffed a couple of folded sheets either side of her and topped it off with three on top. She did her best to close the bag again but it was impossible from inside. Maybe they would put that down to someone having searched in here earlier?

I'm really going to have to stop finding small confined places to hide in, she thought grimly.

She didn't have to wait long for the team to arrive. Once again, she heard the sounds of men conducting a room by room sweep. They reached the linen room and, like her, came in to give the shelves a complete inspection.

'Nothing. They must be outside. Jones, you're with me. Let's search the area by the bins.' Two pairs of boots stomped away.

Raven held her breath. There was a third member of the team and he wasn't budging. 'Sir, I'm just gonna check something.'

'Catch us up!' The commander's voice was some distance away already.

'You're in here somewhere, aren't you?' the man muttered.

Raven's heart pounded so loudly she feared that was what the searcher had heard.

The man pulled the sheets off the shelves, upended the detergent barrel, and then turned his attention to the laundry bags. He kicked the one next to Raven. It fell over with a thump. Hers lurched sideways, revealing the opening was unlaced.

'Got you!' A hand delved inside and grabbed a fistful of hair, hauling her out. She came up swinging. He caught her wrist.

'Sir! I've . . . ' His shout was cut off by a karate-style chop to his throat and blow to his temple. He crumpled, dragging Raven down with him.

'You OK?' whispered Kieran, rolling the man off her.

Relieved beyond words at her rescue, Raven rubbed her scalp. 'Yes. You?'

'Fine. Quickly—tell me what's going on.' Kieran ripped up a sheet and stuffed one end on the man's mouth to gag him before he came round. As Raven filled Kieran in on the details, he tied up the guard's hands and feet and dragged him behind a shelf where he wouldn't immediately be noticed.

'So there's a team outside?'

'Yes. But I'm not sure where.' It was so good to see him again—he looked the same old Kieran, a little rumpled but no sign the brainwashers had got to him. Just being back with him made her a little warmer inside her fear-frozen chest. Things were going to hell but at least they were together.

'And the people here have got Isaac and Joe?' Kieran tidied up so it was no longer so evident that a struggle had taken place. He grabbed a spray can of starch and handed it to her without explanation.

'Yes. Joe's drugged but seemed to be coming round—enough to help me get away. Do you want me to keep hold of this?' She waggled the can at him.

'Yes. Just in case. For the dogs. We've got to move from here. They've taken Siobhan and Johnny to the garage so there's a good chance Joe and Isaac will be there too.' He went to the door and peeked out into the corridor.

'The other men went out to the kitchen courtyard.'

'We'll go out the library window then. Follow me.'

Raven hurried to catch up, but collided with his back when he abruptly paused in the doorway.

'What? Someone there?' she asked anxiously.

'No. I've just got to do this.'

She found herself wrapped in his arms, lifted off her feet, the recipient of a searching kiss that drove all thoughts of the dangers of discovery out of her mind for the moment. He walked her two paces back into the linen cupboard and propped her on a shelf so she could sit, face at a level with his.

'Thank you,' he said, when he broke off, 'for rescuing me.'

She held on for a second longer, then forced herself to let

265

go. 'You are so very welcome. And thank you for my rescue too. Now, get with the programme, Kieran.'

'Yes, ma'am.' With a smile that made her knees weak, he returned to the door. 'All clear.'

With a huff she slid from the shelf, tucked the can in her pocket, and took up her post at his back. He might now feel equipped by the kiss to go face the dragons outside, but she was still reeling.

He reached back and took her hand, thumb brushing across her knuckles. 'Ready?'

She squeezed his hand in return. 'As I'll ever be.'

Raven did not like this game of hide-and-seek one bit, not when the searchers were armed and prepared to kill you. She put her trust in Kieran knowing what he was doing. Clearly, there was far more to him than an exceptional brain and superior kissing abilities: he moved like Isaac, taking advantage of all cover and sensing just when it was safe to pass through the most exposed parts of the house. They saw a number of guards still searching but, by timing their moves across the corridors, they could keep one step ahead. She had counted at least six different men working for Mrs Bain and the Russian and feared there had to be more. They had knocked one out cold in the linen store but the odds were still stacked against them.

They were back by her coat rack again. Kieran pointed across the hall to the far door.

'Library,' he mouthed. 'Exit to garden.'

She nodded. This was the most perilous part of their escape from the building, involving crossing the central thoroughfare of the house. They listened hard before making their move.

Kieran tapped his chest.

She raised a brow. *You first?*

He nodded, putting a finger on her nose in a 'wait there' gesture.

266

So he was being a hero again.

She shook her head.

He frowned.

She leant over and kissed him, putting her hand back in his.

With a roll of his eyes, he held up three fingers. One. Two. Three. As quietly as possible, they crossed the foyer and slid into the library. Their luck held. The room was empty. Two half-empty beer bottles sat on the tables by the fire but the wood had burnt down to ashes. The guards Raven had seen earlier were long since gone, too busy terrorizing Johnny and Siobhan to finish their drink. Kieran didn't spare them a glance as he went to the French windows.

'There's an alarm at night but I'm guessing with the comings and goings out front, it's not set,' he said. He gave the double doors a shove, paused as if half-expecting bells to ring, then breathed a sigh of relief when there was no reaction. 'Good, I was right.'

It dawned on Raven from Kieran's manner that what he was doing was based on guesswork—good guesses, as this was Kieran—but still, he was no more certain of what he was doing than she was. He was winging it, being confident for her benefit. He appeared so self-assured it was easy to forget this.

'You're doing well,' she whispered.

'Thanks. I'm just trying not to get us killed.'

They hunkered down in the shrubbery where Isaac had led Raven only an hour or so before.

'Choices?' she asked.

'Face dogs and try to find Isaac's team.' They both looked out over the dark grounds, neither fancying stumbling about with guard dogs snapping at their heels and only a can of starch to spray in their eyes. 'Or we see what's going on at the garage. They're trying to get rid of all witnesses and, maybe, if we go for help, we'll miss the opportunity to save the others.'

'Or spoil it by trying to do it ourselves.'

'Exactly. I can't work out which decision gives us the better chance of success.'

Raven thought both looked pretty dire. 'OK.' She rubbed her hands. 'Reason doesn't work here so let's go with gut. Mine says "go to the garage". What about yours?'

'Gut?' Kieran looked uncomfortable with the concept.

'You've got to jump one way or another—which?'

He screwed his face up like he was swallowing a very bitter medicine. 'Garage.'

'Good. Two gut instincts equal one rational reason in my book. Do you know where it is?'

'Yes. Round the back.'

Kieran set off at a fast pace. He couldn't shake the feeling that he was running out of time, like sand was pouring on his head as he stood trapped in an hour glass. He was grateful that he had Raven to think about: she kept him centred, helping him focus to make decisions. YDA Owls like him weren't expected to be action-orientated, so his training hadn't included the kind of skills he had to use. He knew he was acting up to a level beyond his normal abilities purely because she was at his side, like when he had taken out that guard. Just seeing the man lay hands on Raven had been enough to unleash the beast.

The first vehicle he saw when they approached the garage was the school minibus the centre used to transport the students to and from Westron. Beyond that was an unmarked black SUV. The doors were open, showing Johnny and Siobhan lying on the seat together, a guard with a gun trained on them. Two more men were just pushing Joe inside to join them. The one Kieran thought of as Handcuff Guy was speaking on the phone.

268

'Yeah, we've got them in the car. No, the others are still loose but I've teams on them. We'll arrange something fatal when we catch them—take them out of the area, do it somewhere they're not known. Can't have too many bodies in one spot. You want us to meet you at Windmill Hill in the lay-by? OK, got that.' He tucked the phone away. 'OK, let's move out.'

One guard got in the driver's seat as Handcuff Man took the passenger side. The one with the gun climbed into the rear seat, not caring if he trod on any of their victims on the way.

'Windmill Hill?' Kieran whispered.

'It's between here and the school—a really steep patch winding down an escarpment. It's wooded.'

Kieran remembered it now from the satellite pictures. 'Who are they meeting?'

Raven shook her head. 'No idea.'

'Mrs Bain, perhaps? She's in charge of making this a plausible accident. A car crash is about as common as you can get.'

'We've got to get there to stop them.' The SUV was already reversing. The men left behind were heading back into the house.

Where was Isaac? Kieran glanced at the manor. Kolnikov did not look the type to let a big fish like Isaac go, not before he had got everything out of him he could.

'Key, we've got to follow!'

Raven was right. Isaac was on his own for the moment; if he were here, he would tell them that their job was to save the other three.

'Right. Let's do it.' He ran across the gravel towards the garage.

'How?'

'Like this.' He got into the minibus and let down the sun

visor. He had noticed on the journey to the manor that the drivers had fortunately developed the bad habit of keeping the keys there. He chucked Raven the set. 'You drive.'

She gaped. 'You serious?'

'You have a provisional licence—I saw it in your room.'

'Yes, Granddad's given me a few lessons.'

'That makes you the expert.'

'But . . .'

'Raven, remember how long it took me to figure out how to dance. Driving is going to be the same. We don't have a month for me to read the manuals and do the maths. This is not yet in my skill set.'

She was already sliding into the driver's seat. 'OK, OK, I can do this.'

'Thank you.' He got in beside her. 'As fast as you can please.'

'Shut up. I will not do this if you start on the backseat driver thing.'

Kieran bit his tongue. She found the ignition without any help and rattled the gear stick to check it was in neutral.

'We'll need to go quickly once you start as the people in the house might hear.'

'Kieran Storm, put a sock in it.'

'Sorry.'

She turned the engine over and it rumbled into life. The clutch grated as she hadn't depressed it enough but then she stepped down fully and got the stick into first. 'Say your prayers. I'm going for take-off.'

The minibus lurched along in first until she managed the transition to second. They circled and left the car park, heading for the main drive.

'I'll look out for any sign of the team,' Kieran said, nobly making no comment as the engine over-revved and went into third with another judder.

270

Raven didn't reply, lower lip gripped by her teeth in concentration.

'You're doing really well.'

'No, I'm bad at this. But what do you expect?'

'You're doing much better than I would,' clarified Kieran.

She gave a choked laugh at that and put her foot down. 'If we want to catch up we'd better not do this by halves.' The minibus shot down the drive, taking the speed bumps as a challenge to go faster.

Kieran gripped the seat belt across his chest. 'You're magnificent, Raven. You'll get us there safely. I have every faith in you.'

'Wish I did,' she muttered.

Chapter 20

Raven pulled the minibus over to the verge just out of sight of the lay-by. 'What now?'

Kieran got out and peered over the barrier at the side of the road. 'Does it get even steeper further on?'

'Yes.' She came round the vehicle to join him.

'They must be planning to make the car go over the edge.'

'So how do we stop them? Drive past and block the road with the bus?' She started back to the bus.

'Then we get a head-on collision. Come on—I've another idea.' Kieran began running down the carriageway. Raven followed, having to push herself to keep up. They came in view of the lay-by and saw two cars parked up—the SUV and . . .

'Joe's car,' muttered Kieran. 'So much for thinking it'd gone unnoticed.' They jumped over the barrier at the side of the road and crawled the remaining distance in the rough vegetation of the verge.

As they watched, Mrs Bain got out of the driver's side. A much better plan to have the accident happen in a vehicle belonging to one of the young victims, Raven acknowledged.

'They'll have to transfer the others,' Kieran whispered. 'That gives us a brief window. Can you get inside, do you think?' Kieran had his eyes on the men hauling Siobhan out of the back of the SUV.

'Yes.' The rear door of Joe's car was open in front of them, with a sizeable footwell for her to hide in. She seized his sleeve. 'But I'm not sure what you want me to do—your brain is several steps ahead of mine.'

'Take the controls. My guess is they are going to tow it down the hill, release the rope and fix the steering so it goes over. They can't just push it or it will never get the right speed for crash investigators.'

'You want me to get in a car that's going over the embankment?'

He caressed her cheek. 'I want you to stop it doing so. Can you do that? I'd try but you stand a better chance of hiding.'

'What are you going to do?'

'Me? I'm going to catch the bad guys.'

'How?'

'Later.' He kissed her. 'Get going.'

The man carrying Siobhan opened the door on the opposite side and strapped her in the rear seat. From the wide-eyed expression over her gag, she was awake and terrified. Her cuffs had been replaced by strips of cloth at her wrist and ankles. The man patted her head and closed the far door on her. Raven felt boiling anger on Siobhan's behalf—bad enough being set up to die, even worse to be patronized while it was happening.

'Put the boys in the front,' called Mrs Bain. 'The bigger one is the driver.'

Raven had only seconds to get in the back unseen. She slid over the road barrier and into the car. Siobhan jolted in surprise but quickly realized this was their last chance of help. She lifted her legs slightly so Raven could fold herself up in the dark gap. Fortunately the man dragging Johnny round to the front passenger seat was in a hurry; he slammed the rear door on the verge side without looking in. Raven started untying Siobhan's legs, which were right by her hands. From the bouncing and swearing, the boys were making life difficult for the men pushing them in the front. Johnny was grunting and shouting through his gag. Raven winced as she heard the dull thud of a body blow.

'Tie the driver to the seat. I don't want him messing with the controls,' ordered Mrs Bain.

Raven had to hunker down as small as possible as a thin nylon rope was thrown round the seat at chest height. Another rope secured Joe's ankles to the seat adjustment lever. Then something wet splashed over all of them. A drop ran into Raven's mouth. A strong spirit. Vodka maybe.

'Should we remove the ropes after?' asked one of the men.

After they'd all gone over the edge.

'I think the fire should take care of them but we'll stay around and check. Have you got the blow torch ready? If the petrol tank doesn't explode by itself, you'll have to help it along.' Mrs Bain sounded impatient. 'Come on, let's get this done. It will be dawn soon. The farmers who use this road will be up and about in an hour.'

'Tow rope secured,' called another from somewhere in front of the car.

The doors slammed, shutting them all together with the reek of vodka in the air. Johnny gave a frustrated howl of protest. Joe was eerily silent. Raven wondered if he had passed out.

The car lurched as the SUV picked up the slack on the tow rope. Raven almost moved but she realized one of the men was leaning in the driver's window to steer Joe's car out on to the carriageway. He then straightened it up so it was pointing directly downhill.

'It won't take long. You probably won't feel a thing,' the man said, glancing towards Siobhan.

The Irish girl screamed at him through her gag. He ran to catch up with the SUV, moment of pity soon over.

The instant he was gone, Raven pushed out from under Siobhan's legs and squeezed through the gap between the front seats. The car was picking up speed, following the tail lights of the SUV.

'Crap, crap, crap,' she cursed. There was no time to get Joe out of her way. The car bounced and she cracked her head on the roof. Johnny had stopped grunting and was looking at her in desperate hope. 'I'm going to take control. Work with me here, guys.'

Siobhan and Johnny groaned their approval. Joe gave a nod. Good, not passed out—just silenced by the horror of what was happening.

Raven had no choice but to sit on to Joe's lap and grope under the seat to shift it back. He helped by pushing down with his heels to move the seat and made a gap for her by spreading his knees. He couldn't do any more, trussed up as he was. He had more ropes on him than the others—a sign he'd given his captors quite a time subduing him.

Raven took the steering wheel, not liking the speed. She knew this road, having cycled down it but a few hours before. The corner was coming up. She found the brake with her foot. She couldn't tap on it to test until the tow ended or the people in front would know something was wrong. Hardest of all was knowing that everyone around her was counting on her to save their necks.

'Say your prayers, guys: this might be a bit close.'

Just then the minibus zoomed by on the wrong side of the road; Raven caught a glimpse of Kieran at the controls. What was he doing? He couldn't drive! She had no time to figure that out as the connection to the car in front was released and Joe's car was left heading for the corner with enough velocity to plough through the barrier. She stamped on the brake, adjusting the steering to skim round the corner.

Beside her, Johnny had managed to get his bound wrists on the hand brake and he pulled hard on that. This proved too much—the car slewed round into a spin under the sudden braking. Siobhan gave a muffled scream, Raven a piercing one. The world whirled as the car rocked and bumped into the high verge on the opposite side from the drop. Raven, not wearing a seat belt, was thrown so she sprawled across the gear stick, head-butting Johnny's stomach. When she pushed up, she saw they had ended their mad spin facing uphill.

But they had survived.

What was the next thing she had to do? The ropes.

Raven untied Joe's hands and the binding around his chest, then turned to Johnny. Joe got free of the remaining bonds, squirmed out from under her and opened his door. He hurried round to complete the job Raven had started on Siobhan.

'Where's Kieran?' Joe asked Raven.

'He was in the minibus.' She had a really bad feeling about what Kieran had planned. 'Said he was going to catch the bad guys.'

Joe swore. 'Get back in, everyone.'

Raven climbed in the rear next to Siobhan as Joe started the car engine. It sounded very loud after the silent freewheeling adventure down the slope. He turned it to face the right way with a sharply executed three-point turn and headed off in pursuit of the minibus.

Kieran gripped the steering wheel with an overwhelming sense that he had bitten off more than he could chew. He had watched Raven carefully, knew the basics about accelerator and gears, but he was trying to do something more than drive the bus—he was attempting to use it as a precision weapon. His brain played out the scenario he had planned. Black car at fifty miles per hour. White minibus reaching sixty. Bend curving at fifty degrees to the right with an incline of twenty per cent. He would need to strike at just the right moment to force them off the road and put them permanently out of the picture.

There was a good chance he would kill himself in the process.

He quickly ran the odds. Acceptable. What was unacceptable was for Raven, Joe and the others to escape death in a fake accident only to have the occupants of the SUV come back and turn their guns on them. He stepped on the pedal and braced himself for the collision.

Joe didn't have far to drive. At the next corner they found the gap in the barrier.

'Oh God.' Raven's blood ran like iced water through her veins.

Joe pulled over and they leapt out, running to the edge. Further down the embankment, having torn up the undergrowth and crashed through saplings until it met with a big tree, was the SUV. It lay on its roof, one headlight still shining crazily back towards them. But far worse for Raven was the sight just below their spot. There was the minibus, nose planted in the brambles.

'He rammed them off the road.' Joe's voice sounded very distant.

You can't pass out now. That's just not happening, Raven told herself.

She slid down the bank and yanked open the driver's door of the minibus. The airbag had engaged. 'Kieran, Kieran?' She was frantic—he wasn't there. She looked around, wondering if somehow he had been thrown clear. 'Kieran?' she shouted.

'Joe, I can't find him. Oh God, oh God.' Tears streaming down her cheeks, she began tearing at the bag in case he was trapped under it somewhere.

'Raven, stop!' Joe pulled her away and turned her shoulders towards the SUV. 'Look!'

She came out of her panic long enough to see someone climbing up the slope towards them—a lanky, familiar shape silhouetted in the headlight. 'Kieran! Oh my God, Kieran— you're alive!'

He waved at her. 'Raven, it's OK. I'm OK.'

She plunged down the slope to collide with him. 'Don't you ever do that to me again!' She hit him in furious relief.

He embraced her, squeezing her tightly, partly to stop her making further attacks on his chest but also to remind them both that they had survived. 'I'm unhurt. I was just checking on the guys in the car.'

She buried her head in his shirt. 'Dead?'

'No, but pretty bashed up. They're hanging upside down in their seat belts so I didn't want to touch them in case it made their injuries worse. I got a phone from Mrs Bain—concussion doesn't make her any more polite—and I've called for an ambulance. Joe, I threw their guns out of reach. Can you get them? I chucked them near the bonnet.'

'Sure. Good driving, pal.' Joe slapped Kieran on the back as he jogged past.

Kieran rubbed the tears off Raven's cheeks. 'I got the calculation a little wrong. Ended up potting myself, like the white ball following the black into a pocket in snooker. Fortunately, most of my momentum had been lost in the collision so I just dropped over the edge. Touch of whiplash though.' He massaged the back of his neck.

Raven wanted to hit him some more—the idiot had played

the angles and almost killed himself. 'You are not allowed in the driving seat ever again, Kieran Storm.'

He nuzzled the top of her head. 'And what about you? You must have done some pretty impressive moves to keep the car on the road.'

'She was great,' said Siobhan. She was standing with Johnny's arms around her. All of them were cold in the pre-dawn chill, but mostly they just wanted comfort.

'Yeah, it was me who added too much brake. Sorry, Raven,' said Johnny.

Raven waved the apology away. 'It worked, didn't it? Whatever we both did. Don't beat yourself up.'

Joe came back with the guns and dumped them in the minibus. 'What now?'

Raven held out a hand to invite him to get a hug too. 'Come here, Joe.'

With a grin, he threw his arms around both of them. 'Man, I can't tell you how pleased I am to see you alive and well. When I came out of my drugged-up haze it was like plunging right into a nightmare.'

'What happened to Isaac?' Raven asked.

'Kolnikov has him. Last I heard, he was taking him to the other trustees to decide what to do with him.'

'So they left the manor?'

'I think so. They wanted to give their men a clear field to get rid of us and look for you.'

Kieran cursed. 'I called in the team after I dialled for the ambulance. They are searching the building now but it sounds like they're looking in the wrong place.'

'Where would Kolnikov go if he left there?' Joe wondered aloud. 'Does he have a plane or helicopter nearby?'

'Kolnikov has properties in London,' recalled Kieran, 'but I doubt he'd want to drag Isaac all the way there—it would tie him directly to whatever they do if harm comes to Isaac in his private residence.'

'The other trustees?'

'Same argument.'

A siren sounded in the distance.

'I really don't want to be caught up in explanations just now,' muttered Joe, 'not with Isaac still in danger.'

Johnny put his jumper around Siobhan's shoulders. 'Look, you've obviously still got stuff to do for this Isaac guy you're talking about. Take the car. Siobhan and I will stay here and talk to the authorities.'

They clambered back up the slope and on to the road, Kieran pulling Raven up the final steep bit, Johnny helping Siobhan.

'OK and thanks. You both are stars, doing that for us.' Joe got in his car, Raven and Kieran in the back. 'You take care. When the police arrive, tell them to contact Scotland Yard and mention Isaac Hampton's name. We'll talk to them as soon as we can.'

Johnny glanced down the road. They could all see the flicker of blue lights approaching from the bottom of the hill. 'Fine. You go.'

'Thanks guys—for the rest of our lives,' said Siobhan, linking her arm to Johnny's.

'No problem.' Joe accelerated away.

'Where exactly are we heading?' asked Kieran as they left their new friends on the roadside.

'My first idea is to get away from the police.' Joe drove with care down the hill so that the squad car would find no reason to stop them. Two police vehicles screamed by, closely followed by an ambulance. 'But I'm thinking that we should try Westron first. If they want to question him somewhere they control, then the school's the nearest place.'

'And Mrs Bain had clearly come from there, as she was so kind as to provide us with your car. How did they know it was yours?' asked Kieran.

'Keys. They took everything, including my phone and keys, when they tied me up.'

'I should've guessed. Yours is still on its original tag, providing them with the make. After that it was just a question of looking in the car park.'

'Yeah, I'm gonna change that as soon as we get out of here. Phone the team, Key.'

Kieran got out Mrs Bain's mobile and waited for a response.

'Rivers here. Who is this?'

Kieran never saw eye to eye with the mentor of the Wolves, but he wasn't a bad choice to have at your back in this situation. 'Sir, it's Kieran again. I'm with Joe. Any sign of the commander?'

'Not yet. We got pinned down in a fire-fight with some of the goons, then had to deal with a bunch of hysterical teens who didn't have the sense to stay undercover. It's taking us too long to search the building but I don't think he's here.'

'Joe thinks Isaac might have been taken back to the school. We're heading that way now.'

'Storm, you are not equipped to take on these people. You will ascertain if he is there but nothing more, understood? We'll be following as quickly as we can.'

'Yes, sir.' Kieran ended the call. 'My orders are to "ascertain" if Isaac is at Westron.' Like that was going to stop him.

'And mine?' asked Joe, turning into the school driveway.

'That's up to you, isn't it?'

Chapter 21

They left Joe's car at Raven's cottage and hurried towards the school buildings. It was four in the morning. Light was bleaching the eastern horizon but it was too early for anyone to be up and around, particularly after the late night of the prom.

'Do you think they're here?' Joe asked.

Raven pointed to the front of the school. A Bentley was parked outside, a chauffeur having a quiet smoke leaning against the bonnet. 'There's someone.'

'That vehicle belongs to Tony Burnham. He's the only one who lives close enough to come and help Kolnikov deal with the crisis.' Kieran frowned. 'So where's the man himself? Mrs Bain's office?'

'I know head teachers' offices are the traditional location for punishment,' said Joe wryly, 'but I'm thinking they wouldn't take this into a building with three hundred witnesses sleeping around them.'

'We can't waste time searching the grounds,' said Kieran.

'We don't have to.' Raven had spotted the lights. 'Look, the orangery.'

'Unless someone is taking an early morning dip, I think we've found our bad guys. Well done, Raven.' Joe took the phone from Kieran and began texting their position. 'Come on—we can see what's going on if we go the far side of the yew walk.'

Leaving tracks in the dew, the three ran through the gardens to take up new vantage points looking into the swimming pool enclosure. With the lights on inside, it was like gazing into an aquarium. Instead of pretty fish floating about, they saw Isaac held up between two men, another standing in front of him flexing his fist and the two trustees, Kolnikov and Burnham, against the wall, heads close together as they talked on the phone. From the slump in Isaac's shoulder blades, he didn't look in very good shape.

'We can't hear anything from here,' whispered Joe. 'Let's get closer.'

They crept up to the door at the deep end of the pool, as close as they could get to the men who had taken up positions in the centre of the building. Raven quietly lifted the latch and opened it a crack, holding on to the bottom so it didn't creak or bang.

'Yes, yes, I agree,' rumbled Kolnikov, 'we must get out of England. Too much interest in our activities here.'

Burnham scowled. 'We mustn't make knee-jerk reactions to this man. He has little on us. With his informers dead—or soon to be so—what does that leave?'

Isaac hung his head. Raven could sense the waves of misery from him—he believed his boys were eliminated.

'Good point. He's the only witness left, and from what little he has told us, his case against us is pure supposition. If we get rid of him, then who is going to come after us?'

'I could relocate for a while—I have businesses in the Seychelles that need my attention,' mused Burnham.

'And I'm due back in Moscow tomorrow in any case. So it is agreed?' Kolnikov waited for the verbal confirmation on the phone. 'Unanimous. Leaving him alive was never an option.'

'You're right, because I'd rip you apart with my bare hands given the chance.' Isaac's voice was low, pained, every word costing him. 'You've killed two of mine. My people won't rest

283

until you pay. Dead or alive, I'm coming back for you to take you to hell.'

'Good luck with that. It'll be your ghost doing that job, I'm afraid.' Burnham gestured to the men holding Isaac's arms. 'A simple drowning I think. The colonel here, on a visit to see his wards, has had too much to drink, got into a fight in the bar and then wandered into the pool. Hold him down.'

They had run out of time. Observing was no longer an option. Kieran moved first. He snapped the whip from his belt loops, jumped up and kicked the doors open, surprising everyone inside. Raven guessed he didn't have a plan—he was doing this her way: on gut feeling. He lashed out at the man who had started for him, catching him across the face. He howled and clutched his eyes. One down. 'I suggest you change your plans, Burnham. There's going to be nothing simple about this.'

Kolnikov drew a gun, putting Kieran in his sights. Kieran swept his arm back, pushing Raven behind him. Joe stood resolutely at his shoulder while she spluttered a protest.

'I hope you've still got that can,' he said in a low voice. 'I can see three attack dogs in front of me.' Her hand groped in her jacket—still there thankfully. Kieran spoke up. 'It wouldn't be very clever of you to start shooting.'

'I can think of nothing better,' countered Kolnikov.

'Were you thinking of making an easy getaway from the UK?' mocked Kieran. Raven saw Joe getting ready with the phone. What were the boys planning? 'Yeah, putting a bullet in a teenager is a great idea. Do that and all airports and borders will be closed to you and your face on all the news channels.' Joe held up the phone and captured Burnham's image, sending it to the team on the outside.

'Thank God,' murmured Isaac, a smile on his battered face. 'I thought you three were dead.'

284

'Too damn stubborn for that, I'm pleased to report, sir,' said Joe. 'And now everyone knows who's here.'

Burnham pushed Kolnikov's gun down. 'Don't shoot.' He gestured to the men. 'What are you waiting for—get them! We'll take them with us and get rid of them later. No bodies, no story.'

Two of the three enforcers ran towards them, not having yet learnt their lesson that small packages could hold big surprises.

'Dogs!' warned Kieran.

Raven darted out from behind him and sprayed the can right in their eyes. Blinded by the starch, they were unprepared for Joe and Kieran's strike—one perfectly timed kick to the stomach, one lash of the whip taking the guy's legs out from under him. Both men ended up in the pool with a huge splash. Raven grabbed the net used to clean the pool and poked them back in each time they tried for the side. One tried to grab it, almost pulling her in. Joe took over and shoved hard, sending the guy back under. The man gave up and swam for the far side.

'I think we have what they call a stand-off,' said Burnham as Kieran stood in front of Raven, rippling the whip, every inch the protector. Burnham spoke into his phone. 'Come to the pool. Bring everyone.'

'We shoot them?' growled Kolnikov.

Raven cringed as guns appeared in the hands of the guys who had taken a dip. They were rubbing their eyes, hardly able to see their targets, but they had every intention of firing when ordered.

Burnham scowled. 'I fear so. Messy, but they leave us little option. You'll have to provide me my alibi thanks to that boy's stunt with the photo.'

'We'll get away before anyone works out we were here.'

Kolnikov walked up to Isaac and levelled the gun at his forehead. 'Easy to deny as it won't be you pulling the trigger.'

The brief hesitation was almost over as the necessary action became clear to the two trustees. 'Exactly. And there are no witnesses if we take them out.'

That gave Raven an idea—mad, but a last throw of the dice as Isaac's team still had not shown up. She moved to the wall, to the little red box with instructions to break glass in an emergency.

'Hey, before you morons do that, I think I should point something obvious out to you.'

'Careful, Raven,' murmured Kieran, seeing the guns now following her.

'Hush up, Kieran, I know what I'm doing. So, mister, you want to murder us without witnesses? Well, unfortunately for you, this is a school.' She picked up metal watering can and used the spout to stab the glass. The fire alarm began ringing in the pool enclosure, and would also now be ringing on every corridor of the castle thanks to the interlinked system.

'Stupid girl, the fire service can't help you!' scoffed Burnham.

'Not the fire service.'

'Do we shoot?' He looked to Kolnikov, whose finger was on the trigger.

'I'd think very carefully before doing that, because in about a minute the first of three hundred children will be gathering just out there.' She pointed to the lawn in front of the orangery. 'If our fastest fire practice is anything to go by, the rest will turn up within the five minutes after that. Even if you've killed us, we will still rather unhelpfully be here—our blood on your hands. Even you couldn't clean the mess up quickly enough, and three hundred witnesses are far too many for you to get rid of in time to get clear.'

'You know what,' said Isaac, standing up straighter. 'I think your plans to do this without witnesses have just gone up in smoke.'

The murmur of students could now be heard outside.

Kolnikov swore fluently in his native tongue.

Burnham's instinct for self-preservation clicked in. 'Forget this—forget them.' He spoke into his phone once more. 'We're going.' His men were already heading for the exit. Kolnikov looked as if he would very much rather shoot Raven but, after of string of Russian curses, hurried after his colleague.

Isaac swayed and crumpled to his knees, only sheer grit having kept him upright until this point thanks to the beating he had taken.

Kieran rushed to his side. 'Don't worry, sir: I've told your team to pick them up. They won't get out of the drive.'

Isaac panted. 'I'd give my firstborn to be out of these cuffs.'

'In that case, you can name him Kieran after me—or Raven if it's a girl.' Kieran produced the key he had taken earlier. 'I think this works on all the sets they have.' He released Isaac's wrists.

Isaac fell against him. 'I might just do that. You were all magnificent. Everyone OK?'

'Yes, the other two students are fine. We left them with the police.'

'Great. I'm gonna pass out right about now so I'll leave the rest to you.'

'We've got you, sir,' said Joe, catching him as he slid sideways.

Chapter· 22

Raven stood by the side of the pool, feeling excess to requirements as Kieran got into the ambulance with Isaac and everyone else buzzed around, fully occupied with the crisis.

'I'll see you later, OK?' Kieran said before the doors closed on him. He gave a brief smile but she could tell he was consumed with worry for his mentor. The ambulance pulled away from the pool leaving tyre tracks on the lawn.

Joe was busy debriefing a huge man in military fatigues and the police officer in charge of the operation. As Joe had predicted, Burnham and Kolnikov had not got out of the school grounds. They were now under armed guard and on their way to the nearest police station. The most immediate problem left for the police was that they had arrested all the resident teachers, leaving three hundred children of various ages unchaperoned, not to mention that some of the young people had been victims of the manor treatment and had to be assessed for the damage done to their minds. The officers were currently shepherding them back to their beds, telling them that everything would be explained in the morning.

Good luck with that, thought Raven.

Siobhan and Johnny arrived in the orangery under the escort of a policewoman.

'Raven, is everyone safe?' Siobhan asked anxiously. 'Where's Kieran?'

'He's gone to hospital with his godfather.' She held up a hand to pre-empt Siobhan's next question. 'Don't worry: he wasn't hurt—it's Isaac who was roughed up. They interrogated him forcibly to find out what he knew.'

'But he's going to pull through?'

'I think so.'

Johnny yawned. 'Sorry, can't help myself. This mess is going to take hours to sort out. Do you think it would be OK if we went back to our rooms until they need us?'

Raven was flattered he looked to her for a lead, especially when she was feeling so confused herself. 'I imagine so. I take it you've already given a statement?'

'Yes. Back at the crash site.'

'I'm waiting to give mine.' She closed her eyes briefly, weariness catching up with her. She wished she still had her phone but that had been left somewhere in the manor, and she doubted she would be reunited with it for quite a while.

'Good, then we'll see you in the morning.' Johnny glanced outside where dawn had arrived an hour ago. 'I mean in the afternoon.'

'Yes, see you then.'

Siobhan gave Raven a hug. 'I know we hardly knew each other before all this happened, but I just want to say a big thank you again. You'll get sick of me saying it. You were so great—so were Joe and Kieran. Friends?'

'Yes, of course, we're friends.' Raven grinned, pleased that she had at least two allies in Westron.

The pair walked away hand in hand.

Joe came over with the man in camouflage. 'Raven, this is Sergeant Rivers. He headed Isaac's team.'

Rivers shook her hand. 'Pleased to meet you, Miss Stone. I hear a lot of the success of today's operation is down to you.'

'I think it was more of a joint effort.'

'Yes—Storm and Stone to the rescue. They made quite a team, sir,' said Joe, ruffling her hair.

Rivers folded his arms across his broad chest, biceps bulging in his tight T-shirt. 'I still can't believe Kieran drove that minibus off the road. I'll have to see if he'll consider a transfer to Wolves. We like recruits who can jump in with the right action at the right time.'

Joe laughed. 'I think he's a total Owl, sir. The most owlish of the bunch.'

Raven wrinkled her forehead in puzzlement. 'What are you talking about?'

'Our organization, Miss Stone,' said Rivers. 'We have nicknames for the groups of young people taking our training.'

'It's good training, Raven—none of that brainwashing stuff they did at the manor,' Joe added.

'I'm in charge of the Wolves, the hunters.' The sergeant cleared his throat, realizing he was saying too much to an outsider. 'But I won't bore you with the details for the moment. You need to get some rest.'

'I don't find it in the least bit boring,' she assured him, pleased to learn something real about Kieran and Joe at long last.

'Ask Kieran about it when you see him,' said Joe. 'Look, Raven, I just came over to say goodbye. I'm going back to headquarters. We've still got a huge amount of mopping up to do on this operation—two trustees still at large and an entire global network of international schools to be investigated. Kieran and I are going to be very busy. But I just wanted to say that it's been an honour to work with you.' He embraced her. 'You've shone from beginning to end.'

'Oh, er, thanks.' So was this it? No, it couldn't be. 'I'll be seeing you again soon, won't I?'

Joe flicked a look at the sergeant's forbidding expression. 'We'll have to see. I'm sure Kieran will be in touch to give you his own thanks.'

She didn't want thanks. He could screw *thanks*! 'He will? You're sure?'

His gaze was fixed somewhere over her head. 'Just stay strong, OK? Oh, I forgot to mention: they arrested your grand-dad along with the other staff members . . . '

'What! You're only just telling me this now!'

'Don't worry—I told the policeman to release him imme-diately. He should be on his way back.'

A policewoman came over and touched her shoulder. 'Are you ready to give your statement now, Miss?'

'What? Yes. Yes, I am.'

Joe patted her back as he stepped away. 'I'll leave you to it then. Goodbye, Raven.'

'Goodbye, Joe.' She caught his sleeve as he turned to leave. 'Before you go, tell me something: were your parents ever in prison or rehab?'

He smiled sheepishly. 'Never. Dad's biggest crime is having a golf handicap lower than mine and Mom is a sweetheart who would be mother to the entire world if she could.'

'Was anything you told me the truth?'

'They do live in New York. Everything else was a smoke-screen,' he gestured around him at Rivers and the police officers, 'for this.'

She let him go, depressed that she had known so little about him and Kieran. It revived all her old fears that her relation-ship with Kieran had been equally fake. 'I'm glad you've got them behind you. Be happy, Joe.'

'You too.'

'Now, Miss, where would you like to do this? Is there a responsible adult we can have sit in on your interview?' asked the policewoman.

Yeah, you just arrested him.

'My grandfather. Joe said he's heading back to our cottage.'

'Shall we take this over there then?'

Raven decided she had had her fill of the swimming pool. She plucked the last rose still hanging on in her hairclip and dropped it on the tiles, petals spilling like drops of blood. 'Yes, let's do that.'

When the policewoman left, Raven and her grandfather sat facing each other across the table.

'Well,' he said.

Raven toyed with the mug she had drunk from while giving her statement. 'It's been quite a night.'

He took her hand. 'You need to know, darling, that my job has gone up the spout. The business behind the school has been suspended pending investigations. The policeman who drove me back said parents were being informed and told to make arrangements to collect their children today.'

'I hope not. Half of them should be in the dock for putting their kids through the manor experience.'

'The manor children are being handled separately. Social workers are coming here to counsel them. The majority of the students never went there though, so they're being sent home.'

'I see.' Raven sipped the last cold mouthful of tea. She hadn't been to bed yet and, though she felt exhausted, couldn't imagine sleeping with so many questions buzzing round in her head, chief of which was whether Kieran was ever going to contact her.

'Do you want some more bad news?' her granddad asked.

'Not really, but I suppose I'd better get it over with.' Her life was one big sigh at the moment.

'My pension was a company one. If the Union of International Schools goes under, I may not see a penny of it. Apparently, they did not organize their finances to protect their staff as they were legally bound to do.'

292

'We'll have no income?'

'And no home. We're going to have to leave here.' His eyes were suspiciously bright. 'But don't worry: I'll find something. I have some other savings and I'm going to the job centre tomorrow and . . . and we'll talk to the benefits people about getting somewhere to stay.'

Raven absorbed this new blow slowly. They were only a whisker away from being destitute.

'I'm really sorry, darling. It's my fault. I've been working for the wrong people—I should've seen it. I should've asked more questions.'

'You mustn't blame yourself, Granddad. How were you to know?' She came round the table and hugged him tight. 'Don't worry—I'll get a job too. I'm seventeen. I'm sure I can find something.'

'But college . . . '

'College can wait a year or so until we are back on our feet.'

He shook with silent sobs. Raven buried her face in his neck, refusing to cry. He needed her to be strong and that's what she would be.

'We'll come through this, trust me.'

'I don't deserve you, Raven.'

'You deserve so much more, Granddad.'

After a much needed shower and sleep, Raven decided to brave the school to see how the students were doing. She went over at supper time to find a very subdued gathering. Many of the pupils had already left in their parents' cars, the celebrities and other important people wanting to put as much distance as possible between themselves and scandal. The media had taken up residence at the end of the drive, police and social workers in the grounds—nothing was as it had been at Westron. The catering crew were still there, with the same shamed, stunned look as her grandfather, but they had obviously agreed to the authorities' request to stay on and feed those left behind. She took a tray and helped herself to a packet of sandwiches and crisps. She could feel the eyes of many of her year on her and wondered just what they were thinking now. It must be so odd to them to find the hate figure of the school had ended up bringing the whole place down around their ears like the Bible story of Samson chained to the pillar. Unlike that ancient hero, she had no intention of going down in the rubble. She straightened her spine and braved the dining room.

'Raven, over here!' called Siobhan. She was sitting with Johnny on the central and most coveted table.

Raven put down her tray. 'Had a good sleep?'

'Yes. Woke to find multiple messages from my parents but I'm not talking to them. I'm thinking of asking my aunt in London if I can go to her for the moment.'

'Which has the advantage that it's near my older sister. I'm going to her,' said Johnny. 'Both of us are divorcing our parents.'

'Can you do that to parents?' asked Siobhan.

'Un-adopting them. There should be a ceremony. My sister hit the roof when she heard what had happened here.'

'And so she should,' agreed Raven. She felt a pang of grati- tude that her own parents had always been perfectly happy with her as she was. She missed them so much. She could do with their help now.

'How about you?' Siobhan's enquiry was interrupted by Adewale, who came to stand beside her.

What now? Raven wondered.

'Raven, can I have a word?'

'Sure.' She pushed her tray away.

'Gina's in with the counsellors.'

'That's good.'

'She had a bit of a meltdown when the police arrived. The cracks were showing, to be honest with you, before then.' Adewale struggled to meet her eye and finally made himself do so. 'Anyway, she confessed that she had no proof that you put my watch in her things—that she might even have done it herself—not that she remembers either way.'

'I didn't take it, Adewale.'

'Yes, I guess I know that now. So I've a massive apology I owe you—not just for accusing you but for what I did afterwards.'

The cricket pavilion.

'You were cruel. I don't know how you could do that to someone.'

'I know.' He swallowed. 'I'm trying to think how I can make it up to you. This isn't enough but I'll make a start now.'

Then to her shock he stood on the chair beside her then got on to the table and clapped his hands. The dining room fell silent; the police officers in the room looked distinctly unhappy, ready to intervene if Adewale did something threatening.

'Can I have your attention for a moment, please, guys?'

Raven tugged his trouser leg. 'Seriously, you don't need to do this.'

'I do. Everyone, you all heard the accusations against Raven. I was one of those who made them. I want to state here before we all go our separate ways that she was innocent—set up by these maniacs who brainwashed our fellow students. In fact, from what I heard, she was a big reason why their scheme was exposed. Without her, the rest of us might have been put through the same thing.' He paused.

Raven squirmed with embarrassment.

'So, that's it. That's what I wanted to say.' As he leapt

down, applause started at the far side of the hall—Mairi and Liza from her dance class. It quickly spread and soon everyone was clapping Raven, or drumming on the table top. Johnny and Siobhan looked delighted.

'See, they love you now!' Siobhan squeezed Raven's wrist.

It had only been a few hours ago when sitting in this same room might have meant she was attacked. Raven was not so quick to take it on trust.

She got up and held up her hand. 'Thanks, Adewale. Thanks, everyone. I'm not one to bear a grudge and I know how it looked, so good luck with . . . well, with wherever you go next.'

Adewale waited for her to sit down again. 'Not enough, I realize that,' he said sadly. 'I don't know what came over me. Madness, the way we behaved towards you.'

She shrugged. That about summed it up. 'It did look bad—the watch and everything.'

'There are no excuses. Will you be OK, you know, now?'

Would she? She had no idea. 'I hope so. You?'

'Mum is trying to get me into Eton or Rugby. She has contacts. I think they'll take me next year.'

Of course he would come out of this better than her, money making for a soft landing.

'I hope you enjoy it there.'

'Yes, me too.'

'Just don't pick on the scholarship kids, OK?'

He winced. 'I think I've learnt that lesson. And Raven, remember, if you need anything in the future, anything at all that I can help with, just call me. I owe you a big favour.'

'Thanks.' But somehow she knew she had no stomach for calling in such debts. This place had put her off that for life.

'How's your friend, Gina?' Siobhan asked as Adewale walked away.

'I don't know. We aren't friends any longer.' Raven took a bite of sandwich but it tasted like sawdust.

'You used to be, you know, like inseparable.'

'I suppose we were. She got re-educated out of that.'

Siobhan grimaced. 'I remember—she was on the same course as me for a time. They really piled on the pressure. She was in pieces for weeks before they glued her back together.'

Johnny stole a crisp from Raven's packet. 'From what Ade said, she might be back in pieces again. You should go see her.'

'You think? I'm not sure it would help.' Raven felt sick at the thought.

'I don't think it would do any harm though.'

Taking Johnny's advice, after supper Raven went in search of Gina. The worse-affected students were in the medical wing being monitored by psychiatrists. They still had drugs in their system, thanks to the top-up doses distributed each day at their reinforcement morning meetings. The longer Raven thought about it, the more she realized she had missed the signs: the clothes, dawn meetings, the weird language, the strange expressions and vicious mood swings—Gina had been showing the symptoms of someone in a cult. The fact that it had been a social rather than religious cult didn't make it any less powerful.

Gina was sitting up in the same bed Kieran had occupied, knees drawn up to her chin.

'Hey,' said Raven, coming to stand by the foot.

Gina turned tired eyes on her. 'I didn't expect to see you here.'

Not exactly an enthusiastic welcome. 'I didn't expect to come but a friend suggested I give it a go. How are you?'

'Confused. Adewale tells me I owe you an apology.'

'You got mixed up. They did some bad stuff to you—made you something you're not.'

'My dad liked me like that.' Gina sniffed.

297

'Yeah, well, between you and me, he's a moron.'

A flicker of a smile curved Gina's lips. 'That's what Mom told him. She's moved out.'

'Can't say I blame her.'

'She's coming to fetch me tomorrow. Take me back to the States.'

'I'm glad. You need to get away from here.'

Gina bumped her forehead on her knees. 'I'm sorry, Raven, for what I did to you.'

'I know.'

'I should never have believed them—but they kinda got inside my head.' Gina twisted the sheet in her fingers.

'I understand. You were drugged too, you know?'

'Is that really an excuse for me? What's tormenting me was that I think I must have despised your background somewhere inside me for it to work.'

So much honesty was hard to hear. 'We all have bad stuff inside us—I've never been too impressed by all you rich kids.'

'But you never hit out at me for it.'

'But if it had been me on that programme, with a message playing to my prejudices, maybe I'd be the one apologizing to you right now. I'm still guilty of stereotyping you all and I know that's dumb. People are people. But they were clever, those brainwashers—clever because what they did made you feel guilty for succumbing to the pressure. It is a form of child abuse you know—not a normal kind but still very sick. It's very common to make the victim feel they were to blame.'

Gina's expression lightened a little. 'Child abuse? Yes, it was, wasn't it? Put it like that and I think I can live with myself.'

'Good.' Raven was pleased she'd found something helpful to say, though it was sad to stand at Gina's bedside; it felt like attending a wake for their friendship. 'Have a good rest of your life, won't you?'

'I'll try. You too. Let me know how you get on.'

'OK. And if you want to prove you're sorry for what happened, do me a favour and don't listen to what that dumbass of a father of yours says.'

Gina laughed a little desperately and shook her head. 'I won't.' But Raven feared she would. Things were never simple with family.

Raven walked out of the medical room, nodding to Hedda as she passed and receiving a stony look back. OK, you couldn't win over everyone. She had to remind herself she and Hedda had never liked each other even before the manor had got hold of the other girl. She couldn't blame brainwashing for every bump in the road at school.

Chapter 23

Isaac's injuries were much worse than they had first thought. He had held on by sheer willpower and only let go when he knew his boys were safe. Kieran sat by his bed in the Intensive Care Unit of St Thomas' Hospital watching the monitors with a hawk's intensity. Internal bleeding. Swelling on the brain. Busted ribs. Fractured fingers. The only good thing about the list was that it gave them charges to slap on Kolnikov and Burnham without having to prove the more tenuous case of corruption. This was their Al Capone charge. No arguing their way out on bail with grievous bodily harm charges pressed and them both being flight risks.

Isaac's fingers stirred. Kieran sat up from his slump in the chair. Eyelids flickered.

'Sir?'

Blue eyes shifted to Kieran.

'You still here?'

'Yes, sir.'

'How long?'

'You've been here twenty-four hours. Are you thirsty?' The nurse had left him with strict instructions to encourage fluids when he woke.

'Like the Sahara.'

Kieran held the straw to his lips. 'I don't suppose this is the right moment to mention that the Sahara has some of the largest aquifers of fresh water under its surface.'

Isaac smiled. 'No. It wouldn't.'

'Good to know.' He put the cup back on the side.

Isaac held his gaze for a while, content just to lie in silence. 'I'm proud of you, Kieran,' he said at last.

Emotions whirled in Kieran's stomach, mostly pleasant but with a generous pinch of embarrassment. 'Thanks.'

'You've grown up a lot during this mission.'

'Yes. Yes, I have.'

'You know I look on you differently from the others.'

Kieran had sensed that. Isaac had always mentioned when he felt proud of him. 'I know that you think I'm bright.'

Isaac closed his eyes as a twinge of pain ran through him. 'It's not just about you doing the job but ... ' he coughed. 'I look on you like a son because that's how I think of you.'

'Just how many drugs have they put you on, sir?'

'Not enough.' Isaac smiled. 'I'm serious. Ever since I recruited you, I thought, that's one fine boy whom no one has cared for. I decided I'd step up to the plate.'

'I ... I ... ' How did you respond to that kind of admission? 'Thank you. You've done a great job. Always been there.'

Isaac frowned. 'It doesn't mean I'm going to let you off easy—no favouritism. You follow the same rules as everyone else.'

'I wouldn't dream of it, sir.'

'You broke them, resuming your relationship with Raven.'

'Ah. Yeah, about that ... '

'She told me.'

'I see. I can't say I'm sorry.'

'We have rules for a purpose. The YDA demands sacrifices. You were told that when you joined.'

'Yes. Yes I was.' Now wasn't the time for long explanations or pleading. For now he was just relieved Isaac was conscious. 'Do you need anything, sir? Shall I call a nurse? I'll see if I can find a pretty one to tuck you in.'

301

'Bugger off, Kieran. Get some rest.' Isaac's lips stayed curved in a smile as he drifted off to sleep, as Kieran had intended.

Kieran got up and stretched, conscious he had been wearing the same clothes for days and not eaten or drunk properly. He went to the window, taking in the view of the Houses of Parliament on the other side of the river. Joe had been left with Mrs Bain's phone, so now he had nothing on which to contact anyone and was reliant on the next visitor from the YDA to bring him some money and a change of kit. He wondered what Raven was doing. She was probably catching up on her sleep and trying to figure out what exactly had been happening in her school. He wished he had a way of messaging her. He still didn't know what he was going to do about her. It looked like it was going to come down to a choice after all: the YDA or her.

'How is he?' Nat stood at the door with a holdall and a take-away cup.

'Much better than twelve hours ago. There were a scary few hours when it looked like he was dipping into a coma, but he's conscious. He's just sleeping now.'

'I'm taking over from you. Your orders are to go to HQ and rest.'

'Is Joe back?'

'Yes, arrived yesterday. Hardly seen him, though, as he's been in meetings with the mentors. I think they're sorting through the international network those people had put in place. He says it's likely they'll miss a few of the guilty but you've made a great start rounding them up.'

Kieran drank the tea Nat had brought him. 'Did he say how the students at the school were?'

'Said they were being looked after by social services.'

'Did he mention a girl—a friend of ours, called Raven?'

Nat shook his head. 'No. In fact, he was very quiet about what happened to him—not his usual life-and-soul self. I think

302

the drugs and the near-death experience has shaken him up more than he lets on. Anyway, who's Raven?'

'She's the one who helped save Isaac.'

Nat settled in the chair to take over the vigil. 'There seem to be quite a few gaps in what he's said then. You'd best go talk to him.'

Kieran found Joe in the meeting room with the mentors in charge of the four groups of the YDA. Rivers was there, leading the session with the usual cut-to-the-chase energy expected of the head of the Wolves; Jan, the mentor for Cats, was making notes, doing a great job of blending into the background, assessing what was said. Taylor Flint, the leader of the Cobras, never seen less than sharply dressed, was flipping through a file of photos on his tablet computer, looking for matches on the international wanted list to the men the trustees had employed. Dr Waterburn was tapping away at her laptop as usual, probably doing most of the actual work thanks to her analysis of the links between the main players.

'Key, I'm glad you've come,' Joe said. 'I'm hazy on some of the details about the manor. I think I may have missed a couple of the guys they had working security.'

Kieran sat down. 'I'll see what I can add.'

Jan Hardy checked her watch. 'To be frank, Kieran, you look like death warmed up. Maybe this should wait until tomorrow?'

'Yes, let's call time, ladies and gentleman.' Rivers rose, closing his file. 'Good work everyone. I take it that Isaac is doing better if you are here?'

'Yes, yes he is, enough to tell me to bugger off.'

The mentors laughed.

'Good to hear.' Rivers took a step towards the door.

'Sir, just a moment, if you don't mind.'

'What is it?'

'The girl who helped us—Raven Stone. I asked Isaac a few weeks ago if we can bring her on board.'

Joe's face broke into a huge smile. 'Great idea! You should've told me!'

He hadn't because Isaac's response had not been encouraging.

'What did he say?' asked Rivers.

'He was thinking about it, but . . . '

'Then let's wait for his decision. She certainly showed potential.'

'So can I contact her, tell her what's going on?'

Rivers shook his head. 'Absolutely not. What if Isaac decides no?'

'But I can't just leave her wondering what happened to me—to us.'

Mrs Hardy sighed. 'So that's what this is about. Send her some flowers to hold her over until you can talk to Isaac. We'll pay.'

Kieran didn't think that was good enough. 'I'll pay for my own flowers, thanks.'

'Just follow orders, Mr Storm,' said Rivers in a formal tone. 'You don't want to risk her recruitment by blowing it too early and, if she's to remain outside, you wouldn't want to break the rules, would you, by resuming contact?'

Kieran swore under his breath. 'No, sir.'

The magnificent bouquet of tiger lilies was still blooming when Raven and her granddad had to move out of their cottage. It was scary heading out with nowhere to go. Her grandfather had made a booking with a bed and breakfast to tide them over, but they couldn't afford to keep that arrangement for long.

'What do you want to do with these?' he asked her, taking

a final look round the kitchen, emptying the vase water down the sink.

Raven thought sadly of their packed car. When she had first received the flowers she had been so excited, but then there had been no more word from Kieran. It was like he had dropped off the face of the earth. Perhaps he had meant them as a farewell, his 'lots of love' message on the little white card a kind of goodbye. She should be used to people walking out and not coming back by now, but it hurt worse each time.

'Put them in the bin. We can't take them with us.'

'I could squeeze them in somehow.'

'No, no. I've got to face up to the fact that some things I can't take with me.' Like her hopes about Kieran. She snapped off one bloom to press as a keepsake, the rest she added to the compost heap at the side of the house.

Her grandfather shut the door to the cottage for the last time. 'When do you start work tomorrow?'

She had found a job sweeping up and washing hair at a local hairdresser's. It catered for older clientele, who seemed a sweet bunch of ladies, but Raven was already feeling the prison of low paid work shutting its doors on her as she faced her first day.

'Nine.'

'That's good.' There was a lot neither of them was saying: the fact that Robert hadn't even got an interview for any job he had applied for, and that Raven would not be able to do her A levels for the foreseeable future if she became the main breadwinner.

'It's going to work out, Granddad,' she vowed. She was going to wrestle their future into submission somehow if it didn't want to come quietly.

They headed out of the drive, not sorry to leave such an unhappy place behind them.

*

'So Mrs Pritchard, are you going anywhere on vacation this year?' Raven asked her fourth client of the day. There appeared to be some disturbance at the front of the shop, but over by the basins she couldn't see what was going on. A Cut Above was busy as Monday was the pensioners' special rate, the entrance crammed with shopper trolleys and two mobility scooters blocking the pavement.

'Already been, love. Had a lovely holiday with my sister in Bournemouth.'

'That sounds nice.'

'They do a very good tea dance at the hotel.'

'Great. I like dancing.'

'So do I! I was a champion at the jitterbug in my heyday.'

'Really?' She smiled down at the lady with new respect. 'I bet you were something.'

'I was a real goer.'

Raven chuckled. OK, she could do this. If her job meant meeting with surprises like this old lady, then it wouldn't be as mind numbing as she had feared.

'I'm good at dancing too. I want to do it at college one day.'

'I wish you luck with that. Hard to get into the business, isn't it? Lots of young girls want a place and so few to go round.'

Depressing much? 'Yes, I guess that's true. Still someone has to make it. I won't if I don't try.'

'That's the spirit.'

Another client took the seat at the basin behind her.

'Raven, when you've finished with Mrs Pritchard, can you do our next customer?' called the owner.

'Sure, Mrs Ward.' Raven wrapped a towel around the jitterbug champion's head. 'There you are, Mrs Pritchard: ready for Julie.'

'Thank you, dear.' Mrs Pritchard walked away with a little skip in her step.

306

Raven turned to the next in the queue and found Kieran sitting in the seat behind her.

'Oh my God, what are you doing here?' She inadvertently sprayed water over both of them.

'Having a shower it would seem. Hello, Raven.'

'But you can't . . . I mean, I'm working.'

'So I can see. I'm your next customer. I've booked myself in for something called a shampoo, cut, and blow dry. Aren't you supposed to wash my hair?'

Raven could feel Mrs Ward's eyes on her. It was only her first day on the job after all. 'OK then. Lie back.' She sprayed water over the crown of his head. Why had he come? Total radio silence and here he was—she would be outraged if she wasn't so pleased to see him.

'I've been thinking of getting a haircut for a while now. You see, I'm not sure how to tell you, but there's this girl I want to impress. Someone new in my life.'

She massaged flowery shampoo into his scalp a little too hard. 'Oh yes?' She hated her, whoever she was. So he'd come to tell her he was moving on, had he? He was leaving the salon with a crew cut. Or a frizzy perm. A shaved crown.

He looked up at her and smiled, giving away that he was teasing. 'She's amazing. Saved lots of lives the other night.'

She gentled her touch. 'Did she? I can't believe that. She's a disaster normally. How's Isaac?'

'It was dicey for a while but he's pulled through.'

'I'm glad.'

'Gave me permission to come talk to you.'

'You needed permission?'

'I did.'

Raven checked the spray was the right temperature on her wrist then began to rinse his hair. Their eyes met, his upside down. She smiled, beginning to hope that everything was going

307

to work out after all. 'You don't need a haircut to impress me. Saving us all from the bad guys kinda did it.' She began on the conditioner.

His mouth curled into a contented smile and he closed his eyes. 'I could lie here all day with you doing that.'

She let her fingers wander over his scalp—all that brain power literally under her fingers, but more importantly, all that made Kieran who he was. 'Now that would really get me the sack.'

'Good, because I've come with an offer—for you and your granddad.'

'What kind of offer?'

'If you'd just rinse the soap off, I'll explain.'

Feeling responsible to her new employer and aware everyone was listening, Raven had to wait until the end of her shift to hear his offer, so Kieran decided to go ahead with the trim. Mrs Ward turned out to be fully capable of styling the hair of handsome young men as well as white-haired old ladies and made a huge fuss of him. The elderly customers were tickled pink to be sharing the mirrors with Raven's beau, as they called him. He charmed them all by displaying his knowledge of Big Band music of the forties and fifties—something Raven had not known he had studied.

Then again, she should not be surprised. This was Kieran after all.

Mrs Pritchard sighed as she paid her bill. 'Your young man reminds me of my Jim.' She leant closer. 'You keep hold of him, love.'

'I hope I can,' Raven said, helping Mrs Pritchard into her coat.

She tied a scarf over her head to protect her newly set hair. 'He looks at you as if he could eat you up, so I don't think you'll have any problem doing that.'

Once the cut was complete, Kieran waited for Raven outside the shop to walk her back to her bed and breakfast. Mrs Ward shooed her out of the salon five minutes early, wishing her a pleasant afternoon with a twinkle in her eyes.

'You're all mine now, are you?' Kieran said, giving her the kiss that had been waiting for her.

'Yes.' And she was. Face buried in his wonderful Kieran-scented jacket, Raven knew that whatever came out of this conversation, she was his, totally and hopelessly his.

They held hands, enjoying strolling together along the high street.

'Nice to have no one shooting at us,' she said as she caught their reflection in the chemist's window.

'It's the simple things in life,' he said solemnly, making her laugh.

'So what's this offer?'

'You know I work for Isaac?'

'Yes, I kinda worked that one out for myself.'

Kieran brushed her knuckles with his thumb. 'He runs a training college in London for young people with a flair for crime detection. The organization then sponsors us through university and we then either graduate and work for the YDA, or go into other branches of law enforcement. The agency is his brainchild, really, as he realized there was no formal training path for investigators like there is for the military or ordinary police work.'

'That's what brought you and Joe to Westron?'

'Yes. We were on a job.'

'So Isaac said.'

'Our agency keeps a low profile. Not secret but we don't advertise. It makes us more useful if we can go in without people knowing we're there.'

'So how do you get to join?'

'Invitation only. And this is one.'

309

'One what?'

'Invitation. Though it's two really, as Isaac says we could do with a caretaker. We've had some incidents of tampering in bathrooms; he thinks a proper caretaker rather than contract cleaners would keep a lid on such behaviour.'

'Kieran, you aren't making a very good job of this.'

'Am I being too obscure again?'

'Yep.'

'All right, let me try again.' He dipped down and kissed her. 'There, I feel better now. Though I'm still not sure what you are going to say when you hear my offer.'

'Kieran, the suspense is killing me.'

The familiar little frown between his brows appeared—his brain noticing an illogicality. 'You do know that suspense isn't actually something that kills a person, unless you mean suspend, as in hanging.'

'Kieran Storm, enough *Oxford English Dictionary* corrections, thank you.'

'Sorry.'

'You have something really important to tell me?'

'Yes, I do.'

'Then go for it.'

He grinned. 'You passed the entry test.'

'I didn't know I took a test.'

'Isaac was assessing your potential during the raid on the manor. I'd already asked him if he would consider your application. He said you did well.'

'Did he?' Raven felt a little curl of pleasure.

'No, not exactly.' Kieran's literal mind corrected him again.

'Oh.'

'His exact words were "that girl can kick ass and take names" which means you make a natural Wolf.'

'Sergeant Rivers's team?'

'That's right.'

'And what are Wolves like?'

'I've already given you that answer: they are like you.'

'Kick-ass name-takers?'

He grinned. 'Yes. I almost cocked it all up by resuming our relationship before Isaac had agreed to let you in but, instead of chucking me out and cancelling the offer to you as the rules demand, he decided to make an exception.'

'Because he needs your brain?'

Kieran bent closer. 'No, because he says you were exceptionally good.' He pressed a quick teasing kiss on the end of her nose.

'Aw.'

'And there's more. Your grandfather also has an invitation.'

'He wants to give a job to Granddad?'

'The YDA needs an experienced caretaker to keep us students in check. The role comes with accommodation and a good salary. He won't have to retire next year but can work on as long as he's fit.'

She stopped by the entrance to the bed and breakfast. 'Kieran, is this all true?'

'Yes.'

'And you think I can do it?'

'Absolutely.' He leant down and whispered. 'And I think you like to kick ass, don't you?' He patted her butt.

'You bet.' She patted his in reply.

'So you accept?'

'I'm not sure what I'm saying yes to.'

'Training in your chosen disciplines, which for you will be criminal law, physical training, evidence gathering, case building. As well as the YDA work, you can finish your A levels in London.'

'Even Dance?'

'I don't see why not, as I've been told you have one hell of a dance partner.'

'Really?' she squeaked. 'You'll do it with me?'

'Yes, really.' Kieran caught her as she threw herself into his arms. He lifted her as she peppered his newly trimmed head with kisses.

'You know something, partner: I love you!' She laughed, face held back to soak in the sunshine.

'I take it that's a yes?'

'Yes to being a Wolf—yes to studying in London for a year—a big yes to being with you!'

He let her drop back on her toes and hugged her. 'I'd love that—and I love you, Raven.' His confession filled her with heady delight.

'I always thought you had exceptional taste.'

He let her pull him towards her front door. 'I'm glad you agreed because Isaac thinks we make a good team.'

'Oh yes? Like you and Joe?'

'Yes, though Joe's having a break for a few months. The manor got to him badly so he's taking a long holiday back home. Isaac wants me to work with you now.'

'Agents Storm and Stone: I like the sound of that.'

He backed her against the banister in the empty hallway, one hand on her waist, the other at the back of her head. Oh yeah, she recognized this manoeuvre. Her insides crinkled with happy anticipation. 'My logic and your gut instincts: that's a powerful combination.'

'You're telling me.'

'So, do you accept the challenge?'

'Absolutely.' Raven went up on tiptoe as he leant down to kiss her. *Yes, mission accomplished.*

BOOKS BY
Joss Stirling

Joss Stirling lives in Oxford and is the author of the
bestselling **Finding Sky** series. She was inspired to write
Storm and Stone by the heroes of British crime fiction
and by years of watching cop dramas.

You can visit her website at **www.jossstirling.com**